THE
RED ABBEY
CHRONICLES

RED MANTLE

THE
RED ABBEY
CHRONICLES

RED MANTLE

MARIA TURTSCHANINOFF

AMULET BOOKS
NEW YORK

Library of Congress Cataloging-in-Publication Data
Names: Turtschaninoff, Maria, 1977- author.
Title: Red mantle / Maria Turtschaninoff.
Other titles: Breven från Maresi. English
Description: New York : Amulet Books, 2020. | Series: The Red Abbey chronicles; book 3 | Summary: "Continues the story of Maresi as she leaves the Abbey at Menos and returns home to the small, oppressed province of Rovas. There, Maresi is determined to spread the knowledge she has gained and start a school—but in the end, she will learn just as much as she teaches."— Provided by publisher.
Identifiers: LCCN 2019035148 (print) | LCCN 2019035149 (ebook) | ISBN 9781419731358 (hardcover) | ISBN 9781683356462 (ebook)
Subjects: CYAC: Magic—Fiction. | Schools—Fiction. | Friendship—Fiction. | Family life—Fiction. | Letters—Fiction. | Fantasy.
Classification: LCC PZ7.T8824 Red 2020 (print) | LCC PZ7.T8824 (ebook) | DDC [Fic]—dc23

Text copyright © 2020 Maria Turtschaninoff
Book design by Siobhán Gallagher

Printed and bound in U.S.A.
10 9 8 7 6 5 4 3 2 1

Amulet Books are available at special discounts when purchased in quantity for premiums and promotions as well as fundraising or educational use. Special editions can also be created to specification. For details, contact specialsales@abramsbooks.com or the address below.

Amulet Books® is a registered trademark of Harry N. Abrams, Inc.

ABRAMS The Art of Books
195 Broadway, New York, NY 10007
abramsbooks.com

FOR TRAVIS,
NOW MORE
THAN EVER

*T*hese scriptures consist of the letters of Maresi Enresdaughter, sent from her homeland of Rovas to the Red Abbey during the reigns of our thirty-third and thirty-fourth Mothers. In Rovas, Maresi became known as Maresi Red Mantle, banisher of frost, tamer of beasts and guardian of the dead, she who brought forth an avalanche and released the dead into the realm of the living.

These letters have been added to the Red Abbey archives by Sister O, archivist and servant to the Crone, and by her successor. These archives are incomplete, but all occurrences pertinent to the Abbey are documented here, lest we forget the events that unfolded in Rovas during the first two years following Maresi's return to her native village. They shall remain significant to Rovas for all time.

FIRST COLLECTION
OF LETTERS

SPRING

Venerable Sister O,

I write this by the light of a crackling fire. Making fire was no easy task this evening. Rain has fallen continuously throughout most of our journey through the mountain pass, so all the wood is wet, as is my woolen cloak. The sounds of the trade convoy surround me: conversation and laughter; the whinnies and bells of horses and mules; the animals' grinding jaws as they endeavor to snatch newly sprouted leaves from among the twigs. I can smell the smoke of the campfires, and spits of meat roasting slowly above them. One of the guards following the convoy had a good hunt today and shared out mountain sheep among the travelers.

It is early evening, the sky is still light, and a pale moon hangs above the low mountain peaks. The convoy reached the crest of the mountain range today, and the lowlands of Rovas extend below us to the north.

I have nearly arrived at my destination, and have formed an idea of how we may arrange the delivery of letters to and from the Abbey, so I am beginning my correspondence now, as we agreed. Annual trade convoys travel the long distance between Masson, the port town of Valleria in the south, and Namar, the walled city of the Akkade people on the high grassland plains north of Rovas. I believe the wisest option would be to send two bundles of letters per year, in spring and autumn. The letters may then arrive within a few moons. I have made sure to speak with several tradesmen and women along the way to let them know that whoever delivers letters from Rovas to Menos can expect handsome payment. I would think it best if the greater portion of this sum were paid when the letters reach their destination.

You told me that you would read my words aloud to the other sisters at mealtimes in Hearth House. This is only right, for they are the ones who have equipped me with the wealth of knowledge I am now carrying out into the world. This and the Mother Abbess's silver will help me to found a school in Rovas. But please, Sister O, will you do me the service of reading my letters alone first? You know my ways: I blather on and write far too much. You told me that I must record all of my experiences, for many things of great significance to the Abbey may happen, even if I am unaware of their significance at the time. But I might also describe events of no relevance, in which case I would prefer that you choose only what is truly important. And perhaps some things will be intended for your eyes only, Sister O. I trust you will know when this is the case.

I am going to view these letters as a continuation of the text I wrote four years ago documenting the spring when the men came to Menos to take Jai away. Now, as then, I do not feel strong enough for the task. Now, as then, I will do my best to fulfill the task anyway, despite my shortcomings. I hope you will share my writings with the novices. It will be good preparation for others like me who intend to venture out into the world and spread the Abbey's knowledge after their education.

I know that everyone was concerned that I might be hurt or robbed on my journey, but everything has gone well. I have joined forces with a number of convoys in exchange for a small payment. This has provided me with protection against highway robbers and other dangers. The convoys are always escorted by several armed guards. Yet we have seen no robbers, and have heard wolves only from afar. They were too distant even to alarm my mule. Of course, I have almost certainly paid exorbitant prices for things at times, like the first convoy I joined that gave me a cart to ride in. Then I made friends with a traveling tradeswoman from Valleria named Ajanie, who told me I should have bartered them down to at least half the price. Still, I have learned a valuable lesson, and plenty of silver remains in my purse. Ajanie advised me to sleep with it under my head.

When this first convoy branched west toward Devenland I had to travel on foot for several days before I managed to buy a retired old mule from a merchant. She has long, soft ears that obscure my view when I ride her, and her broad back is almost comfortable. The merchant who sold her mentioned no name, and perhaps he never gave her one. I call her Gray Lady, in honor of our highest peak on Menos, White Lady Mountain. She has walked this route many, many times before, bearing brick tea and salt on her back to the faraway land of the Akkade people. The merchant said that she is too old to manage that path again. The mountains between Rovas and the Akkade plains are high, and the climb is strenuous for an old mule. My intended route is not as long or difficult, but I still feared that the low peaks that form the southern boundary of Rovas might be too much for her. I dismounted and walked through the most treacherous parts, when stones were slipping under foot and hoof, and it felt as though each step took us as far backward as forward.

The road we are following is known as the Horse Trail, because it is used to herd strong Akkade horses to the south, where they command a high price. We have not encountered any horse convoys, for spring is not a wise time to lead large herds of animals along roads damaged by the rain, snow and storms of winter. The northbound convoys travel in spring, when tradesmen bring sought-after goods from the southern lands to the north, where people are longing for sweets, spices and a little luxury after the hardships of winter. Ajanie showed me the silver jewelry she buys in the markets of Masson. It is too plain for the wealthy citizens of Irindibul, so she undertakes an annual journey to Namar. It is a great distance, but in the walled city people pay well for items considered too modest for Irindibul nobility. When Ajanie reaches Namar she trades her silver jewelry for wool, which she then brings down to the southeast and Lagora, which Ajanie described as a mosaic city by the sea, and trades the raw wool for spun yarn and tapestries. Then she travels back to Valleria and sells her wares for pure gold.

Ajanie has seen so much of the world. For a Vallerian she has traveled a great deal: as far west as the land of the longhorns, as far north as the Akkade plains, and as far east as Lagora.

It has been fascinating to see the landscape change over the course of my journey. From Valleria's archipelago with its rainbow of boats at every little harbor, across vast marshlands where salt is harvested, to the Vallerian lowlands full of grape and olive groves, and the vibrant capital city of Masson. I would like to have seen Devenland as well, but it is too far west. I am trying to imagine the tea plantations on the mountain slopes. I joined a Devenian convoy after leaving Valleria behind, and first smelled the delicious aroma of brick tea. It is transported north to the Akkade people, who drink nothing else.

Of all the people I have encountered, few have heard tell of the province of Rovas. Ajanie said that she has traveled through the region many times but never knew it had a name. To her it was only ever northwest Urundien. Naturally I felt obliged to tell her all about Rovas. The fire is providing a little light yet, so I will write down what I told her, to preserve the history of Rovas in the Abbey's archives.

Long ago Rovas was an independent land, but our nearest neighbor to the southeast, Urundien, was ever hungry for more territory and riches. During one of their military campaigns, Rovas fell under their dominion, and an alliance was sealed through the marriage of their king to the daughter of a Rovasian chieftain. Since then the Sovereign of Urundien has always appointed a nádor, a governor to rule over "the unruly forest folk." The nádor enforces tax collection and trade tariffs. The Rovasians are farmers and woodcutters. The farmers are in a constant battle with the forest itself, which always threatens to reabsorb the cleared farmland, and so they never manage to grow more than the most basic of provisions for their families. The woodcutters, timber-rafters and fur-trappers live tough, solitary lives deep in the forests, traveling wherever they are hired or where game abounds. The people of Rovas are free men and women: the farmers own their farmland and woodland, but the large game belongs to the Crown, and only the Sovereign of Urundien may hunt it and allot hunting rights as a token of his favor. Large hunting parties from Urundien often enter the forest in autumn.

However, our freedom is limited by poverty, ignorance and hard toil. Furthermore, the nádor's levy of taxes is frequent and merciless. The villages often suffer from serious illness and malnutrition. Superstitions and delusions are rife, which is precisely what I hope to rectify when I reach my native village of Sáru and found my school. It feels like a very small step, but it is a start. Ajanie told me that schools are starting to become more common in the cities of Valleria and Devenland, though naturally only for the sons of rich families.

My long journey has given me a lot of time to think about my future school. You said several times that I must have patience, and not expect the villagers to send their daughters to my school straightaway, but I am sure that they will when they see the benefits of true knowledge.

Tomorrow I bid farewell to Ajanie and the rest of the convoy as they diverge to the northwest. They are to cross the flat lowland area, and in seven to eight days, depending on the weather, they should reach the wooded foot of the mountain range that divides Rovas from the Akkade lands. It will surely take them a long time to climb it, but a gentler descent awaits them on the other side, for the vast plains of the Akkade people span a high plateau, with a very different climate from that of Rovas.

I will write again once I am closer to my home village.

Your novice,

Maresi

Dearest Jai,

    I plan to write separate letters to you and Ennike, but that does not mean you cannot read each other's, unless I specifically ask you not to. I cannot say when I will be able to send them, so I have decided to write a series of letters instead of one continuous text. That way I will have them ready to send as soon as an opportunity arises.

Can you believe it? I have finally arrived in Rovas! Well, the southern outskirts of Rovas, in any case. My village is a long way from these gentle, rolling lowlands, deep in the mountainous woodlands. The convoy I have been following took a different course this morning, and I have spent the entire day journeying through the early Rovasian springtime all alone. I am seeing and experiencing everything differently now that I have no one but my mule for company. Each time I cross a gurgling spring stream it is an adventure in itself. Each time I see the roofs of houses peek over the horizon or from behind a bend in the road I feel a tingle in my stomach—whom might I meet today? A part of me always hopes that it is my own village, though I know it is still several days northeast from here, and I do not recognize these surroundings. Yet what if everything has changed in the years I have been away? The village might not be in the same place!

I have set up camp for the night and sheltered under some bushes, and soon I will be sleeping with only my mule and the wind for company. It is overcast tonight, otherwise I would gaze up at the stars; but just the knowledge that the stars are up there is comfort enough. The stars are there, and the moon too, and they are looking down on you, dear Jai.

I will write more once I am home.

Your friend,

Maresi

Venerable Sister O,

It has been raining for seven days now. It never stops. It is a fine, constant rain that leaves everything drenched: me, my mule, my luggage. I am keeping warm inside the cloak Jai gave me, but I have not been dry in a long time. The branches are dripping and the stones are slippery. I have found shelter for the night in a half-ruined cowshed with most of its roof intact, so at least I will not be rained on during the night. I have not succeeded in making a fire, as I have no dry firewood, so this letter will be shorter than the last, because the daylight is fading.

Gray Lady and I have passed many villages that resemble Sáru: several homesteads built in a circle or crescent, dotted with outbuildings, and fields and pastures spreading out into the surrounding forest. In the south every field has its own fence, but as I near my homeland in northernmost Rovas the fields are gathered together, with shared fences.

I have spent many nights sleeping under an open sky. In the summers when I was little, my mother, my sister Náraes and I would sometimes stay out in the forest for a long time picking berries. Mother taught us how to build a shelter of branches and twigs to protect ourselves from wind and light rain, and this is what I have been making each night—beside streams swelling with meltwater and spring rain, beside serene forest tarns, and on slopes with far-reaching views across valleys and mountains, where smoke from unseen chimneys is the only sign of human dwellings.

It is not easy to find one's way through this forest. Though I grew up here, and was toddling through woodland as soon as I could walk, and though I am familiar with this forest and its ways, I am also familiar with its dangers and how treacherous it can be. Rovas is a wooded land for the most part, apart from some rocky, mountainous terrain where no trees grow. Our most important trade routes, indeed travel routes in general, follow the rivers. Yet these rivers generally flow from northwest to southeast, and as I came from the southwest, I have not been able to travel via the waterways. This would have been easier and quicker, as we discussed before I left. The Horse Trail, which I followed to begin with, runs through the western part of Rovas from the southwest to the north. The villages are linked by woodland paths that are often no more than cartwheel tracks, but these go directly from village to village, and so are not best suited for long-distance travelers.

Each time I have doubted the way, when a path has forked or disappeared into the undergrowth, Gray Lady has chosen the way with perfect composure, and each time I have soon realized that she made the correct choice. She is smarter than I, this mule. I do not know what I would have done without her.

I have traveled through the spring and witnessed the first sprouting leaves, and birdsong has followed me along my path. Yet it seems like an eternally timid spring that never manages to take the leap and burst into full greenery and warmth. The farther north I go, the cooler the regions become and the later spring arrives. It never occurred to me that spring, which brings mild breezes and good traveling weather to Menos, is a time of rain in Rovas.

I believe that I am following the same route that I took south eight years ago when I left Rovas, but I cannot be certain. It was so long ago, and everything was so new and frightening that I did not pay very close attention to the route. I was only a child, loaded onto a cart and driven away from Rovas to the southern mountains. From there I was transferred onto a donkey's back, led along the mountain pass and loaded onto another cart for the remainder of the journey to Valleria. I fear I may not be able to find my village. It is an unremarkable settlement, and when I ask the folk I meet in the villages they only shake their heads in answer.

And Sister O, there is another thing I fear, and I can admit this only to you: I fear hunger.

At the Abbey I got used to always having a full belly. Sometimes we had simple, humble fare, but in any case, I have not had to go hungry in eight years. Now I am met by the faces of people who know the true meaning of hunger, and I remember. I remember when we slaughtered our last pig. I remember going hungry for so long that I forgot what it was like to feel full. I remember eating things not intended for human consumption: rotten seeds, leaves and grass, animal carcasses, boiled leather. I remember the taste of bread made with sawdust. I remember how swollen my stomach became, and how thin Anner's limbs were, and how diarrhea weakened her body day by day.

It appears that the recent harvests have been plentiful. The village folk have bread to give me, and sometimes they invite me into their homes and feed me porridge and hard rye bread, and once I was even given salted fish. People only eat meat at this time of year if they have had several good harvests in a row. Approaching the villages, I am met by little flocks of hens and sheep, and pig-men herding long-legged, shaggy pigs while playing willow pipes. I remember making pipes from pussy willow when I was a girl, and still recall the taste of the green willow. It does my heart good to hear them. During the hunger winter all the animals in our village were slaughtered.

Nonetheless, it is evident that these people have known hunger, before I left and while I have been away. The children are stunted and not nearly as round and rosy as our junior novices. No one has any extra body fat. The animal flocks are small in relation to the size of the villages. I am afraid, Sister O. Of course, I knew that life here would be different from the one we lead at the Abbey, but there is so much that I had forgotten.

Most of all I am afraid of what awaits me when I eventually find my village. Is everybody still alive?

I am trying to be strong, Sister O. I am trying to be brave. Yet there are days when my heart is as heavy and dark as the wool of my cloak.

Yours,

Maresi

Dearest Jai,

It was early evening when I suddenly recognized where I was. I saw a babbling brook where I used to play as a child! I saw the meander where we used to race our leaf boats, and the footbridge we would run to to cheer our crafts on. I was tired, and so was my mule, and I was about to set up camp for the night, but the sight of the brook filled my limbs with renewed vigor and my heart with a longing so strong that not even a stubborn mule could stop me. I dismounted to lighten her load, and led her over the footbridge and in among the newly plowed fields. There was no proper road to follow, only a path that ran along various ditches; but even in the fading light, my feet found their way. Jump here; careful of the slippery edge of this ditch;

this is where mushrooms grow in autumn. I led my mule, and she must have sensed my excitement because she was less resistant than usual.

I approached the village from the south rather than from the forest path that runs to Jóla, the neighboring village to the west. I stood on the hillside overlooking two black fields and saw the houses nestled together against a backdrop of deepening dusk. Between me and the village the mill stream flowed, urgent and thick with foam after the rapid rains of spring. On the other side of the stream was a medley of barns and sheds, and beyond them were four houses facing in toward each other to form a protective ring around a central yard. The forest surrounded them like a dark curtain. Smoke was streaming from all four chimneys, but there was not a soul to be seen. Nothing but a little light seeping out from the edges of the closed window shutters. The animals were in their barns and henhouses for the night. My heart had not pounded so intensely since what happened in the Abbey crypt.

My mule snorted and began plodding down the path that runs between the fields, and I followed slowly. The stream was surging, and even slopped onto the footbridge, making the planks slippery. With the rush of the stream filling my ears, I walked in among the houses that leaned into each other, low and gray. The air smelled of manure and smoke and wet earth. I took a deep breath, and it made my chest ache. I tethered my mule to our home's guardian tree. There before me was my mother and father's cottage, gray and dark in the rain, just like the last time I had seen it. I walked to the door and lifted my hand to knock. In that moment, the moon rose above the trees and shone its light upon the worn wood. I opened my fist, ran my fingers along the flaking wood and thought of all the doors in the Abbey: the brown door of Hearth House with its bready scent, the rose-patterned marble door of the Temple of the Rose, and the honey-gleaming double doors to the library in Knowledge House. I leaned on the door and inhaled deeply. It smelled of damp wood.

In Rovas people enter each other's homes freely during the daytime, but come nightfall the doors are latched. I knocked.

"Who goes there?" came a man's deep voice. My father's voice. I was barely able to muster a response.

"Blessings on your hearth, Father."

There was a moment of silence, followed by the sound of the latch being lifted from the inside. Then the door swung open and I was dazzled by light. All I could see was a tall, thin figure before me. Then two strong arms pulled me into an embrace and my father mumbled into my hair.

"My daughter. My daughter, my daughter, my daughter."

Then I heard my mother's voice. My eyes had begun to adjust to the light, and over Father's shoulder, I saw her. She was sitting by the fireplace with knitting in her lap, holding her hands over her heart.

"Maresi. Is it really you?"

I loosened myself from Father's embrace and looked up into his dear face. He was just as I remembered him: warm brown eyes; a large, broad nose; flat, protruding ears. Only he had more wrinkles and his beard was a little grayer.

Mother rose from her chair and came toward me with outstretched hands. Her braid of thick brown hair shone in the hearth light, and she did not look much changed either. She was even thinner than when I had left, if such a thing were possible. I took hold of her hands, and we looked at one another. She tried to speak, but only shook her head, her eyes filled with tears. She pulled me close and held me tight.

"I thought I'd never see you again—never again, I thought. My child, are you home now?"

"Yes, Mother," I replied. "I am home now."

Mother smelled just as I remembered, of flour and cabbage and wool. Immediately I began to weep. I wept like the nine-year-old I was when I left my mother and father and everybody I had ever loved. I never wanted to let Mother go again.

Her bony shoulders against my body. Her hands stroking my hair. I felt them more intensely, more deeply, than anything I had ever felt in my life.

She withdrew suddenly and exclaimed through sobs: "Oh, but you're soaked through! This won't do, you'll get all sooty!"

I undressed in front of the fire while Mother found me some dry clothes, and I looked around our beloved old cottage. Everything was exactly the same: the trodden earth floor with a thick layer of clean straw; the table and benches at the hearth; my parents' and Akios's bedrooms along one side of the house; the little animal pen in the entranceway. The shutters were closed against the night and the rain, and a glorious fire blazed in the fireplace.

"This will have to do," Mother said, handing me a striped skirt with embroidered flowers around the hem and a threadbare, short-sleeved smock. As I dressed, she hung my clothes up by the fire to dry. She eyed the trousers and shirt with an incredulous expression. Then she handed me a woven belt of red, white and black.

"I was thinking of you when I wove this," she said. "With each color I wove in my hope that you were still alive and that we'd see each other again someday."

Just as I tied the belt around my waist, Akios came through the door and stamped the mud from his boots. When he caught sight of me he stopped and his eyes grew large.

"Maresi!" he cried. "My sister!"

It felt strange to be called "sister" by a man, and by someone who truly is my own flesh and blood. I grinned.

"Akios! You have grown a beard!"

He stroked his downy chin and grinned.

"Can't be a farmer without a beard," he answered.

I ran to my brother and embraced him tightly. But Akios embraced me more tightly still. Then he tugged at a wisp of my wind-tangled hair.

"Scraggle-hair," he teased.

"Knobble-knees," I replied, and poked him in the belly, but I realized that the old nickname no longer suited him. I am two years older than Akios, but he has grown a head taller than me, and not even the loose nightshirt he was wearing could hide the fact that his shoulders were broad and his arms were firm with muscles. His hair, once the same shade of nut-brown as Náraes's and mine, had lightened and was hanging down to his shoulders.

"Little brother, you are all grown up!" I exclaimed, and we both laughed until we could hardly breathe.

There was no time to exchange stories at such a late hour. We were all tired and content simply to sit in each other's company and look at each other's faces in the dying firelight, while Mother fed me up with hard bread and the last scrapings of the evening porridge. She kept leaning over to touch my hair, my cheeks, my hand.

"Tomorrow I'll cook something good and tasty," she said. "To celebrate."

"Tomorrow," I repeated with a yawn.

Finally I was warm and dry. Akios offered me his bed in his small room, saying that he would sleep on the ledge above the fireplace. I could hardly wait to crawl under the blanket Mother had woven and sleep to the faintly familiar sound of rain on the wood-shingle roof. But there was something I had to ask first.

"Náraes. Is she . . . ?"

Father looked at me questioningly, then smiled and took my hand.

"Náraes is alive and well. She has her own household and family now. You'll see her tomorrow."

I am writing this in the little bedroom, with one small tallow candle as the only source of light. The others are already sleeping, for dawn brings another day of hard toil. I am almost falling asleep too, but I wanted to write to you first, and to capture this feeling of being safely indoors, full and dry and warm. Home.

It is good to be home, Jai.

Your friend,

Maresi

My dear Ennike Rose,

I am home, and I have spent my first night under my parents' roof. I awoke with a dry mouth and thick head and could not remember where I was. I was lying on a real mattress, and not the bare ground as I had gotten used to on my journey. I could smell clean bed-clothes and wool. I could hear murmuring voices and the dull patter of rain against the wood-shingle roof. For a moment I thought I was back in my bed in Novice House, but the sounds and smells were all wrong.

I opened my eyes when the aroma of rowanberry porridge filled my nostrils. Though Sister Ers cooks up all sorts of delicious dishes in Hearth House, no one can make rowanberry porridge with honey like my mother. I sat up and realized where I was—home! Home in my parents' house, under a blanket woven by my own mother. I threw on a smock, blouse and skirt and tamed my hair as much as I could.

Father and Akios were sitting at the table with a grown woman with a thick, nut-brown braid, and two small children—one on her lap, the other on Father's. Mother stood at the hearth stirring something in a great iron pot, which Father had bought from a peddler when I was very little.

"There she is now," said Father. "Come and say hello to your nieces."

The woman with the brown braid was my elder sister Náraes! Passing the little one to Akios, she stood up and wrapped her arms around me.

"You're alive," she said. "You're really alive! Mother came to tell us early this morning, but I almost didn't believe it." She let go and looked at me in earnest. "I've seen you in my dreams, Maresi. I've seen you walk in the shadows of death."

"I have indeed walked there, but not through death's door," I replied, equally earnest, gazing upon my sister. I barely recognized her. She is three years older than I, and when I left Rovas she was younger than Heo is now. She has aged. Her cheeks are hollow and her eyes appear large in her narrow face. Her hair is still thick and shiny, and she wears it in a long braid down her back with several unruly curls around her face. I used to think that you looked alike, but now she is a grown woman, while you are the Rose, a blooming maiden.

And she is with child.

"Come, you must meet your nieces," said Náraes. "That little savage on Father's lap is Maressa." She looked at me with a hint of shyness. "I named her after you. I hope you don't mind."

I looked at the girl. She is a little over three years old, with fair curls like a fluffy cloud around her face and curious brown eyes that inspected me seriously. I took Náraes's hand and squeezed it.

"Thank you," I whispered.

"And the baby is Dúlan, born last spring. She's teething."

Dúlan was sitting on Akios's lap, gnawing on her hand, dribbling saliva down her chest. She has the same bright, wide eyes as Geja, but her legs and cheeks are not as chubby as Geja's were at that age.

"And when is the third coming?" I asked.

Náraes glanced down at her belly and smiled. "In autumn, after harvest. I'll be at my biggest just when I'm most needed in the fields! Tauer says it's a boy."

Tauer is an old man in the neighboring village whom the local villagers often turn to for advice on ailments and childbirth.

"Come and sit now," said Mother, and set the porridge out on the table. "It's late, and the men have to return to the fields."

When I looked at Father and Akios I saw that their hair was wet. They had already been out working. I felt ashamed.

"It's the journey, Mother. I was so tired, I never usually . . ."

She came and kissed me on the forehead. "I understand just fine. Nobody's blaming you, Maresi."

"I have to go out first," I mumbled.

I took down my red cloak, nearly dry now, from the hook by the door where Mother had hung it up the previous evening. I went outside wearing the cloak draped over my shoulders and Father's great big boots on my feet.

The morning was almost over. It was raining and there was hardly any birdsong. I followed the path around the corner to the privy, which is where it has always been, with one of the best views over the village. I saw the stream running through the valley behind the outbuildings. Around the village spanned the fields, dark and muddy, and beyond them the forest, dark and silent in the falling rain. Smoke was rising from the chimneys and, unlike the previous night, the village showed signs of life. There was a clatter from a cow barn as a girl threw the breakfast leftovers to a flock of pecking hens. She did not see me and I did not recognize her, but by her age I guessed that she must be Lenna Adonsdaughter, who was a babe in arms when I left Rovas. A woman with a sweeping brown skirt was fetching water from the stream, but I could not see who she was from such a distance.

When I was finished in the privy I suddenly remembered Gray Lady and rushed to where she was, still tied to the home tree. She glared at me with her mouth full of freshly sprouted twigs. I rubbed her between the ears and begged her forgiveness a hundredfold before untying her and leading her down to the stream for a drink. We encountered no one, and I hurried her along as fast as I could. My mouth was watering at the thought of Mother's rowanberry porridge.

The house was full of clattering spoons and chatter. I kicked off Father's boots, hung my cloak up by the door and shook the water from my hair. My place at the table was waiting. I took a seat and was presented with a bowl of steaming porridge. My family, my own flesh and blood, were talking and laughing around me, but I was too busy eating to speak.

"Who is your husband?" I finally managed to say through a mouthful of food. Náraes smiled.

"Jannarl."

I looked up.

"From next door?"

She smiled. "Yes. That's where I live now."

I dimly recalled a fair-haired youth with blemished skin who used to joke around with Náraes whenever we took grain down to the mill by the stream to be ground. I looked at my sister. It was strange to think of her as a married woman with two children and a third on the way. Strange that she shared her bed with a man every night, and no longer lived at home with Mother and Father. Jannarl's father had a respectable farmstead, with more fields and a larger house than ours. Now Náraes has moved there, left our family and become a part of his. Now she and Jannarl's mother run the home together.

"Does Máros still live there?" I asked. Náraes nodded. Máros is Jannarl's little brother, around the same age as Náraes. We often used to play together. There was Máros, Náraes, my best friend, Sannarl, Marget from White Farm, and me. Máros is deaf, but we invented all manner of hand signals and used facial expressions and understood each other very well.

"Now Maresi, you must tell us everything." Mother scooped more porridge into a bowl and brushed a strand of hair away from her forehead. She sat down on the bench next to Father and gave the bowl to Maressa, who stuffed the spoon in her mouth without taking her eyes off me. "Where have you been? What has happened to you? How did you make it back to us?"

"On a mule."

Everybody laughed, but Maressa looked at me seriously. "Your *own* mule?" she asked, and I was surprised at how well she spoke.

"Yes, my very own. Her name is Gray Lady."

Father looked surprised. "That one outside? We've room in the animal pen, if you want to bring it in."

"Not now, Enre," said Mother impatiently. "Let Maresi speak!" She picked up her spindle and continued with the thread she had started spinning. I have never seen Mother with idle hands.

So I told them everything. It was not easy to condense eight years into a single narrative, nor was it easy to talk of the most important and difficult of things, like when I opened the door to the Crone's realm and slew all the men who came to Menos to do us harm. I decided to leave that story for the time being. The time for that will come later. Instead I described the island of Menos and my journey there with convoys and boats. I told them how lost I felt to begin with. I described Abbey life and the Abbey itself, the gray-stone buildings (nobody in Rovas has seen such a thing; here they build with timber), the mountains and olive groves, and the never-ending sea. I told them about the sisters and all their expert knowledge, about the different houses and the significance of being called to a house. I explained that we harvest bloodsnails, which bring us the silver we need for provisions. I described my friends—you and Jai and Heo—and how we all came to Menos for different reasons from different lands. I tried to tell them all about Knowledge House and its treasure chamber, and how much I love to read, but it is difficult to explain to people who cannot read or write. I recounted how I came to the difficult decision to leave the Abbey, to return home and share my knowledge.

"A school," Mother said dubiously. "What would you do there?"

"Teach the children to read and write, first and foremost. Then counting, and a little history about the nearby provinces."

"What good would that do?" Mother gave me a bemused look and spun her spindle with increased momentum. "There is nothing to read here, and as soon as the children are old enough they help on the farm, just as you did when you were little. And nobody leaves the village except maybe to marry someone from a neighboring village."

I tried to think of a response that would not offend Mother, who could neither read nor write. But when I looked into her loving eyes, I could think of nothing to say.

"I think it's a fine idea," said Father. "I've always known there was something special about you, ever since you were little and you'd make up all those long stories for Akios."

Mother stiffened at Father's words. I glanced at her and saw a furrow form between her brows and her lips close into a hard line. It was an expression I do not remember from my childhood.

Náraes stood up and lifted Dúlan into her arms. "I have to go and start cooking. Jannarl will be home soon for his midday meal."

"I want to see the mule," said Maressa decisively.

"You can see her on the way out. Come now."

Náraes held out her hand, and Maressa slid down from the bench and followed her to the door, where Father helped them put on their cardigans and caps.

Once they were gone, Father and Akios got dressed and went out into the rain to continue their work. I helped Mother to clear the table, filled a kettle with water from the large tub by the door and sat down to wait for it to boil. Mother put more wood on the fire and wiped her hands on her apron.

My family has changed. Father's beard has turned gray, Akios has become a young man, and Náraes has gone through the greatest change of all: from girlhood to womanhood and motherhood. Yet Mother looks the same as always. Thick, brown hair. Warm, kind eyes. Chapped hands. A tight braid wrapped around her head, and a striped apron tied over her home-woven skirt with the traditional Rovasian pattern of embroidered flowers along the hem. She is thinner than before, and a little more solemn. I remember a mother who laughed heartily and often. Until Anner died.

"How long your hair's grown! It reminds me of my mother's, so thick," said Mother, stroking my head. "You speak differently too."

"They speak another tongue on Menos," I replied. "My mouth is not quite used to our language yet."

"Was it hard to learn?"

I cast my mind back to the experience of arriving on Menos and understanding nothing. I longed for home so much I thought I would die. My only solace was you, Ennike Rose, and your kindness. Have I ever thanked you for that? I thank you now. I do not know whether I would have survived if you had not taken care of me, if you had not taught me the language, sweetly and patiently, if you had not held me at night when I soaked my pillow with tears.

"Yes," I whispered. "It was very difficult."

Mother stood quietly awhile with her hands pressed against her heart. She reached out a hand as though to touch me, but then pulled it back.

"I'll run and fetch a comb," said Mother, and disappeared into her bedroom. She returned with a well-worn comb that I recognized from my childhood.

"I have lost a lot of hair to that comb in Náraes's hands," I said with a frown.

Mother smiled and placed one hand on my shoulder. "Now now, turn around."

She started on my tangled mound of hair. I shut my eyes and enjoyed the feeling of my mother's hands in my hair, the smoke from the hearth in my nostrils and the lingering taste of rowanberry and honey on my tongue.

"You weren't here for your hair-braiding ceremony," said Mother thoughtfully. "You were too little before you went away. And now you're far too old."

"My moon blood flows now."

"Yes, of course it does, you're seventeen after all."

Mother can count. Most people here can, to count the animals in the evenings and the eggs in the baskets and the sheaves in the fields. But few can count above twenty.

The braiding ceremony is performed when a girl receives her first moon blood. On the fourth day they comb and braid her hair and then she wears it bound forevermore, as a sign that she has become a woman. I do not want to braid my hair. We never do on Menos, and I choose not to here either. I decided to change the subject.

"Tell me a story, Mother."

"Me?" Mother scoffed. "You're the one with stories to tell."

"A ballad, then. Any one you like."

Mother was quiet for a moment. She had reached my neck, and the comb was scraping my skin and making me wince. She started to sing.

A great strong silky paw
Honey paw all alone
Up in the sky so black
Sought a stronger groom . . .

It was almost like a dream: to hear my own mother's voice; to feel her loving hands in my hair; to hear her sing to me, like she always used to when I was little. There is no ballad that Mother does not know. It was a while before I could steady my voice enough to speak.

"Have you been to Murik to visit Auntie lately, Mother?"

"No. We haven't been there in a long time. You know how much there is to do here on the farm, and whenever I've got time to spare, Náraes needs help with the children. The roads have been so bad this spring, and we had a lot of snow this winter. We don't have a horse anymore, you see, so we can't ride the sleigh like we used to. The roads aren't as safe as they were either. But we've had word from Kárun Eiminsson that they're alive and well in Murik. Do you remember Kárun? He's a woodcutter and hunter and lives in a little hut near Jóla, so he gets about more than the villagers."

I shook my head. I remember no one called Kárun. There is so much I have forgotten.

"Have you no animals to tend to?"

"No. Not anymore. We had to slaughter them all last winter to avoid famine. It was a hunger winter."

"But . . . Did you not buy a pig after that? Just before I left."

Mother's combing hand paused. "We've had more than one hunger winter, Maresi. Three years ago the drought claimed even the rye. We were forced to borrow seed and food from the new nádor to survive."

"We have a new nádor?"

"Yes. After the second famine, the Sovereign of Urundien decided to replace the old nádor. We don't know why—they never tell us anything." I noticed that she lowered her voice as she spoke of the nádor, as if someone might overhear. "Maybe because nobody could pay their taxes after all the famine. The new nádor's not like the others. The last one mainly kept to his castle and left us in peace, save for when the taxes were due. But this one now . . ." She hushed her voice, as if the very walls were listening. "We're all in debt to him."

I turned around so abruptly that the comb tore at my hair.

"How large are Father's debts?"

"Large. But don't you worry yourself about them." She leaned forward and squeezed my shoulders. "We're so glad to have you home again, Maresi. Let's not speak of hardships on your first day home." She leaned back and lifted a strand of my hair, which was now smooth and tangle-free. "I see no harm in skipping the ceremony and simply braiding your hair now. Got to be done sometime. Would you like one braid or two?"

I turned around and gently took my hair out of her hand. "I no longer bind my hair. It is not done on Menos."

She regarded me for a moment. She dropped her hand to her side. "The water's boiling. Do you want to wash or dry?"

We spoke no more of it, but I can see that my refusal to bind my hair worries Mother. Or else it irks her, like an itching mosquito bite.

Now it is time for me to curl up in bed.

Yours,

Maresi

Dearest Jai,

I have been home for a handful of days now. I am not yet sure what to make of it. I am tired—please forgive me if I come across as bad-tempered.

I spent the first day helping Mother around the house, and kept mainly indoors. I was tired and feeling fragile. I wanted to avoid people's prying eyes. Instead I asked Mother about everybody else in the village. She said only that everything was the same.

"What would change here?" she said. But she is wrong. Nothing has changed in her eyes. To me, after leaving and returning, much is different.

My friend Sannarl, whom I used to play with almost every day, died shortly after I left Rovas. Her father was a woodcutter, and their family lived in a little cabin outside the village with no farmland. When the hunger winter came, after an early frost had claimed most of the rye and heavy rain washed away the remainder, there was no longer anyone to sell them food. By autumn the whole family had taken to the road to beg. Only the mother and Sannarl's younger sister returned. My father's mother also died the year after I left, weakened by hunger and age.

I miss Grandmother. I remember her soft, wrinkled cheeks and the gentleness of her voice when she spoke to her grandchildren.

Babies have been born in my absence, here and in the neighboring village. The village itself is the same. The buildings are where they have always been. They have not changed since my father was a boy. Jannarl's father has built an extra room for Jannarl and Náraes and their children, but for the most part the houses look the same as they always have, though perhaps a little shabbier. There are fewer animals than I remember from my childhood, but more than there were when I fled the famine. My playmates have grown up and their parents have grown old, but life continues just as before: with hard toil from daybreak to nightfall.

On the evening of the second day, after we had eaten, Mother cleared the porridge pot from the table and told me it was time I thought about visiting the neighbors.

"So they know our daughter is well and truly home."

I understood that this was important to her. She had sheltered me from curious visitors so that I might rest, but now she wanted to show me off to the village as an honor on our home.

"I cannot go empty-handed," I said, and Mother and Father nodded. Everyday visits do not require gifts, but this was no everyday visit. Rovasians always exchange small gifts to mark special occasions.

"You can go tomorrow," said Mother. "That'll give you time to prepare."

Later that evening I unpacked the salt I had bought in Valleria, and the red woolen fabric our Mother Abbess had smuggled into my bag before I left. I cut out four pieces and sewed them into small pouches. Then I embroidered some simple shapes on them, the first that came to mind: a rose, an apple, a shell. I used black and white yarn from Mother's stash. I can picture you raising your eyebrows in surprise, thinking, "But Maresi is useless at sewing." Well, embroidery is in fact a time-honored Rovasian tradition, and my mother and Náraes taught me the techniques from a very young age. I filled the pouches with salt, which is an expensive commodity here. All salt trade has to go via Urundien, and all the mines in Urundien and its vassal states are owned by the monarch. The Kyri River (which flows to the east of our village, and alongside the city of Kandfall, the seat of the nádor's castle) is commonly known as the salt river, because it is used to transport the salt from the mountain mines all the way to Irindibul.

The following day I was ready to set out with my pouches. I went to visit the neighboring farm first. It felt like the least intimidating option. I knocked and stepped inside without waiting for an answer, as is the custom here. Máros was the first to bid me welcome, making the sign we would use as a greeting when we were children. He lost his hearing after a bad fever as a boy, but we never let this get in the way of our games.

Their house had not changed but for the new door that led into the new room where my sister now lives with her family. The earthen floor was firmly trodden and covered in crisp straw, a fire burned in the hearth, and there was a long hearthside table laid with a gaily embroidered tablecloth. Jannarl's mother Feira was well-known for her skill with a needle.

"Well now, here she comes, our special guest," said Feira, rising from her seat by the hearth, where she had been spinning. She looked just as I remembered her: gray hair tightly braided and pinned up around her crown, a linen blouse and brown-striped skirt covered with an embroidered apron. Around her wrists and ankles she wore brightly colored woven bands twisted together in the old Rovasian style. She was as thin as ever, and as slow to smile. "Father, fetch the horn."

Maressa came running from the newly built little room where she lives with her parents and little sister, closely followed by Jannarl and Náraes. Dúlan had been sitting on her grandfather Haiman's knee, but Haiman stood up, put her down on the floor and went to fetch the drinking horn from where it hung on the wall. Then he lifted down the jug of moonshine from a shelf, filled the horn and limped over to me. Haiman has limped ever since I have known him. His leg was injured in an accident involving a harrow when Jannarl was a boy.

I drank from the horn, feeling very ceremonious. This was a new experience for me. Father has offered the horn to our guests many times, but I had never been the honored guest invited to drink first. The horn was then passed around, and even Maressa was allowed a sniff of the contents. She wrinkled her nose. "Blurgh!"

I offered the red pouch of salt to Feira who accepted it stolidly, but Náraes's eyes grew wide. Feira gingerly placed the pouch next to the jug of moonshine.

It was oddly formal sitting at the neighbors' table and talking about the spring sowing and the past winter. I noticed Feira looking at my unbound hair, but she said nothing. Máros's gaze did not leave my face for a single moment, and I wished I could tell him everything about my journey and my time on Menos. But when I made an attempt to signal "island" to him with my hands, it became clear that our shared symbols fell short. How could I describe land surrounded by water to a person who has never seen anything beyond our village and the nearby forest? The farthest he has been from home is the offering grove and burial grove in the hidden valley. He knows trees and fields, but we do not share the vocabulary to describe the ocean.

After a while I thanked them politely and continued to White Farm, so called because the doorframe is carved from real silverwood from the burial grove. Nobody would ever lift an ax or knife to one of the rare white trees of the burial ground, for fear that it would bring bad luck to their home and family for generations. But sometimes skilled carvers pick up storm-fallen branches and carve knife shafts or candleholders or other smaller objects from the ever-white, stone-smooth wood. I have never seen a doorframe made from silverwood other than the one at White Farm.

The moment I knocked, Marget opened the door and threw her arms around me.

"Maresi!" she cried in my ear. "Maresi!"

I held my old friend at arm's length and looked at her. I am a head taller than she is now. Her eyes shone as she looked at me, just as Ennike's always do. She has a broad, determined chin, large nose and dark eyebrows.

"Mother told me you were home again, but I didn't quite believe it," she said, inspecting me as closely as I was inspecting her. "You haven't braided your hair?" she said in wonder, fingering a brown strand. "And what a cloak you have!"

For a moment I felt embarrassed about wearing it. It is so costly and fine, so unlike anything the folk of Rovas are used to seeing.

"Let the girl in," came an old woman's voice from inside the house, and Marget led me inside. And there, seated around their red-painted table as if they had been expecting me, the whole family was gathered: Marget's little sister Lenna (who is younger than Akios), their mother Seressa, and grandmother Kild. Only the father Ádon was missing.

"Father's out tending to the animals," Marget explained before I could even ask. "We've a cow and a pig," she continued proudly.

"Bought with borrowed money," muttered Kild, but nobody seemed to pay attention to the old woman's words.

The woman of the house raised a horn of moonshine to me, and once again I drank and passed the horn around before presenting my gift.

"Goodness me!" exclaimed Seressa. "You've clearly done well for yourself out in the big wide world. We thought we'd never see you again, Maresi, so we did."

Lenna set the drinking horn aside, sat back down and returned to her handicraft. "Else we didn't think you'd return with virtue and honor intact. That's what Grandmother said anyway." She looked at me innocently. "Do you, Maresi? Have your honor intact?"

She did not know what she was asking, but the elder women did, and I caught Seressa looking me up and down. Marget hushed her sister angrily, but I looked her straight in the eye.

"Yes I do, Lenna. According to your definition and mine."

I sat down at the table and looked at the other women. They each had something in their hands: Lenna was engaged in some simple needlework, Marget was working on a beautiful embroidery and Seressa was spinning. Only Kild's eyesight was too poor to manage crafts. It felt strange to sit there as a guest, taskless, while everyone else was working.

"So I said to her, I said, your eggs aren't worth *that* much," Seressa continued the conversation I must have interrupted with my arrival. "I gave her a bit of cheese, and told her that would have to do!"

Kild nodded. "She's always been one for high prices. It's just her nature, but she's no stranger to a bit of haggling."

"Maresi, what did you wear in that abbey of yours?" asked Marget.

"Certainly not what you would call beautiful clothes," I said slowly. "We dressed simply. Trousers, a linen shirt and a headscarf. White scarves for the novices and blue for the sisters."

"Does everyone have cloaks as fine as yours?" Marget looked longingly over at the cloak, which she had hung on a peg on the wall.

"No. My friend Jai sewed it for me as a farewell gift. She said it would keep me warm and dry on the journey home, and she was right."

"How did you *dare* travel all that distance alone? Weren't you afraid?" Lenna brought her needlework closer to her face and concentrated as she stuck the needle through the fabric.

"Sometimes. But not too much. I knew I would survive the journey." I had no desire to explain the ways of the Crone and that when she opens her door for me, I will know. I did not want to speak of all the things that made me different from them. I changed the subject.

"Marget, what is that you are embroidering?"

Marget's cheeks flushed red. "A bridal bonnet," she said quietly.

"Marget's planning on marrying your Akios," said Lenna saucily. "She wants to become the housewife of Enresbacka."

Surprised, I turned to look at Marget, who was leaning so far over her embroidery that all I could see was the crown of her fair head.

"Akios is only fifteen! Is that not a little young for marriage?"

"It is," her mother answered firmly. "And Akios hasn't even asked her." She looked pointedly at her youngest daughter, who scoffed. "Lenna, don't meddle in things you don't understand." Then she looked at Marget. "But a girl can sew herself a bridal set, there's no harm in that. It'll be a few years before it's ready. A lot can happen in that time."

"I hope you don't mind," whispered Marget.

"No, of course not," I replied, but only later did it occur to me what she meant. If Akios married Marget, or indeed another, my status as the unmarried sister in the family would rank bottom of the hierarchy after Mother and Akios's wife, and I would hold the least sway in all matters concerning the organization and running of the household.

"Go to the storehouse, Marget," said her mother, "and fetch some of Lenna's lingonberries."

"I picked the berries myself last autumn and preserved them in water!" Lenna explained proudly. "*And* I milked Clover and skimmed the milk, so we have cream to go with them!"

ᛒ

Eventually I bid my farewells, left White Farm and headed for the last remaining house in the village, Streamside Farm, so called because of its proximity to the stream. Only two people live there: the widow Béru and her son Árvan. I was dreading this visit the most. I had not often been inside their home, and Árvan is the only other young man in the village besides Jannarl and Máros. I am not used to the company of men. My father and brother are one thing, but—after what happened in the crypt when the Crone devoured every last man who had invaded our island—I find it difficult even to hear male voices. They frighten me. For eight years I saw no men other than those who came to the island hunting for you. I still remember the shaved heads, the tattooed hands, their weapons and cruel laughter. I remember your father's silken, ice-cold voice. The smell of the men's blood when they were dragged through the door of the Crone—the door that I held open.

Although the men here in the village are nothing like those who invaded our island, they conjure up the memories nonetheless. Their voices have similar tones. Their bodies are male bodies. It is not fair, and I am ashamed of these feelings, but sometimes I flinch and recoil if a man approaches me with a sudden movement. When two men call to one another outside our house in the evening, I do not hear their talk of rain and compost; I hear words of violence and blood and . . . and what they did to Sister Eostre when she still served as the Rose. Then my heart begins to race and I hardly dare breathe, I am so afraid.

Streamside is the largest homestead in the village. The house has a real floor of planed wooden planks, covered in woven rugs. There are three bedrooms and one family room with a large brick fireplace. Béru's husband came from a large family with many sons and daughters, but they are all deceased now, apart from some daughters who married into other villages. Béru had only one child, her son, Árvan, before her husband died. I do not know him particularly well; he is some years older than I and did not take part in our childish games because he had already started working to help his mother.

I was welcomed in by Béru, whom I was always afraid of as a child. The same stern, dark eyes met mine now from under a wreath of brown braids as she handed me the greeting horn.

"Blessings on your journey, Maresi Enresdaughter."

She said no more and returned to her rocking chair before the white-mortared hearth. Béru is always very well dressed, in a gray blouse, plain gray-striped skirt and an apron with simple embroidery on the hemline. I have never seen her wear anything else. She has real curtains in her windows, and thick knotted rugs on the walls to keep out drafts. Her son, Árvan, is so unremarkable that I almost did not see him sitting there on a bench by the wall, resoling an old boot. He nodded at me but did not meet my gaze. I sat down timidly on the edge of a bench by the table and set down the greeting horn.

The conversation did not flow smoothly. Árvan said nothing at all, but I saw him glance in my direction from time to time. It was Béru and I who spoke, and the conversation consisted of her asking me questions. What had I learned at the Abbey? What embroidery stitches did I know, and was I deft at spinning and weaving, and what did I know about plant dyes, and pickling and juicing? I answered as well as I could, embarrassed both by her questions and by her son's silence. As soon as possible within the restraints of courtesy, I gave her the salt pouch, thanked them for their hospitality and headed for home.

I was exhausted. I suppose I am not used to meeting new people, and though these are the neighbors I grew up with, they feel like strangers. It is nighttime now and I will blow out my candle soon. I am sending you my thoughts. If you were lying in bed next to me now, my tiredness would surely disappear and we would lie here talking long into the night! Instead I must curl up alone, without your breathing to listen to.

Your friend,

Maresi

Venerable Sister O,
I have been home for nearly a whole moon now. I am beginning to slip back into the daily routine of my childhood, but some things remain foreign to me that were once so familiar. The earthen

floor of our house is damp and cold. The lack of cleanliness is making my skin crawl—I miss the Abbey's morning wash more than I could have imagined! The people here only wash their hands and face occasionally. The children bathe in streams and rivers in the warmest of the summer months, but the adults never do. I cannot get used to the odors. I leave the door ajar on purpose and my mother looks offended. Yesterday she calmly asked: "Can you no longer stand our smell?" So I shut the door on the cool spring night, while secretly thinking that she was absolutely right: I can no longer stand it. But it is more than just bodily odors. Mother has a few hens that live in the animal pen at one end of the house, and the smell of chicken droppings permeates the building. Chicken droppings and cabbage, and the rancid grease on Father's newly greased boots, and smoke from the fireplace, and everything is so *musty*. Mother is cleanly; she makes sure we have clean clothes and changes the straw on the floor at least once per moon. Her pot and pan are scrubbed and well kept, and she airs out the bedclothes, and every autumn we have new straw in the mattresses. Yet it is always musty. No fresh ocean breezes sweep through the village, and there is nothing like Body's Spring where we can bathe in hot water and then cleanse in cold.

I go out into the central yard every morning to wash myself in rainwater and perform the sun greeting facing the eastern forest, despite the fact that the sun has rarely shown itself since I arrived. Last year Rovas was plagued by drought, and now rain threatens to be equally damaging. I hear the men mutter about seeds rotting in the ground. Ever since the hunger winter the people have been in debt and unable to save up a store of seed or flour. There is just enough and no more. I hear Mother and Father talking early in the mornings, when Father gets up to sow the last of the spring seeds. Their debts are greater than they led me to believe. They are behind on their payments. If the seeds rot away now . . . I do not know what Father will do. And I am yet another mouth to feed, an unexpected addition to the family.

I think of the purse of silver that the Mother Abbess gave me before I left the Abbey. It is at the bottom of my bag, under my books. It is the silver I am going to use to build a school.

I gave Maressa the shell necklace that Heo gifted me. She loves it and wears it around her neck day and night. Please tell Heo. I hope she does not mind. Shells are rare here and considered very beautiful. I am wearing the snake ring you gave me on my finger, and it attracts many looks, though nobody mentions it.

I am not alone. I have my family around me, and my friends. Marget and I see each other every day. But our friendship is no longer as effortless as it once was. When I talk about the First Mother and her three aspects, or about the Crone and her door, Marget listens politely for a while but soon starts gossiping with my mother about the neighbors, or discussing the best remedy for diaper rash and colic with Náraes, who often comes to see us and brings the children. I am no longer one of them. I am an outsider, an oddity they can inspect and muse over, but who is completely disconnected from them and their everyday lives. I have put off visiting the nearest village, Jóla. I have no desire to relive the experience of interest and well-meaning curiosity transforming into utter bewilderment because I do not braid my hair, or no longer speak as they do here.

At times I feel as lonely as I did during my first year on Menos. But please do not tell my friends. I do not want anybody to worry about me. I am sure it will be fine—everything turned out well at the Abbey after all. I made friends with Ennike, I learned the language, and I learned what was expected of me.

I will start work on founding the school soon. However, there is so much to do during spring and summer that no one would let their children join a school at this time of year anyway. The children have to help on the land. Even the little ones can be of use picking harmful insects off the vegetables. Autumn after harvest will be a better time to start a school. Now my family needs me. I cannot expect them to simply provide for me.

I am not going hungry, not yet, but there is little to eat. Mother makes stew from the last of the autumn's cabbage, which is in bad condition and does not taste good. Sometimes she adds beans, turnip or onion. We have no meat. Sometimes Akios has time to go fishing in the river, and then we get fresh fish to eat, which is a real feast. I would gladly go with him, but Mother wants me at home to help with the housework, so I do as she asks. I have only just returned, and I do not want to displease my mother so soon. During winter, Father and Akios went out hunting for the small game that we are allowed to hunt, but they will not lay traps now that the animals are tending to their young. My stomach aches often. You can tell Sister Nar that the peppermint leaves she gave me have been very beneficial. Akios has helped me dig a little herb garden along the southern wall of the house where I have sown the seeds I brought with me. Mother cannot understand why I am wasting energy on growing anything other than food.

The evening meal is stew. Breakfast is rye-flour porridge. We have no other meal and no bread. The hens are not laying much, but we hope that they will later in spring.

I did not celebrate Moon Dance. Was that wrong of me? It felt far too strange to go outside and dance alone without my Abbey sisters. There is no Maidendance to dance at, in any case, and no feast to celebrate afterward. The First Mother is not here—she abides on Menos. I do not think she would have heard my song.

Still, on the night of the Moon Dance I went out to relieve my bladder and saw that it was one of the few clear nights we have had since I came here. The moon was full and hung just above the horizon, larger than usual. I stopped in the yard and bowed to her. I was fully clothed and neither sang nor danced. A kite called from the darkness and its wailing cry sent shivers down my spine, and at once I was overcome with cold—the same cold as I felt in the presence of the door of the Crone.

I miss the Crone. I miss the chill of her crypt. I miss the snake on your door. I miss our lessons in the treasure chamber, which you taught for me and me alone. At the Abbey I could speak with the Crone, and sometimes even hear her answer. I no longer feared her and even grew to enjoy the feeling of being her chosen one. She shared her secrets through you, and only I was party to them. Here I learn nothing new, and fear has crept back into my heart. Sometimes I think about the winter that, though still far off, approaches nearer every day, and then it becomes difficult to breathe.

There are soldiers in the forest as well. I do not know why they are there; no one will talk about them. They only warn me not to stray too far from the village alone. When they mention them, in brief snatches and hushed tones, I can almost hear the clattering weapons of the men who came to our island, and their voices, and the hissing whisper of the Crone. I become so frightened that I can barely move.

There is no one I can talk to about all these things.

You will not tell anybody else what I have written, will you?

Yours,

Maresi

Dearest Jai,

I am going to send this first bundle of letters to the Abbey soon, to let you know, at long last, that I have arrived safely. A whole moon has passed since I returned home, and the worst of the rain has been and gone. The roads should soon be dry enough for travel. It may be that the best route for letters is via Irindibul. Goods are transported from Rovas to the city several times a year, usually along the Kyri River.

Gray Lady is doing well. She is pleased that she no longer has to walk constantly, and the land is teeming with grass and other good things for her to eat. We also give her the straw that we sweep out from the house. She could live inside with the hens, but she seems happiest outside, even in the rain. She can shelter under the roof where it protrudes from the wall, or under a tree, where she gazes out at the falling rain surrounding her like a curtain and appears content. Sometimes we employ her for farm work, but not often. Mainly she helps us to carry water, or wood from the forest in panniers.

Yesterday I made the decision to finally visit our neighboring village, Jóla. It was necessary, because I need to know how many girls there are for my school. I think that the school will initially consist mainly of the daughters of our village and Jóla, and then once it is all up and running I can accept pupils from other villages as well. The air was misty and my cloak was soon damp, but it kept me dry inside. I wore Father's old boots, for there has not yet been time to make a pair of my own. They kept getting stuck in the muddy path, and I had to lean on Gray Lady for support as I pulled myself free.

I passed the shabby cabin that Mother—by which I mean my own mother, not the Mother Abbess—said belongs to a woodcutter by the name of Kárun. I have no memory of him, but I do remember his house. It is a small gray hut with a single window, not far from the stream. No smoke came from the chimney, so I supposed Kárun was out chopping down trees or whatever it is that woodcutters do. Water was dripping from the roof, which was green with moss, and I saw no vegetable garden. I wonder what he lives on.

The path between our villages is not long. It crosses the fields, rises onto a ridge and continues through woodland until the landscape opens out on to more fields, and there lies Jóla. It was a short, easy walk, despite the muddy path and my unsteady steps. It felt right to go on foot, with Gray Lady by my side. Finally I was on my way—finally I was beginning the work I came here to do! Spring birds were singing despite the miserable weather, and I saw a snake wriggle across the path. It must have just awoken from its winter sleep, for its movements appeared sluggish and slow. I greeted it with respect and asked it to pass on my greetings to the Crone, and for that moment I felt close to all of you in the Abbey again.

Jóla resembles our village but is a little larger, with four fine houses in a circle around a central yard and a number of additional outbuildings. Every homestead I visited received a pouch of salt, which was most welcome and considered auspicious by all. Then I counted the number of children in each home and asked whether the girls might want to attend my school in autumn. I was met with expressions of surprise and polite mumbles, but no straight answers. They probably need time to get used to the idea.

"That's all well and good for you, Maresi, all that learning and reading," said Rehki, a young man with a pretty, dark-haired wife. They have three children, one of whom, Jannorin, is of school age. "Your father always did say there was something special about you ever since you were little. And there's certainly nothing wrong with being able to read and write. But who needs any of that here in Rovas besides the nádor and his scribes? Can you teach Jannorin to be a good housewife? Can you teach her how to make the flour rations stretch, or to care for a baby? Thank you for the salt anyway, and may the Great Bear grant you the strength of her paw, the cunning of her small eyes and the courage of her heart."

I wanted to answer that I could indeed teach her all those things, and more. Sister Nar and Sister Ers taught me many methods of making flour stretch, and I know a great deal about herbs and curatives for small children. But I did not know how to make them believe me. As far as they are concerned, education has no practical purpose. Books and figures are for the likes of the nádor in his castle. They see education as something that belongs to the overlords, and therefore something almost wicked.

After Rehki's I went to the house of my childhood friend Péra, her mother, father and beautiful elder sister, who resembles Eostre. Then I headed to the smallest farmstead, where a couple lives with their three sons. I felt embarrassed and did not stay long. After what happened at the Abbey, I still find it somewhat difficult to be in such close proximity to so many unknown males. There was one in particular called Géros, the middle son, a little younger than I, who looked at me with laughter in his eyes and made me feel very uncomfortable. The final house I visited belonged to old man Tauer's son, his wife and their four children. They were a pleasant but rather wild gaggle, and my questions about school attendance were met once again with friendly smiles and evasive words.

Every house offered me moonshine. It is not too strong, only slightly stronger than wine, but I had eaten nothing since my morning porridge and ended up as intoxicated as at the feast after Moon Dance. I was grateful for Gray Lady's back to lean on when I reemerged into the cool spring evening. I may have sung a little. I longed to head home, but one salt pouch remained. So I walked around the corner to the final house, the annex built for Tauer and his aged father when Tauer became too old to work the land and his son took over the farm. I sang the "Song of the Bear," which we always sing at every festival and naming ceremony, in praise of the wise bear who watches over us. It felt like the natural thing to sing. I thought about how much I love my village, and the people in it, even though I feel like an outsider right now. They may see me as something other, something different, but no one has shown me anything but kindness since I returned home. And it is painful to see how hard their lives have become. I do not remember it being quite this hard when I was little, but perhaps I have simply forgotten. I see deterioration; I see hollow cheeks. I see children ten years old laboring as hard as their parents, and I want to offer them something better—something more. The absolute worst thing I see is resignation. They believe that this is how life is, and how it always will be, indeed how it *should* be. I must show them something else. I must open a window in their world, but I do not know how.

I knocked and entered through the unpainted door.

I had never been inside Tauer's and his father's home before. The only house in Jóla I ever visited as a child was Péra's, because we sometimes played together. But I know Tauer—everybody in these villages knows him. Tauer is the one people go to when they have a festering wound, or a stubborn wart, or relentless pain, or a husband straying from the marital bed. Tauer has concoctions and prescriptions for everything. He helps to bring new lives into this world and accompanies others out

41

when their time comes. He is full of superstitions, and the folk around here swallow them willingly. They believe warts can be removed by rubbing them with vole skin soaked in saltwater under a full moon at a crossroads, and that it is even more effective if done at a crossroads in a different village from one's own. They believe that a woman can change the sex of her unborn child by walking under a rainbow. They believe that they can ensure a good harvest by baking a bread from rye, corn, salt and honey in the shape of a five-pointed star, blessing it in running water, smoke and dust, and then burying it in a field.

They have so many delusions that I will hardly know where to begin when I eventually come to teach them the truth of how the world works.

Tauer's home was not like I imagined. Herbs and rye bread were hanging from the rafters to dry. The straw on the floor was clean and fresh. There was a small table and two carved wooden chairs, and a wall-mounted bed with embroidered curtains. There were bright copper pots hanging on the wall and a shelf lined with bowls and jugs of mysterious contents. It could have been any ordinary farmhouse. Lying in bed was Tauer's father, an old man as wrinkled and crinkled as laundry that has been crumpled up and left to dry. A small black-haired girl sat under the table rattling around with a pot and a wooden spoon, accompanied by two brown hens. Tauer was standing by the stove on the other side of the room, busy with some task or other. He is an old man, older than Father, but still has a straight back and more brown than gray in his beard, which he keeps neat and trim. He is short and stocky but not fat. He reminds me of a little bear.

I was sleepy after all that moonshine. Sleepy and hungry. A quick horn of moonshine and then home. I would ride the mule, so I could half-sleep throughout the journey.

"So, here you are at last!" Tauer's voice was dry and warm, like a hill in summer heat.

"At last?"

"Yes." Tauer wiped his hands clean. "We've been waiting, haven't we, Father?" He spoke in the direction of the bed, and a rustling sound came in response. "We knew you'd come, sooner or later, but we understood perfectly well that you had your own matters to see to. Unbound hair too, I see. But that shouldn't really come as a surprise."

I sighed. I had to hear about my hair even from Tauer. Why should it matter so much that I do not braid it like the other girls?

Tauer took down a bundle of herbs from a rafter, lifted a small pot from the hearth and crumbled the herbs inside. A fresh scent spread through the room. The girl under the table banged on her pot, causing the hens to cluck nervously. Tauer made small talk as he expertly plucked various jars and packages from the shelf and added an array of ingredients into his pot.

"Custom doesn't dictate moonshine, you know. Only that a guest be offered a beverage, and that the host then drinks from the same receptacle." He poured the contents into a wooden bowl and came over to me. "Drink now. You need it."

I sipped at the hot drink. It was sweet and bitter.

"Honey?"

"Wild honey. And mint and wandflower and fir sprigs and a few other bits."

I thought of Sister Nar and her brews. Tauer pulled out a chair for me and shooed the hens away.

"They should be out in the pen with the goats and my daughter-in-law's hens," he said, and looked at them with concern. "But they're so attached to me that they refuse to lay eggs anywhere else. And Father needs his eggs, don't you, Father?" He lowered his voice. "It's practically the only thing I can get him to eat these days. Raw eggs."

I held out my bowl and he took it, sniffing the air around me as he did so.

"It is lavender," I said. "From Menos." I still have bunches of dried lavender between my clean clothes in the chest at the foot of my bed.

"Lavender?" Tauer looked at me with an expression I could not interpret. "Indeed. I'd never have thought it."

The hot drink was very refreshing and my head soon felt clearer.

"Will you not invite your daughter to drink as well?" I asked, and pointed under the table.

Tauer laughed.

"Oh no, she's my son's youngest. But it's such a bustling din in their house that I often bring her here. She likes a little peace and quiet, does Naeri." The girl punctuated this point by banging the pot again, causing the hens to cluck and the old man to groan in his bed. "Do you know how many grandchildren I have, Maresi Enresdaughter? Ten! Seven of whom are in this village. Three children was enough for me, but they spawn like anything. In any case, the drink is too strong for her, you understand."

I fished out the salt pouch. He looked pleased when I handed it to him.

"An excellent gift. Powerful. Not everybody got an embroidered snake, I hope?"

"No. Shells, apples, roses, all sorts of things."

"Good. I would have chosen something longer-lasting than salt, but at least they'll all make use of it."

I stared at him.

"As will I," he hastened to add.

I was so confused that I hardly knew what to say. "I am planning on starting a school in the autumn," was the first thing I could think of.

Tauer leaned back in his chair and furrowed his brow. One of the hens flapped onto his lap.

"There's much to be done first. Will you manage?"

This irked me. Nobody seems to understand how important this school is, not for me, but for the girls of the villages! They think that sowing and reaping and embroidery and daily chores are all that matter. I stood up abruptly.

"Thank you for letting me rest awhile. And thank you for the tea. Now night is approaching and I must return home."

"Are you walking?"

Anger prevented me from honoring Tauer with a reply. I no longer felt in the least bit tired, only irate. I said a short farewell, left the house and called to Gray Lady. Naturally she did not come, and I had to walk around the house to look for her. I found her munching on a few strands of straw next to a shaggy gray goat. She was extremely reluctant to leave her new friend, and when I finally managed to lead her to the gate in the farmyard fence I saw Tauer standing there and watching, so I could not mount her. I had to push her through the gate instead.

"Go straight, go strong," Tauer called after me.

I stomped away, angry and irritated. Nobody understands the importance of the school. Nobody understands that I am doing it for their own good!

I heard the old man start singing the "Song of the Bear" behind me. He came to the verse about the bear's wrath:

And her jaws snapped at the fiend
And her claws ripped into his flesh
And her steps caused the ground to tremble
And no one dared approach her lair

I started humming along involuntarily, and then found myself singing the most fiery of the verses all the way home. I even threw in a few lines of my own about the Crone's ice-cold wrath and dreadful vengeance. When I arrived back home I was surprised that the walk had passed so quickly, and I gave Gray Lady straw to chew on and ate a bowl of porridge myself before crawling into bed. I slept a deep and dreamless sleep, but have felt a little drowsy and lethargic today. I hope I am not getting a chill. Spring chills are always so drawn out.

Tomorrow I will head out into the forest to bring home the wood Akios has chopped, and I need to be fresh and alert for that. I will write more again soon! Please remember to tell Geja stories about me, so she does not forget me.

Your friend,

Maresi

My dear Ennike Rose!

Today, as Akios and I were out collecting wood in the forest, I met a most peculiar person.

We rose at daybreak and ate yesterday's cold porridge while Mother packed us a small lunch. I went out before my brother and tied the panniers to Gray Lady's back. I was excited—how I had been looking forward to getting out into the forest! Mother has kept me cooped up at home too long, and I have missed the trees and fresh air and silence. Akios came out carrying his ax and our food package, and off we went.

It was a pleasure to walk side by side with my brother at dawn, into the forest to the east. Akios is one of the few people whose behavior toward me has not changed in all these years. Father looks at me with excessive admiration, I think, and Mother's thoughts are something of a mystery to me. Sometimes she is warm and joyful and all is as it was before I left, but she dislikes it when I talk about the time I spent away, about the Abbey or anything that happened there. Whenever I bring it up she immediately grows quiet and withdraws. Náraes is cordial, but absent and occupied with her children and her own problems. We cannot have the same relationship as we used to, because she is not the same person as she used to be. Perhaps neither am I, though I feel like exactly the same Maresi I have always been—which is strange, if I think about it. I have opened the door to the Crone's realm. I have sacrificed my very blood to sate the Crone's hunger. I have been inducted into knowledge and mysteries unimaginable to these people. Still, I feel just as lost and confused as I did on my arrival at Menos, when I understood nothing and always did everything wrong. I seem to have forgotten how to live in Sáru, and even though this lifestyle is in my blood, and has been since birth, it feels as though little of its influence remains. I am different, and no one will let me forget it. They do not speak to me in the same way as they speak to each other. They show me respect, as one does a scholar, but at the same time they treat me as though I am ignorant of the things that truly matter. I am not a foreign weed, but neither am I a grain of rye among the others. I am . . . no, I know not what I am, Ennike Rose, my friend, and it is very difficult.

But Akios's way with me is the same as ever. He teases me as before, and turns to me with questions and worries as before. He may be standing on the threshold of manhood, but he still behaves like a little boy. A boy who works hard. We walked on either side of Gray Lady's head and listened to the birds singing in that way they do only at dawn and dusk. We saw animals as well: long-eared hares; an earth fox poking out of its burrow at the edge of a ditch; voles that darted out of the way of Gray Lady's hooves. Above our heads a flock of cranes flew north, sounding their solitary calls to one another. I believe I also heard the harsh cry of a kite. Perhaps the same kite I heard before.

"Remember when we wanted to catch an earth fox to tame it and teach it to catch mice?" asked Akios. I laughed.

"We were going to hire it out to all the villages and get rich!"

"It would have worked as well, if you weren't petrified at the sight of a little blood."

"It nearly bit your thumb off! Náraes was close to fainting when we came home."

"Ah, my thumb was fine," said Akios with a grin, waving his left hand in my face. A smooth scar gleamed at the base of his thumb. "You were always too easily frightened by small things."

"You can talk! Remember how you screamed when you thought Mother had burned the wooden horse Father whittled for you?"

"That was no small thing! Been breaking it in for months, I had. A spirited stallion who shunned me at first, but then became my trusty steed."

"What was it you called it? Steel Tail?"

"*Silver*tail, actually. Yours was called something stupid, like Apple Sauce."

"Apple Blossom." I smiled at the memory. I had named her after the most beautiful thing I could think of. Akios and I used to have a lot of fun with our horses. I sat steeped in pleasant memories, and his next question took me by surprise.

"Do you ever think about Anner?"

"Yes, of course." I glanced at him. "Often. Not every day, perhaps, but almost."

"I think about her constantly, but sometimes it feels as though nobody else does."

"Do the family not speak of her?"

He shook his head. "It makes Father too sad."

"I think . . . he feels guilty. He believes it was his fault, because he was unable to scrape together enough decent food. But of course it was not his fault. It was those seeds we were given by the nádor— they were bad. I do not know if you can remember the smell, but they were completely black. We all got sick from them, but little Anner was so small and weak to begin with."

"I've always thought it was my fault."

"How could it be your fault?"

"Mother had some cheese hidden away, did you know that?"

I shook my head. Akios gazed out into the forest, where the first morning rays were beginning to filter through the trees.

"I saw her hide a round, yellow cheese in an old pot on the highest shelf. I don't know how she got it—there certainly wasn't anything to buy in the village. I was so hungry, and one night while everyone was asleep I crept up and took it. I was only planning on cutting off a little morsel, but when I tasted the salty, fatty cheese I just couldn't stop myself." Akios swallowed, as if he could still taste it on his tongue. "Mother never mentioned it. But I've often thought that that cheese could have saved Anner's life."

I did not answer straightaway. I thought about it. "When was this?"

"A few days before she died."

I laid an arm around my brother's shoulders. "Akios, she was already sick with diarrhea by then. Nothing she ate stayed inside her. I have learned a little about starvation and such things during my years at the Abbey. We did not know it at the time, none of us did, but the Crone—by which I mean death—had already set her sights on her." I thought about the Crone's shining door that appeared in our house during those days. I had thought that it was me she wanted. But Anner was the one she was waiting for. Anner was already dying.

"Are you sure?" Akios did not look at me, but his tensed shoulders relaxed a little.

"Entirely sure."

I did not want to think about Anner any longer, or about how I might have been to blame for her death. Would the Crone have taken me instead, had I offered myself in place of my little sister? The Crone did want to take me later, except she did not demand I come; she invited me.

We entered the shade of the tallest tree in the forest, where the light and soundscape shifted. It became damper, dimmer, and the wind that had been whistling in our ears was now rushing through the leaves of the canopy overhead. The moss was soft beneath my feet. Deciduous and coniferous trees both grow here, and the fir sprigs are dazzling at this time of the year. Akios removed his cap and bowed before the tree. We hold the forest sacred in Rovas and perform our festivals, offerings and ceremonies in consecrated tree groves. Without thinking, I too found myself greeting the forest with respect, as I was taught to do from childhood. You do not suppose the First Mother will be angry, do you, Ennike Rose? The old teachings are returning to me now that I am back home.

We walked along the barely visible path that Akios had trodden previously, and before the sun had reached its zenith we had arrived at the glade where he had been working. Everything between our village and the Kyri River is common land, and we are free to take firewood and timber for our houses, graze cows (before, when the village still had many cows), pick berries and plants, and so forth. On the other side of the river the forest belongs to the Sovereign of Urundien, and the common folk are only allowed to hunt small game. No Rovasian may hunt large game. But it was a poached deer that saved our lives during the hunger winter. We did not travel as far as the Kyri River, but through the trees we could hear the rush of its flow. A small stream ran along one side of the glade, where we could slake our thirst. Akios scanned the woods vigilantly.

"What is it, Akios?" I asked with a chuckle. "Scared that Ovran will come and take you away?"

Ovran is a female entity that people believe in here in Rovas. She lives in the woods, has long birds' legs and chases solitary men, brandishing razor-sharp claws. Akios looked at me with a frown.

"There are real dangers in the forest now, Maresi. I'm not afraid when I come here alone, but now that you're with me . . ." He trailed off. I stared at him. "The nádor's men," he clarified anxiously. "They patrol far and wide, supposedly to protect our land against intruders and robbers, and to keep Urundien safe. But all they really do is take whatever they want." He lowered his voice, just as Mother had done when she spoke about the nádor. "Animals, food, silver . . . women."

My heart began to race. Just as it did that time in the crypt, when the men came and wanted to hurt Heo and the other little ones. My mouth was dry and tasted of metal. I could not move. I clenched my fists so tightly that my snake ring bore into my flesh. *They must not come here*, I thought. *They must not intrude on my family or my village.*

Akios noticed my expression. "They haven't been seen around here for a long time, Maresi. And I have my ax. I can protect you, don't you worry."

A fifteen-year-old boy with an ax against seasoned soldiers on horseback.

But there was no time for me to stand about worrying. The wind whistled through the treetops. I have always felt safe in the forest. My anxiety soon loosened its grip. Akios had built up a sizable pile of firewood, and it took us a long time to fill the baskets efficiently. We worked in silence for the most part, and when we were finished we sat down to eat the boiled eggs Mother had packed for us.

I inspected my hands. They were covered in scratches, and I pulled a long splinter out of my thumb with a grimace. Akios laughed and held up his hands. His skin was tough and smooth.

"Splinters don't bother me. You've spent too much time sitting around with those books, Sister."

"Have you seen me read a single book since I arrived?" In truth I have been doing physical work ever since I returned, just like the rest of the family.

"No. But I know you have them with you. Why aren't you reading?"

I was silent.

"I thought you loved reading? At least that was the impression you gave when you spoke of the Abbey. The treasure chamber and all that."

"I love to read. It is my favorite thing in the world. But . . . everybody thinks I am strange enough as it is. I have no desire to remind them that I can do something that no one else can."

"But they'll know all about it when you start your school. Then you'll *have* to know things that no one else does. Otherwise how can you teach them?"

I was silent again. He was right. I have missed my books more than I realized, Ennike Rose. Perhaps I need to make some time for them again.

Suddenly the silence of the forest was broken. My eyes darted around and I tensed, ready to flee. Akios laid his hand on his ax and pricked up his ears. A man's deep voice came from between the trees, singing a song. Akios relaxed and smiled, relieved.

51

"It's Kárun. He sings to let us know it's a friend approaching and not a foe. Kárun often visits to see how I'm doing. He's a woodcutter and timber-rafter. He knows everything about the forest and how to float timber all the way to Irindibul. I'd like to try it, I would."

Soon the singer revealed himself. He appeared walking through the trees with long strides and an ax over one shoulder. He was shorter than the men in Sáru, around the same height as me, but broader around the shoulders than Father. He was wearing the same brown trousers and striped waistcoat as most men do in Rovas, and he had long, straight hair that fell to his shoulders, but he was clean-shaven, which is unusual among men here. He did not stop singing when he saw us, but continued until he was standing right in front of where we were sitting and peering down at Akios.

"Is that a new song?"

Kárun nodded. "Aye. Learned it from three woodcutters I met upstream." He looked at the baskets filled with firewood and the pile of wood still left. "Been working hard, I see," he said, and I saw Akios sit up a little taller. "Has your ax stayed sharp?"

"Oh yes, ever since you helped me sharpen it."

Kárun glanced at me. "And who's this? Have you found yourself a girl?"

I frowned. I still do not like being around unknown men.

"My sister Maresi. She's been away for many years, but she's home again now. She's going to open a school to teach the girls to read and write."

For some reason I wished that Akios had not mentioned the school. My frown deepened.

"I see." Kárun looked at me searchingly. He has thick dark eyebrows, but his deep-set eyes are a very light brown. "And why is that?"

"Because knowledge is important," I said hesitantly. I swallowed in an attempt to rid my mouth of the taste of the fear that flashed through me once more. "Because there is much to learn about the world that no one here yet knows. And because people who know how to read and write can take control of their own lives."

Kárun crouched before me and listened closely.

"Naturally. But why will your school be for girls?"

"Why not?" A rush of anger prodded me to meet his gaze, and he seemed less threatening now that he was no longer towering above us. "Why should girls not learn knowledge and skills?" I wished he would leave me alone. I have learned much in the Abbey, from Sister O and Sister Ers and Sister Nar, from the Mother Abbess herself and everybody else. But I have never learned about men. I do not know how to look at them or talk to them. I cannot understand their jokes and gestures and movements.

It is not so with Akios. His body is a part of my body, and despite his beardy tufts and deepened voice he is still my brother, not a man. Do you see the difference?

This man, this Kárun, he is not really much more than a boy. He is a similar age to Náraes. But he sat before me and looked at me with a man's gaze, and questioned my school, and showed no signs of relenting.

I stood up and brushed the eggshell from my skirt.

"I am going for a walk in the forest," I announced, and hastened away without looking back. I hope they did not notice that my legs were trembling. I heard them talking behind me. Akios asked something, and Kárun muttered a response. He really has an uncommonly deep voice, even for a man.

It occurred to me that I should pick some forest thorn, which Sister Nar taught me can be very useful. It is an unremarkable little plant but it can both stanch blood and fortify women who have just given birth. It might come in handy when Náraes's time comes. I do not trust that old man Tauer and all his superstitions. I removed my headscarf and filled it with shoots. The forest was full of birdsong and the late-spring scents of budding life and damp moss. Slowly my galloping pulse was soothed.

Akios found me before long.

"Why did you go off like that? Kárun was only curious about your school."

"No, he was not." I tied the ends of my scarf together and stood up. "He just wanted to tell me how I should run *my* school."

"He was asking me all sorts of questions after you left."

"Like what?"

"Where you're going to hold it. What you're going to teach. If you're going to build a dedicated schoolhouse. If it's only for the children of Sáru or for the children of other villages as well. For the *girls* of other villages."

I glared at him, but then I saw that he looked sad. Offended.

"I'm a man. If I were a child you wouldn't want to teach me to read."

"You're no man!" I playfully punched his arm, but he did not smile. "Do you want to learn to read?"

"I don't know what use it would be for someone like me. I have to take over Father's farm and work the land. But . . ." He gazed into the forest. "When you talk about all the things you've read in books, of all the worlds you can visit through those black marks on paper, it makes me wish I could go on those journeys too." He smiled at me uncertainly. "It's beautiful here, don't you think? Are there forests like this on your island?"

I looked up at the tall, whispering trees above our heads. I felt the great boundless expanse of the forest stretching to the east and north and south.

"No. The tallest trees on Menos are not half as big as these. There are some narrow cypress trees that can grow quite high. And then there are harn trees, knotty with gray leaves. And olive trees and lemon trees, but you would call them bushes. The soil on Menos is not robust enough for giants like these."

"I like trees. I like being in the forest, working with an ax, being alone. If only I had brothers I could've become a timber-rafter, like

Kárun. He's helped me a lot over the past few years. Shown me which wood is good, taught me how to make a tree fall where you want. Have you seen the cabin by the stream where he lives? His father built it, and he has plans to build a new house, but something always gets in the way, he says. Kárun does what he wants, when he wants. I wish . . ." Akios trailed off. "It sounds like a good life," he concluded feebly.

"Grandmother always said the life of a timber-rafter is the hardest of all. They have no crops to eat so they must always trade or hunt. When the winds and the currents are going in the right direction they must work day and night, almost without rest, to take the felled timber downriver. The rapids are terribly dangerous, and logs get stuck and have to be pried loose. Rafters often die in rivers. Many cannot even swim."

"Kárun can. He's going to teach me this summer, as soon as the river is a little warmer. Kárun hunts when he isn't timber-rafting, and he sells the furs. He picks berries and sells them to the castle for a good price. He travels all around the forest and knows all its secrets. Sometimes he works for a few moons in Irindibul, once he's floated his timber down there. I think that must be freedom."

We started back toward the glade. It had never occurred to me that my brother might have a dream, or at least a dream of something other than what was expected of him. That is so unusual here. At the Abbey we are encouraged to discover what we are good at and follow our own paths. But in Rovasian villages all paths are mapped out from the moment you are born. Boys take over the farm from their father, get married and have children, then their sons take over the farm. Or you work at the castle and follow in your father's or mother's footsteps as a scrubber-woman, cook, washerwoman, cowherd boy, stable boy or guard.

Nobody here has dreams. Perhaps that is why they have so much difficulty understanding the point of my school. Life is tough and there is no point in moaning and groaning. Nothing can be changed, not even through hard work, because everyone already works hard from a young age. Life is what it is, and you should consider yourself lucky if you do not die a drawn-out, painful death when your time comes.

Not everyone is so lucky.

Akios interrupted my thoughts.

"You know, Maresi, if you insist on being so contrary and unfriendly to people who take an interest in your school, you're going to have a hard time finding pupils."

Akios is right, of course. I must get used to talking to men. And I must learn not to immediately assume that all questions are challenges and attacks.

He was quiet for a moment. "It was Kárun who killed that deer we were given to eat just after Anner died, remember?" I shook my head. "His father had just died. He was around the age I am now. He risked his neck to save the lives of everybody in Sáru. He brought meat to Jóla as well. If the nádor's men had caught him he would have paid with his life."

We worked together to attach the panniers to Gray Lady's back and tie more bundles of wood on top. She was heavily laden, and I felt a little sorry for her, but she was sparing Akios several days' work. It did not seem to bother her; she was more interested in the green leaves on the branches Akios had lopped off when felling the trees. We set off homeward. The rain has relented over the past few days and now the ground is not nearly as wet. It was afternoon and the sun would soon sink into evening.

"I ought to have practiced," I said. Akios looked at me questioningly. "Teaching. I have never taught anybody to read. Could I possibly practice on you?"

Akios looked at me dubiously at first, but when he saw that I was serious he smiled widely.

"You're a sly one, you are. How can I say no to helping out my sister?"

"And how could Mother and Father object?"

He gave me a friendly shove that almost sent me straight into the nearest ditch. He has grown strong, my little brother. I think you would like him. He has a warm and sunny nature, like you.

Missing you is made a little easier in his company.

Yours,

Maresi

Venerable Sister O,
  I have found a potential location for my school: very close to the village in a common pasture that is hardly used now that livestock is so scarce. It cannot take too long for the children to walk there, else their parents will be reluctant to excuse them from farm work for a sufficient length of time. The field is on the western side of the village, so eventually the children of Jóla will be able to come too. I intend to begin after harvest, and hire workmen using the silver the Mother Abbess gave me. We have access to free timber from the forest, but there are other necessary materials, not to mention paper and writing implements. Of course, the children can practice on planed boards to begin with. We will need books too, but we can manage without for a while. We will need a hearth to heat the school, and enough firewood to see us through winter. There is much to be obtained and arranged, but I believe I have enough silver.

I have a clear and detailed plan—I am grateful that we discussed it so often and so thoroughly during my final year at the Abbey. I will slowly gain the villagers' trust, and show them what benefit my knowledge may have for their children. At first they will find it difficult to understand what purpose it serves, but I must not be discouraged. I will pray to the Crone every evening for strength and tenacity.

There is another thing bothering me, which no one can help me with. I miss the routines of the Abbey terribly. The comfort and familiarity of greeting the sun every morning, together as one. All the festivals. Our lessons. Though this is my homeland, I do not feel at home here, not yet. Sometimes I even forget to call it "home." I feel like a ship with neither anchor nor harbor, bobbing through unknown waters, braced to hit land at any moment.

I am finding it incredibly difficult to apply myself to my great task, Sister O. The days come and go, and I am doing far less for the school than I ought to. So much of my energy is spent navigating the expectations put upon me, and finding my place in my family and village. I did not count on this, and it is frustrating me.

Your novice,

Maresi

My dear Ennike Rose,

I have been thinking about the Maiden a lot this spring. Everything is burgeoning and new: seeds are awakening; buds are bursting. It is the season of the Maiden, so I carved out a little labyrinthine Maidendance in the mud by the stream and danced there alone one night. It was not the real Moon Dance—the time for that is long past. Besides, I am not servant to the Moon, and the Moon Dance must be led by one whom she has called upon. Neither could I undress, for fear that someone might see. So I danced my own dance instead: a dance for the Maiden and the spring and all things budding and new. But it felt strange, almost wrong.

I serve the Crone, even though I never officially became Sister O's novice. The Crone's domain is the opposite of the Maiden's—it is endings, death and decay. In many ways springtime feels awkward and contrary to me. Or else it is I who am awkward and contrary, but I prefer to blame the season.

Inevitably someone *did* see me dancing. It was a new moon, yet the night was not dark enough, and I should have been more careful. You cannot imagine how much gossip there is now. It is not as if I blended in particularly well before, with my "men's clothes" and unbound hair, flame-red cloak and talk of schools—but now! Maresi Enresdaughter making a spectacle of herself, alone outside at night! Seressa and Feira lean in close to whisper when they see me. Mother returns from visits to friends' houses with a furrowed brow. She says nothing, but I can see her lamenting that her daughter should be so eccentric and odd. Generally, it seems that the warmth she showed me on my return is beginning to cool. She talks to me less, and I often catch her watching me with an expression I cannot interpret. Once I saw her touching my cloak, but as soon as she noticed me she quickly turned away.

But not quickly enough to hide the tears in her eyes.

At the Abbey everything was so simple because we always did everything together. Nothing felt remarkable or strange when we all took part in the same tasks and rites. I took it for granted that I would naturally continue in the same vein here in Rovas.

However, nothing here is simple or natural. Nothing at all. Everything about me is freakish and wrong.

I have started taking walks around the village at night in an attempt to rediscover the person I once was when I lived here, and recreate the feeling that this village is the whole world, and that I have my own natural place within it. I walk a wide circuit, between the forest and fields. I breathe in the scent of wet earth and moss, marshland and softwood forest. I listen to birdsong and the calls of the bucks in the woods. The stream burbles and gurgles, and the trees' young leaves whisper in the wind. I discover flowers I have not seen, or even thought about, since I was little. My boots get stuck in muddy ditches and twigs snap where I tread. I walk and I try to remember what it felt like to be just Maresi Enresdaughter, one of the village children, in no way remarkable.

Yet now I know that the world is so much greater than Sáru— greater than the whole of Rovas—and the place I once occupied has become overgrown without anybody noticing.

The absolute worst event of late was today at dawn, when I encountered that Kárun man as I was returning from my early-morning walk. I often go out in the mornings, when no eyes are on me and I can be alone. Besides, during the day I always have so much to do, and in the evenings I sit out in the yard with Akios and practice teaching. I hate to complain about my mother, for that is not good daughterly behavior, and I am aware of how many of you at the Abbey have lost your mothers, or live in the knowledge that you will never see them again. Still—my mother wants me to do everything her way. I learned a lot at the Abbey and have performed many household chores there. I have my own methods now, and Mother has hers, and both are equally valid. But Mother refuses to recognize this. Every time I make soup, I have to take careful note of where the pot and the ladle are kept so that I can return them to exactly the right place. Then I have to spice it exactly how Mother does, and make sure it tastes the same, and wash the dishes using her method and not the method I was taught by Sister Ers. It means that everything takes a lot longer than necessary. If I make the smallest deviation, Mother says: "Why did you put the pot here?" or "I wouldn't use so much chervil" with a pointed tone.

Yes, I know, I am babbling. Forgive me. I was supposed to tell you what happened this morning, but it was so embarrassing! Kárun emerged from behind our house just as I returned to the central yard. I was damp from the fog, and hot and tired after my long, brisk walk around the fields. Mother had silently remade my bed shortly after I had made it, and I had gone out to calm the irritation smoldering inside me. In other words, I was not in the best of moods.

Kárun's long hair was damp and clinging to his head. He had not shaved in several days and his chin was dark with stubble. I came to a halt, taken aback.

"Have you been out dancing?" he asked, and I could feel my face boil all the way up to my scalp.

"That is none of your business," I said, and stared at him with cheeks ablaze. Can you imagine how I felt? Yet again I was being taunted for my nighttime dancing. I wonder who gossiped to him. Could it have been Akios? Or perhaps he saw me himself that night! I wished I could disappear into the earth.

"It's none of *theirs* either," he said seriously. I saw that there was no hint of laughter or mockery in his eyes. "Whenever a person is different, or doesn't follow exactly the same path as everybody else, all the villagers begin to talk. You must learn to pay them no mind."

"Do you manage to pay them no mind?" I asked, raising my chin. He smiled softly. "Sometimes."

"What are you doing here?" I asked. In hindsight I realize this was probably unnecessarily hostile.

"Helping the White Farm sow give birth. She's had trouble in the past, but last night it went well."

Then he left. I watched his broad back as he disappeared into the dispersing morning mist.

Now I will sleep, my Ennike Rose. Sleep and dream. I hope I can find a way to send these letters to you, and soon.

Maresi

Dearest Jai,

I am not quite sure how to recount what happened yesterday! I have laughed until my stomach ached, but I must admit I am also rather pleased.

It was evening, and now that the weather is warm and fine, we usually sit together out in the yard after the evening meal. Mother sews or spins and Father mends some tool or other. Náraes often visits around this time and lets Maressa wreak havoc on her aunt and uncle while Mother and Father play with Dúlan. Pregnancy is exhausting Náraes, even without two children. Jannarl sometimes comes too and sits quietly. He is not much of a conversationalist, my good brother-in-law, but his silence is amiable. I expected to dislike him. Another man— one of these strange creatures I do not understand—who has taken my sister from our home and impregnated her. Yet Jannarl is so kind that it is impossible to think badly of him. Perhaps that is why Náraes married him. It is certainly *not* for his beauty! He still has the same blemished skin and skinny frame as he did in boyhood. He says little and is neither fun nor interesting, but he does everything Náraes asks of him, and he is a loving, patient father. In fact, he reminds me of my own father. He has the same kind, calm eyes. I have never heard him raise his voice or say a bad word about anybody, just like my father. The only person Father ever criticizes is the nádor, and even that is very seldom.

Jannarl was not with us yesterday evening, but Náraes and the children were. Akios and I were sitting in the central yard on the bench along the outside of our house with our planed planks and coal. He already has a sound knowledge of the alphabet. Maressa came running over and asked what he was doing. She is a lively child who rarely sits still, but she watched attentively and said she wanted to try. She learned three letters before she lost interest, took a plank and started drawing on it. Dúlan was toddling around and stuffing various leaves and twigs in her mouth while Mother shadowed her and pulled them out again. The cool evening air was filled with the smell of smoke.

Evening is the time for visits, so it was no surprise to see a figure approaching from the other side of the yard, but we were somewhat surprised when we saw that it was Árvan from Streamside Farm. He is the one who lives alone with his mother here in the village.

Mother and Father exchanged a brief glance. Náraes looked at Árvan and then at me, and a crease appeared between her eyebrows, though I did not understand why at the time.

"Blessings on your hearth," said Árvan.

"Blessings on your journey," Father replied. "Sit down, Árvan." He moved his tools so that Árvan could sit next to him on the graying wooden bench.

"Can I offer you something?" asked Mother. "We have a little soup left over from supper."

"Thank you, no." Árvan raised his eyes to the sky, then lowered them to the ground. He looked in every direction other than at the bench where Akios and I were sitting. Árvan's hair is very light brown, which is unusual for Rovas folk. His eyes are pale too, and the spring sun has sprinkled his long, narrow nose with freckles. Náraes scooped Dúlan up in her arms and positioned herself in front of me.

"So, how's everything on the farm?" she asked, almost angrily. I looked up at her, but she had her back to me so I could not see her face.

Árvan looked up, surprised. "Oh well, it is how it is. We've got the spring sowing done anyway. And Mother's back isn't troubling her quite so much now."

"Has she been to see Tauer?"

"Oh yes. She was given an ointment that needs rubbing in every night. Then it's complete silence until sunup. It's really helped."

I scoffed. This is exactly the sort of quackery the old man uses to fool the villagers. Complete silence—as if that would make a difference!

"What is the problem with your mother's back?" I leaned forward to try to see Árvan past Náraes. "Perhaps I could—"

"Jannarl was wondering just the other day if you could help him to repair a shaft in the mill," Náraes interrupted me. "He needs an extra pair of hands."

"Oh yes, certainly I can. Will I come by tomorrow? I'm sure Mother can do without me for a bit while she takes her midday nap."

"Náraes," Mother said with a warning tone in her voice. She turned to Árvan. "Was there something on your mind?"

Náraes spoke no more, but her tensed shoulders told me that it was an involuntary silence.

Árvan wiped his palms on his brown trousers. "Oh well, there was one thing. It's about Maresi."

"Me?" I stood up to get a better view of him past Náraes. "Does it concern your mother's back? I am sure I have some herbs that could help."

"My mother?" Árvan looked up and accidentally locked eyes with me briefly, which made his neck flush a deep scarlet. "It's not to do with my mother. Oh well, it was Mother's idea that I should . . . that is, it's time I ought . . ." He cleared his throat. "Streamside lacks a housewife.

Mother can't manage much anymore, and I've got my hands full with farm work and there's no time for anything else: the food and clothes and animals . . ." He swallowed, utterly befuddled.

It slowly dawned on me where this was going, and I retreated, aghast.

"Árvan," I began to protest, just as he finally arrived at his point.

"Yes, well, I was wondering if Maresi might want to marry me."

The yard fell deadly silent. Maressa looked up from her drawing.

"Why do you want to marry Maresi? She's not pretty."

"Oh well, she's healthy and strong. And not altogether unpleasant to look at." Árvan's entire face was now bright red.

"Are you gonna get married then?" Maressa looked from Árvan to me.

"No, we are *not*." I raised my hands, appalled at how bluntly I had blurted out the words. "What I mean to say is: thank you for your kind offer, Árvan, but I cannot accept."

"We've a fine homestead." Árvan's eyes were downcast, but there was a certain determination in his chin. "Not large, I know, but well kept. It will provide just fine for a small family. I'm soon to be debt-free."

"You're a good man, everybody knows that," Father said, and patted him awkwardly on the shoulder. Father can never bear to see anyone sad or disappointed.

I wished I could run away and hide, like Heo does when Joem scolds her.

"You see, I do not ever intend to marry. But thank you once again for asking."

Then I sat back down on the bench with a thud, picked up the wooden board where Akios had written his letters, and stared at it as though it were the most interesting thing in the world.

Árvan thanked us politely and slunk away across the yard while I hid my face in my hands.

"That was the worst thing that has ever happened to me," I whimpered. "How could he get such an idea in his head?!"

"He's a young unmarried man, with a farm and a sick mother to care for. There's nothing strange about it," said Mother.

"The village girls have been fawning over him for the longest time," said Akios, poking me in the side. "Now you've missed your chance!"

I glared at him as fiercely as I could.

"Does no one in this village understand that I have no intention of getting married? I have work to do: I am going to found a school—I have said so from the beginning!"

Mother looked at me seriously. "Do you really mean to stay unmarried for the rest of your life, Maresi? Who'll take care of you? What will you live on, and where? And who'll take care of you in your old age if you have no children? It isn't possible, you must understand. You don't have to marry the first boy who asks. But if you did marry Árvan you could stay here in the village, and we could see each other often. That would make me so happy, after all these years apart."

"You sent Maresi away for nothing then?" Náraes hitched Dúlan a little higher up on her hip. I could see her face now, and rarely have I seen her so angry. Her entire body was shaking. "Eight years she has been away; for eight years I haven't known whether my sister was alive or dead. And all this time she's been getting an education that no one here could even dream of. I would have done anything for such an education. But no, it'll all be for nothing, she'll get married and start squeezing out babies and taking care of a hypochondriac tyrant of a mother-in-law to boot. So what was the point of sending her away? What was the point of sending *Maresi* away?"

Dúlan started to cry, frightened by the anger in her mother's voice. Mother and Father stared at Náraes. "Oh, my darling daughter." Father stood up but did not know what to do, so he just stood there with his arms limp by his sides. "I never knew that *you* wanted to go."

"You never asked. No one asked me. You just decided, you and Mother. And it was only right that Maresi was chosen. I know you could afford only one journey, and Maresi always wanted to learn about the world. She was always the curious and inquisitive one, whereas I was always happiest at home." She had started crying silent tears that rolled almost unnoticeably down her cheeks. I stood up and wrapped my arms around her. "I'd never have been brave enough to go anyway," she sniffed. "I'm too afraid of anything new. But she mustn't waste everything she's fought for, everything *we* have fought for."

Mother took Dúlan in her arms and comforted her. Her expression was cold and hard, and she said nothing to me or my sister, but her gaze lingered on Father, and there was something in her eyes that frightened me.

I held my sister, inhaling the scent that always clings to her: babies, cooking fumes, flour and sweat.

"I will not waste it, I promise," I mumbled into her hair. "Never fear."

"For my sake?"

"For your sake. For Maressa's and Dúlan's too."

ω

I never knew that my sister envied me. I have been so self-obsessed that I never even considered the possibility. Now I know. That evening I asked Akios if he had also wanted to go away. He did not take my question lightly. I like that about him. Though we bicker and he teases me often, he does take me seriously.

"No, I don't think so," he answered. "I was so young, I probably wouldn't have wanted to leave Mother. Besides, it wasn't an option. In all the songs about the Red Abbey, in all the tales and fragments of legend that have found their way here, it's abundantly clear that only girls and women are welcome there. So it didn't really cross my mind."

"There are other places for boys though. Monastic schools, apprenticeships in Irindibul."

"The only son of a farm leave his parents to take an apprenticeship? It's impossible, you know that."

I knew he was right. "Men have come to Menos several times in the history of the Abbey. But only when they needed help and protection, and even then, they were not allowed to stay long." I looked at Akios for a long time. It is not right that he never had a chance to leave. I have to think this over carefully, Jai. There is so much to think about that I have never considered before.

Still, someone proposed to me! Can you believe it? It is utterly ridiculous. Akios and I laugh about it every time it comes up in conversation. Poor Árvan! It must have taken him a long time to summon the courage to come and propose, and we really should have treated him with more courtesy and respect. I hope no one else asks for my hand, but Mother says that it is a possibility. There are unmarried young men, and older men besides, both in our village and the other villages nearby. Now at least I am somewhat prepared and will try to respond with more dignity if anyone else ventures to Enresbacka Farm to woo me.

There is something I must admit, Jai, my friend, before I blow out the candle and snuggle under my blanket. Sometimes I do think about what it would be like to have a husband. To have a man lying in my bed at night, waiting for me. I am not sure what to make of it. It is frightening—and quite exciting.

But that is not my path, so there is no need to speculate more on the subject. I have had an education. I have to prove myself worthy of it.

Your friend,

Maresi

Venerable Sister O,
I have come up against an unexpected problem. I have started teaching my brother Akios letters, but I learned to read and write in a different language from the one we speak here in Rovas. The sounds that the letters represent do not entirely correspond to the

67

sounds we have in our language. We also have sounds I do not know how to spell. These are the issues I have to contend with now, as I lay Akios's foundations. I am glad to have realized this early on, before opening my school. If you have any sage advice, please write and tell me! For example, we have a short *u* that does not sound like the long *u* we use at the Abbey. How can I represent it in writing?

Your novice,

Maresi

My dear Ennike Rose,

Summer is coming in, and the villagers say it is the most beautiful early summer in many years. There is sunshine nearly every day, and enough rainfall to keep the crops well watered. Everything is growing at a tremendous rate. My little herb garden is doing very well, and I have started digging up a new patch of ground for more plants that I plan to transfer from the surrounding forest. This way I will not have to walk so far every time I want forest thorn or wild catmint. I spend as much time outside as possible. I missed the Rovasian early summers when I was on Menos: the sustained, luscious greenery, when all things are in bloom, and the air is thick with fragrance and alive with the buzz of bees. Náraes, who tends to several beehives, is delighted. If all goes well she predicts a record yield of honey. The apple trees are blossoming, and they look just as I remember: a sheer, cascading river of petals behind our compound. I take every opportunity to sit beneath the trees and feel the caress of the falling petals in my hair.

Mother is still having difficulty coming to terms with my refusal to braid or bind my hair. Unbound hair is not forbidden, but it is simply not done. She comes out with little comments: that it looks ugly; that I have a beautiful neck and if I only tied my hair up people could see it. I have a headscarf that keeps my hair away from my face, like we wear at the Abbey, and that is all I need.

We are grating on each other's nerves more and more, Mother and I. When I first came home it was so wonderful to be mothered again. I had missed her so. And she enjoyed making a fuss of me. But it is becoming more and more difficult to conform to the daughter mold that she has created for me. I have my own thoughts and ideas, and when I express them she enters into a steely silence that can last for several days.

ᵹ

I met that Kárun again. I went to the forest to dig up a few women's bicker plants. The roots of the women's bicker are an excellent way to bulk out meals to make provisions last. We have less flour than we did at the Abbey, due to several meager harvests in recent times. So I grind the roots and mix them with our flour rations to make dumplings for soup. There is not enough flour to bake bread. Father laps my soup up, whereas Mother eats very little of the food I prepare, and says nothing of it. Was she this closed-minded and contrary when I was a child? I have no memories of her acting this way.

Akios was busy working the land so I had to go alone. I took Gray Lady with me, not because she would provide any help or protection if I encountered trouble, but for the company. I found no women's bicker at first and had to delve deeper into the forest than was my intention. This did not bother me, for I love walking in the forest. There is always much to see and hear. I feel the presence of the First Mother there, just as I always did on Menos when gazing out across the ocean. All my worries about the school, about Mother's cough (for which even raspberry-leaf tea is no remedy)—in other words, worries about all the things I have no control over—simply disappear. It is easier to breathe in the forest. It is easier to hear my own thoughts. It is only the knowledge that other people, other men, make it unsafe that makes me anxious.

I eventually found a large growth of women's bicker at the river's edge. I dug up the plants and packed them into a sack, thinking all the while about the rites of the upcoming summer offering. I was utterly absorbed in the earthy scent, the swish of thin leaves against my hands, and fantasizing about the delicious food we ate at the celebrations. This meant I did not hear Kárun approach until he was directly in front of me.

"You should listen more closely in the forest," he said as I jumped with a startled shriek.

"I make noise to ward off wolves and lynxes," I said indignantly, and picked up the scissors I had dropped.

"I wasn't talking about animals. The nádor will send his men out on the summer hunt soon. They take whatever prey they can find."

I looked up and saw the gravity in his light-brown eyes. I swallowed.

"Thank you. I will bear it in mind."

He looked out over the river. "Have you started your school yet?"

My heart was still racing from the shock. I sat down on the damp earth with my sack on one side, and he sat down, uninvited, on the other side.

"Not yet. There is much to do on the farm, and then it will be harvest. I believe autumn is the time to begin."

"Hmm."

He said nothing more. Nothing about how I ought to get married, or how a school would be of no use anyway, or that the whole idea was mere fantasy. I glanced at him. That day he had tied his hair up with a leather band, revealing his jawline and his tanned, sinewy neck. For some reason, I was not afraid.

We sat quietly awhile. The river rushed past, wild with rain and mountain meltwater. I brushed earth from my fingers and skirt absentmindedly.

"I'm traveling downstream in a few days. There's a large felled area with lots of timber ready to be transported to Urundien. The river's strong enough now. We should reach Irindibul by the end of the summer."

"How do you return afterward?"

"I usually stay in Irindibul for a while, taking what work I can find. Earn a little before winter. Then I go with some tradesman or other northward as they make their way to the autumn markets."

"I see." I did not know what to say. "Well, perhaps we will see each other again in that case."

"Perhaps." He rose. The sun was shining on his chestnut hair as he looked down at me. "If you could check on the White Farm sow and piglets from time to time, I'd be grateful. She's a good mother for the most part, but sometimes she lies on her piglets and squashes them. And don't forget to keep your ears open when you're alone in the forest."

And he disappeared between the trees downstream.

I am not sure why I am telling you this. It was just such an unusual encounter.

I think I will avoid walking alone in the forest for the rest of the summer hunting season.

Yours,

Maresi

Most Venerable Mother,
      I have a terrible confession. I have done something I could never have foreseen. I pray that you are not angry. I pray that you can forgive me. Furthermore, I pray that I can forgive myself. I believe I made the correct decision, but I cannot be certain. Perhaps it was mere selfishness.

First I must explain a little about Rovas, the land where I was born and to which I have returned. We are not an independent nation but subject to Urundien and its sovereign. Whoever the current sovereign may be rarely affects us. Local rumors have led me to believe that a new one was recently crowned. However, the sovereign's choice of nádor, the governor of our province, does hold great sway over our lives. To Urundien, Rovas has never been more than a near-forgotten little vassal state, worthy of attention only for its good hunting grounds and easily accessible timber. Plus the river provides a good trade route for wares from the Akkade folk, as an alternative to their trade convoys. Be that as it may, we have largely been left to our own fate and suffered only minimal interference from the nádor.

Until now. The nádor who was appointed a few years ago is not content with sitting in his castle and having his enforcers collect the taxes once a year. From what I understand from snatched whispers between villagers, this nádor has a thirst for wealth—and will stop at nothing. He saw an opportunity to squeeze the Rovasians dry, taking advantage of the shortfall caused by hunger winters to sell seed on credit at extortionate rates. He lets his soldiers run wild and sees us Rovasians as little more than livestock. Father has toiled on the land harder than ever before, and yet I can see in the furrows of worry on his brow that he is far from able to pay back the loan he has taken from the nádor to see his family through the winter, and to have seed to sow in spring.

The event I must recount took place five days ago in the daylight of the early evening. The men of the village were coming in from a long, full day in the fields. We awaited their return in the yard as we usually do: women, children and old folk; dogs, cats and chickens. Once the men had returned, the housewives served them bowls of fresh water from the stream. It had rained earlier that day, but only a light summer rain. I was on my knees, weeding my herb garden—most of my herbs are growing very well!

At first I felt a tremor in the ground. It must have been hoofbeats, though it is inconceivable that I could feel the vibrations so distinctly. My body trembled with them, as though hundreds of ants were scuttling all over my skin. I rose and tried to brush them off, but it did not help. A sudden chill made me shudder. Gray Lady, who had been standing tethered to an apple tree lazily flicking her ears, suddenly pricked them up toward the edge of the forest in the northeast. She stamped one front hoof on the ground, and the sound merged with the approaching tremors and spread throughout my body. I knew I desperately needed to react somehow, but I simply did not know what to do.

The men were brushing the worst of the dust and mud from their clothes, and readying themselves to retreat indoors for their evening meal. Gray Lady and I stared at the edge of the forest.

Maressa looked up from her game, which consisted of trying to herd all the chickens into one corner.

"Someone's coming," she said, and looked around.

At the forest edge, on the path that leads toward the river, there appeared four men on horseback. When I saw the evening sun glint upon objects hanging by their sides, it was as if my heart stopped beating, Venerable Mother. It reminded me of the moment when the men's ship emerged through the Teeth and I saw the morning sun's first rays reflected in the men's drawn weapons as they sailed toward the Abbey. I wanted to crawl into the soil and disappear. *Go,* I breathed. *Go away.* The horses slowed a little, and I saw one of them shake its head. Gray Lady stamped her hooves, and there was a ringing in my ears. The rest of the village had noticed the riders by now, and all was quiet in the central yard.

The horses neither stopped nor diverted their course. I pushed myself up against the outside wall of our house, wishing to melt into the rough gray planks. With a rattle of bridles and swords they rode into the yard. Everyone stepped silently and anxiously to the side to make way for them. Mothers picked up the littlest ones while fathers tried to hide the elder children behind their backs. There were three soldiers on horseback, dressed in the colors of Urundien: black, white and gold. Their shirts each bore the royal symbol of the crowned tower. Their muscular brown steeds were foaming at the mouth. The men's black beards were clipped short in the Urundian style, and they were tall—we Rovasians are short in comparison to Urundians. Though they had not drawn their swords, their hands rested on the hilts as they watched us coldly. Then there was a fourth man; he was not a soldier. He carried no sword and was elegantly dressed. His thick fingers were heavy with rings.

The well-dressed man produced a scroll of paper from his cloak and read it aloud.

"Ádon, Jannarl, Haiman and Enre," he read in an authoritative voice.

The four men took one step forward in silence. I saw Marget and Lenna, standing behind their father, Ádon, reach for each other's hands. Náraes gripped Dúlan even more tightly. Mother held Maressa closer. The man looked down at the villagers who had stepped forward.

"You are behind on your loan payments, every one of you. The nádor, in his infinite benevolence and mercy, has granted you respite from repayments over winter, to spare the need to eject you from your homes and farms into the winter cold. However, the period of respite is at an end. Three years have passed. It is time to pay."

"We're working the fields as much as we can," said Ádon in an exhausted voice. "It's the weather—it's not been favorable."

The unarmed man on horseback appeared not to be listening, but one of the soldiers was looking intently at Ádon. Then his gaze passed to Ádon's daughters standing behind him, and there it stayed. I could not breathe. My mouth tasted of metal and ice. Though I could not see the Crone's door, I felt its presence, Venerable Mother.

The leader continued to read. "Ten Urundian silver coins due from Jannarl and household. Five silver coins due from Haiman and household. Seven silver coins due from Ádon and household. And thirteen silver coins due from Enre and household." He looked up from his paper. "Now the time has come to pay."

The men stared down at the ground. I saw shame weigh heavily on their shoulders. Resignation. Thirteen silver coins is an enormous sum, Venerable Mother. The nádor is demanding a staggering interest rate simply because he can. Who could stop him? There was no way for Father and the other men to understand the payback rates attached to their loans. They cannot read. They did not know what was written on the papers before they signed them with crosses.

One after the other the men shook their heads.

"Then I have no choice but to seize all that is yours, and in exchange you may walk free from your debts. Thus spake the nádor, in his merciful justice."

"Everything?" Jannarl asked slowly. "The animals?"

"The animals, the tools, the farms."

"But won't that make us homeless?" cried Jannarl's mother, Feira. "My husband's father's father built this farmstead with his own hands. He burned the ground and cleared the fields. These farms are ours by right."

"And now they are the nádor's by right." The man spat disinterestedly on the ground. The phlegm almost hit my father, but he did not move.

"Where will we go?" asked Seressa from White Farm. Only the women asked questions; only they dared. The men were crippled with the shame of not being able to protect their families. "Are we to wander the streets like beggars now?" She raised her chin high. She held the soldiers' gaze.

"I have my orders," said the man, and his indifference was as harsh as a smack in the face. "The loan must be paid, and it must be paid now."

I watched the soldiers ride into the crowd and scatter everybody, like Maressa's chickens. I watched my father fall to the ground. Dúlan was crying. One of the soldiers charged straight toward Marget and Lenna. Their grandmother, Kild, saw what was about to happen and leaped in the way of the horse. She was trampled. The soldier leaned down and lifted Marget onto his lap. His hands wandered over her body, hard and hungry, right there before everybody's eyes.

After what happened in the crypt at the Abbey, I never thought that I would experience such terror again. But the same fear gripped me this time, Venerable Mother. I was so afraid that my legs refused to obey me, just as in the crypt. Gray Lady stamped her hooves, and the impact set me in motion. I slipped along the wall like a shadow. In through the open door of our cottage. Into my bedroom. I opened the chest by my bed. Pulled out the purse you gave me. Counted the remaining silver. Stuck two coins into a crack in the wall. Pressed the heavy purse against my chest.

When I reemerged I could smell smoke.

"We would have permitted you to move in peace," shouted the leader. "But such displays of obstinacy evoke the wrath of the nádor." He had lit a torch and thrown it onto the roof of the barn. The wood shingles caught fire immediately. Women were screaming. Inside the barn I could hear the pigs squealing. One of the soldiers had dismounted and opened the barn door, so all the pigs and one cow came rushing out. They saved the animals because they could be sold. Our homes and barns were of no value to the nádor and his men.

"Stop!" I screamed, but neither the villagers nor the soldiers heard me. Gray Lady stamped her hooves. I was trembling. I closed my hand around my snake ring and felt the hard metal against my skin. The woven belt Mother gave me was heavy around my waist. I stamped on the ground as well: once, hard.

"Stop!" I screamed again. This time my voice resounded across the yard and made the horses rear in shock. The leader twisted around in his saddle. His gaze stung. I held up the purse.

"Here is your payment. For the whole village. Thirty-five silver coins."

I threw the purse at him. He caught it, opened it abruptly, and counted. I did not look at the villagers: not at Marget sobbing on the soldier's lap; not at Lenna and Seressa, bent over Kild where she lay on the ground; not at Náraes with desperation in her eyes. I looked only at the man on the horse.

"Where did you get this from, girl?" He pulled the purse strings slowly shut.

"I have been away to teach. This was my pay."

"It certainly was a lucrative teaching post." He smiled scornfully. "And you can count."

"You must write a document to say that you have received full repayment of all loans. Otherwise you will no doubt return demanding more silver."

How I mustered these self-confident words and commanding tone, I could not say. It was almost as though the Crone were working through me for a brief spell.

He looked at me with disdain. Then he scoffed, dismounted smoothly and opened his saddlebag. He took out a quill and paper and scribbled down a few words using the horse's side to lean on.

"Never let it be said that the nádor would deceive his people." He handed the paper to me.

Slowly, with all eyes on me, I walked over to him. I was close enough to smell the sweat and horse and metal. Or else the hint of metal was a taste in my mouth. I looked at the paper. It was not all that easy to discern his handwriting, and I was unaccustomed to reading in my native language, as opposed to the coastal tongue of the Abbey. After a while I looked up.

"You have written that we did not pay and that you will return next moon."

The man squinted. He had laughter lines around his eyes. Hence he was capable of laughter. I could not imagine such a thing.

The burning barn roof crackled. Ash drifted down on the yard and all the people in it. My hands trembled as I handed the paper back to him.

With jerky movements he wrote a new document and tossed it at me. Then he remounted his horse. He did not take his eyes off me. I am watching you, they said. You cannot hide from me. Then he rode away from the village, in a southerly direction, and after a moment's hesitation the soldiers followed suit. The last man was holding Marget in a tight grasp at the front of his saddle—even though I had paid, even though I had written proof—and there was nothing we could do, Venerable Mother, nothing at all.

ᛒ

We quenched the fire, but the barn will need a new roof. Kild is alive, but badly injured from being trampled by the horse. The next day Marget came walking along the path with her skirt ripped and a broken look in her eyes. We all know what happened to her. Nobody speaks it out loud.

I do not know why the man wrote a real document for me. He was not compelled. Perhaps he thought it made no difference. He can return anyway. He can do as he pleases, and there is nothing we can do about it. Perhaps I sacrificed all the silver you gave me for nothing, Venerable Mother. Yet if there was the slightest chance that I could help my family and my village, what could I do but try? We need not leave our homes, and we still have our animals and fields. You told me once that I must protect the little ones and take care of them. I believe that is what I am doing. However, I do not know what will become of the school now, Venerable Mother. I do not know what will become of us. And I cannot shake off the look in that man's eyes, the look that said: I am watching you; I know where you live; you cannot hide.

Respectfully,

Maresi

Venerable Sister Eostre,
I am writing to you as the former Rose, servant to the Maiden. I could have written to Ennike, who currently serves as the Rose. But she is my friend, and always has been. Besides, she is young, and has not experienced the things you have. I hope you do not mind my asking you to keep this letter a secret from the Rose. I know that your affinity lies more with Havva, the Mother aspect of the Triple Goddess, now that you have borne a daughter. But you channeled the Goddess on that occasion when the men landed on Menos and penetrated the Temple of the Rose. With your body as her instrument, she saved us all.

Now there is a young girl in my village who has undergone a similar ordeal. She was carried away from our village, and at least one man forced himself upon her. I do not know exactly what happened—nobody does. She refuses to speak of it. She is the same age as me, Sister, and this burden is destroying her. She no longer leaves her house. She does not show her face when visitors come to her home. Nobody gossips about her in the village, and I have heard no one speak ill of her, yet everybody averts their gaze at the mere mention of her name. They become silent. They do not know what to say or do.

Rumors are spreading among the other villages, however: that she was asking for it; that she smiled at the soldiers; that she did not fight back, or that her resistance was feeble.

I must help her, Sister Eostre. There must be a way. Tell me how. These men must not be allowed to determine her fate forever. How can I help her to reclaim her body?

Every evening I comb my hair with the Goddess comb that you bequeathed to me. I gather all the hair that comes loose and bind it into a braid. The braid is thin but long. Strong. As I braid, I think of the soldiers that harmed Marget. I bind them tight and hard to prevent them from returning here. I place the braid under my pillow at night. The knowledge that it is there affords me some comfort.

I remember the way the soldiers' captain looked at me. They can come and take whatever they want, Sister Eostre. They can claim people like livestock. They can argue that Father is still in debt to them, and my sacrifice will be in vain. I braid and bind and pray to the three aspects of the First Mother for her protection. Please would you add your prayers to mine?

Respectfully,

Maresi

SECOND
COLLECTION
OF LETTERS

SUMMER

Dearest Jai,

I sent the first bundle of letters to you shortly after writing one final letter to Sister Eostre a moon ago, and I am already starting a new batch. I have tried to restrain myself, but I need to feel close to you all, even if it is a waste of precious paper.

I wonder whether we will ever sit together again under the lemon tree in the Knowledge Yard, you and I and Ennike the Rose? Drinking cool spring water and watching seabirds fly as we talk of everything and nothing. When I close my eyes I can imagine being there with you. It is strange: I can see it all as clearly as if I were there. The walls of my parents' house melt away, and I am caressed by salty breezes and shaded by the glossy, dark leaves of the lemon tree, and I rest my cheek on the smooth grain of its tough bark. I can hear the bleats of the goats grazing on the mountain slopes, and the patter of sandals running across the stone-paved courtyard. A cat lies asleep in my lap. You are there, and Ennike, and we have just eaten, and the taste of nirnberry sauce lingers in my mouth.

How I miss nirnberry sauce!

The letters cannot possibly have reached you yet, but I like to think about them making their journey closer and closer to Menos. The donkey convoy came winding past from the north just before the summer solstice, with bales of wool stacked high on the donkeys' bony backs. They had traveled through the mountain pass and stopped very close to Sáru for an afternoon to rest and water their animals. As soon as I heard tell of them, I dropped what I was doing and rushed to gather my letters, not forgetting a small coin I had set aside for precisely this purpose. I ran so fast that I lost my headscarf, my hair was flying in my face and my heart was pounding. I was afraid that I had missed them. But they had set up camp for the night in a dell, and when I found them I was met by the smoke of many fires, and talk and song. Having traveled in a similar convoy myself, I searched for a solitary woman among the multitudes. I saw no familiar faces, but I did find a woman tending to three hinnies at the edge of the camp. Her hair was bound in many tight braids that she had then tied together into a knot on her crown. She wore a necklace of coral, amber and bluestone wound several times around her neck. Her animals looked well kept, which encouraged me to approach her. She was from Devenland, and spoke an almost unintelligible dialect of the coastal language, but with gestures and repetition we managed to understand each other. When I mentioned Ajanie, she became instantly more amicable, realizing that we had a mutual friend. She promised to take my letters as far as Masson, where she would find someone reliable to carry them farther to Muerio and send them on a boat bound for Menos. When she heard the letters' destination she became very serious and looked at me intently, as if to figure out whether I was telling the truth. She examined my clothes and my unbound hair. I held up my hand to show her Sister O's snake ring, and then she smiled and nodded.

"The symbols of the Goddess: rose, apple, snake."

If I understood her correctly, her grandmother had spent her childhood on Menos. Have you ever heard the elder sisters speak of a novice by the name of Dakila? The tradeswoman refused payment for taking the letters, but she allowed me to buy some of the wares she had not been able to sell to the Akkade people: cinnamon bark, which is delicious in food but also helpful against infections; ginger, one of the most useful plants Sister Nar taught me about; and ink, because my supply had nearly run out. Then I bought a little candied ginger for Maressa and Dúlan. Now one silver coin and a few copper coins is all that remains from the money the Mother Abbess gave me.

By the time you read this letter I suppose she will have told you what happened to the rest. The whole Abbey surely knows of my failure. I feel profound shame when I think of it, so I try not to think of it at all.

Now my letters are moving south in the travel pack of a Devenian merchant. When I lie in my bed at night, I follow their journey in my mind's eye. I recall a small lake where convoys often stop, so perhaps this convoy will stop there too. I remember a bridge across the rapid river there, and how frightened I was to cross it. Perhaps they have reached Masson already and the tradeswoman has already passed the letters on to another. I have asked Sister O to pay a handsome sum to the fishermen who deliver them to Menos in the hope that word will spread: it pays to bring letters from this little place in the far north to the solitary mountainous island in the south.

Oh Jai, I am rattling on. Please forgive me! Nothing I have written in this letter is of any consequence. A waste of ink and paper, not to mention your time spent reading it. I can imagine where you are now—in your favorite spot in the Knowledge Garden, surrounded by Sister Nar's fragrant herbs? I picture your head bent over my pages, your squinting eyes in the bright light, your already fair hair lightened in the summer sun until it is as white as snow. Butterflies and Sister Mareane's bees are fluttering around you, aren't they? Tell me they are!

Writing this letter has let me feel close to you. I hope that is enough of an excuse.

Now I can hear Father snoring. That is my signal to set aside my writing implements and let myself be enveloped by the night. Akios is mumbling in his sleep. He sleeps in front of the fireplace and not on the ledge above it now that it is too warm. A mild summer breeze is whispering in the apple trees, which have already shed their blossoms.

It is not only nirnberry sauce that I miss, Jai, my friend.

Maresi

Venerable Sister O,

I have no silver left. How will I found my school now? I could work to earn more, but that would leave me no time to help at home. Besides, I am a grown woman; I cannot expect Mother and Father to provide for me. My days are filled with hard labor, and I have no time or energy left for anything else. How disappointed you must be in me! All my plans have amounted to nothing. Nobody here wants to send their children to my school. It is summertime now and everybody has to pitch in with the farm work, young and old alike. Perhaps they were right: education has no place here.

Your novice,

Maresi

My dear Ennike Rose,

Yesterday we celebrated one of the biggest festivals in Rovas: midsummer's eve. It is the shortest night of the year, which here we call the summer offering, when Rovasians dance through the evening in their sacred offering groves, light fires to chase evil spirits away, and praise the fruitfulness of the earth with offerings and rituals.

I am currently sitting beneath the apple trees to write this, though it is so dark that I can barely see my own words. I hope you can read my writing. If indeed you ever get the opportunity to read this. I am not sure whether I will send these letters. I am not writing about what is truly important. I touch upon the important things, but dare not go further. I have no silver and have become little more than a farm girl. I have accomplished nothing with all that I learned at the Abbey. I am wasting the knowledge that all the good sisters worked so hard to impart, and that I worked so hard to learn. Now only my body works, not my mind.

Indeed, it is my body that has stories to tell you this evening— things I can tell no one but you, my friend, because you are the Rose. Writing does not do it justice. I wish we could talk about this. I wish I could visit you in the Temple of the Rose and address you formally in your role as the Rose, all the while knowing that you are also Ennike, my friend with the chestnut curls.

Something is pulsating inside me, something new and strange that I do not understand.

We gathered in the circular central yard early in the morning of midsummer's eve. The whole village, old and young. Náraes was there with her family, and Mother and Father and Akios, and Árvan, who was carefully avoiding looking at me, and everybody else. I saw Marget too, with gaze downcast. Even she could not stay indoors on a day such as this. Everyone was dressed in their finest clothes. The women wore beautiful aprons with elaborate embroidery, with their hair freshly braided and flower wreaths on their heads. The men wore embroidered waistcoats over clean shirts, and gleaming, well-polished shoes. The children ran around barefoot, squealing with impatience and excitement. Everyone was carrying sacks of food. I had attached Gray Lady to a cart, which was beautifully decorated with leaves in honor of the day, and we loaded it with much of the village's food, along with barrels of malt drink and soured skim milk. There is still a food shortage in the village from last winter, and the grain is nowhere near ready to be harvested yet, but we had plenty of eggs, and fresh vegetables from the kitchen gardens, and wild strawberries and waterberries the children had gathered from the ditch banks. Akios, Jannarl and Máros had gone out on several morning hunts for the summer offering and come home with birds and hares from the forest. Father and I had also ventured all the way to the river, where we managed to catch some great shining salmon. Árvan contributed several round yellow cheeses his mother had prepared. We could hold our heads up high as Sáru made its contribution to the shared feast. Of course, it is nothing compared to nadum bread and the flaky pies Sister Ers makes for Moon Dance and the other festivals at the Abbey.

We sang in procession out of the village and along the fields toward the forest. We left our homes behind us, scrubbed spotless from threshold to rafters, with clean bedclothes, new straw on the floor, and all the fireplaces freshly polished. Old grandmother Kild stayed at home. She is recovering from her injury, but she will never walk as she did before.

It was a beautiful day with a clear-blue sky, and already warm when we set out early in the morning. Still, I wore my red woolen cloak. I wanted to be well dressed too. Mother watched as I hung it over my shoulders, and then looked away. I cannot imagine what problem she has with my cloak!

In Rovas they do not believe in any god or goddess, but the forest and earth and sky are divine in their own right and venerated and worshipped as such. There are also animals attributed with godlike qualities: the bear is the guardian of the forest and hunters; the waterbird Kalma spans three territories—earth, air and sea—and is therefore sacred; the black fox outwits the other animals time and time again when they attempt to kill her.

We arrived at the offering grove after midday. The grove is in a valley where ancient trees grow—all the broad-leaved trees that exist in Rovas are to be found there, except the silverwood, of course. Giant lindens, birches, maples and oaks reach for the heavens, their vast canopies creating a dappled-green ceiling. The ground is strewn with fallen leaves, and few plants grow but the arctic starflower. Another village was already there when we arrived, and everybody was greeting relatives, comparing sowing experiences and exchanging news of this and that, while a long table was set up at the edge of the grove. We did not venture too far in to where the elder oak stands. Another two villages joined us in the grove, one of which was Jóla. I saw Tauer with his children and grandchildren, but supposed his elderly father could not manage the journey.

Once everything was set up and several fires were blazing away, the village elders gathered by the elder oak to perform the rites and whisper the holy words into the tree bark. Then finally they sacrificed a river duck, slitting its throat and letting the blood drip into the black soil at the base of the oak's trunk.

I stood close to my family as we watched the ceremony, and under my breath I muttered the Abbey's words of thanks to the Mother aspect of the Goddess for the blessing of her summer bounty. And Rose, do you know something? For a moment I thought I felt her respond in the vibrations beneath the soles of my feet and the wind caressing my unbound hair. I looked up, surprised, and met my mother's inscrutable gaze. I quickly looked down again. She must have heard me, and I know that she does not like it when I continue with the traditions and rites of Menos.

Once the sacrifice was complete the women took down the pots that had been hanging over the many fires, and it was time to eat! We sat on benches at the long table and helped ourselves to all the delicious things on offer: cheeses, sweet bread, sausages, pots of tender spring cabbage, and smoked wild salmon served whole and topped with boiled eggs, fresh berries, newly sprouted peas and soured skim milk. One of the villages had even brought a barrel of beer. We all ate and ate until the little ones fell asleep and the rest of us leaned back-to-back and stretched out our legs. It was the most satisfied my appetite has been since coming here. The men lit pipes stuffed with homegrown tobacco, and the women cleared away slowly, chatting amiably and carrying all the bowls and pots down to a nearby stream to be washed. I helped, and washed in silence beside Marget. Then I spread my cloak out under a birch tree and invited her to join me, and together we slept away the rest of the afternoon, with Marget between me and the tree so that she might feel safe.

Many others slept also. When we awoke it was early evening, but still daylight, as is always the case in northern Rovas at midsummer. I walked down to the stream to drink the cold water and splash my face to wake up properly. With stream water dripping from my hair, I returned to the grove, where the musicians were gathering in the middle, though still at a respectful distance from the elder oak. Someone had mounted two old bear skulls onto stakes on either side of the musicians. They dated back to the times when we were still allowed to hunt large game in the forest. The children had picked starflowers and other blossoms to make wreaths to adorn their heads, the trees and stakes, so the whole grove appeared as though in full bloom.

The musicians struck up the "Grain Tramplers' Song," and all the old women took each other by the hand to form a circle in front of the musicians and started singing, as is our custom. They stamped their feet in measured rhythm, and sang about how the Old Lady in the sky sent grain to the people of Earth to cultivate and eat, then how Samarni the Foolish lost the grain but her sister Agarne found it again, and carried it in her mouth through the burning plains and the weeping caves and the forest of ice and mist.

Then all the old men took each other by the hand and formed a circle around the old women. Father was among them, and I clapped to the rhythm and smiled as I saw his brown boots stamping in time with the other men as they sang the verse about Rókan, the youth who wanted the grain and made a number of attempts to steal it from Agarne's mouth before finally succeeding through a kiss.

As the shadows lengthened beneath the trees, many old songs were played and sung. They were the songs unique to this time of year, when summer is in full bloom and grain is ripening in the fields, when balance must be maintained and all important things must be remembered. When twilight came we lit the fires once more, as a sign to the earth and the sky that the villagers of Rovas still honor those to whom honor is due. And it also marked the beginning of the free dance.

I took Maressa by the hand and led her in among the dancing couples. We danced "Maiden's Kiss"—and it made me think of you, Ennike Rose—then we danced "The Merchant's Silver Pitcher" and "Stream Hop" and "First Snow." Then Maressa wanted to dance with her father, and I stepped to the side of the dancing crowd to catch my breath. Náraes passed me a jug of cool water and I drank gratefully. The summer evening was warm and mild, and the wind had calmed down. I was hot from dancing, and the air was heavy with sweat and the smoke of many fires. Akios came to find me and pulled me back up, and we danced so many dances that I lost count. Finally, we lay laughing in the grass, looking up into the tree branches.

"Can we continue our lessons soon?" Akios asked quietly when no one else could hear. "I really do want to learn to read, Maresi. There must be more to life than Sáru. Tell me there's something more?"

I sat up, leaned back on my elbows and watched the people dancing. The fires cast a flickering red glow upon the swirling couples, and I was suddenly reminded of the Moon Dance. I reflected before answering.

"There is more," I said quietly. "But I do not know whether I am the right person to show it to you, Akios."

The families with small children had set up camp around the grove, and the elder folk had also retired for the night. It was the young people's turn to dance, and young men and women with flushed cheeks were holding hands and waists and necks, and smiling and laughing and dancing in a flutter of waistcoats and skirts. I saw Árvan dance past, stiff and serious, with a very young beauty who had thick brown braids and a richly embroidered skirt. Péra from Jóla ran over to pull Akios to his feet, and as he laughingly gave in, I saw Marget's face darken and turn away. She did not dance at all. Everybody paired up, boy and girl, and perhaps those same pairs would get married and have children, or perhaps they would simply find a little happiness and comfort in each other's arms that night.

Suddenly I no longer felt happy. There was no part for me to play in this game. I stood up and picked up my cloak. It was time for me to go home to bed.

Then a young man approached me. I hardly knew him, just that his name is Géros and he lives in the neighboring village, Jóla. Géros is a little younger than I, and I know that he and Akios played together when they were younger. He is tall and slim with distinctive dark eyebrows.

"Why aren't you dancing?" he asked.

I glanced at him to see if he was mocking me, but his smile was friendly. His face was full of freckles.

"I am already exhausted from dancing," I said. "I think it is time I went home."

"Not yet, surely?" Then he took my hand.

I was too surprised to protest. His hand was warm and dry. He pulled me into the ring of dancers. I saw raised eyebrows and meaningful glances, and my cheeks started burning, but then the music took hold of me and I no longer noticed anyone else. Géros is a good dancer. He is quick and nimble and never lost me among all the other dancing couples, even when we spun apart. My feet were moving at lightning speed, stomping and kicking, turning and jumping, and Géros's hands kept spinning me around, catching me and spinning again. It was great fun, dear Ennike Rose, and soon I was breathless, and felt hot and wild.

We danced to a few more songs before Géros grabbed me, laughing, and pulled me out of the crowd of dancing couples.

"You're insatiable, Maresi Enresdaughter," he said, and fell to the grass, panting. He smiled up at me. "Insatiable and pretty."

No one has ever called me pretty before! I am sure I blushed terribly. I stood there, uncertain what to do, but he reached up a hand and drew me down beside him. I landed on my knees and felt the damp of the grass seep through my skirt. Still holding my hand, Géros interlaced his fingers with mine. The air was still full of flutes and drums and the ground was vibrating from the dancers' heavy footsteps. The evening was cool, but I was struck by the warmth emanating from Géros's body. He smelled of countless things I had never encountered before and could not put my finger on. I had never been so close to a man who was not a member of my own family. For a brief moment I thought of the men who came to the island, and became conscious of the scar on my abdomen where the fingerless man stabbed me with his blade. But then I looked into Géros's dark eyes, and it was not the Crone I heard whispering in my ear. It was another whisper altogether, one I had never heard before.

He pulled me toward him and kissed me—in front of everybody! He kissed me, and it felt like being inside the Temple of the Rose, or no, it was not like that at all. It was like nothing I could have ever imagined. It was heat. It was a tremor in my body, a squeeze, a fire. I do not believe I was ever truly alive before that moment. I had only ever known one aspect of life, and that was death, but now I know the power governed by the Rose, the first aspect of the Goddess. It is the power that lives in my own flesh.

I could not get enough of his lips. I could not get enough of the feeling he awoke inside me. I am blushing as I write this, but I know that you understand because this is the power you serve. And it is strong, Ennike Rose, it is stronger than the power of the Crone. More irresistible. I never understood it before now. I used to believe that nothing was more powerful than the Crone, that nothing could be more inevitable than death. I believed I had chosen the strongest aspect.

I was wrong, oh how wrong I was.

His body pressed against mine. His hands in my hair. My hands on his strong, bare neck.

I am trembling as I write this.

Maresi

My dear Ennike Rose,

I am so glad that the harvest has not yet begun, because sometimes I can snatch a little time to myself, and that means I can see Géros. Some days he comes to our village early in the morning so that we can spend some time together before the day's tasks begin. We meet behind the hay barn. On other days he walks the path from his village to mine as soon as he has finished his duties on the farm. Sometimes I run to meet him. We seek out a secluded ditch or walk deep into the forest where we can be alone.

We explore each other with lips and hands and it is wonderful—wonderful! I never knew anything of this body I possess. I had no idea that my body could do such things. When we are together, all I can think of is Géros's hands, lips, neck, throat, cheeks, legs, chest, body . . . It is like being drunk on sweetened wine. My head spins, my hands tremble, my heart beats fast and hard.

Akios teases me relentlessly. Father just mutters and gets on with his work. Mother has a satisfied smile on her face. She has thawed out and become more talkative with me. It is like when I first returned. But, more remarkable still, everybody in the village is now treating me differently. The girls stop to chat when we cross paths fetching water at the stream, rather than squeezing out a polite hello and continuing on their way, as before. The older women in the village give me advice about chicken feed and offer to teach me various embroidery patterns. The boys wink and chuckle as they pass by.

I have made that infusion you taught me to prepare. The one with the plant with the pointed leaves that you called Goddess Tongue. I drink it every morning. You know what that means. Thank you for insisting, despite my laughter and dismissal when you brought it up in conversation. I do not want to become with child now.

Géros fills my thoughts. It is bizarre—I have been more intimate with him than with anyone else in my life, yet I know so little about him. I know how the color of his eyes deepens when he looks at me. I know how weak I become when he touches my waist. I know the taste of his lips, the feeling of his tongue against mine, the smell of the skin in the hollow of his throat. I know the feeling of him inside me. But I know little about Géros the person, and neither have I asked him much. How odd that one can be so intimate with someone who is essentially a stranger.

I feel like a stranger to myself too. The thoughts in my head are changed. My body is changed. Everything is new and amazing and I do not speak to the Crone and I do not go for walks around the village in the evenings anymore, because I have no time. I pray to the Maiden and the half-moon that hangs pale above the horizon.

Soon it will be harvest time.

Yours,

Maresi

Dearest Jai,

Today Náraes and her family came for a visit. Mother put down her sewing the moment they came breezing into the cottage, but it did not escape my sister's keen sight.

"What are you sewing, Mother?" she asked with furrowed brow. Jannarl unwrapped the large blanket he had wound around Dúlan for the short walk across the yard.

"Is it raining?" I asked.

"No. What are you sewing, Mother?"

"Just a little something that we need. For Maresi."

I had indeed guessed a long time ago, but I had never brought it up with Mother. I had no desire to talk about it now either, and tried to think of a way to steer the conversation elsewhere, but just then Maressa ran over to me.

"Do you have time now then?"

"What for?"

"To teach me those letters. You promised!"

"Yes, Maresi does seem remarkably busy, doesn't she? The sowing is long finished, and everybody else is enjoying a rest before harvest time. What could possibly be keeping you so occupied? Could it be that you're finally working on that school you were planning to open?"

Náraes's voice was pointed. I gave her a sour look.

"You know I have no silver with which to build a schoolhouse, or to obtain all the necessary provisions."

"You could always begin with Maressa and the other little ones right here, at Mother's fireside. Why must it be in a special schoolhouse? Why do you need more than a lump of coal and a smooth-planed plank?" She turned abruptly to Mother. "What are you sewing for Maresi?"

Mother crossed her arms across her chest. "Bedclothes. Towels. A bonnet."

"Náraes. Darling." Jannarl laid a calming hand on his wife's arm. She shook it away, irritated.

"A *bridal* bonnet?"

"Yes, if you must know. Maresi was away for several years; she hadn't the chance to sew her own bridal set."

Náraes turned to look at me. We are the same height now, but in that moment it felt as if she towered above me, like when we were young. "You need a bridal bonnet? You need a bridal set?"

I thought about Géros. About his mouth on my neck. His hands on my . . . I blushed. I had given no thought to marriage. Honestly. I had only thought that I wanted to be with him all the time. But, well, is that not what marriage is? Being together all the time?

"I will probably marry at some point," I said, and looked to Mother for support. "Everyone does eventually."

"But you aren't like everyone! You've had something no one else has! It's your duty to share it with those of us who never got the chance!" Náraes's fists were clenched in frustration. "Oh, if only I could go back in time and convince Father to send *me* in your place!"

"Náraes!" Mother cried in a fearsome voice. Everybody fell silent and looked at her. "Think of what you are saying," she said quietly. She looked at my father. He avoided her gaze and withdrew.

"It's true! I could have made life better, for me, for everybody in the village." Náraes's voice had softened somewhat, but she would not relent.

"I can still teach even if I am married," I said weakly. But I was not wholly convinced it was true. Náraes scoffed.

"Really? When you have your own home to care for? Do you ever see Mother take a half-day off her work for any purpose whatsoever? Do you ever see me do that? We clean, scrub, sew and patch, spin and weave, pickle and juice, dry and salt, we carry water and wood, we make sure the fire keeps burning—and just wait until you have children!" She stopped suddenly. "*Are* you with child?"

I blushed. "No!"

"When you have children you have no freedom left. None! You nurse and cook, you attend to illness, you keep watch, you worry." She gasped violently for breath. "I love my children. I love all three of them. But you know nothing, Maresi. Nothing."

ᚹ

The atmosphere was tense after that. Maressa did not seem bothered by her mother's outburst. I sat with her in a corner practicing letters on a plank stub all evening long. Akios joined us when he came home. Then I had them practice with each other and asked Náraes to come outside with me for a talk. She stood there with arms crossed, looking just like our mother. The same sharp wrinkle in her forehead, the same beautiful lips drawn down at the corners into a deep frown. The nocturnal birds were singing and the air was both warm and cool at once, in a way that it never is on Menos.

"Don't be cross with me." I put one arm around her and leaned my head on her shoulder. "Please, my sweet sister. Don't be cross."

She sighed and stood still for a moment before putting her arm around my shoulders. "I'm not cross."

I looked up at her and raised my eyebrows. She laughed.

"All right, I am. Maresi, why are you throwing everything away?"

"I do not see it that way. You must understand . . ."

I searched for the words. I had not really thought about it, and neither did I want to. I would rather not put it into words. Some things are better left in the realm of pure experience. But I owed it to Náraes to at least make an attempt.

"When I went to the Abbey I was just a little girl. I thought nothing of men or boys at all. I devoured knowledge; I always wanted to learn more and more. It was the only thing that kept homesickness at bay. And when men did come to Menos, they were wicked. They had wicked intentions, they did wicked things. Then I came back here, where men and women live together, and the men here are good men, like our brother and father, and your husband."

Náraes held me a little tighter.

"I had no idea how to be with men."

"And now you do?" Náraes had the hint of a smirk in her voice. I pinched her in the side.

"Oh, hush. You understand . . . Or perhaps I do not really understand it myself. I thought I had dedicated my life to the Crone, the third aspect of the First Mother, who reigns over the realm of death, guardian of mysterious wisdom, mistress of tempests, the cold and dark. I was convinced that this was my destiny—my whole destiny. And then . . . then came Géros, and he looked at me and suddenly there was something more. There was life. There was desire. There was another power that was just as strong, if not more."

"Love?" Náraes turned to look me in the eyes.

"I am not sure. I think so."

She sighed. "Promise me you're not throwing everything away for a man. Promise me that."

As soon as she said these words, the promise was easy to make.

"I promise not to devote time to love before I have made something of my life."

With that she was satisfied.

Yet I am not even sure what I meant by that.

Yours,

Maresi

Venerable Sister O,

It has been calm in these parts ever since I paid off the village's debts. The soldiers have left us in peace, which everybody says is a wonder. However, a patrol appeared just south of Jóla recently. Without so much as a word, they stole three pigs from a young boy as he was herding them along, and when he tried to protest they beat him very badly. I called in today to see if he needed help, but Tauer had treated his injuries expertly. Still I worry that the boy's right hand will never be the same again.

As I walk home from Jóla in the light summer evenings I listen intently for hoofbeats and the clink of weapons among the trees. We are not safe here. We are at the mercy of the nádor and his whims, of his soldiers and their violence. The people here have no way to defend themselves. I must help them, Sister O. There must be a way I can protect my people. But how? If only I could ask you for advice!

Your novice,

Maresi

My dear Ennike Rose,
Meeting Géros is more complicated now that the harvest has begun. The days are filled with work. I have been going to Jóla in the evening to try and see him after he has finished working. Yesterday I found him by the hay barn, alone and eager. He pulled me into the near-empty barn and undressed me immediately, without a word. It has become more and more pleasurable every time. The first few encounters were nothing special, but now I know my body better and know what to ask for.

Afterward, we lay tangled in each other's limbs. Géros's fingers played in my hair and I floated in and out of a blissful stupor.

"My beautiful Maresi," he whispered hoarsely into my ear. "Mine, mine, mine." He kissed my neck between every word. I paid little attention to what he was saying; I was just enjoying the sensation of his hands in my hair. It has grown longer now and soon will be as long as Jai's (except hers must have grown too, of course!). Géros's fingers coiled and caressed. I shivered with pleasure.

"I've been thinking that I should build a house for myself here in our compound," said Géros after a while. "Nothing big. One room only. We've already got a larder and all that."

"Aren't you a little young for that?" I mumbled. "Don't you enjoy having a mother who takes care of your food and washing?" I yawned. "I do."

His fingers stopped. "You do?"

"Yes. Though of course it would be nice to make my own decisions about my own household. No, don't stop." I pulled his hand back into my hair. He had propped himself up on his elbow and was studying my face keenly.

"Do you mean it? Would you really like that?"

Suddenly I realized where this conversation was heading. I tried to keep my voice steady and my face straight. "Well, yes. But not yet. Not for a few years."

"Oh." He sounded disappointed. Slowly he continued to play with my hair.

We said goodbye shortly afterward. I kissed him on the forehead. I had never done that before.

When I emerged I realized that he had braided my hair into a thick, tight braid. I felt it with my hands. It was strange having my hair bound that way. I have not had it braided since . . . well, since that night when we bound the calm and then brought forth the storm.

Mother raised her eyebrows in surprise when I came in, but said nothing. She set out a pot of steaming soup and bowls. Akios came in from chopping wood on the hillside, and Father put down the basket he was weaving. We sat down at the table and began eating. Then Akios looked up.

"Your hair! You've braided it!"

"It suits you," said Mother calmly with a little cough. "Now we can see your pretty neck."

Father said nothing, just looked at me with a mildly inquisitive expression in his eyes. I shrugged.

"I am just trying it. It is tight. It pulls at my scalp."

"You get used to it," said Mother. "And if it's too heavy you can always cut a little hair off."

I gave the braid a chance and kept it for the whole evening. But by bedtime my temples were tense and throbbing and my head ached. I loosened the braid and listened, but no storm lashed at the cottage walls. It was a relief to have my hair free again. I took out the copper comb and realized it had been a long time since I had used it. Several dry lavender flowers fell to the floor—Jai's gift. I picked them up and inhaled the scent deeply. They smell like the dormitory in Novice House. They smell like Sister Nar's garden. Like home.

I pulled the comb through my hair. It crackled and sparkled, but nothing happened. No howling storm. I gathered the hair that had fallen out and bound it into the braid I keep under my pillow. Then I undressed and crawled into bed.

I do not have much Goddess Tongue left, but that is no matter. I do not think I will need it anymore.

Yours,

Maresi

Venerable Sister O,

I no longer wear the clothes Mother gave me: the blouse, embroidered apron and gray skirt. I now dress as we do in the Abbey: in my own shirt, trousers and headscarf, which Mother had washed and put away in the chest at the foot of my bed. For even if I do dress like the women here, it does not make me one of them. They have treated me differently since I started spending time with Géros, but still not as one of them. Ironically, it seems that the silver I paid for everybody's debts has become a barrier between us. Nobody here had ever seen so much money. Few had even seen a silver coin. The idea that Maresi Enresdaughter, who used to play down by the stream as a child, suddenly had so much money is too bizarre for them to comprehend. I share a name with the girl who once played here, but as far as they are concerned we are not the same person.

Of course they are my people, and I have missed them, and I am happy to be reunited with them. The women here are kind and friendly and clever. But all they talk about is men and farm work, marriage and housekeeping. I understand. I do not blame them in the least. Larders and looms are their domain, and they measure their worth in how well they care for their homes and children. It is not their fault that their world is so small. Neither is there anything wrong with this world.

Yet I want more.

I am blowing out my candle now. Goodnight, Sister O. I wish I could speak these words to you. I wish I could be with you, just for one moment, standing beside you by the outer wall, watching the moon rise over the sea.

Your novice,

Maresi

AUTUMN

Venerable Sister O,

I am at a loss. I am devastated. My sister Náraes is with child, as I must have already mentioned, and some days ago we were rinsing laundry down by the stream, and I helped her up because it is becoming difficult for her to move, and I accidentally touched her belly, which is already full and firm, and an icy chill shuddered through me. The same chill as I felt in the crypt beneath Knowledge House.

What will I do, Sister O? Where do I turn?

Now I feel it every time Náraes is nearby. I am doing all that I can for her: helping with the children; making sure that she does not lift anything heavy; preparing food that I know to give strength to expectant mothers. I have resumed my walks around the fields and village, and sometimes I bring her along, because it must do her good to get a little exercise and respite from cooking fumes and children's screams. Jannarl is a good man and never complains about being left alone with the children after a hard day's work.

But nothing helps, and our walks around the village leave me not only exhausted but chilled to the bone. Náraes does not seem to notice anything is wrong. She is grateful and happy, if a little pale around the cheeks. She often takes the opportunity to lecture me, repeating that I must ensure that my life does not turn out like hers.

One evening she came to our house and asked Father and Akios to excuse us for a moment.

"Women's things," she said, and then they could not leave quickly enough.

Mother helped to deliver both Maressa and Dúlan, so now Náraes had come to ask for advice about this pregnancy. I was knitting myself a pair of winter socks, reusing the yarn that Mother had unraveled from a tattered old pair of Father's. Throughout Mother and Náraes's conversation I felt the chill emanating from my sister, and I did not know what to say or do.

Mother fussed over Náraes, giving her the best seat by the hearth and sitting on a stool to massage her swollen feet.

"How's your strength holding out?"

"Well, mostly. I no longer feel nauseated and can keep food down. Maresi is feeding me all sorts of fortifying things." She smiled at me, but all I could feel was that icy chill deep in my bones. "I was just wondering if you could check that everything's how it should be. I have a sort of pain in my chest when I go to bed at night. Might that be dangerous? It never happened with the other two."

Mother lowered Náraes's foot from her knee, rose and stood before her. She placed her hands on Náraes's belly. At once she became completely still. Her expression softened and she looked into her daughter's eyes.

"It's a boy. Without a doubt." She moved her hands expertly and firmly over Náraes's swollen belly. "Here's the head, and here's the bottom. Does he kick upwards?"

"Oh yes." Náraes laughed. "Sometimes I can hardly sleep."

"There'll be less of that as he grows and it gets a little cramped in there." Mother's voice was gentle and calm, just as I remember from childhood. "The pain in your chest is nothing to worry about. I'll get you a tea from Tauer, the one he gave me when I was pregnant with . . . when I was last pregnant."

She was thinking of Anner, and both Náraes and I knew it.

It made me feel very alone to be excluded from their conversation. They share something, an experience that I have never had nor ever will. And I felt alone because I knew something that they did not.

"Are you scared?" I asked Náraes.

"No. I was the first time, but now I know that no matter how awful the birth is, I can handle it." She leaned back against the mortared wall and sighed. "I worry about the baby, of course."

"No point in worrying about something you can do nothing about," Mother said, and gave me a sharp look.

"I can make you a tea," I said. "Chamomile and perrak, that should help the heartburn."

"Probably best she goes to Tauer anyway," Mother cut me off. "He knows what he's doing."

We locked eyes, and the look she gave me told me that she *knew*. She knew, and I knew, and neither of us could say anything. A little later, Náraes got up and waddled home. Mother and I were left sitting in the dusk-lit cottage, with the fire crackling in the hearth and our handicrafts sitting untouched in our laps. I wanted to ask if she could also feel the mark of death on Náraes, and what we should do about it, if there was anything she could do about it. I wanted to hear words of solace.

Yet I did not know where to begin, and I could not be sure whether she realized that I knew too.

But Sister O, this means that my mother shares my ability to feel the presence of the Crone, or hear her whispers—what does this mean? I did not believe that the Crone was here, Sister O. I believed she was present only on our island. I should have known better—after all, it was here that I first saw her door.

Is there anything I can do, Sister O? I wish somebody could cast some light on the whole thing. I have opened the door to death's realm. I wish for the power to keep it closed as well.

I have started talking to the Crone again. I do not hear her whispers, but I whisper to her instead. I whisper with every step I take along the paths around the village. I whisper as I pull weeds from my herb garden. I whisper in Gray Lady's ear as I give her hay and water. I whisper as I fetch water from the stream, as I weave fabric with Mother, as I rub soothing salve into Father's knee.

She is not yours to take, I whisper. *She is not yours. She is not yours.*

Maresi

Venerable Sister O,

I need to write to you urgently, as if you could receive this letter straightaway and write back to me, despite the fact that I have not heard from the Abbey at all. You must not have received my letters yet. I miss you and your good advice more than ever. Oh, why must I be so far away from you all?

Náraes came to see us yesterday evening. She is as big as a house now and walks slowly. As soon as she sat next to me on the bench, I felt it.

The icy chill was gone.

It took me a few heartbeats to understand what this meant.

The Crone had taken what she wanted.

My eyes filled with tears.

"What's the matter, Maresi?" Náraes laid her hand on my arm in concern.

I shook my head and tried to think of something to say. "Oh, everything is so difficult," I said.

"You're thinking of your school." Náraes leaned back against the wall with a groan.

I swallowed. She had given me a way out, and I took it. "Everyone is happy and this harvest looks to be the best in many years, but my days are filled with work. I have to contribute—I cannot let Mother and Father keep me, a grown woman. Especially not now that . . . Well, now that I must start from nothing. I have no energy left for the school."

Náraes sat quietly awhile. We were surrounded by the murmurs of the early-autumn evening: crickets, mosquitoes, the cackle of hens. Mother bred a hen last spring, and now we have seven hens and a rooster. The air was crisp.

"Sometimes I feel like one of those beautiful horses that belong to the nádor," she said thoughtfully. "A proud animal: wild and free. Born to run through fields with fluttering mane and thundering hooves." She shut her eyes. "But I'm harnessed to a donkey cart. Forced to trudge and haul while I dream of galloping free." She sighed, her eyes still closed.

The worst part of it is that I am relieved—relieved, Sister O!

I feared it was Náraes who was going to die. I cannot lose another sister. I refuse to.

ω

This morning Mother and I were standing on either side of the large washtub, stirring its contents. Father and Akios were out in the turnip field, and Mother had decided it was time to wash our bedclothes. It was a chilly morning. Mist hung over the fields, and lay thickly in the dell where the stream flows. We had built a fire in the central yard, and our neighbors were passing to and fro, busy with their own tasks. The mist dampened all sounds, making it feel as though Mother and I were alone in the world and everyone else was merely a phantom.

I needed to talk to Mother about the things I had felt. I cut a piece of soap into the washing water and looked up at her through the steam rising from the pot.

"Náraes's baby is dead."

Mother's hands, holding the washing paddle in a tight grip, came to a halt. She stopped stirring the pot and sighed deeply. She gave a barely perceptible nod.

"We both knew this would happen."

"You knew?"

"Didn't you? I thought that was the sort of thing you learned in that abbey of yours. To master life and death, that's what they taught you. I thought you knew everything."

"Why are you so hostile, Mother? What ill have I caused you?" I dropped the remaining soap into the pot and swallowed to force back the tears. "You become curt and cross at every mention of the Abbey. You act as though it were my fault that you sent me there!"

Mother dropped the washing paddle onto the ground and clasped her hands beneath her apron.

"When you returned to me, Maresi, I couldn't believe it. I thought I'd lost you forever. Every day without you was torment. I didn't know if you had come to harm, if you were even alive. You were just a little girl when we sent you away—how could you survive all alone? I've lain awake night after night with daggers in my flesh thinking: how could I send my own daughter away? It may have been the right thing to do, but I regretted it immediately, and ever since. Nothing can have been worth all that pain."

Mother had never spoken about this before. Never uttered a single word about it. I thought she was glad that I had gone. Or if not glad, at least relieved. It meant one less mouth to feed.

"And now I look at you and I hardly know you. You speak differently, in a way I don't recognize. You talk of strange things: opening the door to death's realm, a Crone and a silver door. You call another woman Mother!" She gasped for breath and coughed. "You are my own flesh, and I don't know you!"

She turned around and hurried into the house, leaving me alone in the yard with laundry and sorrow and tears.

Why must everything be so difficult? Why must life be this way? Forgive the running ink. I cannot stop crying.

ω

I will continue writing. One day has passed.

In the evening, after we had eaten, Mother came into my room. She stared down at the floor, avoiding my gaze. The evening sun filtering through the window illuminated the graying hair at her part.

"You wear the snake on your finger. Now, I might not know everything you've learned from books and fancy folk, but I know what the snake represents: the beginning and the end. Helping new lives into this world is the beginning. Accompanying the dying on their final journey is the end. Both are things you must learn. Or have you already learned that on your island?"

I shook my head but then realized that she was not looking at me. "No, Mother."

"Then come with me now to see Náraes."

Mother portioned out some herbs that might come in useful, and I quickly gathered them up along with a selection of the same herbs that Sister Nar used to aid Geja's birth. Mother briefly told Father and Akios where we were going, and then we walked the short stretch to Jannarl's farmhouse. Mother uttered not a word along the way.

Mother started by asking how Náraes was feeling, then tentatively brought the child into the conversation.

Náraes froze. "He hasn't kicked in a while. He's usually so lively. I . . ." Suddenly she looked at her husband with increasing fear. "Jannarl, when was it you felt my stomach?"

"Must have been yesterday, in the morning," he said.

He came and sat down beside Náraes. He laid his hands on her belly. They both sat still in silence. Náraes started running her hands over her belly, rubbing and pressing. She grew paler. I could not watch.

"Eat a little honey," said Mother. "We'll see if that gets him moving."

But both she and I knew that he would never move again.

We waited out the evening. We made no hasty decisions. Jannarl took his daughters to stay with his parents, then returned. We waited. The boy moved no more.

We waited until morning. By that time Náraes was sure. Mother started to prepare the tea that would help to induce birth. Náraes looked at me.

"Maresi. Stay with me."

I did as she asked.

I wished I could have left, and walked and walked and disappeared into the forest. Mother boiled water, and I brewed a tea with the herbs I had brought with me. Mother quietly instructed me at every step: which herbs to use, how they brought on the contractions, and what to do next. I helped Náraes out to the privy to relieve herself. It was early morning and veils of mist covered the fields. We exchanged few words. I wanted to say something, I truly did, but I could not find the words. Sister O, what is there to say to one's beloved sister who is bearing a dead child?

Sometimes silence is best.

I have witnessed birth before, when Geja was born. Yet Eostre was fighting through the pain knowing she would soon have a warm, living baby in her arms. The Mother aspect of the Goddess was close throughout Geja's birth. I felt her power and warm breath.

This time not even the Crone was with us. She had already claimed what was hers. All that remained was emptiness. Náraes fought through the pain and labor and knew that no reward awaited on the other side. I felt for her so badly I thought my heart would break.

When the boy was born Mother washed him with warm water. He was so still. I searched for the softest little blanket I could find, and wrapped it around him with care. Then I laid him at Náraes's breast, and she caressed his fine little nose and thin eyelids and bluish cheeks.

I went outside and down to the stream, where the creak of the mill wheel concealed my sobs.

Mother saw to the little body after that. She rubbed the boy with oils and wrapped him up properly, and then Jannarl brought a basket and laid him inside, on a bed of dried grass. I covered him with late-summer flowers before the lid was lowered.

Mother stayed with Náraes all day to make sure she had not suffered any injury or complications during the birth. I returned in the evening and prepared food for them: boiled eggs and porridge. Náraes sat at the table, quiet and pale, and ate.

"I can't believe I'm eating," she said afterward. She looked at me with blank eyes. "I'm sitting here eating, and then I'll go outside to empty my bladder. As if nothing happened. And I'm thinking about the garden and what needs harvesting."

Mother gave me a look. But I had nothing to say.

"It is what it is," she said. "It is how it must be. The end of his life doesn't mean the end of yours." Her voice was soft. "You will live on, and do what must be done, and that doesn't mean forgetting about your loss."

"It's my fault." The expression in Náraes's eyes was unbearable; I had to look away. She continued speaking. "I did something wrong. That's why he died. That's why he was taken from me."

"Don't be silly." Mother's voice remained gentle and kind. "You mustn't feel guilty. It only takes space in your heart away from all the love you need to be feeling."

"Love?"

"For the children you do have. For the child you did not get to keep. For your husband. For the world."

"You don't think he is in a better place now?"

"Could there be a better place for him than in your arms? At your breast? No. I cannot tell you that, my darling. I cannot give you answers. But I can assure you that the fault is not yours, and your child had a peaceful death. He never knew anything other than warmth and softness and love."

Both Náraes and I knew that Mother was thinking of Anner and the drawn-out death she suffered. Mother must have feelings of guilt also. Náraes rose and embraced Mother, and again I sensed their mutual understanding of something that I, the Crone's chosen one, will never know.

I went outside. Jannarl was standing in the yard all alone. He stared at me, his arms hanging helplessly by his sides. I went and put my arms around him, and in the quiet evening he wept on my shoulder until my shirt was soaked.

Jannarl blew his nose and went inside to his wife. Mother came out and we walked slowly home.

"Perhaps I know less than I thought, Mother," I mumbled. "We learn about the First Mother and her three aspects at the Abbey. The Maiden, the Mother and the Crone. That which blooms, bears fruit, and dies. I have opened the door to the realm of the Crone. But I did not think that she was present here too."

"Death exists everywhere, as does life. You talk of the Crone and her realm. Here in Rovas they speak of the realm beneath the roots of the silverwood trees. Elsewhere folk believe that one is born into a new body after death, or that the gods have a great hall in the clouds for all who have left this life. Don't you see that it's all one and the same? We only have different words for it."

ᛟ

I used to think that the Abbey was the only place where I could learn about life, through books and lessons. But I am learning new things here, things that are not written in books.

I wish I had not had to learn this.

Please write to me. Tell me what to do. Help me understand.

Your novice,

Maresi

Most Venerable Mother,
        Yesterday we buried my little nephew.

The only mourners were our family and Jannarl's parents. When an old, respected member of the community dies, the whole village follows them to the burial grove, but this tiny baby, known to none but his mother, had few companions on his final journey. We set out very early. Gray Lady was harnessed to a cart belonging to Jannarl's father. Náraes and the girls sat in the cart with the little basket between them, and Akios and I walked on either side of the mule. Father headed the procession, cutting marks into the trees along the path leading to the burial grove, to help the little one find his way to death's realm, which Rovasians believe exists under the roots of the silverwood trees.

Mother brought up the rear alongside Jannarl's parents, and I was struck by how she has aged, even in the time since I returned. She has become so thin.

The acorns are still green and late-summer blossoms abound. The fields we passed were yellow with stubble. We have reaped the flax, barley and rye. Now the flax must be cut and retted, which entails a great deal of work. We are hoping for a rainless moon so that everything has time to dry.

Mother and Feira carried bags of chopped juniper slung over their shoulders. They strewed juniper on the ground behind the cart and sang the mourning song, which bids farewell and prevents the dead from wandering back into the world of the living. I heard my sister mumble something to herself in the cart. I let go of Gray Lady's halter and fell in line with her.

"I don't want to stop him from coming back," Náraes whispered to me. "There's nothing I want more."

"I understand." There was nothing else I could say. Náraes took my hand and squeezed it, then let go to grab hold of Dúlan and stop her from falling out of the cart. She sighed. She was not crying, but her face was swollen and red.

We were deep in the forest by this time, and dry leaves were crunching under feet and boots and wheels. It smelled of the autumnal forest and decaying foliage.

Eventually Mother and Feira stopped singing, and the only thing to be heard was Father's ax as he chopped into the trees along the path. Dúlan slept in her mother's lap, and Maressa was quietly eating the nuts I had picked for her.

It is a long way to the burial grove, and the forest was bathed in twilight by the time we arrived. The offering grove where we perform rites and hold festivals is used only by the immediate villages, and other villages have their own. But the burial grove, which lies northeast of our offering grove, is ancient and used by all of northern Rovas. It is set in a deep valley where I had been only a few times as a child. The forest parted, and the valley lay before us like an ocean of white foam, set against the dark backdrop of the northern mountains.

Silverwoods grow only in this valley. They are the most sacred tree in Rovas, and this valley is the most sacred site in Rovas. Silverwoods are entirely white, with white wood, bark and leaves. The leaves never change color and never drop. Generations and generations of my people have been buried at their roots. As soon as we started on the path down into the valley, I heard a voice.

Maresi, it whispered clearly. It was a voice that I would recognize anywhere. It pierced my heart. My mother was right. The Crone is here too. Of course she is. I am not alone, as I had thought. The Crone's whispers coiled around my feet, and her breath tickled my neck. We were reunited.

That evening we committed the boy to the earth in the part of the valley where our family has laid their dead for centuries. He was buried with a copper coin and a snow-white silverwood spoon, as is our custom, and Jannarl sacrificed a chicken before lowering the basket into the hole Father had dug. It was such a small hole. Such a small grave. We filled it and I threw my flowers on top.

The Crone continued to mutter and sigh among the tree trunks. This site is even more infused with her power than the crypt in Knowledge House. So many of the Crone's devotees are here. So many generations have worshipped her here, though by a different name. The Crone takes her due. She is not too particular. The First Mother is not demanding. She understands that we fragile humans are confused and vulnerable in this big, wild world, and we try our best.

We set up camp for the night under our family's burial tree. Feira and Mother lit a fire, and we sat around it to warm ourselves and eat our provisions. There was a bounty of food following the harvest, and we had thick egg pancakes and beer and small pastries filled with green beans, salmon and egg. Dúlan and Maressa snuggled up to their father and fell asleep. Presently, Náraes wrapped herself up in a blanket and lay down on the ground by her son's grave, with her head among the flowers I had scattered. Jannarl came to lie behind her with his arm around her waist, and there they slept throughout the night.

The older generation lay down to sleep as well. I sat wrapped up in my bloodsnail-red cloak and stared into the embers of the dying fire. My skin tingled and crawled. The ground was humming and trembling beneath the soles of my feet. The snake ring on my finger was freezing cold. Then the full moon rose over the valley and cast her white light over the silvery forest.

Suddenly a handful of stars detached and shot across the firmament, flying away like darting swallows. I held my breath. It was the most beautiful thing I had ever seen, Venerable Mother. And there, under raining stars, I wept.

"The world is so cruel, most venerable Crone," I whispered. "And I am so small. There is so little I can do."

I had never spoken to her in this way before.

Maresi, replied the Crone. *My daughter.*

There was warmth in her voice, but there was also a caution. A thought struck me: if I truly am the daughter of the Crone, if I am hers, perhaps I am capable of more than I believe. Perhaps I am more than just myself.

The next day I took a fallen branch from our family's silverwood tree. I am keeping it and carving a staff. I need some support, for I have the feeling that a storm is on its way.

Respectfully,

Maresi

Dearest Jai,

Yesterday marked the beginning of the harvest festival celebration in Sáru. All the essentials are now harvested and preserved: dried, jammed and juiced, pickled and soured, baked and salted.

Mother is beaming and says she cannot remember the last time her larder was so well stocked.

I have been too busy to write to anyone in half a moon. When I have not been taking part in harvest labor or picking mushrooms, plants and herbs in the nearby forest (I dare not venture far), I have been walking around the village with my silverwood staff, on the lookout for signs of the soldiers. No one has come to collect the taxes yet, and the whole village is holding its breath wondering whether, as if by miracle, they might leave us be this autumn. What with all the taxes imposed on us, we just barely have time and strength enough to scrape a meager living from the rocky Rovasian soil. However, this year the weather has been kind, and the soldiers and authorities have left us alone since the summer. Everyone, old and young, has been free to work on the land, and we have finally managed to fill our larders and storehouses properly. In the evenings I comb my hair and bind the strands that come loose into a braid that grows thicker with each passing day. As I do it I direct my thoughts to the soldiers and their commander, and imagine that I am binding them hard—so hard that they cannot come here and harass us. I have the feeling that these tasks are extremely important, but I am always surprisingly exhausted after my walks. I hope I am not falling ill. Maybe I am just fatigued from all this physical work. Mother makes sure that I take my walk in the morning or evening, no matter how tired I am or how much there is to be done at home.

"Take that cloak of yours," she says without so much as a glance, "and go out. I'll take care of the dishes."

I am grateful for the opportunity to be alone for a while. But in truth I have a suspicion, like a thorn in my heart, that Mother insists on it because she needs space away from me.

Maressa and Dúlan have been constantly tugging at Mother's skirt hem while she works, in the hope of being given a bowl to lick clean, a crumb of honey cake to nibble, or a jam spoon to taste. Mother lets them stay so that Náraes can have a little peace. My dear sister will not be defeated, Jai. She is getting on with her life, smiling and laughing, doing her work, cuddling her daughters and helping her husband at the mill, now that the flour needs grinding. I see what effort it costs her and adore her all the more for it. Her laughter is without heart, and she smiles with sadness in her eyes. Then she notices me looking at her and I avert my gaze. She does not want sympathy, but she does appreciate help. So Mother and I ensure that she gets it.

The harvest festival begins with the village making a sacrifice in the offering grove as a thanks for the bounties of the earth. However, the actual festival is not celebrated there; it is too far away and too sacred. Instead the festivities are held on a common between our village and Jóla. We walked there, with Dúlan in Jannarl's arms and Maressa holding my hand, but Náraes chose to stay home. Akios followed us to the festival ground but then soon went off in search of his friends. It was afternoon, with a warm, dry sun and pleasant breeze, and dogs were trotting among the tables in search of scraps. The harvest festival begins with a great feast, where all the households bring something from their harvest bounties, and the tables are loaded with food. Even my ravenous appetite was satisfied! Tell Ennike that she would have loved the soup—with proper meat and thick flour dumplings. There was blood sausage, bread and pastries, preserves and crispy bacon, and salted fish and fried piggies, which are a type of Rovasian pastry rolled in ginger and cinnamon. On separate tables stood barrels of malt drink and beer and jugs of moonshine. The young men who were able had been out hunting, and had caught wild birds and hares and gleaming silver salmon, which their mothers and sisters then smoked and salted and prepared in various ways.

We ate until we could barely move, the girls and I, and all three of us took equal delight in eating our fill without having to worry about minding our portions, for once. Dúlan fell asleep on her father's lap with a piece of cake in her hand. Maressa leaned on me with a contented little sigh, and I pulled my headscarf over my forehead to shade my eyes from the sun. Everybody sat around, talking and digesting, and Dúlan was not the only one to fall asleep.

Once the sun had sunk a little and the air had cooled, we stirred to help clear the tables and put away the leftovers so that they would not spoil. The village folk do not always understand that certain foods must never sit out in the warmth. They must be put away in cool cellars or stored in bowls of cold stream water as soon as possible. Neither do they understand that they are poisoning themselves by heating up the same meat soup day after day until they fall badly ill. They usually blame it on a curse someone has put on them.

Today there is a market in the hills, and I am so looking forward to it! I hope traveling merchants come, and that some of them might bring books. What I wouldn't pay to read something new! Now that the harvest is over I might even have time to read.

There is also the small chance that some merchant has come traveling from the south, and that letters from a distant island Abbey might have found their way here. I am bubbling with excitement and anticipation!

ᛟ

Evening:

What a disappointment this day has been! Here I am in my room, close to tears. No merchants came. Not a single one. Such a thing has never happened, according to old grandmother Kild, who managed to join in the celebration despite her injury. No books, no letters. I miss you, Jai. I miss everyone so much my heart is fit to burst! It feels like an eternity since I saw you last, when the boat sailed out of the Abbey's little harbor and all the sisters and novices stood on the steps and cliffs and sang me off. I watched your fair hair flying in the wind, and Ennike's brown curls, and little Heo's straight black tresses. That was the last I saw of you.

Your forgotten friend,

Maresi

My dear Ennike Rose,

The market has been quiet today, and was quiet yesterday. The villagers have had to make do with trading their wares among themselves, paying in kind. I set up a small table where I displayed my herb clippings and the little jars of salves I have been making when I have had time. I had a salve for swollen, aching joints that I traded for paper, which Péra's grandfather was once given as payment for a piglet but never had any use for. Then I traded an herb mixture that aids digestive trouble for several beautiful beeswax candles, which I will use this winter when I write to you in the dark. Other than that, most people walked past my table with polite smiles.

The same could not be said for Tauer's table. He stood there with his jars and pots and herbs, and people flocked around him. They paid with eggs, pastries, a live rooster, an ornate knife and even salt. When it became apparent that I would sell no more, I packed up my things and placed the sacks next to Gray Lady, who was munching on a shrub. When I passed Tauer's table, I heard him doling out his medications accompanied by the most ridiculous prescriptions. "Speak not a word before taking this each morning," he said to a pregnant woman, "and then walk, still without talking, three circuits around your garden." "Stand at a moonlit crossroads and rub this into your wart," he said to a young man and handed him a little pouch. "If your heart is pure the wart will disappear within a moon."

Now that the harvest is over I will make sure to pay Tauer a visit and ask him to teach me what he knows about herbs and healing. For he does have some genuine knowledge—I have witnessed his tinctures help people. I want to know how and why.

I walked home afterward. There will be a dance this evening to conclude the harvest festival and growing season, and to salute the coming of the darker season that is spent mainly inside, when we occupy ourselves with all our hundreds of indoor chores. Yet I had no desire to take part; I was missing everyone at the Abbey too much. Instead I walked aimlessly through the fading daylight along the fences and streams. The air was cool and the night is bound to be cooler still, but I never feel cold in my red mantle.

I happened to pass Kárun's cabin. Smoke was rising from the chimney, so I already knew from a distance that he had returned from his travels. As I came closer I saw Kárun standing outside and whetting his ax. He was barefoot, wearing trousers and a shirt with rolled-up sleeves. As I approached he caught sight of me and called me over.

"Enresdaughter! Come and crank the grindstone for me."

Cranking the grindstone is hard, tiring work, but I knew it must be difficult for him to keep his tools sharp on his own. Sharpening scythes and other tools is a two-person task. Without a word, I took hold of the grindstone's handle and started to turn. Kárun sharpened his ax, tested the edge and then sharpened it some more. I was getting hot and had to push back my hood. His eyes flickered to me and then back to his hands. I did not stop turning until he had finished with both axes. Dusk had deepened, but I saw no warm yellow light spilling out from his cabin. The stars above us began to ignite.

"So, Enresdaughter," he said slowly, and sat down on the chopping block by the grindstone. His forehead was glistening with sweat, which he wiped off with his arm. He sat with legs wide, sure and comfortable in his body. I fiddled with the hem of my cloak.

"Are you chopping firewood for winter?" I asked, looking up at the starry sky. I tried to find as many constellations as I could recognize: the Red Bear, the Burning Star, the Long Dance and the Roebuck and Faun.

"Winter is harvest time for a woodcutter," answered Kárun. "Time to head into the Crown forests again. The new nádor is a greedy man. I expect he wants to stay on the right side of the Crown by being the governor to bring in the most taxes and provide the most riches from his province." It was the most I had ever heard him speak. I tore my gaze away from the stars. It was so dark that I could not see his face clearly, but he was looking directly at me. "But before that I'm going to start building a new house."

"Yes, your cabin has seen better days," I said, but he just hummed in answer. "Where will you build it?"

"I was thinking of the hill beyond the South Field, you know? Where three paths meet."

"A visible place," I said, and looked at the old gray cabin nestled by the stream, half-hidden in greenery.

"Easy to find from several directions. And near the forest. As a woodcutter and timber-rafter for the Crown, I can take timber for my own use."

"Did you go to Irindibul last summer?"

"Yes. I stayed for half a moon, taking work where I could. Earned a few coins too, for nails and tools."

"You never thought of staying?" The stream gurgled over the stones, and a magpie squawked irately from a bare birch tree. The moon had risen above the treetops now and Kárun's yard was bathed in a pale light. He brushed a little sawdust from his trousers, which I noticed were patched at the knees. He did not spend his earnings on new clothes, that was for sure.

"No." He looked at me. His gaze is always so earnest. I find it hard to look away. "I can't live without the forest. Cities are fine to visit, but it's only in the forest that I can breathe."

That is exactly how I have always felt! And I have used those very words to describe the same feeling. Before I had time to respond he got to his feet.

"Shall I walk you back to the village?"

I shook my head. "No, thank you. I can manage fine on my own. The nádor's men have not been seen in these parts for a long time, and in the darkness I can hear them coming before they catch sight of me."

"As you wish, Enresdaughter," said Kárun. "Thank you for your help with the grinding."

I nodded to him and walked back up toward the path. When I turned around again the yard was empty and the door was closed, but still no light peeked out.

I walked home slowly. I was not in the least bit afraid to be alone in the dark woods. I know the path well enough to walk it even in darkness. When I am surrounded by trees I can breathe. I am not seen, not weighed on a scale and found to be wanting. I am just myself: Maresi of Rovas. This forest has witnessed the growth and life and work of my father and his parents and their parents, and it knows me profoundly.

Yours,

Maresi

WINTER

Venerable Sister O,

I have not written in a while. Life is uneventful in Sáru during winter. It is cold and snowy, and we mainly sit inside doing tasks such as spinning, weaving, sewing, embroidery or repairing tools and utensils. I have never much enjoyed being inside. I am happiest outside on the seashore or mountain slopes of Menos, or in the forests of Rovas—with the exception of the treasure chamber, of course.

You cannot imagine how much I miss books here! I have read the ones I brought with me so many times that I know them by heart. At first my family thought it was strange that I spend my winter afternoons reading, but that is the time when there is enough daylight to forgo candles. I have my spot by the window where I drag over a stool, wrap up in my cloak to protect myself from drafts, and read. The books I brought with me were mainly chosen for their benefit to the school: one each about the history of the coastal lands, agriculture, constellations, mathematics and healing. Then I also brought some of the poet Erva's collected legends and tales from his travels through Lagora, Lavora, Urundien, the Akkade plains, Rovas, Devenland and all the other lands along the southern coast. I have read this one over and over again.

Mother is not best pleased about me sitting idle, as she sees it, and Father—well, Father rarely says much. He busies himself greasing boots or knotting baskets or repairing tools. Then one afternoon when Náraes and the children were visiting and everybody was occupied— Mother was patching a pair of trousers, I was knitting a pair of socks for Akios, Akios and Father were weaving baskets, Náraes was nursing Dúlan and Maressa was playing with leftover yarn—Father said something quite unexpected.

"It sure would be nice to know what's in those books you read, Maresi."

Mother looked up.

"I agree," said Akios. "I can already read a little, but it takes me a long time. And most of them are written in a language I don't know."

"Would you like to hear?" I looked with surprise at my family.

"Oh yes!" Náraes's face lit up. Seeing her excitement, there was no way Mother could object. Náraes has had a difficult autumn and we have all done what we can to ease her burdens and bring her a little happiness. I put down my knitting and fetched Erva's collection. It is the book containing all the most ancient legends of Lavora: Landebast, who founded the capital and named it after his white-haired daughter Laga; the hero Olok, who slew the terrible sea monster Keal; Unna the Seafarer; and Arra the Raven-Haired, whose song brought mountains crashing down on her enemies and who went on to become Lavora's most beloved queen. It is the same story that Heo always used to ask you to read, Sister O. I decided to start with that one.

I sat by the window, wrapped in my cloak, crossed my legs, placed the book on my lap and started to read aloud.

I read and read and read and no one in the room uttered a word. I read until the light outside began to fade and the words became harder to see. Then Mother got up from her seat, lit two candles and placed them on the table. I moved into their light and read on while Mother prepared the evening meal. Once the food was served I looked up in a daze, my head swimming with the blue-and-white mosaics of Lagora, and Arra's nocturnal meetings with Prince Surando.

"I can see the pictures in my head," said Náraes. "It's like I'm there in the forest, and in the city, and at the harbor, and in Evia's house."

"It's like our ballads," said Father thoughtfully. "You can know things that happened in places you've never been."

"And long ago, besides," I said. "The legend of Arra is very old."

"Nobody could remember such a long song," said Mother. "But in those black marks it's preserved forever."

"Some songs are very old too," I said. "But they change over the years. Every singer adds their own touch."

"Carry on, Maresi!" said Maressa. "More!"

"We're eating now," said Mother. "Come and sit down, everybody."

But once we had finished eating, Mother lit another candle so that I could continue reading.

Now I read aloud from Erva's collection every day. Náraes and Jannarl come with the children when the day's tasks are done, and then the whole family sits together while I read. It makes me happier than anything—maybe even happier than sitting in the treasure chamber and reading alone, because when I read aloud we experience the events of the story together. We can discuss them afterward. And I love looking up from the book and seeing Maressa sitting with her mouth agape, hanging on every word, and seeing my mother bent over her sewing yet so engrossed in the story that she looks up the moment I stop reading and silently demands that I continue. This is the closest we have ever been. It makes me wish that the winter would never end.

Yet I cannot sit inside interminably, although this is how Rovasians traditionally spend the long winters. It is not in my nature. I do go out as well, in the morning when the sun sparkles on the snow and casts long, bluish shadows. Of course, that just makes me all the more peculiar in the eyes of others. Apart from Mother, strangely enough, who hands me my socks and gloves and makes sure I go out every day, whatever the weather. I have gloves that I knit myself and woolen socks and Father's old felt boots and my lovely warm hooded cloak. I have whittled a staff to lean on when I get tired during my walks, and I am in the process of engraving it with shells and snakes, apples and roses, and all the phases of the moon. It is no masterpiece, but it is a good thing to have.

First I usually walk one circuit around the village, wearing Father's felt boots, and then stop in to see Tauer in the neighboring village. I have taken to assisting him with his daily tasks. Many people turn to him for help, but few offer a helping hand in return. They give him gifts in gratitude, and those gifts are his sustenance. When I was there at the end of autumn he gave me a young goat, one of his own goat's yearling kids. I believe I grew in Mother's estimation when I came home with the animal. At last I am contributing something substantial to our table!

When I came here last spring I thought that Tauer dealt in mere quackery and willingly deceived the poor village folk. Now I know better. He has very patiently taught me what he knows, and explained his methods. There is certainly one area in which Tauer's knowledge is far greater than mine, and that is about the people of Jóla, Sáru and other villages nearby.

He gives them what they need to cure their ailments if he is able—herbs, ointments, good advice—but then he flavors it with a little mysticism.

"It tends to help more if there's an element of magic," he explained to me the other day. "Rubbing ointment on a wart is nothing, but if I tell them to go out at midnight and wait at a three-way crossroads, then they feel like they've really done something worthwhile." He chuckled. "Then, if the wart-sufferer happens to be a particularly uncouth young man, I might add that it will only disappear if his heart is pure. Then I give him a weaker salve, and when the wart is slow to disappear, it might encourage him to examine his conscience just a smidgen."

He is wise in a way that I did not see before. He makes use of everything he knows about the villagers and their families, like with Árvan's mother. He gave her a salve for her bad back that contained many of the same pain-relieving herbs and roots that I have learned about. But he told her she must apply it in the evening and then stay absolutely silent until dawn.

"And that wasn't for her sake so much as for that son of hers," he smiled. "So that his poor ears might get a little respite from her nagging and complaining, at least at night."

Once finished at Tauer's, I leave the village and resume my walk. It has not snowed much yet this winter, so walking is not too difficult.

I can be alone with the wind and the animal tracks and the cawing of ravens and crows, in sun or cloud. I often walk through the forest. How I love the woods in winter. Frost on the branches, green patches under the densest trees, the translucent winter sun filtering through the branches.

The only human sounds I hear are the chopping of Kárun's ax and the blows of his hammer, coming from the construction site. He is building himself a new house on the hill between Sáru and Jóla. Sometimes, when I hear that he is up there I sneak into his cabin. Naturally, it is never locked. Kárun has nothing that anyone would want to steal. I do not know why I go there, but it feels so exciting and forbidden! My heart beats wildly and I jump at every tiny sound, even though I know that he is busy building.

His cabin is very simple. It is made of unstripped, unsealed logs. His father built it, or so I heard from Akios, who knows all sorts of things about Kárun. There is a wide bed in one corner, without any curtains. It must be where Kárun's mother and father used to sleep. I do not know where he slept as a child. Maybe with them. The bed has a straw mattress with a coarse linen cover. Kárun has no bedsheets, only a thick woolen blanket to cover himself with and another smaller blanket folded up as a pillow. The house is sparsely furnished: a table and bench; a small clothes chest; a home-woven mat on the floor. Perhaps his mother made it. A fireplace, some pots, a bucket, a drum of salted fish. A few circles of rye crispbread hang from the ceiling. Timber-rafters are indeed even poorer than farmers. In winter they chop down trees, and in spring and summer they float the timber on to cities and boatyards and other places where wood is needed. They get paid, but not much. Kárun only lives in his house for part of the year. The cold part.

Sometimes I sit on the bed and listen to the wind whistling through the cracks. I wonder why he has remained in that drafty old cabin for so long.

My fingers itch to tidy up for him. Wash the mat. Scrub the pots until they shine. Bring some bedsheets. Of course I cannot, because then he would know that I had been there. I am careful to erase any traces that I have even sat on the bed.

ϖ

I am writing to you all, but it feels like nothing more than shouting into the night sky. Nobody hears me, and I receive no reply. The winter is relentless, never-ending. I have been home for nearly a year, and I have done nothing. I used the Mother Abbess's silver to pay off the village's debts to the nádor. But that is not what I came here to do. I wanted to open windows and doors. I wanted to show the people of Rovas that the world is wide, that their lives are not predetermined and their futures are in their hands. Yet I am unable to influence or help even my own family. Náraes lost her son. Akios is learning to read, but for what purpose? He is destined to take over the farm. What good will literacy do him? I have become a storyteller, a stay-at-home daughter who turns down marriage proposals, ever waiting. For what? I do not know. I no longer know anything. I feel lost and alone.

Forgive me. I probably will not send this letter. I do not want you to know of my failures. Maresi, who was supposed to go forth and change the world, has accomplished nothing. My whole being is one big failure. All I can do is entertain my family with tales, teach Maressa and Akios to read, and make cabbage soup. According to Mother, I cannot even do that right.

Géros has a new girl, Tunéli. It comforts me to know that whatever he felt for me was not true love. He was driven by lust, as was I. Driven by the desires of our bodies. I am glad, because it means neither of us is suffering. Still, I do feel a little prick in my heart when I see them together in the afternoons, not because I miss him but because it is a blow to my vanity, every time.

I enjoyed feeling desired for a while.

Here is the reason why I am so downhearted: one evening Father suggested that I should open up our home as my school. We could gather the village children at our hearth during the times of the year when their work is least needed around the farm. Mother said nothing to support or contradict the idea. So I visited each local farmstead in turn and asked if the families would send their little ones to our house for three afternoons a week. None came but Maressa.

On the third afternoon little Lenna from White Farm appeared too. She stamped the frost and snowy grit from her boots and slammed the door shut.

"Well, is there a school here or not?" She looked around. Maressa was sitting by the window writing letters on a board. She has become very good at it now, and can write her own name.

I stared at her. Lenna was the last person I was expecting. She is practically a little housewife already. She cooks and sews and embroiders and is interested in gossip and hairstyles.

"Of course. If you . . . if you could just sit down next to Maressa."

"She has already begun learning?"

"I have been teaching her letters since last summer."

"Well, I'm older, I'll catch up. Where can I hang my cardigan?"

Lenna has proven to be a very enthusiastic pupil. She thoroughly enjoys learning, but has very little patience and wants to be able to do everything at once (just like Heo!). She chatters incessantly, but asks all sorts of questions with equal zeal. Sometimes I feel like you must have felt, Sister O, when I used to ask you at least a hundred questions per day. I am trying to show the same patience as you always did, and to answer all the questions I can.

However, two pupils—one of whom is my own niece—is no school. It is nothing. Lenna and Maressa are my pupils, but I only teach them to read and count, and I cannot bring myself to take any payment.

The villagers suspect that I want to fill their children's heads with intellectual nonsense of no practical use that only takes time away from their real work.

There are so many things I need to talk about that no one here would understand. On the occasions when I have tried to speak about what I did in the crypt, or how I heard the Crone's voice on Menos, and again in the burial grove, Mother withdraws from me. She changes the subject. She turns away. I wonder if she might be afraid of me. Sometimes I think she is. Once, when I was telling Maressa about life on Menos, about the bloodsnails and the morning wash and the sun greeting and other entirely normal things, Mother stared at me for a long time.

"I can hardly believe that I bore and raised you," she said. "Who are you, Maresi Enresdaughter?"

Her words hurt terribly. I have asked myself this ever since. Who am I? And why is Mother so angry? Or is it that she is afraid?

So there are certain things I keep to myself.

Mother is disappointed in me too, both because I am so strange, and because despite all this strangeness I achieve nothing.

"If they aren't coming to your school," she said, "maybe you should consider making some changes to your behavior here in the village." She did not look at me as she said this. "Act a bit more like everyone else. Like Náraes or Péra. Then once they've got used to you maybe they'll send their children to your school. It's not as hard as you think, to change yourself, to imitate others and fit in."

I did not respond. I did not want to show her how much these words hurt me. I am not good enough for Mother, and she believes that it would be better for everyone if I tried harder to conform.

Perhaps she is right. Perhaps it would be better for everyone. But if I become like them, and stay indoors sewing and cooking, and welcome the courtship of some village boy, then I will not be myself. How can I teach others if I lose my own self? I would slowly become one of them, and become complacent. People who are complacent do not try to change things. I must remain strange. I have to make a difference. I have to *be* the difference.

I know that I am contradicting myself. I already am different, but I get nothing done.

Oh Sister O, please do not tell the others of my failings.

Your novice,

Maresi

Dear Jai,

Winter continues. More snow has fallen and the nights are bitterly cold, but the sun is already bringing a little warmth and light to the days. Now is the time to take to the woods for hunting and fishing. It is usually only the men and boys who ski out on hunting trips with sleds full of supplies, but Father has always taken out whichever of us was old enough to cope with the hardship: first Náraes, then Náraes and me, and finally all three of us. I had been looking forward to this hunting trip for a long time. I am itching all over from these endless days spent inside, though reading aloud and my little "school" have helped to pass the time. Besides, I have always enjoyed these ski trips and missed them even when I was at the Abbey.

Mother and I packed food for the journey: rye bread; matured goat's cheese Tauer had given me; a cured sausage we obtained through trade; a small pouch of salt. The hens are not laying currently, so alas there were no boiled eggs. We were counting on mainly eating what we could hunt or fish. Father made me a new pair of skis. They are beautiful, with fur on the underside of one so they slide well on the hard snow crust but are not too slippery on the slopes. We wrapped ourselves up in every warm garment we own, and I was glad for the long woolen underpants Mother had knit for me. I had knit myself a pair of thick gloves and a cap, and then I wore trousers of homespun wool and two shirts, one very thick woolen sweater I inherited from my grandmother, and my woolen cloak on top of it all. Thus equipped, off we went: Father, Akios and I. Jannarl had considered joining us, but opted to join Máros instead and set off a couple of days before we did.

Father pulled the sled behind him, so Akios and I were free to just ski and enjoy the fresh air in our lungs. The sun was shining as we set off, and the magpies were chittering in the bushes around the frozen, snow-covered stream. We followed the stream eastward into the forest. There were no ski marks to follow on the hard snow crust, and it was so smooth that it was a constant struggle to prevent the skis from slipping and sliding in all directions. It had snowed a great deal, and the forest was beautifully adorned: the snow-laden branches bowed deeply toward the ground. It was quiet—as quiet as only a forest under a blanket of snow can be. A kite flew silently overhead. And yet, when I pulled down my hood and listened very closely, I could hear a tone resonating from the very earth. At first I thought the freezing cold must be causing something to reverberate, but the tone followed us throughout the forest. The others did not seem to hear it. It sounded like a string someone had plucked long ago that was still vibrating with a barely audible tone. It rippled through my skis and boots and into my body, causing my teeth to hum.

I think it was the tone of Rovas itself, and as the day rolled on and we skied ever farther my whole body began to hum with it as well. It was a pleasant sensation, and it gave me the strength to keep up with Father's pace even when my legs and arms were shaking with strain.

Father returns to the same place every winter, a whole day's ski from the village. It is not far from the offering grove. He built a little shelter there long ago, situated close to the river but far upstream, where few pass. It is good hunting ground, and one can fish in the river too. Night was falling by the time we arrived so it was too late to fish or set traps. We pulled off our skis and Akios removed the pack from his back. Akios and I fortified the shelter with fresh, dense fir branches, and Father chopped wood and cleared a place for a fire in front of the shelter. Then he took some dried kindling from his sled and before long we had a lovely blazing fire. I took the little kettle out of our pack, filled it with snow and hung it over the fire, then once the snow had melted I dug out some herbs to make tea. It was wonderful to sit by the fire warming our hands on the wooden cups we had tied to our pack, while steam rose from the brew, darkness tightened around us and bright winter stars lit up one by one. Our breath hung like clouds around our faces, and the fire crackled and fizzled as it melted the surrounding snow. My toes were cold in Father's old boots and the air nipped my nose, but I was content sitting on an old hide rug between my father and brother, nibbling on rye bread. It was like old times, when I was little and knew nothing of hunger winters or travels away from my family. For that time I was simply Maresi Enresdaughter, on a winter hunting trip with my father, and it felt good, Jai.

Sometimes I wish I had never gone to Menos. I have not dared admit this to anyone else, but I think you might understand. Yes, the Abbey gave me so much—safety, food, knowledge, reading, and the chance to meet all of you—but at the moment it is making my life so difficult. So . . . convoluted. Before I left, everything was much simpler. I used to fit in. Now my head is too full of thoughts and questions that I would not have, had I never gone away.

Writing this, an even more painful thought just struck me. Perhaps I do not regret being sent to the Abbey as a child. Perhaps I regret leaving it, and all of you, behind. Still, it is too late for regrets now.

ᴡ

I know that you have never slept in a snowy forest, Jai, so let me indulge you. First we laid out a dense mat of fir branches in the shelter. Then we spread an animal hide on top and slept tightly snuggled together with a second hide over us. It was as warm and cozy as anything. We put wood on the fire before going to bed, and Father woke twice in the night to feed it, to keep wild animals at bay. I was awoken when he stirred, and lay for a while listening to the crackling fire and the murmuring tone resonating from the ground before sinking back into a deep, dreamless sleep.

We rose before the sun. My hood was stiff with frost and both Father and Akios had icicles in their beards, but none of us had felt cold during the night. We shook the frost from the hides, and I made us some more hot tea.

"Let's lay the traps first," said Father, "so we can collect the catch this evening, if there is any. Not likely though. More likely to get the first catch tomorrow. But we can spend the day fishing."

We scooped snow onto the fire and set off each in our own direction. Akios has been hunting with Father several times and knows all the best places to set traps. I was nine years old the last time I went out hunting and had no memory of where the animals tend to go. The hard snow crust revealed no tracks as clues either, but I chose three places that looked promising and set up snares.

The day was sunny and cool, and melted snow dripped from tree branches, but the crust held out well and I did not fall through it once. I hate breaking through the crust, as it is difficult to free oneself again. I skied down to the river and found Father already fishing with a long line through a small hole he had cut in the ice. I borrowed his ax and cut my own hole in the ice a little upstream, then found a small tree stump, dragged it onto the ice and sat down. Then it was just a case of sinking the hook into the hole and slowly pulling it up again, over and over . . .

Though I enjoy sleeping in a wintry forest, I do *not* enjoy ice fishing. Sitting still is unbelievably cold and boring—especially if you get no bites, which I did not. Akios joined us a little later in the day and immediately caught a trout and two big fat female perches full of roe. I caught nothing. The hum of the earth was intensifying in my body and making me squirm where I was sitting. Eventually I tied my line to the stump and called to Akios.

"You can keep an eye on this. I have to ski to warm up a little."

He raised a gloved hand in answer.

"Don't stray too far," said Father. "I saw the scratch marks of a bear on a pine trunk to the north of here."

"So I will ski to the east," I said. Then I pulled on my skis, picked up my staff and crossed the river. The way up the riverbank was tough, despite the squirrel skin providing some grip on the underside of one of my skis. I had soon left my family and the river behind me and was skiing directly eastward. There was a humming vibration in my feet and ears. Soon my blood was pumping faster and I began to warm up. The sun had just about cleared the treetops to my right. I heard my breathing resound between the trees as rhythmically as ax chops. A kite surprised me with a sharp shriek overhead. Then suddenly the forest ended.

I looked out across a long, treeless hillside where I was dazzled by the sun glittering on the snow. On the far side, at the forest's edge, I saw a handful of working men and a large, shaggy horse attached to a cart. I had forgotten that winter is the time for felling timber, when logs can be easily transported to collection points along the river to be moved downstream when the ice breaks up. These were not the nádor's men, but ordinary woodcutters like Kárun; yet my body tensed with alarm. Woodcutters are often freelanders, living alone and traveling from one timber-felling area to the next. Unknown men, unaffiliated with village or province. I became aware of how lurid my red cloak must be against the white snow. The kite circled above the men and screeched several times in quick succession. It felt like a warning. I had to flee at once.

As soon as I regained control over my shaking legs, I turned around and skied faster than I have ever skied before, back to Father and Akios.

Father looked with concern at my flushed cheeks as I swooshed onto the icy river.

"Bear?"

I shook my head and caught my breath. "Woodcutters. Not far from here, to the east."

"Did they bother you?"

"No. I skied away as soon as I saw them."

Akios had come over to boast about his recent catch, but when he overheard, a wrinkle appeared in his frost-white brow.

"A timber-clearing area this far north?"

"Hasn't happened in living memory," Father said slowly.

"Awfully close to the offering grove," said Akios.

"And the burial grove."

"But this land does not belong to the Crown," I said. "They cannot fell trees here."

"All of Rovas belongs to the Crown, Maresi," Father said coolly. "The only rights we have are those issued to us by the Crown."

ϖ

After that I found it difficult to relax. The strange men were so nearby, and it made my skin crawl. We had caught a decent amount of fish—or rather Akios and Father had. I had no luck with the fishing at all. Akios and I skied back to our camp with the catch while Father did a circuit to check the traps. We spent the afternoon cleaning the fish and removing their spines to make them easier to hang up to dry once we got home. I lightly salted a medium-sized trout and then Akios grilled it over the fire while Father and I flayed, skewered and cooked a hare from one of his traps.

As darkness fell we sat down to eat delicious, oily trout with our hands. Suddenly something moved at the edge of the sphere of firelight. Father's hand flew to his ax and Akios leaped to his feet. I had no time to think at all, because the appearance of a fur-clad figure directly in front of us filled me with fear.

"That smells good," came a voice, and Akios visibly relaxed.

"Kárun!"

Kárun came to a halt, leaned on his ski pole and peered down at us. He was on skis, and dressed in a fur hat and waistcoat that looked like wolf skin.

"Blessings on your hearth," he said, and smiled. The skin around his brown eyes wrinkled amiably.

"Blessings on your journey," answered Father. "What brings you here?"

"I saw Maresi in her red cloak earlier today so I knew you must be nearby."

"Sit, please!" said Father, scooting over. "Plenty of food to go around."

Kárun removed his skis and leaned them against a tree. My heart was still pounding from the shock and my mouth was all dry. I took a piece of fish, my hands shaking, and passed it to Kárun once he had sat down between Father and Akios. He took it and looked me in the eye.

"Did I frighten you?"

"A little. I saw the woodcutters today and I thought . . ." I trailed off. Kárun nodded.

"Sorry about that. But they are good men this year. Rovasians, no vagabonds. The foreman is from Urundien, of course, with orders from the nádor. But you have nothing to fear from them."

I swallowed and felt the tension melt from my body.

"You've come very far north." Father wiped his mouth with a gloved hand.

"Yes." Kárun popped a piece of fish into his mouth. "And I don't like it. The land here is sacred. The nádor is sinking his teeth and claws ever farther into Rovas. But we would never raise an ax against a sacred tree, you know that, Enre."

Father poked the fire. "Are they paying well this year then?"

"The pay has remained the same for many a year. I manage. I've no one else to feed." He swallowed the last of the fish and gave Akios a friendly shove. "And how are you? Has it been a long winter?"

"Not as long as usual. Maresi's been reading to us, and it feels like we've traveled the world from our own home!"

Kárun smiled. His face changes a lot when he smiles. It becomes lighter, more likable. Akios gestured in my direction with his gloved hand.

"And Maresi has a school now!"

Kárun looked at me. "Now, that is good news!"

I squirmed. It was difficult to receive praise for a failure. "It is only my sister's eldest, Akios and Lenna who come," I muttered. "I teach them to read and write and a little counting. It is hardly a real school."

Father poured some of the tea I had made into his cup and handed it to Kárun, who took a sip.

"I've come on far with my building project," he said. "I got the roof on before the snow came. Last spring all I had was stripped logs and uncleared ground." He looked straight at me, and it felt as if his eyes burned right through to the heart of me. I can still feel it. "Then I laid the first log."

Father smiled. Akios yawned, and Kárun set his cup down in the snow.

"Well, I'd best leave you now. I still have a way to ski to our night camp." He got up and tied on his skis. As he took hold of his ski pole it seemed that something occurred to him. "I almost forgot," he said, and reached for an item that was bound to his back.

It was a pair of boots. Brand-new and thick-soled, made of fine, soft leather, with buttons of white bone.

"You've been walking around in your father's worn-out boots," he said quietly. "I had some tanned leather left over, and I inherited my mother's cobbler tools, and maybe a bit of her knack as well."

"She was deft with the leather needle," Father agreed.

Kárun handed me the shoes. They smelled pleasantly of leather and shone in the firelight. Kárun had greased them well.

"Been working on them by the fire through the winter evenings. We can't fell trees after dark, so there's plenty of fireside time. When I saw you today I rushed to finish them off." He rubbed his cold-chapped hands together.

I have not had footwear of my own since I left the Abbey, where we only ever wore sandals. I looked up at Kárun with my jaw dropped.

He cleared his throat. "Well, I'll be off then."

Kárun turned around and skied away between the snow-covered firs. He was gone.

I thought that my father would make some sort of pointed comment, but he just washed Kárun's cup out with a little snow.

"Remember last hunger winter?" he asked my brother. "Kárun brought game to all the homes that were struggling, until the snow made hunting impossible."

Akios nodded. "He never asked for anything in return either. Even though he has so little himself."

"His father was a terrible man. Wicked toward wife and son alike. As long as he lived I wouldn't let your mother go to Jóla alone, because that meant passing Eimin's cabin, and you never knew what he might do. Remarkable that Kárun turned out to be such a decent fellow."

"How did his mother die? He doesn't like to talk about it." Akios washed the fish from his hands in the snow.

"She was sick. His father refused to call for help, and when Tauer came to their house Eimin chased him away with bludgeon blows and foul words. Kárun was only young at the time, not much older than Maressa."

I looked down at the boots in my lap. There was so much work behind them. To get all that leather together. To cut everything just right. The even, patient stitching. I thought of him as a little boy, alone with a violent father. I quickly blinked away the tears before Akios could notice and tease me for them.

Later, as I lay between Akios and Father, beneath fragrant fir branches, wrapped so tightly under the hide that only my eyes and nose peeked out, Akios whispered in my ear.

"Do you realize that you didn't even say thank you, Maresi?"

That was unforgivably rude of me. I have to visit Kárun next time he is in the village and thank him properly. To think that I got new boots made specially for me! I have tried them on and they fit well, but there is also extra space inside for thick woolen socks. My feet will never be cold or wet in these. I will wear them as I walk around the village, wander in the forest and work in the garden and fields. It is a greater gift than he probably even knows. I can hardly believe that he made them just for me. It has the marks of a proposal gift, but without the proposal. We have only spoken to one another a handful of times. And he has never made an attempt to approach me in the way a man does when he desires a woman. As Géros clearly did.

He truly is a peculiar man, that Kárun.

ω

We came home with masses of fish and a fair bit of game, and have been busy hanging fish to dry up on the barn roof where the animals cannot reach. It is perfect drying weather. The snow crust is no longer holding as firm, so that was our last hunt. Timber-felling must also come to an end now, and the woodcutters are making their way home in anticipation of the breakup of the ice, when they can float their timber downstream. We have dried some of the game, but we gorged on most of it in delicious roasts and stews. I showed Mother how Sister Ers taught me to prepare birds, stuffed and skewered, and for once she let me prepare the food my own way. We ate three whole white grouse, and Father boasted that it was the most delicious thing he had eaten in a long time. Akios poked me in the side and said that I would make a fine housewife someday. It made me angry.

"Have I not made it clear to you and the rest of the village that I do not intend to marry? That there are other things I must do?"

"I was only joking," said Akios grumpily.

"Well, I am not joking."

"Your school doesn't take up so much of your time," Mother said coolly. "There's time for other things as well."

"This is only the beginning of my school," I said despondently. "It is only the first stage. You will see."

I am not sure I even believe my own words, Jai, but I want to believe. I want to believe that I will make the school a success.

Only, I do not know how.

Your friend,

Maresi

My dear Ennike Rose,

The sun is warming my cheek as I sit by the window and write this. Icicles are dripping from the roof and the stream is gushing wildly under its thin cover of ice. Small flecks of bare ground are already appearing near the southern facades, and the birds are beginning to return from their winter homes. Birdsong is ringing out from the leafless branches around our house. It is afternoon. Father and Akios are outside investigating the ditches that need clearing now that the snow is melting. I am writing at the hearth table, where Mother is also standing and kneading dough. It smells faintly of sourdough, and Mother has rye flour all the way up her arms. She says nothing, but I know she thinks I ought to be helping her. There is no need for her to say it out loud. I can see it in her tensed lips and jerky movements and deliberate avoidance of me. She thinks I am being lazy when I read and write, except for when I am reading aloud for the whole family. Father thinks I should be left to my own devices, so she has stopped saying anything. I have tried reading her excerpts from my letters in the hope that she might understand. But it only makes things worse. A sadness appears in her eyes, and she looks at me as if I were a stranger. So I have stopped trying.

The weather has been sunny and fine for a long time now, and everything speaks—no, sings!—of spring. There is still a lot of snow, but it shrinks with each day the sun shines. It is coarse and crunchy and impossible to walk on now, but I continue my walks around the villages along the paths I trod during winter. I always bring my staff, which keeps me from getting too tired.

When I was out hunting with Father and Akios I heard a tone being sung by the forest, or by the earth itself, but I have not heard it at home. It appears in my dreams. It calls to me, luring me out of the village and into the forest, where some terrible thing is waiting and drawing me in—some nameless thing with teeth and claws—and my heart pounds and I wake up breathless and sweaty and am too afraid to go back to sleep.

Gray Lady has become completely impossible. I often bring her on my walks, at least where there are tracks already trodden in the snow, but she acts wild and keeps trying to pull me off the paths and into the forest. She lumbers astray, headstrong, and there is nothing I can do to make her turn around. What does she think she will find in the forest? A handsome stallion? I would rather avoid the forest. I think of my dreams about the formless danger lurking in there, and keep to the paths.

Perhaps it is the spring sun making the old mule act so silly. I should ask Sister Mareane about it. Now I feel like I have to leave her at home when I go out, and she gives me awfully angry looks. I am sure you doubt that a mule could make such an expression, but it is true, I swear!

Akios pointed out that I acted very rudely when Kárun gave me a pair of boots (maybe Jai read you that part of her letter?). I did not even say thank you. It has weighed on my conscience ever since, meaning the boots have not brought me as much pleasure as they otherwise would. I wear them all the time, and every time I lace them up I admire the craft behind them. Not a single stitch out of place. I think of Kárun's large hands holding the tiny leather needle. Making shoes is no easy task, and few can do it alone. Kárun claimed that he happened to have leather "left over," but I cannot believe that—shoe leather is not something one simply happens to have.

I knew I must give him something in thanks, so I have sewn a pair of rabbit-skin gloves made from several beautiful rabbits I caught during a hunt earlier in the year. I have turned the fur inside out and embroidered some protective words in the coastal tongue on the outside.

Rovasians would think them nothing more than decorative squiggles. I finished them yesterday, then this morning I shook off Mother's gaze and set out. I have not heard the sound of work coming from Kárun's construction site over the winter, so I took the path directly to his dilapidated cabin. Smoke was rising from the chimney, so I knew he must be home. I knocked and entered.

There, in the gloom, Kárun was standing by the hearth stirring a large pot. He looked at me with surprise as I entered.

"Blessings on your hearth," I said, and stamped the muddy snow from my boots.

"Blessings on your journey," he answered absentmindedly. "Wait."

He put down the stick he was using to stir the pot and wiped his hands on his shirt. He took down a little clay cup from a shelf and filled it from a jug. Then he came over to me and offered me the cup. I took it, looked him in the eye and drank a small sip of moonshine. He took a sip after me and put the cup down on the solitary table. He looked at me questioningly but said nothing.

"Should you not be keeping an eye on the pot?" I asked, just for something to say. He turned around, looked at the pot on the fire and laughed.

"It's laundry," he said. "Mother taught me to boil linen to get it truly clean."

I pulled out the gloves and presented them to him. "Here. I never thanked you for the boots. You . . . I was so surprised. So I made these, as a thank-you."

It was awful, Ennike; all of a sudden I had no idea what to say! I could hear that I sounded brusque, almost unfriendly, but I could not stop myself. Kárun looked in astonishment at the gloves in his hands.

"Try them on. I am not sure if they will fit."

He tentatively pulled them on. "They fit," he said quietly. "They're very soft." He looked up. "Thank you."

His gaze drew me in. It burns its way straight through me every time. I blinked.

"Those signs are for protection, you see. Against ax slips."

"Won't you come in? Sit down?" He pointed to the bench. "I have nothing special to offer. A bachelor like me . . . it's only ever porridge, and a little meat sometimes."

"Yes, I can sit for a while."

I walked gingerly over to the bench and sat down, still with my cloak on. I was wearing a leather waistcoat underneath but still did not feel too warm, for the cabin was chilly. The only light came from a single window and the fire in the hearth. But I already knew what the cabin looked like from all those times I had visited in secret while Kárun was away. My cheeks felt hot when I thought about it.

"I have some bread that Tauer gave me," Kárun said, and produced a loaf and a knife that he placed directly on the table. "Helped with his father when he had to visit a patient downstream."

He poured a little more moonshine into the cup and presented it to me. Then he sat across from me and cut me a piece of bread. I took it and chewed gratefully on the dry crust. I could not be expected to speak with bread in my mouth.

"So, how's the school going? Are they learning?"

I swallowed the dry bread. "Some. Maressa is the quickest, but Lenna is bright too. They can already read simple phrases and write their names and some short words. They are very good at counting also."

"And Akios?"

"He has had less time to practice than the girls, but he is progressing too."

"You changed your mind, then?" Kárun was playing with the knife. "About what?"

"About boys, in your school."

"Akios hardly counts," I said. "He is my brother."

"I see."

"Are you off again soon?" I asked, just to change the subject.

"No, not yet. As soon as it dries up a little I can finish my building project. Then it's time to make timber rollers."

"Rollers?"

"Yes, to transport the logs to the river. Once the ice is gone and the river is high, but not too wild, we roll the timber we have felled over the winter."

"And then you transport it downstream?"

He nodded. "One team sets off first and waits at the places where the timber tends to get stuck in logjams. I belong to the rolling team, which remains until all the wood is in the river."

"So you will spend the summer in Urundien?"

"Some of it. I expect we'll reach Irindibul in high summer."

"What is Irindibul like?" I asked curiously. People in Rovas rarely leave their homesteads. No one has the time or opportunity to travel. Women move only when they marry, and men hardly move at all. The timber-rafters and hunters are the exceptions.

Kárun shrugged. "Big. Lots of people, lots of soldiers. I never feel truly safe there. Never truly at home."

"But there must be so much to see, so much to experience!"

"Not really. We toil from dawn to dusk with few breaks. Even the nights are short, for timber must reach Irindibul before the river has lowered." He raised his little liquor cup thoughtfully. It was almost engulfed by his huge hand. I thought about that hand working on my shoes. Holding them. "When we reach Irindibul there's no need to even step inside the city. We're paid at a collection point. I usually stay in the sawmills around there, work a little, earn a few coins. I only enter the city to buy necessities. Salt, a new grindstone, an ax head, some fabric for clothes. That sort of thing." He rubbed his chin. I like that he shaves, unlike most men here. He does not hide behind a beard. "Then it's a case of finding a boat to take me back upstream. Or a cart to ride in. It's too far to walk."

"Yes, but . . ." I did not know what to say, so I said nothing more.

"But you, you have really traveled," said Kárun, looking at me. "You've seen things, learned things. You're like no one else in Rovas, Maresi." His eyes were deeply dark in the gloom of the cabin.

I sighed and looked away. I will never fit in. I stick out. I am strange and different. Mother is not the only one who thinks so.

"Yes, so it is. Many thanks for the shoes, Kárun. I wear them every day." I rose.

He looked up at me. "I'll wear your gloves every day."

"Soon it will be too warm for them," I said, for no intelligible reason. I pinched the edge of my cloak in my hands. "Thank you for the bread."

I trudged out and slammed the door shut behind me. My heart continued pounding until I was halfway home. I was pleased to have my staff with me. I ran my fingers along the hard wood.

Missing you.

Maresi

SPRING

Venerable Sister O,

Yesterday I began work on my herb garden. The soil is exposed now, but it is not yet time to start working the land because the earth below remains frozen. But my little garden along the south wall is frost-free. White Farm's sow has been in there, snuffling around and eating roots and the like, while also contributing fertilizer to the soil, so now it is well processed. I went out after breakfast and started hacking up the final clumps and evening out the soil, and when Mother was finished with the washing she came out and helped me.

It was very pleasant. It is still cold in the shade, but the sun warmed our stooped backs as she climbed higher in the sky. I pulled my head-scarf down to shade my eyes from the dazzling light. Snowdrops and other early spring flowers had sprung up here and there, and the air was filled with birdsong. Mother had her old brown cardigan on, carefully patched several times over. Her thick braid swung in time with the blows of the hoe. We worked in amicable silence. She coughed from time to time. This cold winter has been tough on her health.

When we had finished, Mother stood up straight. "We have a lot of chicken droppings from winter that should make good plant food. What are you going to grow?"

I was pleased that Mother was showing interest in my garden.

"I have seeds saved from last year, so I am going to grow the same things. The perennials are still there in that corner, where I made a little fence to keep out the sow. There is mint and parsley and other such things. I was planning on lots of herbs and cabbage, and plenty of beans this year, as they store well."

"True. Carrots are good to have also. Onions?"

"Yes, and garlic."

Mother grimaced. "Ugh, I'll never get used to the taste."

"I know, but it has medicinal qualities. And Father likes it."

"He likes all the strange things you brought back with you," Mother said shortly. Then she stepped forward to the edge of the garden. "We could extend it here. I liked those sweet peas. Do you think they could be dried and saved?"

"Good idea, Mother. I think I have enough saved from last year for a small patch. But then we will have to construct some sort of support for them to climb up."

"We'll need a fence all around as well," said Mother, glancing at the sow sunbathing in the middle of White Farm's yard. "She's to give birth soon, and I'm worried the piglets might chew everything up."

"Father and Akios brought home a few fence poles over winter, so we can start right now if you have time."

Mother nodded, and we spent a good portion of the remainder of the day building a sturdy fence. When we were finished I made us tea with the herbs I know are to Mother's taste: mint, raspberry leaf and sweet honey flower. We sat inside at the table and drank, with earth still under our nails.

I looked at my mother, still so youthful with her thick brown hair and kind eyes. She is the same age as Sister Ers, I believe. She still wears the same cardigan as she did when I was little, and has the same braid, same chapped hands. She saw me looking at her, coughed and reached out to pat my hand.

"It's good to have you home, Maresi. My daughter."

I smiled. "It is good to be home, Mother." And I really meant it. It is rare that I feel that way, but in that moment all was right with the world.

Mother leaned back and drank deeply from her cup. "You're a great help also, I can't deny that. The food your garden provided last summer helped us through the winter. You get a lot done, despite that school of yours."

There it came, the jab, the little thorn that destroyed my good mood. But nothing could have prepared me for the next blow, or how painful it would be.

"You know, I've started looking forward to having a stay-at-home daughter, despite everything. It's a comfort to know that Father and I will not have to age alone. Náraes is close by, but she is fully occupied with her own family and household, of course. Akios will likely bring home a wife in due course, but it is never the same as having a daughter of one's own."

I stared at Mother, and she waved her hand in mild irritation.

"Yes, yes, I know you'll have your school and all that."

"But . . . what are you saying, Mother?"

"Well, you've made it clear that you won't marry and have a family of your own. So you'll stay where you are, here."

ᗡ

And I had no response to that, Sister O. I could think of nothing whatsoever to say.

I had not given it any thought, if I am honest. About where I will live, how I will survive. In other words: what to do with my life. I knew that I would found a school, but my plans never stretched beyond that. I have not dedicated a single thought to what shape my own life will take. I cannot live alone—it is too difficult in a land and climate such as Rovas. One needs other people. But does that mean I must live at home? Here with Mother and Father until I grow old and die? Taking care of them while Akios and his wife run the farm and I live in some tiny little room, on charity?

That vision of the future does not appeal to me at all, Sister O.

But neither can I envision another to replace it.

Your novice,

Venerable, missed Sister O,

Tauer was the bearer of the good news. It is a miracle! He spoke nothing of it to begin with. He came to see us this evening, the customary time for visits, and was met with the respect and courtesy due to men and women as wise as he in Rovas. Father pulled up a stool by the fire, for the evenings continue to be chilly, and Mother set about taking out the best that the house has to offer. Stores are sparse at this point in spring, but the hens are laying, and Mother had made a fresh batch of cream cheese with milk she had gotten from Árvan's mother, and Akios went over to Náraes with word of the visit and she soon arrived with some bread. I brewed an herbal tea that I know Tauer likes, and Father went out to the storehouse for the smoked sausage Árvan had given him in exchange for help during the planting season. Maressa and Dúlan sat wide-eyed, watching all the delicacies being served.

"Egg!" whispered Dúlan excitedly. There is no limit to how much egg that girl can eat.

"Mama, I want egg and cheese on bread!" whined Maressa, to which Náraes snapped: "Guests first."

"It's good to see children with round cheeks," said Tauer. "Not like years past. I've seen far too many little ones wasting away." He drank deeply from his cup of tea. "Do you see how far spring has come now? The thimbleweed is in bloom—the sign of a long and fine summer."

"That would be a blessing," said Father as he sliced up the sausage. "If all goes well, this promises to be the best harvest we've seen in many a year."

"If only the nádor allows us to keep it this time." Tauer furrowed his brow. "No one collected the taxes last autumn. I fear that this year they may demand double."

"Our villages have been extraordinarily guarded from harm over the last year," said Mother.

She looked at me for an extended time and then away. I noticed that Tauer was also looking at me more keenly than usual.

"Have you heard from that Abbey of yours, Maresi?" he asked, wiping his mouth.

"No," I responded sadly. "Not a word."

"Oh, well perhaps there's something in here," he said, and produced a thick roll of letters from inside his waistcoat. I stared at him in astonishment. His eyes glittered.

"My son-in-law Gézor went to visit his parents in his home village of Arik—that's two days' walk west, did you know?—because his mother has been doing poorly all winter and I received word that she'd taken a turn for the worse. Well, by the time he arrived she was recovered, so he only stayed a day and a night before setting off back home. But on the way he came across a group of soldiers and made a big diversion to the north to avoid them. He came to the old crossroads, the one where the council would meet once upon a time."

"The one by the standing stones?" Mother asked as she put out the final dish. She sat next to Náraes and started to slice more bread.

"The very same," confirmed Tauer. "Anyway, when he arrived there was a group of traveling merchants from Devenland."

My heart was pounding. I could not tear my eyes away from the roll of letters.

"He greeted them courteously and helped one whose horse had gotten a stone stuck in its shoe. Gézor is good with horses, as you all know. His father's father kept horses since Gézor was a lad." He leaned forward and helped himself to a large portion of eggs with cheese. "Well, when they were finished with the horse the merchant asked Gézor if he knew one Maresi Enresdaughter of the Red Abbey, for he had a delivery for her. And Gézor said he did indeed. Then the merchant handed over these very letters, and a little something extra that I have in that bag over by the door." Tauer pointed to a small pouch he had brought with him, which I had barely noticed. "Gézor regretted that he couldn't pay the merchant. He's got a head on his shoulders, my son-in-law, despite his many faults and shortcomings—pride, for one—and he knew that if he paid well, the rumor would go around that deliveries to Maresi of the Red Abbey pay better if they reach their destination than if they're sold to the highest bidder. But the man said he wanted no payment, for he considered it an honor to ensure that the letters reached their intended recipient. He was from a small village by the coast, he said, and last summer he sent his young daughter to the Abbey in the hope that they might rid her of the ailment that had plagued her throughout her childhood, and lo, she returned with the autumn wind, healthy and strong. He also said that he was on his way to the Akkade land beyond the mountains to buy their spring wool, and would travel back down to Valleria around midsummer. So if you have letters to send south, he said he can take them when he passes through, and you are to seek him out near the standing stones when the liverleaf blooms, he said."

He looked at me and laughed in a way that made his eyes almost disappear among his wrinkles.

"Yes, yes, you can have them now. Stop looking at me with those hungry eyes."

He handed me the letters, which I took into my room at once, and I shut the door, so great was my excitement, Sister O. I could not get a single word out, nor even look at my family. I must spend the evening with you all, and no one else.

I will write more once I have read all the letters.

Your novice,

Maresi

Dear Jai,
    Thank you for your letters! I understand perfectly that you waited until you had heard from me and knew I had arrived safely before writing. And thank you for the red thread you sent! How could

you know that I had ripped a hole in my cloak? Not to worry, it is very small. I can fix it with this thread and no one will guess it was ever torn.

I will do as you say, and hold you in my thoughts every new moon, and know that you are doing the same. Thank you. It will make me feel much less alone.

How dare you laugh at my marriage proposal! You ought to know that it was certainly the first and only of my life so I must cherish the memory fondly! In all seriousness, though, I do so wish that we could sit beneath the lemon tree and laugh about it together.

I am terribly envious of all the books you have read in the treasure chamber! You cannot imagine how much I yearn for those books. I miss them almost more than I miss all of you! I am joking, of course.

It is incredible to think that it was a girl who came to the Abbey for convalescence—whom you helped to care for—whose father brought your letters all the way here to me. It is difficult to imagine new novices coming to the Abbey, novices I will never have the chance to meet. I hope you make many friends among them, Jai, truly I do. Yet I hope that there always remains a small place reserved in your heart for me alone. There is, isn't there, Jai, my friend?

Your friend,

Maresi

Venerable Sister Nar,
    I thank you from the bottom of my heart for all the seeds that you sent. I have greatly missed turmeric; it is such a useful plant. I will sow radishes too. I wonder what my mother will think of their peppery flavor! We have had problems with snails here—do you have any advice for getting rid of them? I am sending you a bag of honey-flower seeds. Is that a plant you have ever come across? The flowers make a delicious tea, and I believe they have an invigorating

effect. If you study the properties of the plant, I would be most interested to know your findings.

Yours faithfully,

Maresi

Venerable Sister Mareane,
I now have a goat and kid to care for. Any advice you might have about caring for these animals would be gratefully received!

Yours faithfully,

Maresi

Most Venerable Mother,
Thank you for not castigating me for giving away the silver you entrusted me with. You have lifted a great burden from my conscience. I will do as you advise and try to trust the people around me, as I trusted you all when I lived at the Abbey.

I believe the omen you received at Moon Dance foretold the death of my sister's baby son last autumn. There have been no other deaths since, and neither have I seen the Crone's door. She is here nevertheless, I understand that now, and I can feel her presence. She is everywhere, as are the Maiden and the Mother. Though different people give her different names and forms, we are all children of the First Mother.

Respectfully,

Maresi

Venerable Sister Eostre,
Thank you for your letter, brief though it was. I knew you would be the only one to understand. You accurately predicted Marget's behavior over the past year: she has withdrawn from everything and everyone, kept mostly at home, not wanting to participate in

shared tasks or celebrations. No one blames her for what happened, but I believe that she blames herself.

You wrote that the solution is simple, and that I already have all I need to help Marget. I believe I do understand, and I am ashamed that it never occurred to me before. I will do my best.

Yours faithfully,

Maresi

My dear Ennike Rose,

Thank you for all your words of encouragement. You are a great friend, do you know that? It makes no difference to me that you are now the Rose, servant to the Maiden. To me you will always be Ennike, the first friend I ever made at the Abbey.

You are too funny with all your questions about Kárun! I have only met him a couple of times since returning home. He is no one, you know, just a neighbor. Well, you will see when I send the second bundle of letters—and you will be able to read about Géros and see how wrong you were! Strangely, I have not thought about Géros in several moons. The things we did together creep into my dreams sometimes, but he has been replaced with a sort of faceless man. I wish that you were here, so that we could discuss these dreams. They are the type of thing that can only be discussed with the Rose.

Thank you for sending me more Goddess Tongue. I may need it again at some point in the future, if I choose to warm my bed with a man again. For a mother is something I never want to be.

I can stand close to the Maiden and the Crone, but the Mother demands so much energy. Do you understand what I mean? I want to remain free to work and study. Besides, if I do not use it myself there are others I can give it to, other women who do not wish to fall pregnant again, or at all.

Geja has grown so big! It was wonderful to receive a letter and drawing from her. Jai truly has a way with her.

But I expect that she will forget me. For her and all the new novices, Maresi Enresdaughter will become little more than a myth. A story to tell on dark winter evenings.

Yours,

Maresi

Dear Sister O,

I saved your letters until last. I sat and read throughout the evening, paying no heed to Tauer or the evening meal or my family. I started my replies at once, writing several letters in one go, because I wanted the feeling of immediacy, as though I were truly talking to you all, in genuine conversation.

It was very wise of you to send me more paper.

I was most taken aback by what you wrote about my mother. With all due respect, I did take offense at your words. I am trying my best to listen to all she has to say. And I do understand that it was difficult for her to send me away. But why must it be so difficult for her to have me back? You say I must continue learning from her. Yet she taught me everything she knew during the first nine years of my life. What can a farmer's wife from Rovas teach me, who has studied at the Red Abbey? It is your teachings that I miss!

When I sent those first letters, which you have now received, I had not yet come across the tone that sings and resonates through the forest, both luring and frightening me. Do you know what it is? Certain phenomena occur that seem connected, but I do not understand how. The calling kite, Gray Lady's desire to go out into the wild, that tone . . . It is as if they are trying to speak to me in a language I do not understand. I have prayed to the First Mother for guidance, but have received no answer yet.

I miss being able to ask you all the questions that swirl around in my mind. You have always taken the time to try to answer them.

Thank you for everything you wrote in your letters, and all your guidance. I will hold it close when storms are raging, and when I feel uncertain and weak.

I no longer feel like as much of an outsider as when I first arrived. I am sorry that I complained so much. You are right: I can never be like everybody else here because I have had experiences that no one else shares. But I will take your advice and try to use this to my benefit—if I can. Sometimes Tauer gives helpful advice. His knowledge is not of the same sort as yours, for he has not studied it in books, but he has lived a long life, seen much and helped many. He is a friend to life and death alike. That is something I also choose to be. Currently I am of the opinion that life is the more frightening of the two.

Has the Mother Abbess told you about the vision she had at Moon Dance? The one where she saw me standing by the opened door of the Crone? I wrote to her saying that I believe the vision foretold the death of my nephew, but I fear that this may not be the case. It was not I who opened death's door for him; it was not I who let him through. I have not seen the door of the Crone since coming here, I have felt only her breath. What do you think the vision means? It worries me.

I agree with the Mother Abbess: you do need to take a novice. Your stubbornness is incomprehensible. I am in Rovas now. My life is here. There must always be a servant to the Crone at the Abbey, and therefore you must train a novice. You are not old, and there is time for a new girl to come to the Abbey, one whom the Crone calls, as she did me. You will teach her all you taught me about the Crone's mysteries, and more besides, and she will be your support and your aid in all the tasks you now do alone.

Your novice,

Maresi

Most Venerable Mother,

It is late evening, but still light, as always at this time of year in Rovas. I am sitting in a room that is new to me, but which, all of a sudden, is my very own. It is mine in a way that no room has ever been before. My bare arms are covered in mosquito bites, and the scent of fresh wood fills my nostrils. I love the smell. My heart is full of . . . I know not what, Venerable Mother. Gratitude.

Kárun came to our homestead earlier this evening. I am sure Sister O must have read aloud the letter in which I mentioned him. I was sitting in the central yard and keeping an eye on Dúlan and Maressa while unraveling one of Father's old sweaters. Mother wanted to reknit the yarn into some garments for the girls. Náraes and Jannarl were on a visit to the neighboring village and their daughters were impatiently awaiting their return.

Rovasian late-spring evenings are truly special, Venerable Mother— the light, the lingering warmth from the day's sun, the scent of the soil and slowly awakening summer. Mosquitoes were buzzing around us, the sow and her piglets were grunting and snuffling around the yard, and Maressa was practicing writing the names of all the members of her family. Náraes is the most difficult. She just writes "mama" instead.

Kárun appeared at the gate just as Mother came outside to empty the dishwater. His words of greeting were almost swallowed by the pigs' eager grunts as they rushed over to see if Mother was throwing out anything edible.

"Blessings on your hearth," he said.

Mother peered at him with wariness and suspicion.

"Blessing on your journey," she answered curtly. She does not think much of woodcutters and other solitary folk. She says she does not trust them. "Akios isn't home."

"I have a matter to discuss with Maresi," said Kárun quietly. I looked at him in surprise. He was leaning against the gate with his shirtsleeves rolled up, and the sun-bleached hair on his forearms glinted gold in the evening sun. His deep-set eyes gazed at me with absolute earnestness.

He was not mocking or playing with me. His hair was tied back, and his skin was already brown from the spring sun.

"Will you come with me? I have something I want to show you," he said. "If your mother can spare you."

Mother looked disapproving as I put down the sweater.

"Would you look after the girls?" I asked. She bobbed her head in answer and did nothing to stop me. Then she turned around and marched straight into the house, only to return a moment later with my staff. She handed it to me without a word. I gave her an appeasing smile as I took it.

"No need to worry, Mother. He is a friend of Akios. He is no threat to me. I will be back before long."

But I know that it is not violence she fears. She sees Kárun as a suitor—regardless of my feelings on the matter—and does not wish to see a daughter of hers wed to a poor woodcutter without farm or field.

Kárun led me along the path toward Jóla, and I asked no questions. It was pleasant to walk, pleasant to move. I have spent most of my time at home recently, rereading your letters, milking my goat, experimenting with making cheese and cooking the whey into whey cheese. The garden also needs much attention at this time, when everything is sprouting, including weeds.

The trees have started blooming, and the forest was a marvel of beauty: shiny white tree trunks under a thin veil of pale green. The stream surged, joyful and wild, to the left of the path, as melodic as an instrument, and to the right there grew a dense carpet of snowblues, which is a small spring flower in the shape of a bell. It is common in these parts and gives off a divinely fragrant nectar.

"I heard you got letters from your abbey," said Kárun. "That must've made you happy."

"Yes." I smiled to myself. To this day your letters make me happy whenever I think of them. "It was good to know that everybody back there is well, and that they are thinking of me and have not forgotten me."

Kárun peered down at me. "And are there really only women there?"

"Yes. Is that so strange?"

"Quite strange. I'm not used to men and women being divided in such a way."

"You freelander types who hunt and fell trees and float timber are exclusively male," I said.

He nodded and thought for a moment before answering. "True, but many have wives and children waiting for them back home in a cabin somewhere. They long for home and talk often of their families. They have mothers and sisters. Perhaps I don't go among many womenfolk myself, but I certainly wouldn't like it if I never saw any of them. Any of you."

"I had to reaccustom myself to men when I came home," I said hesitantly. I had never spoken to a man about this. About how strange I felt on first hearing male voices again and seeing men everywhere on a daily basis.

"It can't have helped, what happened to Marget," said Kárun.

I glanced at him. Nobody talks about it openly. He is the first person not to avoid the subject.

"It is true. But it started long before, with things that happened at the Abbey. Wicked men did us harm. Great harm."

"What happened to them?"

"I killed them."

I did not intend to say it, Venerable Mother. It simply slipped out. The only person who knows about those terrible events is Náraes. I cannot even bring myself to tell my parents about what happened with the door and the Crone and my blood. I regretted the revelation at once, suspecting that Kárun would see me in a new light. I realized in that moment that I did not want to lose that searching, serious look he always gives me. I looked down at the ground, stumbled over my own feet and swallowed the lump stuck in my throat.

"So that's what's been weighing on you," said Kárun calmly. "I knew there was something."

I looked up, my eyes a little misty. He had stopped before me on the path, with the evening sun illuminating him from behind. He looked at me with a steady gaze, without fear or disgust. I could not answer, and only nodded. We stood there awhile.

That instance of pure honesty and ensuing acceptance was one of the best moments of my time in Rovas, Venerable Mother.

We walked farther and came to a place where the path divided and a newly trodden path led uphill to the north. We waded through a small sea of thimbleweed, then through a hazel shrub and emerged in front of Kárun's building site.

However, it was no longer a building site. It was a completed house. It was beautiful and golden, steeped in evening sun and surrounded by wonderful scents. Kárun has cleared away all the timber and waste, but the ground around the house is covered in sweet-smelling shavings. It is a small building, just one room, but with a window to the south and one to the west, and a real chimney—not just a smoke hatch like many old houses here still have. It is lovelier than any house in the village, up on its little hill with a view across a field of grazing Jóla sheep, and a view of the little stream where it meanders in a merry curve. Behind the house, to the north and east, the forest is at its most beautiful, full of fanning leaves and birdsong.

I leaned on my staff and beamed. "This is so beautiful, Kárun," I said. "To think that you did all this alone."

"Oh, well, a few of the lads from Jóla helped me with the roof," said Kárun, running his hand over his head. "And I had help to lift the final logs." I gave him a playful shove in the side, and he laughed in surprise. "But yes, it's a fine setting. That's why I chose this place. Do you want to come in?"

I followed him inside. Sunlight poured through the western window and made the fresh-wood walls appear as though daubed in honey, or gold. It is not a large room, about the size of Mother and Father's cottage, but without a separate bedroom. There is a small mortared fireplace on the north side and some wall-mounted shelves beside it. That is all.

"It is wonderful," I said, and the dimples in Kárun's cheeks deepened. I could see that my approval was important to him, though I did not know why. "You are yet to move in though, I see?"

"I don't intend to live here."

I turned to him. He cleared his throat and started rubbing his hands together.

"I've built this for you, Maresi."

I stared at him.

"For your school." He looked at me searchingly.

"My school?" I whispered. "I have no school. Only three pupils."

He shook his head. "You needed help to lay the first log, that's all. Here, I've laid it for you. Now it's up to you to continue building." He looked around the room. "I didn't know what the right furniture for a school would be, but you only need tell me and I'll try to put it together before I have to travel south down the river. That day is fast approaching now."

"A long table," I said slowly, picturing it. "With benches."

I looked at him, and perhaps it was the first time I had truly *looked* at him. An entirely ordinary man, a little older than I. An entirely ordinary man, grown from Rovasian soil, like my father and brother. Yet not really like them. No, not like them at all. Broad shoulders, arms strong from swinging an ax through summer and winter, coarse hands—hands that he has used to build me this incredible gift. Furthermore, he wants nothing in return, Venerable Mother. I know this. I have communed with the Maiden enough to know.

"Why, Kárun?" I asked.

He hesitated. "Sit down, Maresi," he said, and gestured to the floor. He sat opposite me with crossed legs. He searched for the words awhile. "My father was a wealthy man when my mother married him. But one night, when he'd been drinking, he played a game of dice, not understanding what was written on the paper that defined the stakes. He lost our farmstead, the livestock, everything." Kárun stared blankly out of the window. "Afterward he was a changed man. He took out his anger and shame on everyone else."

"On your mother," I whispered.

"Yes. Father and Mother moved away from the farm, far enough away that no one would know of Father's shame. As a child I always had to be on my guard, so that he'd never have reason to direct his anger at Mother or me." He took a deep breath. "When I was a little boy my mother became very sick. Father said it was because she was a sinful woman, and the sickness was punishment. When I too fell sick, he said that it was Mother's fault." He clenched his fists and pressed his knuckles into his knees. "When Mother died he finally allowed Tauer to come and take care of me. I recovered." I could see the muscles in his jaw tensing. "When I first worked as a timber-rafter there were several in the team who contracted the same sickness. We had reached the outskirts of Irindibul by then, and a healer was sent for. With a few concoctions he cured them all, and explained that it was an easily curable disease, but if left untreated it could be deadly."

He leaned forward and took my hand. I was utterly taken aback but permitted him to hold it between his hands. They were coarse and warm. "Knowledge is protection, Maresi. My parents' lives could have been different."

"Thank you, Kárun Eiminsson," I said, looking him straight in the eye. "Thank you for believing in me. Thank you for your help. I will do my best to be worthy of it."

ᚹ

Then he left me alone in the building, and now here I am breathing in the scent of my own school. I do not know how to go about filling it. But a gift such as this must be used, and used well. I cannot waste it or take it for granted. I am duty bound to continue building on the foundations that Kárun has laid.

With love and respect,

Maresi

Venerable Sister O,

Now I must recount what came to pass the day before yesterday. I have not written in a while.

Spring is a hectic time here. We have been working hard to cultivate and fertilize the clayish, stony soil, and singing the ancient songs to the earth and sky asking for warmth and water in equal measure, and retreading the old furrows. For a time I have gone back to being simply Maresi Enresdaughter, with a place in our community. It has felt good to work side by side with Mother, Father and Akios. Spring came early and was beautiful, with light rain at night and warm sunny days—weather in all ways perfect for early sowing.

The seeds sprouted well, and spring passed into early summer. Everybody in the village has been gazing contentedly at our green fields and predicting a record yield. Finally hunger and starvation are beginning to fade into a mere memory. The growth in my herb garden has picked up speed and everything is flourishing. The early evenings have been full of the sound of frolicking frogs, which is a sign of a long summer, according to Tauer. He is full of superstitions, but sometimes he is right. My little "school" has been put on hold during these busy times, despite the fine new schoolhouse I have acquired (I trust the Mother Abbess read that letter aloud?). We have all been busy with our spring activities, adults and children alike.

On the evening I now want to recount, I went out for my usual walk around the villages. I have continued the habit since last autumn. The solitude does me good. I always bring my staff with me, and sometimes Gray Lady. When I feel tired, Mother usually chases me out, as indeed she did on this occasion. She had been standing out in the yard with her eyes fixed on the forest edge for a long while. She appeared to be listening to something. Then she sniffed the air and turned to me. I was sitting on a bench and resting my tired back. I had been weeding my garden all day and everything ached.

"No time to rest now!" she exclaimed in vexation, jabbing the same familiar spike into my heart.

I am not my own person here; I do not have authority over my own time. Mother will not suffer laziness or idleness. She went in to fetch my staff and cloak, which she handed to me with the same indecipherable expression she always makes when she looks at the cloak.

"But Mother, I am so tired," I said, though I knew it would serve no purpose.

"Work must be done, tired or not," Mother said sharply. Her lips formed a hard line. "You know very well what's on its way."

I had no notion of what she was referring to, but was too tired to protest any further. I took the staff, wrapped my cloak around me and pulled up the hood so that Mother would not see my sour expression. It was a beautiful evening. Perhaps it is best to be out of Mother's way when she is in this mood, I thought.

I walked the path around our village and on toward Jóla. There the path descends into a valley where the stream meanders away. I leaned heavily on my staff with each step, sunken in thoughts of my herb garden and how I might procure more paper and new books to read. I was awoken from my musings by that same humming tone that resonates from the earth. I looked up.

Mist was rising from the valley. It seeped out from the ditches and stream, groping with white, swirling tentacles up toward the hills and fields. And in that mist I recognized the unmistakable odor of iron and blood and icy chill: the breath of the Crone.

It was you who taught me of the Crone's dominion over not only death and wisdom, but also over cold and storms, darkness and ice. I have felt this icy chill before, streaming out from behind her door.

"No," I said, and banged my staff hard on the ground. "No."

I took one step and heard the newly sprouted grass crunch beneath my boots. Frost was coming. It is already summer. I have heard of frost coming this late in the year, but not in living memory. Frosty nights in the approach to midsummer are known as Iron Nights. A frost now would cost us our entire harvest. No seed remains for a second sowing. If we lose our crops now we will have no alternative but to borrow seeds from the nádor at extortionate rates yet again. Frost now would mean starvation.

"No," I said, and slammed the silverwood staff into the ground in time with my steps. "Not now. Not here. No."

Jóla is situated on a high ridge and is less vulnerable to frost than the low-lying fields of our village. I turned around and hurried homeward. On reaching our first field I saw more whitish, ice-cold mist come creeping up from the valley. I was exhausted, but I dug deep to gather my strength and beat all my own warmth and life force into the ground with both foot and staff. I know perfectly well that the Crone is too powerful for me to subdue. I know that she takes whatever she wants. But there was no choice: I had to try. I thought of those who would be worst affected by starvation: the little ones—including Dúlan—and the elderly. I walked around the fields, between them and the mist, muttering, "No!" with each step. I slammed the staff into the ground to reinforce my words. I refused to surrender. I saw people from the village come out and look on helplessly as the freezing mist rose higher and higher from the stream, from the icy realm of the Crone. But I did not stop to speak to them. I continued walking.

Once I had walked the whole western edge of the fields, I heard footsteps behind me. Heavy, stamping steps. A voice broke into song. It was an ancient ballad that I had not heard before, but I recognized the voice, and it felt like a fire ignited inside me.

It was Mother.

She was singing an ode to the black swan known in Rovas as Kalma. She presides over death's realm, and escorts the dead beneath the silverwood trees and over the great dark lake that rests in stillness beneath their white, shining roots. It was a song of darkness and cold and death, but also about how everything has its season, and how, now that it is summer, the swan ought to tuck her head beneath her wing and hide her face until her time comes. Her realm of cold and ice will return when the days are shorter than the nights.

After hearing the ballad several times, I was able to join in. The song and Mother's voice gave me the strength to continue. Step by step. I wove my own words into the song, words to the Crone: my teacher and friend; my foe and dread. I begged her to leave us be. I begged her to bide her time.

White icicles had already formed on my staff.

People appeared between the fields. They walked along the edge of the ditches, silent and resolute, watching the frost creeping ever nearer. Father and Akios were there, and so were Jannarl and the children, everyone from White Farm and even Árvan. They saw Mother and me. They said nothing, only looked on with expressions of grim concern.

Then, from behind Mother and me came a beautiful, deep woman's voice. I recognized Náraes, and my heart was filled with indescribable joy. The grass rustled and crackled under my feet and the sky was already darkening, but I continued to raise my knees high and stamp my feet hard on the ground. The earth trembled in response. I heard Jannarl join in with the song. Then Akios. More and more voices joined us and everyone followed me through the cold, dark night. Father sang, and Marget too, and Lenna as treble. The earth rumbled and hummed beneath our feet. My staff was like ice in my hand, but my heart glowed warm. Everybody in the village circled our fields and homes again and again, and I walked at the head of them all, beating and stamping and singing.

All night long we walked, Sister O. Some carried lanterns and torches, but for the most part we found our way by the light of the waxing crescent moon. When morning dawned and the sun's first rays crept over the forest edge, we saw that the fields between Sáru and the forest lay white with frost. Yet the sprouting green of our fields remained untouched, but for a narrow belt on the southern edge nearest the stream.

I stopped walking, and I remember no more. Mother says that I was covered from head to toe with a thick layer of frost and had icicles hanging from my hair. Father caught me when I fell. He carried me home in his arms, and Mother heated water to warm me up enough to remove the staff from my stiff hand. My limbs were like ice, and my family feared I might lose some fingers or toes, or worse. But when Mother undressed me she found my torso glowing as hot as an oven, and this heat slowly diffused into my arms and legs, and my skin was not blue-black and frostbitten, but rosy and smooth.

I slept all day yesterday, under a pile of blankets and furs in my room, and Mother woke me from time to time to urge me to take hot drinks. My sleep was dense with dreams: black and cold, but also boisterous and full of laughter—a laughter that still echoes in my mind as I write to you now. At times it felt as if someone were stroking my hair, and sometimes as if a familiar voice were whispering my name, both tender and stern.

It was like your voice, Sister O, and yet different.

Today, when I awoke and emerged, our table was loaded with food. Akios was busy eating and could only nod at me, his mouth was so stuffed. There was freshly baked bread, honey-scented cakes, a small smoked ham, fresh eggs, sausage, mead and even salted butter. I looked at Mother, who was tearing between hearth and table with flushed cheeks.

"It's for you," she said. "Everybody in the village has been coming with gifts since yesterday."

I ate and ate as if I had never seen food before in my life, like after Moon Dance. I still felt that wonderful glowing warmth in my heart, and I know what its source is, Sister O. It is my people. Rovas itself is glowing inside me.

That evening there came a knock on the door. The fathers from Jóla, among them Tauer's son and son-in-law, came tramping inside. Gézor, who is married to Tauer's daughter, spoke for them all.

"The spring sowing is over and done. Don't need the children on the farm for some time now. So if Maresi still wants to teach them reading and such, that'll be just fine," he said, and the other men muttered in agreement. "We can pay in food, if that's all right with you."

I had just come out of my room and was met by Tauer's tall son Orvan. "We want our children to know all the things you know."

"I cannot teach them what I did last night," I said carefully. "That was not knowledge, but a gift."

"Be that as it may," answered Orvan. "You know one thing that none here knows, and that's reading. The nádor's fooled us many a time with his written words. But he's not gonna fool our children."

"No, he is not," I answered seriously. "So it is agreed."

Once they had gone, Mother looked at me. "So it's to be a real school now, then."

"Yes, Mother. And I can still contribute to the household if they come with food as payment."

"That doesn't worry me. But what of your other work? It's so important to us all."

She was standing with her sleeves rolled up after washing the dishes. Her apron was damp, and I suddenly noticed how tired she was. She had walked with me and sung with me before anyone else. All night she walked, and then she took care of me, prepared the food and cleaned the house.

What strange things she was saying, Sister O. She had been saying strange things ever since my return. I sank down on a bench without taking my eyes off her.

"What do you mean, Mother?"

"You know perfectly well!" She dried her hands on her apron. "What you've been doing this whole time, all the more so since autumn." I stared at her. "What you did yesterday!"

"Yesterday I drove away the frost," I said slowly. "What did I do last autumn?"

Mother frowned. "Do you really not know?" She came and sat down beside me. She studied my face carefully. "You don't know. By the bear's paw, you don't know!" She let out a short laugh. "Your walks around the village. The staff. And that comb I've seen you with." I shook my head. "You're protecting the village, Maresi. I thought you were doing it on purpose! Why do you think last year's harvest was better than ever? Why do you think the nádor's men haven't been here to collect the taxes, or harass us common folk?"

"That was me?" I whispered.

"Did you learn nothing in that abbey? Of course it was you. You have more power inside you than anyone I've ever seen, Maresi. And with your steps and your staff you've pushed a protective barrier deep into the ground around the village. No merchants could even find us last autumn, don't you remember? You've hidden the entire village from the world."

"That is why you have chased me out every evening. That is why you have been looking at me so strangely."

Mother's face softened. "Have I?"

I nodded, unable to speak.

"It's frightened me, that's all. All the things you can do. I've seen it before, as a child. It frightened me then, too. I thought it was something they taught you at the Abbey."

"No. Not this. I thought you wanted to be rid of me for a while every evening."

"My daughter." Mother took my hand. "I'd never want that! I never want to lose you again, you must understand that."

We sat quietly for a long time. Eventually I remembered that Mother had mentioned the comb.

"What am I doing with the comb then?"

"That I don't know. But when you comb your hair it feels as though something's being bound very tight. Sometimes I find it hard to breathe." Mother coughed, as if the memory alone constricted her chest.

I thought about how I imagined binding the nádor's men tight with all the strands of hair I wound into the braid beneath my pillow. "I believe I am binding the nádor's men," I said slowly. "Holding them tight. That is a part of the protection."

Mother nodded. "The protection waned during summer. I don't know why. Then you made it all the stronger after the soldiers beat that boy so badly."

"It was because of Géros," I said, and felt my cheeks go hot. "I stopped doing all those things when I was with him." Mother nodded, without looking angry. "But Mother, how do you know all this? You knew that the frost was coming, you were the one who made me go out to meet it. How can you sense what I am doing, when I never understood it myself?"

Mother released my hand and turned away. "I learned to recognize these things when I was very little. It was a matter of survival." She pulled a cardigan over her shoulders, still facing away from me. "Time to shut the chickens in for the night. I'll do it tonight so you can get to bed." She hurried out before I could ask her any more questions.

ϖ

Today I walked to the schoolhouse Kárun gave me, and saw the children coming up the hill. Every single child in Sáru and Jóla over the age of five was there, timid and wide-eyed. There were ten of them altogether, boys and girls. I admitted the boys too, for what else could I do? I still had no table or benches, so the children sat cross-legged on the floor, and I gave them all planed wooden planks and pieces of coal, and the sun poured in through the open window shutters, and thus my school began.

Your novice,

Maresi

THIRD COLLECTION
OF LETTERS

SUMMER

Dearest Jai,

Not long after the Iron Night, one of Tauer's grandchildren rushed over to tell me that a trade convoy from the Akkade plains had been spotted in the north. I hurried to the crossroads with the standing stones, but there was no one there. I was terrified of missing "my" merchant, so I set up camp by the stones with Akios for company (and protection, I must admit), and there we slept and lived on foraged birds' eggs, and some cheese and bread Akios had packed, and felt right at home. It was a welcome break from the endless chores of village life.

On the second day the convoy arrived, trailing horses and mules fully loaded with high, swaying wool bales. I found my merchant friend and gave him my letters. He refused to accept payment, and gave me a sack of the finest lamb's wool instead. And since then, well, I have been working harder than ever before.

I run the school for four days, and then close it for two so the children can take part in necessary tasks at home, and then it is four days of school again. I try to mirror Sister O's methods, teaching the children to read and write and think. But it is difficult to teach them to write without proper writing implements. The wooden planks and coal soon became impractical because one cannot rub out what has been written. I show them the letters, and teach them to sound them out and put words together. I read aloud often because most of my books are in a foreign language and I have to translate as I read. Only Erva's book is in the local tongue. We do a little simple counting as well, with stones and fir cones. Many of the children are very good at counting because they have herded pigs and goats in the woods and know how many animals they have on their farms. I am frustrated, not at their pace of learning, but because there is so much I would like to teach them and do with them, but cannot because I lack the tools. Sometimes we go out into the forest and I teach them about different medicinal plants. I teach them to wash themselves as well, and that cleanliness is essential for one's food, household and body in equal measure. I know that this is not always popular among their families, but it is one of the most important things we had to learn when we first came to the Abbey, wouldn't you agree?

Maressa and Lenna are not very pleased about having to share me with all the other children, and Maressa in particular is getting up to all sorts of mischief to show her discontent. Several of the children have a very difficult time sitting still and listening, because it is not something they have ever done before. But there is one boy called Édun—Tauer's grandson and elder brother to little black-haired Naeri—who is my special favorite. I know that a teacher should not have a favorite pupil, but you could not resist Édun, Jai. He has big, brown, almost completely round eyes and curly brown hair, and though he rarely speaks, he never takes his eyes off me. He can already read better than both Maressa and Lenna.

Akios is somewhat disappointed that he cannot join in the school. There is far too much to do on the farm. I practice reading with him in the evenings, if I have the energy.

But there is so much else to be done—as if the school were not enough in itself! Since the Iron Night the villagers' attitude toward me has changed. I worried that they might fear me or consider me even more of a freak after what I did that night. And it is true that they certainly do not see me as one of them, but now they are glad of my presence. Many who previously turned to Tauer now come to me with their ailments, injuries, pregnancies, lame goats and whatever else. I help them as much as I am able. Sometimes I really can help, while in some cases the best I can do is provide a little comfort or sound advice. I am understanding more and more what an important role all Tauer's strange prescriptions and rituals play in his work to help others. My little herb garden is in constant use, and I spend a lot of time weeding and caring for it because I foresee needing a lot of dried herbs this winter. I try to find time to make concoctions and salves as well, to keep in store, but it is difficult to fit everything in.

It has been a fine summer, with enough rain and plenty of heat and sunlight, but I have not had much time to enjoy it. I barely took part in the summer offering this year; I contributed only a little nut bread that I had baked (which came out nothing like Sister Ers's nadum bread) and went home early. Géros is betrothed to Tunéli now. The wedding is to take place in autumn after the harvest. I saw them dancing together before I went home. I wish them all the best. Personally, I was too tired to dance. Honestly, Jai, I swear, I felt no sorrow, nor even wounded vanity! It is only that I am so very tired all the time.

I am happiest in the early mornings when I go to my little schoolhouse and the grass is still damp with dew and the birds are so full of life that it seems the whole forest is singing. Then, for a while, I can enjoy the beauty of the Rovasian summer. Mowing season grows near, and the school will have to close its doors for a while, for the children will be needed at home on the farms. I must say that I am looking forward to it, for I have so much to do all the time that it will be a relief not to have to think about the school, at least for a while.

I have my mule and goats to look after as well. They provide me with fertilizer for my garden, and I have become skilled in milking the elder goat and making delicious cheeses. Mother said recently that I make better cheese than she does, which is no small praise. Some days ago Akios and I were out in the forest collecting birch branches to dry as winter feed for the animals. I took the opportunity to pick some wild plants as well, both the edible sort and those with healing properties. The school was closed, so we were free to stay out all day. Gray Lady was with us, loaded with panniers, and once again she was being impossibly obstinate and trying to drag me deeper into the forest. But people say that there are soldiers in these parts, so we dared not venture far. They still have not found us, thanks to the shield I have created.

In the evenings I still walk around the village, however tired I may be, with my white wooden staff in hand, beating protection into the ground.

Your friend,

Maresi

My dear Ennike Rose,
   I am writing this at the edge of the forest, where I have come for a little peace and quiet. I can see the village from here, slightly below me on the other side of the stream and fields. I do not believe anyone can see me. My brown trousers and unbleached linen shirt blend in with the pine-tree trunks. The afternoon sun is blazing, and I have pulled my headscarf over my eyes, just as Sister Loeni always used to chide me for. My skin has turned very brown from all this summer sun. A warm, dry, spicy smell is seeping out from the grass all around and from the smooth yet rough bark of the pine behind my back. I am trying to save paper by writing in small letters—I hope you can read my writing.

You are welcome to read this letter aloud to Sister Eostre. I specifically want to tell you both about what has happened with Marget.

I am ashamed of my behavior toward her. I feel I have betrayed her. She was my friend before I left Rovas. Why did I turn my back on her?

So I have started visiting her more. She has been glad of my company, I believe, for she has mainly stayed at home since she was taken by the soldiers. I have not been able to think of anything redemptive to say to her, no way to erase what has happened. But we have spoken about everything imaginable. She has shown interest in my time at the Abbey, and I have told her about our lessons and so forth. It has been beneficial for me also. I miss you so much, my sisters.

She never speaks of Akios anymore, nor do I see her embroider anything for her bridal set. I asked her cautiously about it one evening after the Iron Night, when we were doing laundry together in the stream, because I was concerned that perhaps she feared that he would reject her because of what happened.

"I can't bear the thought of any man," she said simply as she pensively wrung out one of her father's shirts. "I mean no offense to Akios, but I find men vile now."

"I felt the same way when I first left the Abbey," I said slowly. "Men's voices scared me. They still do at times, if I am honest."

"What was it that happened there?" she asked, and brushed her damp hair from her forehead.

So, for the first time, I recounted in detail what happened at the Abbey when the men came, when the Goddess used the Rose's body as her channel to spare the other sisters and novices from the men's violence. I told her about the men in the crypt who meant the junior novices harm. I told her about the man who stabbed me, about the blood, and the door to the realm of the Crone.

She listened calmly, without taking her eyes off my face. Around us the summer birds were singing from the green birches, the sun seemed not to move from where she hung above the forest edge, and our laundry lay forgotten on the stones. It was wonderful to talk about all of this with someone who listened without judgment.

When I was finished she leaned forward and took hold of my hands. Her brown eyes looked steadily into mine.

"I felt it, as we walked around the fields, Maresi. I felt an immense power in you, and in the earth. No one can withstand such a force. No soldiers. No one. I want to learn about it, Maresi. I want to be able to do all that you can do."

"I will teach you all I can," I said solemnly. "Not even I know how I do it all, nor whether it can be taught. But I will try." I smiled at her, and it warmed my heart to think that I might be able to help her. "Sister Marget."

Since then Marget has followed me everywhere. She has become my shadow, just as I was yours when I first came to the Abbey. I am doing my best to be as good to Marget as you were to me. She seems filled with some new energy, like a strong wind that knows precisely which direction it is blowing. She has started coming to my school. There are many who raise their eyebrows at this, and I know that her parents are far from pleased. Marget is not of school age—she is of marrying age. She ought to be sewing linen and embroidering aprons and visiting the neighboring houses that are home to young men of the right age. But Marget does not care about what she ought to be doing. And I am glad of her company.

Now I must return home and help Mother with the cooking.

Yours,

Maresi

Venerable Sister O,

We have had a good summer. The weather has been favorable for the harvest, after the Iron Night. I have been extremely busy with work, and we have had plenty of food to eat. More of Mother's chickens have brooded and our flock has grown. We ate the cockerels, which was a rare luxury. My garden has provided us with beans and peas and an array of vegetables, and I am now the person the villagers turn to for advice concerning ailments and worries, which means my family is always receiving gifts (a basket of eggs, wild strawberries from the forest, a small firkin of salted meat, a freshly caught trout, a few cubits of home-woven linen fabric). I have taken on many responsibilities that I never imagined when I left the Abbey: draining abscesses; pulling shoulders into alignment; brewing anti-wart medicine; alleviating severe moon-blood cramps; helping women prevent further pregnancies; helping others to conceive; smearing ointments on the aching backs of old men; helping to bring a child into the world. However, the most difficult cases are when I have been unable to help. I had to tell Péra and Tunéli's grandmother that there was nothing I could do to save her sight. Árvan cut himself badly with a knife, and though I prevented him from bleeding to death, I could not save his finger.

Tauer is pleased to share the burden of responsibility for the villagers' health. His elderly father takes up a lot of his time, and the people of Jóla still rely on him for advice rather than me. He has enough work as it is.

Now it is harvest, which means I have closed my school for the time being. I am delighted with the school, though it has cost me a great deal. I want my school to become the equal of yours. I want to think that you would be proud of me. You always maintained composure, answered all of our questions, and knew how to teach us. I use the same methods as you: reading or reciting to the children, then asking them to relay what they have just heard, and discussing it together. I spell out words and have them repeat them back to me. I try to help them see things contextually and holistically. Though I struggle to stay as calm and collected as you when the littlest ones have trouble sitting still and start running around chasing bees that have erred into the schoolhouse, or pulling each other's hair, or crawling around pretending to be kittens.

Today a shipment arrived at our farm from Jóla. All the households whose children I have taught gathered together two sacks of rye flour, a jar of honey, two chickens, four skeins of wool in gray and green and—the most precious thing of all—a score of beeswax candles. Our own village also paid handsomely for my teaching, and even included payment for the education I am expected to give this winter, weather permitting. Mother and I have been busy all day unpacking everything and organizing the storehouse and larder.

Our relationship is different now that I know that I am protecting the villages with my walks. Mother no longer speaks ill of my school. She can see that I have continued protecting the village, and she is pleased that I am contributing to the food stores. But I am bursting with unanswered questions. How did Mother know what I was doing when even I did not understand? And why does she avoid my questions on the topic? She only coughs and turns away.

I spoke to Náraes about it not long ago. She knows Mother better than I do, after all; they have been together this whole time. Mother and I lost a lot when I traveled away. Náraes was sitting and sewing Maressa's trousers (she has asked to wear trousers now, like me) and raised her eyebrows when I brought up the subject of Mother.

"You know she's always been a bit of an odd one," she said with a shrug. "She isn't from these parts after all, so she's never really fit in. I don't think she wants reminding of her former life. She always says that what's done is done and there's no use dwelling on it."

Mother is not from Sáru or any of the nearby villages. I always knew that, of course, but it is not something that I often think about. Her hair is a lighter brown than that of most Rovasians, which Akios also inherited. We have never met our maternal grandparents or any of Mother's relatives.

"Where does she come from?"

Náraes snipped off the thread and inspected the trousers critically. "Maressa wears out the knees quicker than I can sew them up. It wasn't like this when she wore skirts! Mother comes from somewhere in the west, but she's never said where."

Náraes was not especially interested in discussing Mother, so I brought my questions to Father. I wanted to talk to him in a place where Mother would not hear, so I sought him out that afternoon as he was sharpening his scythe and ax behind the woodshed. He was grateful for help with the grindstone.

"I found your mother in the forest, you know that," he said, and smiled at the memory. "You all loved hearing the story as littl'uns."

"But surely that was just a story," I said. "She cannot have appeared out of nowhere."

He examined the scythe's edge and shook his head. "Not sharp yet. Well, she did. It was winter and the ground was hard with snow. I'd skied out alone to hunt. This was in the time of the previous nádor, not the one you grew up with, but his father. The one they called the chicken-hunter, because . . ."

"I know why he was called that." I could not listen to that chicken story one more time. "You skied out and the moon was full so you stayed in the forest for a while and found something in one of the traps. At first you thought it was a little bear."

"She growled like one," he said, and I could hear the tenderness in his voice. "And was dressed in layers of furs. But it was your mother, so it was, and I had to spend a long time calming her down before I dared approach and free her from the snare. Then I took her home, and me and my mother took care of her until she came around and got a little meat on her bones. She was so thin, she probably wouldn't have survived long alone in the forest. But it all worked out and we married the following summer."

"But where did she come from? What was she doing there in the forest in the middle of winter?"

"I asked a few times, at first." Father stood up straight. "But it soon became clear that she didn't want to talk about it, so I stopped asking. And it wasn't easy to ask her much to begin with 'cause she hadn't learned our language. Then, as time passed, it didn't seem so important."

I stopped turning the handle. "She spoke a different language?"

Father nodded. "But she soon learned ours, and you'd never know it wasn't her first language. She soon learned all of the customs and traditions of Rovas as well. I doubt it even occurs to people anymore that she isn't from here. It doesn't to me."

"She never tells me anything! She knows about all sorts of things that I have never learned about. And she has acted so strangely toward me ever since I came home—distant and cold!"

In that moment Father looked aged and stooped in a way I had never noticed before.

"Did you know that your mother tried to get you back? The same evening you left she rushed out with neither hat nor cardigan. Akios and Náraes were alone in the house and told me when I came home. I ran after her, not knowing where to search. I found her the next day. She was still walking, but had no idea where she was. She barely recognized me. When I got her home she was frozen through and lay in bed for many a day. We didn't think she'd make it. I'm not sure she even wanted to. That chill that she picked up has never really left her. When you came home to us I thought she might get better, but I think it's too late for that."

He rubbed his eyes. "She blames me for sending you away. She let herself be persuaded but then regretted it. She's never forgiven me."

This was another thing I had never realized before. There is so much that I do not know about my parents, Sister O. It is as if I am seeing them for the first time.

Your novice,

Maresi

Most Venerable Mother,
Summer continues, but the cooling air and darkening evenings indicate the coming autumn. Tauer has predicted a cold autumn and early winter. Yet I know that we will manage; our stores are filled to bursting.

We will manage, but I do not know what will become of everybody else. Venerable Mother, I am continually learning new things here in Rovas, seeing things that I had been blind to before, and what I see strikes fear in my heart. I have been so intent on protecting my village that I have had no concept of what is happening in the rest of the land. I have willingly closed my eyes.

ᴡ

About ten days ago a beggar came to our village and went from house to house. He came to us last, as the sun was setting. We gave him the typical beggar's bread, and then Mother served him a bowl of porridge and I cut him a decent wedge of goat's cheese. He sat on the bench outside the door and devoured it all greedily, though he must have been given food at the other houses as well. He was unwashed and long-haired, his beard hung down to his chest in a tangle of brown and filth, and he did not smell good. His skin was sunburned and dirt was deeply ingrained in the lines of his face. Mother wanted nothing to do with him, but I had to shell a basket of peas to dry for winter, and preferred to sit outside so as not to make a mess inside. So I sat next to him and tried to breathe through my mouth.

"Ain't had such fine food all summer," he said, and slurped down the hot porridge. "These here houses have given me more to eat than I managed to scrape together from ten villages." He peered at me from over the edge of his bowl. "I could barely find this place, you know. The paths that I knew should be there in the forest had faded and disappeared. But my wife's mother was from Sáru, so I knew the village was here, oh yes. I didn't give up. Followed the river, I did, and then on to the west. Kept pushing on slowly. There was something resisting, but you can't keep out the likes of me. No soldiers have bothered me here, oh no. Not like on the country roads. Not like in them other villages."

I wanted to get up and leave. I wanted to block out his truths. Deep down though, Sister O, I already knew. Something prevented me from leaving, and I continued husking peas without looking up. "Are there many soldiers on the roads then?" I asked, almost managing to maintain composure in my voice.

He scoffed, but it sounded almost like a laugh. "Many? An honest man can't walk from one crossroads to another without bumping into them, being ridden down and struck with the broad side of a sword. They tend to leave the likes of me in peace though. They've already taken everything I got. The nádor took it all." He spat on the ground, and I looked up in surprise. Nobody dares criticize the nádor openly. One never knows who might be listening. "He took my farm and my animals when I couldn't pay my taxes. But the harvest had failed— what could I do? So we took to the road, my wife and daughter and I. Spring before last, it was."

I quickly looked down at my peas again. The husks were green and healthy, and the peas I squeezed out of them were round and sweet. The pig and goats would get the husks, and I would dry the peas by the hearth, where the animals could not reach them.

"Now I'm the only one left. Does the young lady have any more of that cheese?"

I got up, spilling pea husks from my lap, and ran inside for more cheese. When I came out again I could not sit down and remained standing with arms crossed. The beggar gobbled up the cheese in several large bites and then carefully picked every crumb out of his beard.

"Life is hard in the villages, you know. Soldiers hound them. Count every hen, measure every field, weigh every sack of flour. The taxes are gonna be brutal this autumn. Mark my words." He peered at me with shrewd eyes. "But not here. No, the young lady sees to that."

"And what do you know about that?" I snapped.

"I may be old and I may be poor," he said, and sucked air through his teeth in a particularly unpleasant way. "But there ain't nothing wrong with my nose. The young lady smells, she does. Can't hide the smell from the likes of me."

I did not understand what he meant at the time. But one night, as I was lying awake, it struck me that Mother had also sniffed me on occasion. My powers, the things that I do, leave a scent on me, and Mother, who is clearly aware of much more than I gave her credit for, has recognized it. I always thought she was smelling the lavender that I keep with my clothes. Now I know the truth.

Others recognize it too, and not only women. It is a great surprise— but I see now that there are many ways in which I have been mistaken.

ɯ

My homeland is suffering, Venerable Mother. Suddenly everything is overwhelming and difficult—the world is too vast. There is so much to be done. I was feeling content with my school, but now I see that it is not nearly enough.

I ask myself: what would Sister O do? What would the Venerable Mother advise me? And the answer is here somewhere, very close. For I know that you would do something and not simply crawl into a hole and hide, like the hare that hopes the fox will carry on by.

The fox is approaching ever nearer, already sniffing the mouth of the burrow, as I lie inside quivering with fear.

Respectfully,

Maresi

AUTUMN

My dear Ennike Rose,

The harvest is over, and soon it will be time to open the school again. Many families remain busy with various tasks, and the harvest festival is still to come. But when all that is done, finally I will be able to stand on the crest of the hill again and see my little students come traipsing up the grassy slope. Frost has started to cover the grass in the mornings. Autumn certainly is coming early this year, and, alas, the frost took all our winter apples. They did not have enough time to ripen.

Speaking of which, do you know what I have been missing of late? Lemons! It is far too cold here for lemon trees. I remember how you and I used to grimace when Jai would sink her teeth into the sour yellow rind, but lemons add a wonderful flavor to cooking. Sister Ers's succulent whole-roasted chicken stuffed with lemons, olives and thyme! Oh, sometimes I long for Abbey food so intensely that my mouth waters. We always used to get so many delicious treats in the autumn. Well, you still do, of course. Sister Ers's honey and nut cakes! And that fish stew with mussels and korr-root and masses of spices . . .

As thanks for relieving Feira's toothache enough for Jannarl to help pull her tooth out, Haiman gave me some coarse brown linen that I am trying to sew into a pair of trousers for myself. Mother refuses to help because she is still of the opinion that I ought to wear only skirts and braid my hair. She has come to terms with everything else by now, but not my appearance. At least she has stopped picking on me for it. She has become very fatigued over harvest time; her cough shows no signs of improvement and none of the teas I make her help. Sometimes there is a nasty wheezing sound when she breathes. I wish Sister Nar were here to advise me. And how I wish Jai were here with her nimble fingers! She would have finished sewing these trousers long ago. I have been struggling with them every evening for several days now. There is always a point at which the frustration becomes too much for me, and I toss my sewing in a corner and swear never to touch it again. And yet I must have a new pair of trousers, for my old ones are too worn and will not survive another winter.

However, this was not at all what I intended to write about. Yesterday, early in the morning, I went to my little schoolhouse for the first time in a while. I wanted to check that all was as it should be before leaving it unattended for the first time. My parents are going to the market that takes place after harvest festival in the village of Murik, and they want me to go with them while the school is still closed. My father's sister married into a large farmstead in Murik, where her son Bernáti has taken over the farm. He is married to Jannarl's sister, so Jannarl and Náraes want to come as well.

Murik, which lies two days' walk to the west, is a much larger village than Jóla or Sáru, and its market attracts tradesmen from near and far. Seeing as no one can find their way to our villages these days, we are in want of certain things. Father needs a new ax head, Mother a new kettle. Náraes hopes to buy some sheep, for we are in desperate need of wool for clothes. I want to buy more paper and ink, as usual. A little sugar would be nice, if there is any to be found, and our salt supply is nearly finished. Salt can only be bought from the nádor's official merchants, whose store is strongly guarded by soldiers. I feel a little uneasy about this journey, but I understand that it is necessary.

Anyway, I was going to write about what happened yesterday. Off I went to my school through the frosty grass, past wild-rose bushes heavy with rosehips. I was wearing gloves that Mother had knit for me, and my red mantle, and my boots.

The rays of the autumn sun fell on my frost-covered schoolhouse, making it glitter like the palace of Irindibul. To my surprise, smoke was streaming from the chimney. I hurried over and threw open the door.

"Hello? Who is there?" I called sternly.

The room smelled of smoke and fresh timber. I stopped in the doorway, astonished. In the center of the room was a long table with benches, yet it was a most peculiar table, with a raised edge all the way around, like a shallow box.

"It's only me, Maresi," came a quiet voice.

Kárun was standing over by the fireplace and stacking firewood. He brushed bark from his hands and smiled at me. He was wearing a new shirt, a blue one, which he must have bought in Irindibul. It made him look foreign. Like a blue bird that flew here instead of south for the winter. His shirtsleeves were rolled up. I had forgotten how broad his shoulders are. The blue brought out the warm color of his eyes. I was happy to see him, I must admit. I misjudged him when I met him that first spring. He is a good man.

"Kárun!" I exclaimed. "You are back!" I beamed at him, which immediately made him smile too.

"Well, I've been back a while already, but I've been busy here. Wanted to arrange a few things before it was time for you to open the school again." He nodded at the table. "It's not really finished yet."

"It is very handsome!" I said, and admired the beautiful light-wood table. "But why is the edge like this?"

"I heard tell that the rich boys' teachers in Irindibul have them practice their writing in sand. So I got a few sacks of fine sand from the riverbanks down by Lady Falls." His enthusiasm was growing as he spoke. "And that's why I built these edges. You can fill the space between them with sand, and then the children can write with sticks. And I'll build a couple of light covers for the table, so it can also be used as normal when they're doing something else."

"Kárun!" I exclaimed, too amazed and astonished to say anything else.

"Is it a very silly idea? Perhaps that's not how you teach writing at all." He crossed his arms over his chest. I rushed over to him and touched him on the arm.

"It is a wonderful idea," I said, unable to prevent the tears from welling up in my eyes. "It has been such a headache figuring out how they might practice writing letters and words. This is perfect. Absolutely perfect."

Kárun looked down at my hand on his arm. I quickly removed it. We were standing very close to one another. I could feel the warmth radiating from his body. I could clearly see the beard stubble on his chin. He looked at me, and I felt my cheeks start to heat up. Suddenly I wished I had left my hand where it was.

"I built some shelves over here," he said, without breaking eye contact. "And there's a few things I bought in Irindibul."

I looked over at the woodpile. Behind it stood a slender, chestnut-brown bookshelf. On one of the shelves was an abacus with brightly colored beads, painted in the typical ornate patterns of Irindibul. But I paid little attention to that, for beside it were two books! I let out a cry and rushed over to them. Two leather-bound books, Ennike! I was speechless as I ran my fingers over the spines. I carefully pulled out first one, then the other, opened them and read the beautiful handwritten title pages. One was entitled *Sovereigns of Urundien and Their Reigns*, and the other thinner book was called *Four Plays by Andero and a Selection of Ofoli's Wisdoms and Aphorisms*. Brand-new books. Books I had never even heard of—that not even Sister O knows of. I could hardly wait to sit down and start reading.

But you know the price of a book, Ennike. You know how much work goes into every single page.

"There wasn't much to choose from," Kárun said from behind me. "I hope these can be of some use."

I swallowed a few times before turning around.

"This is too much," I said, and looked up at him. "You must have spent all your earnings on these books and the abacus. I cannot accept them."

"They're not for you," he replied, looking me straight in the eye. "They're for the school."

And I could not argue with that.

"Besides, they weren't all that expensive," he said softly, and started pulling on his leather waistcoat. "Now I'll go out and make a cover for the table. If you think it's a good idea."

I am convinced that he was lying about the books not being expensive, but I did not say so. I told him that the sand-filled table was an excellent idea, and I would be very grateful if he built a cover. He pulled on the gloves I had made him and went outside. It felt remarkably cool inside, despite the fire. Taking a look around, I discovered something I had not seen before. Next to the far wall, by the fireplace, a mattress was laid out on the bare floor. A coarse blanket lay on top of it. Was Kárun sleeping in the school? And if so, why? But I had no time to think about it. I grabbed the books, hugged them to my breast and rushed home with such haste that I stumbled several times and nearly fell. I hid in my room and sat reading late into the night, and I have been reading all day today. Mother and Father can say what they like. To read a book I have never read before, to see completely new words and discover new thoughts and worlds—I have missed it *so much*, Ennike! I must write and tell Jai about it also, for I know she would understand how I feel. Or maybe you could read her that last part about the books, so that I can continue reading now instead.

But you could leave out some of the things I wrote about Kárun.

Yours,

Maresi

Venerable Sister O,

I have two new books! Or rather, the school has two new books. They are from Irindibul and are written in the language shared by Rovas and Irindibul. One is a rather thin volume containing four short plays by a man named Andero, who I believe lived around a hundred years ago. They are entertaining as stories. I am pleased to have some plays to teach my pupils about drama, and perhaps even stage a little performance. But the second section of the book is of greater interest to me because it contains the aphorisms and wisdoms of a man by name of Ofoli, with exquisite illustrations. Have you heard of him? I am studying them carefully, for it seems that a greater, more complex truth is hiding among his often banal and commonplace maxims.

The larger book, bound in midnight-black leather, is called *Sovereigns of Urundien and Their Reigns* and is very informative. I realize that it must have been commissioned by some monarch or other, and accordingly I am taking some of its claims with a grain of salt. For example, I hardly believe that a hundred thousand Lavorian warriors stood against Bendiro's army during the time of Arra and Surando. Lavora was a small land and would have struggled to mobilize so many men. But I am learning much of our realm, most of which is new to me. There are maps also—the first I have seen that include my province. The book contains a list of sovereigns, several myths about the conquest and rise of Urundien, who married whom and why, how various regions were conquered (or in some case, like Lavora, escaped conquest), and the great achievements of various rulers. One interesting thing I have learned is that Evendilana, who is named in the legend of Arra in Erva's book, does seem to have been a real person. As a woman, her mention is only brief, but fascinating and utterly perplexing.

When Bendiro the Truthful perished, his daughter Evendilana was the only heir to the throne. For a time the realm was governed by Bendiro's second wife and his principal adviser, the Duke of Marena. The Princess was expected to marry the Duke but thenceforth came to rule the kingdom in her own right for ten years. It was said that she was greatly skilled in all musical instruments and that her playing could bring grown men to tears. Thereafter the land was ruled by Kamarel the Righteous, who conquered the Tungarian mountains and the nine silver mines.

Curiously, it does not say that Evendilana died when her rule ended. The deaths of all other sovereigns have been carefully recorded. Neither does it say that she married Kamarel, for the book goes on to mention his three wives and the children he had with them. It would appear that Evendilana was Bendiro's daughter with his first wife, who is mentioned a little earlier in the text.

On his twenty-first birthday, Bendiro wed Venna, daughter of a governor of the province of Rovas, thus sealing the union between the poor province and mighty kingdom. Venna was known for her beauty, but she was against the alliance, more between Rovas and Urundien than between her and Bendiro, and she perished a few years after marriage. Bendiro then married the daughter of his aunt's husband's sister, Tarenna of Tandari. She brought thirty horses, seven warships and a peacock with her into the marriage.

This means that Evendilana, the unfortunate little princess from the stories, has Rovasian blood! This discovery has delighted me greatly.

Your novice,

Maresi

Dearest Jai,

So much has happened since I wrote to you last. I still have not fully recovered. All the things I have seen and experienced are hugely important, but I do not yet know how to act, nor what they mean for me or for Rovas.

As Ennike may have told you, Father and Mother wanted to go to the Murik market to buy various items, and seeing as Jannarl's sister also lives in Murik, Jannarl and Náraes came along too. Traveling in a big group felt safer. Before setting off I visited the schoolhouse with some bed linen the villagers had given me as payment for teaching. Since Kárun donated the furniture and books for the school, I thought it was the least I could do in return. It seems that he is currently living in the school while he makes the final preparations for winter, and I can understand why. His own cabin is of the old style, with a smoke hatch and no proper chimney, and it is dark and drafty. The autumn has been very cold and there is frost every night. When I arrived at the school Kárun was nowhere to be seen, but a high, neat pile of firewood was stacked against the eastern wall. I made his bed and left a little food on the table: some boiled eggs, rye bread and goat cheese I had made myself. After all, he is a bachelor without farmland, and I imagine that his diet is rather monotonous.

We set off at dawn six days ago. Gray Lady pulled a little cart we had borrowed, while I walked by her head with my staff as support. I was wearing the new trousers I had sewn. They do not fit well, but at least they are warm and have no holes. But I had made an effort to look presentable, as the market is a festive occasion. I chose a day with somewhat milder weather to wash my body and hair with homemade soap in a tub of heated water in the barn. I had used my Abbey comb to tame my hair. I was wearing a linen blouse that Náraes had embroidered, a gray sweater Mother had knit and the boots Kárun had given me. I also had on a headscarf of fine wool that I had received as payment for teaching, and Mother's white, black and red belt around my waist. Your red cloak is still the finest thing I own, and no one else in Rovas has anything to compare.

Maressa and Dúlan rode in the cart with the adults walking behind them. We brought some goods to sell or exchange: a few sacks of flour; two full baskets of eggs; my goat cheese and a little boiled whey; Náraes's pickled berries; Father's fine wicker baskets; and a selection of my dried herbs, spices, potions and ointments. We headed to Jóla first and then farther along the paths and cart tracks to the southwest. It was a sunny day but very cold, with frost everywhere. Rowanberries hung in heavy clusters, which Tauer says is a sign of a harsh winter. Gray Lady followed the path obediently, and for once I did not have to fight with her at all. We were finally doing what she had wanted to for so long: leaving the village. As soon as we left Jóla behind I heard it. That tone. The tremble in the ground that spread through my legs and into my body and made my teeth tingle. I knew that it had been waiting for me, and it surged into me with incredible power, filling me from head to toe, and for a while I had trouble hearing anything else.

It frightens me. I know that it is the sound of the Crone, and of Rovas. Perhaps they are one and the same. It is the Crone's way of speaking to me here. I cannot hear it in the village, and I have started to suspect that this is another effect of the protective barrier I have created. It seems nothing can penetrate it. The Crone is using this tone to tell me that she wants something of me, and I have started to suspect what it might be.

Only I do not want to face it.

Other sounds returned before long: grass rustling under my boots; cart wheels creaking; Maressa eagerly pointing things out to her grandfather. The kite called triumphantly above us. The last migratory birds trumpeted overhead. They are heading south. My desire to join them on their southward journey is not nearly as strong as it was this time last year. The trees have shifted colors and now display red, orange and gold leaves that shine out from the muted green of the pines.

We walked until hunger caught up with us, and then we sat at the foot of a scintillating orange rowan and ate some of the provisions that Mother and Náraes had packed. Then we continued walking. We had to cross a stream, and at one point we came to a small river that necessitated a lengthy search upstream before we managed to find a rickety old bridge.

We walked past many fields, yellow with stubble. Later that afternoon we came to a small village of four gray wooden cottages huddled around a central yard. We saw no animals, but smoke rose from the chimneys. Mother approached one of the houses and knocked on the door while Jannarl lifted the girls out of the cart and I sat down to rest my legs.

Mother was about to let herself in, as is our custom in Rovas, but just then the door was opened by a thin woman in a gray cardigan and unbleached linen skirt. She stared at Mother without speaking or inviting her in.

"Blessings on your hearth," said Mother.

The woman in the doorway relaxed a little when she heard our ancient greeting, but she remained in the doorway and did not step aside to let Mother in.

"Blessings on your journey," she said quietly. "What brings you here?"

"We're on our way to the Murik market," Mother said politely. "And we were wondering if we might heat some water over your hearth and let the little ones warm up for a spell." She pointed to Maressa and Dúlan. When the woman saw them she smiled and stepped aside.

"Of course. Excuse my rudeness, but you never know who's on the roads these days. Do come in and warm yourselves up, but we've nothing to offer."

We all stepped inside and found ourselves in a simple room with real wood floors and worn woven rugs. Four wall-mounted beds ran along two of the walls, and there was a long table of dark wood, scrubbed clean, and two narrow benches with embroidered cushions. Everything was old and faded and tattered. I brewed some tea in a kettle the woman lent me. She had two daughters, one of Akios's age and one a little younger. They were very beautiful, one fair and the other dark, with thick braids but skinny arms. I understood why their mother feared soldiers.

As we drank our tea and the little girls played with a coal-black kitten, the woman and her elder daughter told us briefly about their lives. Sickness had claimed the man of the house the winter before last and now they worked the land themselves, with help from an uncle in the neighboring farm. They had no animals, not even chickens.

"The nádor took some in taxes and we had no choice but to eat the rest," said the woman without a hint of bitterness. She may as well have been talking about the frost—something inevitable, a force of nature. "He's already taken this year's taxes. I just don't know how we'll survive the winter."

The younger girl had severe red rashes. I looked at them closely.

"If you come across some oats, you can use them to relieve that rash. Cook a porridge, let it cool and put it on your skin."

She shrugged and looked away.

Before we continued our journey Mother and Father exchanged a brief glance. Then Mother went out to the cart and fetched an apronful of eggs, which she gave to the woman of the house.

"As thanks for your hospitality."

The woman looked at the eggs for a long time but shook her head.

"We've never put a price on hospitality in Rovas. I won't be the first to take payment for a little warmth and water."

"Then consider it a neighborly gift," said Mother stubbornly. Eventually she convinced the woman to accept the eggs.

ᚹ

We continued in silence. The girls slept in the cart, wrapped tight in furs. When it grew dark, we camped on a beautiful slope from which we could see the smoke of Murik in the distance. We were set to arrive shortly after noon the following day. Akios and I lit a fire, and Mother shared out the provisions. Gray Lady's chewing guided me into sleep, along with the persistent murmur of the tone of Rovas.

ᚹ

This has become a long letter—forgive me, Jai. Too wordy, Sister O would say. Stick to the point! But this is how I must write, to capture all that has happened and how I have felt. This is my nature. This letter is going to be so long that it will take several days to write. Now it is too dark and my hand is too tired. Good night, Jai, my friend. I will continue tomorrow.

ᚹ

It is afternoon and I have some time to myself. Everyone else is out, for a change. Sometimes it feels like I can never truly be alone, except when I walk around the village to fortify the protection. I do this more than ever now. I do it so often that Mother says I am going to tire myself out. It is true that I am very tired. My legs are shaking. I would happily sleep until late morning.

If I lived with Jannarl's sister Selas and our cousin Bernáti I would never have any solitude. Murik is the largest village I have seen here in Rovas, with around twenty farmsteads. It is situated in a beautiful, fertile valley, which has been cultivated for so long that the forest has been pushed back and subdued. How wonderfully lush it must be in the summer! Even now, when the bare fields are dark with muddy ground, it is a beautiful region. The village itself consists of about fifty buildings, which was, understandably, an overwhelming sight for Akios and the girls! Even Náraes looked around with wide eyes as we walked among the houses on our way to Bernáti's farm. There were also lots of people out and about, on account of the market. We could see it in the distance.

Tables and tents had been erected on one of the stubbly fields outside the village, horses and oxen were tethered around it, and smoke was rising from the forges of traveling blacksmiths and various fires where food was being cooked. Music and distant chatter traveled on the wind.

Maressa stood up in the cart and almost fell out in her eagerness to see better. But first we were going to see Bernáti. He lives on a hill at the edge of the village, away from the noises and odors of the other farmsteads. I knew that they had a large and lavish home, but I was still astonished when I saw it. It is like one house upon another, Jai! Can you imagine? There is another floor where the roof should be, with walls around it and windows, and then the roof is on top of that. And their compound contains so many buildings that it looks like a little village in itself. They are arranged along three sides, and then there is a real fence with a gate through to the yard.

The first thing we saw was a soldier. He was guarding the door to one of the sheds, looking bored. A sword hung by his side. We all stopped at the gate, confused. Father immediately came to stand in front of us women, and Jannarl joined him. They spoke quickly, in whispers. The soldier glared at us but did not move.

Then the door of the farmhouse was flung open, and Aunt Míraes stepped out onto the doorstep.

"Brother!" she called, loud and clear. So that the soldier would hear. "Blessings on your journey!"

"Blessings on your hearth," Father answered with some uncertainty.

"Come in, come in," said Aunt Míraes. "You have traveled far. And you've brought the little ones, Míos will be pleased! Míos is the youngest of my grandchildren. Come on then, in you get."

Father opened the gate and we went inside. My aunt looked just as I remembered her, bony with protruding ears, like Father. She was wearing a white blouse with a high collar and red and green embroidery around the neck, a striped linen skirt and a large, impeccably clean embroidered apron tied around her waist. I never went to see her when I was little, because she and her husband, Tan, would always visit us. They had a horse and cart of their own and could travel the long road between villages in a single day. They would always bring gifts for us children: toys that Uncle had carved for us, some yummy cakes Auntie had baked. Their children, Bernáti and Tessi, were older than us and mainly spent time with the adults, but I was very fond of them. Tessi especially was very kind and always told Akios and me wonderful stories. She is unmarried and lives in the family home. She used to bring a huge lump of butter for Mother, and several cheeses she had made herself from the milk of all their cattle, and sometimes even sweet, delicious cream.

That was all before the famine, of course.

The soldier was watching us, still in silence, as we unhitched Gray Lady and I tethered her to a ring in a wall and gave her some straw to munch on. Then we went into the house. I will describe it to you, for it must be one of the largest farmhouses in all of Rovas. Well, in the cities they surely have larger and finer houses, but in the countryside two-story houses with so many rooms are highly unusual.

Downstairs is the main room, with a large brick hearth and bread oven, where Aunt Míraes and Jannarl's sister Selas do the cooking in large pots hanging from chains. Their household is large, so their pots must be too. The main room is enormous, with a great long table in the middle and benches on either side, and wall-mounted beds along two walls behind exquisite curtains, where the farm boys and milkmaids sleep. They have three lads and two girls working for them. The room is majestic, just imagine, with wooden floors and several long, striped home-woven carpets and shag rugs on the walls. There are only two windows, so it is a little dark, but very clean and neat. There is even a large table leaning up against a wall that can be folded down and used for the men's carpentry during winter when it is too cold to work outside. Then there is a bedroom where Selas and Bernáti sleep together with their little boys, Míos, who is around the same age as Maressa, and Kunnal, who is ten. There is a cold room as well, or the milk room, as they call it, where they store food.

From the entrance, a staircase leads up to the second floor, where my aunt and uncle have their private room. In another larger room lives Bernáti's unmarried elder sister Tessi, and Bernáti and Selas's daughter Unéli, who is twelve. There is also a chair loom and spinning wheel.

Altogether there are thirteen people living in the same household. On our arrival everybody except Aunt Míraes was out at the market. She had stayed home, not wanting to risk leaving the farm unsupervised. She explained why briefly when we had sat down at the table and she had presented us with a large bowl of delicious hot porridge and a beautifully carved wooden spoon each to dig in with.

"The salt merchant is here," she said in a low voice with a furtive glance at the door. "That's one of his soldiers guarding some of the salt stores while the merchant himself is at the market with the other two. As the largest farmstead in the village we've had to accommodate them, as usual. The soldiers have been sleeping in here with the farm boys, and the merchant sleeps in Bernáti and Selas's room. They sleep with us, and the milkmaids have moved in with Tessi." She looked at us somewhat worriedly. "We'll have to move the farm boys and soldiers into the hayloft, which should be warm enough for the time being, so you can have space down here. We can't move the salt merchant."

"Don't worry, Sister," said Father. "We'll manage just fine." But he and Mother exchanged an anxious glance. The salt merchant always travels surrounded by soldiers. And common folk like us want as little to do with soldiers as possible.

"It can't be helped," said Mother quietly. "There's no other accommodation to be had."

"We won't need to stay more than two nights. Maressa and Maresi can sleep up with Tessi, and the rest of us can fit down here."

"You must be very friendly and polite to the merchant and his men, girls," said Náraes to Maressa seriously. "Keep out of their way as much as possible, and only speak to them if they speak to you first."

"Yes, Mama," said Maressa through a mouthful of porridge. "Can we go to the market now?"

"Soon," replied Jannarl. "How has your summer been?"

"Mostly good," said Míraes, who was still standing at the head of the table to make sure we had everything we needed. "Some of the fields were affected by the late frost, but only the small ones. We've had a good harvest, and healthy piglets have survived from all three of my sows. There are more soldiers in the village than just the salt merchant's, of course," she sighed. "They do take their taxes—I lost nine piglets. Not to mention the flour they took. Year by year it's becoming more and more arbitrary how much the Crown thinks we ought to be taxed. This household has a lot of mouths to feed and it looks like a bleak winter ahead." She shook her head. "We'll manage, but it'll be a tough winter. And there are many who are not as fortunate as we."

"Has the harvest been worse for others?" asked Mother.

"No, not exactly. But many still haven't recovered from previous hunger winters. And with these harsh taxes recovery is impossible for most. You'll see for yourselves at the market."

"Shouldn't you be a little careful, Sister," Father said quietly. "Don't voice your discontent so loudly with the nádor's men in earshot."

"Oh, but it isn't the nádor who has decided all this," said Míraes, surprised. "He is only following orders from the Crown. The Sovereign of Urundien is the true extortioner."

Once we had eaten we went to the market. We were tired, but the children were eager, and we had only two days to fulfill all our tasks. We left our wares at home with Míraes and walked into the flurry of sounds and scents.

The market was wonderful—until I saw what was happening at the edge. But up until that point, I was able to enjoy all the festively dressed people, the delicious smells and the wonderful products displayed on tables. There was fabric, yarn and thread for sale, and lots of pots and pans. There was a metalsmith and a blacksmith, each with an anvil. There were basket-makers, musicians, jesters, medicine men, spice merchants, and there in the middle of the crowd was the salt merchant's stall with its blood-red canopy and a soldier stationed at either side. There were plenty of soldiers moving through the crowd, taking what they wanted without paying and staring at all the beautiful young girls. I was in constant fear of seeing the ones that had been in our village. The ones that took my silver and defiled Marget's body.

We moved as a group, Maressa on her father's shoulders, Dúlan in her mother's arms. Like a little flock of rural chickens we made our way through the stands. Náraes was the first to notice something strange.

"See how hardly anyone is selling livestock. And few are selling food either."

It was true. We found one man with a few skinny young pigs for sale at a ridiculous price. One woman was selling duck eggs and another was selling chicks. A merchant from the southwest had various smoked sausages on offer, and there was a large, red-cheeked woman selling aromatic fried piggies. Father said he had never seen food so expensive at a market. Everyone feared the coming winter and their stores were sparse. And sheep, which Náraes was after, were nowhere to be seen.

"I suppose I'll just have to buy wool then," my sister said disappointedly. "I'd so hoped I could start keeping my own sheep."

I found neither paper nor ink. I suppose I should not be surprised. Literacy is practically unheard of in Rovas.

It was as we were walking along the edge of the market, where the few animals that were for sale were kept, that I saw them. A group of soldiers were taking aim at something small that kept poking out of a rubbish heap with weasel-quick movements. One soldier threw an apple core at the moving figure, and a mop of dark hair disappeared into the pile. Soon it was back, and another popped up beside it.

They were children. More than two. Emaciated children in ragged clothes, swiftly rummaging through the waste in search of something edible. I saw one—I could not say if it was a boy or a girl—nabbing the scrap the soldier had thrown and swallowing it in two bites. The soldier swore and picked up a stone, a big one. He threw it, and it hit one of the children on the leg. The child did not make a sound, but just crawled away and stayed out of sight.

I had my staff, but no silver door appeared for me to open. The soldiers were many, and we were unarmed. I looked at the soldiers and I cursed them, summoning the Crone's wrath and the Maiden's curse and the Mother's spleen. One of them turned around.

It was the one who took my silver that first spring, the one wearing finer garments than the others. I turned my head quickly and hid my face in the hood of my cloak, but not before I saw him frown, as if trying to recall something. I positioned myself behind Mother, but he followed us with his gaze as we made haste to disappear into the throng of people. My heart was pounding—with rage and with fear.

And that is what I saw during this trip, Jai. I saw destitution. I saw starvation. Not only those children. There were grown beggars too, and families forced to walk from village to village after being thrown out of their homes, driven away by the nádor because they could not pay their taxes or debts, or because they could no longer survive on the meager provisions of the soil.

Suddenly I saw them everywhere at the market, where at first all I had seen was woolen fabric and black pots. They drifted between the stalls with hungry eyes. They sat on the ground, wrapped up in threadbare blankets, with hands or wooden bowls outstretched to the passers-by. Often without saying a word. The worst was seeing the families with small children. I could barely bring myself to meet the parents' gaze. Their eyes were full of the pain of failing to feed their own little ones.

ᛒ

The evening meal was excruciating. The salt merchant and his soldiers joined the family table, and all the women in the house had to wait on them. The atmosphere was formal and heavy with unspoken words. What bothered me the most was that Maheran, the salt merchant, a tall, gray-haired man from Irindibul, would not stop complaining about Rovas—about how lazy people are here, and how the nádor does his best to help anyone affected by hunger, illness or accidents, but it is almost impossible to help people as foolish and stubborn as the Rovasians. And nobody contradicted him! Quite the opposite—Aunt Míraes's family all agreed, especially Cousin Bernáti. They blamed the high taxes on the Sovereign of Urundien and made the nádor out to be an intermediary who did the best he could but received only ingratitude from all sides.

"The nádor is doing what he can for Rovas," my cousin said to the salt merchant, who was wearing a black velvet jacket with pearl embroidery and sucking the meat from one of Míraes's cockerels. "He lends money liberally to those in hardship. But it's clear that they are loans, not handouts, and then people seem to be in an uproar about having to pay them back."

I exchanged a brief glance with Father. We said nothing. We said nothing about the children being pelted with stones by soldiers. We said nothing about Marget and all the girls like her of whom we had heard tell. We said nothing about the sky-high loans. Nothing about how we were almost forced to leave our home and land. We looked down at our plates and all the delicious food that this wealthy household had to serve even in a time of hardship such as this, and we said nothing.

ᛒ

That night when I was in bed with Tessi, and Unéli and Maressa were already sleeping in Unéli's bed, Tessi told me that the children we had seen were orphans whose parents had died from sickness or starvation, and now had no one to take care of them. This is a new concept in Rovas. We have always taken care of the vulnerable. If a child loses their parents they move in with a neighbor. If a widow finds herself alone with several children to take care of, neighbors and friends help with the sowing and reaping. That is the way it is—the way it has always been, until now.

Now there are too many people who are hungry, weak and alone. And nobody considers themselves in a strong enough position to take care of them. Tessi said that she sometimes leaves food out for those little children, but only when Bernáti and her parents cannot see. They are too concerned about their own fate this winter.

"We have our own little ones to think of, they always say," she whispered in the warm darkness of the room. "We have to take care of our own first. But I can't agree with them."

ᛒ

After this conversation I sat awake for a long time with a shawl wrapped around my shoulders. I recalled the taste of bread baked with wood shavings and bark, and the feeling of hunger so intense that I tried to eat twigs and grass. I thought about the children being pelted as they tried to eat refuse.

Finally I got up and dressed, careful not to wake anyone, and went downstairs. I moved as quietly as possible in the darkness, but when I came down into the living room someone grabbed my arm.

It was Mother.

"Not a sound," she whispered in my ear. "Follow me."

She led me out through the back door. "The soldiers guard the salt store at night as well," she whispered. "Hurry." We sneaked past the privy. My heart almost stopped when a shadow separated from the darkness and came toward us. "It's Father," whispered Mother when I froze. "He's brought some food."

I swallowed my fright. "The children," I whispered. "I cannot sleep."

"I know. We're going to help them."

Father came to us with a bag under his arm. "We'll have to hurry."

I had gotten up with the intention of helping the starving children, but I had no plan. Mother and Father, on the other hand, had made up their minds as soon as they saw them. "They were so skinny," whispered Father. "They looked like you kids did during that terrible winter. We can't just leave them here. But my sister mustn't know of our plans."

"She's too anxious about her stores," Mother tutted when we had left the yard. "We took a little of her food and a little of ours. We don't need anything from the market, not really. I overheard people talking yesterday, and I know where the children usually spend the night."

We found the orphans in a barn outside the village, buried deep in the hay. The first we found was a girl who looked around ten years old, though perhaps she was older and only appeared younger due to malnourishment. She regarded us silently, expectantly. She looked at Father.

"As long as he leaves the little ones alone, I'll do him for three copper coins." She looked at the bag under his arm. "Or bread. I'll do it for bread too."

Father did not know what to say. Neither did I. Mother took the bag from Father, stuck her hand in and pulled out a loaf of bread. She crouched before the girl, who had hay in her hair and smelled indescribable.

"Here. Eat. You don't have to do anything in return."

The little girl looked at her, then at the bread. Then she grabbed it and shoved it in her mouth piece by piece until she could fit in no more. While she was chewing, clutching the bread tightly, she looked at Mother.

"How many of you are there here?" Mother asked.

The girl did not answer. She just continued chewing.

"Do you want to come with us? We're from a village in the east called Sáru. You can have food there, and a warm place to live."

"Why? What you gonna do with us?" She eyed Mother, not suspiciously but calculatingly. Would it be worth it? Worth the risk of going with these strangers? It was a terrible expression to see on the face of a child. I will never forget it.

"Because I have watched my children starve," said Mother slowly. "If their father and I had died, I would hope that someone would have helped them."

The girl swallowed the last crumb of bread. "There's Mik and Berla and me. And Mik's little sister, dunno her name, he just calls her the littl'un."

"Are any of your parents alive?"

The girl shook her head. "Mother died last winter, and I ain't seen Father for years. Mik and the littl'un's parents died last spring for sure, the soldiers killed them. And Berla, I dunno where she comes from, but if anyone cared about her she wouldn't be here."

"Tell them to meet us tomorrow at dusk by the footbridge over the stream. Do you know where that is?"

The girl nodded. Mother took more food out of the bag: bread, cheese, sausages and carrots.

"Share out the food, but don't eat it all at once or you'll get sick."

The girl stared silently at the food. She took the cheese in her arms and caressed it.

"What's your name?" I asked. She looked up at me with wide eyes. "Silla," she said.

We walked back in silence so as not to attract attention. I could not ask Mother and Father what they were planning to do. But I was incredibly grateful for their courage and initiative. And I was proud. Proud to be their daughter. I squeezed Mother's hand in the darkness before climbing back upstairs, and she patted my hand in response.

ᗯ

We visited the market again the next day and bought and exchanged what we could. There were only everyday items and tools on offer, such as ax heads, nails, a kettle for Mother, yarn and carded wool for Náraes, linens and some spices—no animals or food. There was a visible lack of anything edible. We had planned to sell our eggs and flour and my cheeses, but Mother, Father and I looked at one another and wordlessly agreed to bring our food back home again instead. The children would need it. I sold only a few pieces of cheese.

When we had bought everything we needed, we gathered in the little square in the center of the marketplace, around which the vendors were clustered. Father had promised Maressa and Dúlan a fried piggy each, and they were disappointed at the lack of goods. But before they could complain, three soldiers barged through the crowd to get to a post that stood in the middle of the square. Two of them were dragging a half-unconscious man between them. My stomach clenched into a knot of fear. The square went quiet. Náraes tried to turn her daughters around, but curious folk were pressing forward from behind us, and more soldiers were behind them. We could not get away. The two soldiers lashed the man to the post, on his feet, and the third, who was wearing expensive leather gloves, unfurled a scroll and nailed it to the post above the man's head.

209

"In the name of the Crown, our most benevolent and esteemed nádor punishes this man for his heinous crime," read the soldier in a loud voice. "He has been caught stealing salt from the Sovereign-appointed salt merchant's stores, one of the worst crimes that can be committed. The nádor, in his infinite mercy, has decreed to spare the man's life, but to take his right hand, so that he will always be recognized as the thief and criminal he is."

"By all the spirits of Rovas," Akios swore quietly.

I gave him a little shove to tell him to keep quiet. Looking at the soldiers' faces, I saw the same ruthlessness, the same love of violence and power as I saw in those men who forced their way into the crypt that spring on Menos. I did not see the door of the Crone. Yet my entire body was humming, my teeth were aching and my vision was blurred.

We averted our gaze as the soldiers carried out the punishment. But we could not block out the man's screams. We could not avoid the smell of burned flesh when they singed his arm stump to stanch the blood. Akios squeezed my hand. Father stood close to me, and I leaned against him with my eyes fixed on the ground, trying to fill my nostrils with the smell of wool and sweat from his sweater. I thought of the girls, but could not bring myself to look at them.

When it was over they loosened the man's binds and he fell to the ground. A woman rushed over to him and fell to her knees by his side. She cradled his head in her lap and cried and screamed. The soldiers stood a short distance away and watched the woman. They laughed at a private joke. I walked slowly over to the post and the man. The woman holding him was younger than him, perhaps his daughter. I crouched beside her, with the soldiers' eyes boring into my back.

"Do you have somewhere you can take him?"

She sniffed and nodded. Her face and hands were dirty.

"You must keep the wound clean. Do you understand? Never touch it with dirty hands. Wash your hands every time you touch him. If he gets a fever, give him a brew of boiled willow bark, can you manage that? Or lime blossom. I have some at home, but not here."

My words were whispered and rushed. She sniffled.

"He didn't take any salt. It's not salt we need—it's food! But no one believes him. No one would help us."

I grabbed her by the shoulder, felt how bony she was beneath her thin linen blouse.

"Remember! Lime blossom or willow bark. And wash your hands."

Suddenly a child's voice cut through the air.

"That isn't what it says here. It says: 'The salt thief must pay a fine in the form of one cow, or equivalent, or bear five lashes.' It says nothing about death or cutting off his hand."

Maressa was standing in front of the post squinting at the paper the soldier had nailed up. The paper with the real orders directly from the Sovereign of Urundien.

The soldiers stopped talking and looked at Maressa. Straight at her. Jannarl came running and scooped her up in his arms, but it was too late. The commanding soldier, the one with the fine leather gloves, approached in long strides.

"What did the girl say?"

"Nothing," mumbled Jannarl. "She's always making things up. She's at that age."

"No I'm not!" Maressa roared. She looked at me. "I can read! Maresi taught me, didn't you? Maresi, *tell* them!"

I rose slowly. There I stood in my fire-red mantle, the likes of which no one in Rovas has ever seen. I wished fervently that I was not wearing it at that moment. I wished I had not shown compassion for the condemned man and his daughter, and had not been seen talking to them. I wished I was in my bed at Novice House, safe under my blanket.

"Of course the girl can't read," I said slowly, almost as if I were slow myself. "No one can, apart from the high lords in the nádor's castle."

Maressa's eyes filled with tears. She hid her face on Jannarl's shoulder and sniffled. "Stupid Maresi," she whispered. "Stupid, horrible Maresi." Jannarl held her tight to prevent her from saying anything more. The soldiers forgot about the little girl and directed their attention at me. Jannarl and Maressa managed to slip unnoticed into the crowd.

"Maresi," said the soldier. "And where do you come from, Maresi?"

He knew my name now. My whole body was shaking. "From Assa. In the north."

"Do you know this criminal?" He pointed at the unconscious man on the ground. I shook my head. "Why were you speaking to that woman?"

I could think of nothing to say. The young woman on the ground looked up. There was fire in her eyes.

"She was trying to rob him! To see if he had any coins or salt in his pockets."

"I see." The soldier laughed. "And your cloak, did you steal that too?"

Suddenly I knew what I must do. I whispered the name of the Rose, stood up straight and smiled straight at the soldier. "No. It was given to me by a salt merchant. For my services. I am his special favorite."

The smile that spread across the soldier's face made my stomach turn. "Is that so? You must be very talented in that case." He straightened his trousers with a gloved hand.

I swished my cloak and stuck out one hip in a way I hoped was alluring. "You can ask him yourself."

"Maybe you could show me your talents? Tonight, once I'm off duty. I can't give you a cloak like that, but I can pay well."

I smiled at him suggestively. "Where will I find you?"

"At Gennarla Farm, you know where that is?"

With a pounding heart I nodded, curtsied and disappeared into the crowd. No one followed me.

When I reached the edge of the market square, I could no longer hold it in. I fell to my knees and vomited. Mother found me there and helped me to my feet. She pulled off my cloak and rolled it into a bundle under her arm as she dragged me back to my aunt's farm. We set off at once, without waiting for cover of darkness. I had to hide under yarn and linen and sacks in Gray Lady's cart until we were well away from the village. Maressa lay curled up among the bundles and cried the whole way home. Because she had not gotten the fried piggy she was promised, because she had to leave her relatives' wonderful farm and the exciting market, and because her beloved aunt had betrayed her.

We set up camp when we reached the forest, and Mother and I walked back to the footbridge over the stream in the dusky evening light. Three children and one toddler waited for us there, silent and frightened, and we brought them back to our camp as quickly as we could, and gave them all something to eat. They traveled with us in the cart back to Sáru, and Maressa soon put them at ease. Full bellies helped to put them at ease too.

I think that perhaps Silla could make the journey south to Menos in the spring. We cannot send her now that winter is coming, but it is the right place for her—I can feel it. She needs the knowledge and protection that only the sisters can provide. I have already started planning the journey, and Mother and I are sewing and knitting clothes for her and the other children. Silla and Berla are staying with us, while Mik and his little sister (whose name turned out to be Eina) are living with Náraes and Jannarl. Mik adores Jannarl and follows him everywhere, keen to show off what a little man he is. Dúlan and Eina are of a similar age, and Náraes says that taking care of two little lasses is much the same as one. I cannot say I believe her, but she seems content enough. Only Maressa is not entirely pleased about the newcomers, but Mik is her obedient servant and does everything she asks and demands, which placates her somewhat.

And Berla, black-haired Berla. She is around nine years old. She says very little. She is difficult, always pilfering food and other items, or hiding in hay barns and drying houses, going missing for a day at a time, or longer. But she always comes back. She will talk to no one but Silla.

Your friend,

Maresi

Venerable Sister O,

When we returned home from our trip to the Murik market, the soldiers had found their way to Jóla. I am certain that my absence was to blame. I have only been intentionally protecting my home village of Sáru, but I believe that the protection has extended to Jóla, for no one has demanded taxes or harassed the inhabitants there for a long time either. As soon as I left the villages the protection weakened. It must have retained its integrity around Sáru, but for a short time Jóla was exposed, and that was all it took.

The soldiers plundered barns and sheds mercilessly in the name of taxes. As luck would have it, Géros had seen the soldiers approach and managed to beat them back to the village via the quicker forest trails. Forewarned, all the young girls had time to hide in the underground storehouse that they have dug into the side of the hill, and which is so overgrown with grass and bushes that the soldiers would never find them.

In Sáru we held a council in Jannarl and Náraes's home and decided to donate what we could to our neighbors in Jóla. Thus our stores are not as well filled as they were at the beginning of autumn, but we will manage.

Now I walk around both villages morning and night. I slam the protection down into the earth so hard that my whole body vibrates for a long time afterward. I comb my hair so vigorously that it is starting to feel a little thin, but my protective braid is thick and long. I am frightened, Sister O. I am frightened for the future of my homeland—of this world. And I do not know what I can do about it, or whether I even can do anything other than protect those nearest to me.

I have reopened the school, which is good, for it gives me something else to think about. It is much easier to teach the children to read and write now that I have the sand table for them to practice on. I fear that the nádor may hear tell of my school. I know that he would not allow it. I am quite sure that he has learned my name by now. Maressa revealed my name, and the fact that she can read. I managed to divert their attention, but the soldiers may yet have realized that she really was reading what was written on the notice. My hope is that they themselves cannot read, or at least not very well, and that they were simply given the paper and an indication of what it said—or rather, what it did not say.

I dare not think about what might happen if the nádor finds out that there is someone in his province who not only can read, but is teaching others how to read as well. I do not believe the salt merchant's lies. The nádor is not an innocent intermediary; he is the root of the people's suffering. He will show no mercy to those who try to lift the Rovasians from their ignorance.

I have three new pupils in the school: Silla, Mik and Berla. Mik is overjoyed to be freed from responsibility for his younger sister for part of the day and is making a genuine effort to learn. Silla disturbs my other pupils a great deal, but I have hope that she will calm down with time. Berla mainly sits quietly and stares out of the window, but she has started to answer questions when asked and, strangely, it always turns out that she has been listening and, if she chooses to answer, she is always correct.

Yours,

Maresi

M y dear Ennike Rose,
It has become truly cold now. It is still autumn, but the weather is oblivious to this, and not only are the nights frosty but the days too are bitterly cold. The wind is unusually strong as well. Every morning the schoolhouse is freezing, and even though I go in as early as possible to light the fire, the children still have to wear their outside clothes for half the school day to keep from freezing. And still their fingers are chapped and red as they hold their sticks and practice writing letters. I make them run several times around the long table now and again, to keep their body temperatures up.

Marget has a way with Silla, and since the two have become friends Silla has calmed down and stopped distracting the others as much. Often Silla goes home with Marget after school and helps around the house. Sometimes she stays there for the evening meal as well.

Marget accompanies me on my walks around the villages sometimes. She does not disturb me, but having her there does make it different. When I asked her what she was doing she answered: "Listening. Learning."

She wants to understand how I am guarding the villages, how I drive my energy into the earth. I wish I could explain, but I have no words to explain it. Naturally this would be the thing she finds most fascinating. For the first time since returning home, I feel like I have gained a true friend. She wants to be my friend not simply because we knew each other as children, but because of who I am now: Maresi, banisher of frost, wearer of the red mantle, teacher, foreigner.

Marget spends the evening at our cottage sometimes, and helps with whatever I am doing: repairing a garment, boiling whey, grinding roots for some concoction. If I read aloud to the family she sits at my feet, wrapped up in a large cardigan that used to belong to her father, listening intently. Her eyes glisten with emotion, even when the text is not sad. It is almost like having Heo here. I like it.

ᛒ

I walked past Kárun's cabin in the first light one ice-cold morning, before the sun had risen and when it was still gloomy beneath the trees. I saw that several shingles were missing from one corner of his cabin's roof. It must have been that way for a while, but I had never noticed it before. It was still early so I knew he would be home. Without thinking, I walked straight up to the door, knocked and entered.

It was not much warmer inside than outside. Kárun was in the process of lighting a fire, but I saw that the water bucket by his door had iced over. He must have just risen but was fully clothed, in a leather waistcoat and boots. I suspect that he sleeps in his day clothes. I quickly shut the door behind me but still felt drafts being drawn in through the cracks.

Kárun brushed the bark from his hands and shut the smoke hatch. "Is all well with the school?" he asked.

He has a very deep voice, and I can almost feel it vibrate inside me. I quickly averted my gaze from the hole in the roof. Rain must leak through it into his house.

"All is quite well. The table you built makes it much easier to teach the children. I have three new pupils now; maybe you heard about the children we brought home from Murik?"

"Yes, your father mentioned them when we met in the forest the other day. That was a good thing you and your family did, Maresi."

"It was Mother and Father's idea. They could not stand back and watch children starve."

"They are good people, your parents. It's no surprise that you turned out as you did."

There was tenderness in his voice and it made my cheeks hot.

"The books you gave me come in useful daily, and the abacus likewise," I said suddenly. "Only . . ."

"Yes?" He came a little closer, for it was dim in the cabin and difficult to see properly in the half-light. I took one step closer to him as well.

"It is cold in the mornings. I have to light the fire long before the children come, and still it is so cold that I struggle to hold their attention." I wriggled my toes inside the boots he gave me. My feet are never cold when I wear them.

"I've done all I can to seal the gaps," said Kárun. He withdrew from me a little. Suddenly I was very aware of the growing distance between us. Everything I said was coming out wrong. That was not at all what I had meant to say.

"It's not that," I stammered. "I was just wondering . . . it would be a great service and kindness to the children if you would consider moving back into the school. Then you could light the fire in the morning and it would not be so cold when we arrived. You are out working during the day anyway, which is when we use it."

He looked at me questioningly. "I won't say no to that," he said slowly. "I haven't had time to do up the cabin here as much as I'd have liked before winter. The rain and wind get in."

"What a blessing it would be to arrive in a ready-warmed building," I said, suddenly aware of how formal and stiff I sounded.

"As long as I'm not in the way," said Kárun. I shook my head but could not bring myself to look at him. I was in no hurry to leave, but could think of nothing else to say, so I backed out of the cabin with a few mumbled words.

Yesterday the school was closed so that the children could rest. Then, as I was going to school this morning, I saw smoke rising from the chimney from a long way off. There were footprints in the frost on the stone staircase up to the door, and when I came inside it was warm and cozy and smelled faintly of porridge and smoke. I think he lives on porridge, Kárun. Up against the wall was a roughly hewn bed. It was neatly made with the linen I had given him.

I think I will bring him some food from time to time, as a thank-you. He cannot manage for long out in the forest on nothing but porridge day after day. Even after sharing our stores with the villagers of Jóla, we have enough food to survive. Mother will not miss a sausage here or a piece of bread there. And my goats are still producing good milk, so sometimes we have cheese. Sometimes I wonder whether we will have to slaughter my goat kid this winter—well, she is hardly a kid anymore. It would be wonderful to have two goats to milk in the future.

Yours,

Maresi

Venerable Sister O,

Your letters have arrived! They came to me via a most unexpected route—I had not dreamed I would receive letters from you twice in the same year! Kárun was waiting for me outside the school one day when I opened the door to send the children home. He grinned, revealing deep smile lines. It was plain to see that he had something special to share with me but that he was waiting until all the children had gone running down the brown hillside. Then he entered and retrieved something from his coat sleeve.

"I was given this by one of the fur-trappers traveling upstream from Kandfall," he said, handing me a thick roll of papers. "The ice hasn't formed yet. He got it from a merchant who had sailed north, he didn't say where from. It's for you."

I was overcome with such joy that I had to sit down, because I knew at once what it must be, and I took the roll and pressed it against my cheek. To hear from you again, and so soon! Kárun smiled at me.

"Welcome news, I see."

I nodded happily with tears in my eyes. "Letters from home," I whispered.

"From home," he repeated, and looked down at his hands. He turned and walked outside, toward the forest.

I was grateful for a place to read in peace. But this time I have not started my replies straightaway; I am savoring the prospect instead. I know that these letters will have to wait until after winter to be sent. I have plenty of time. You all write such long, beautiful letters! I am so ashamed of my sprawling, incoherent scribbles.

Your letters are a special treasure, Sister O. I can feel your encouragement about my school and the importance of inclusion. As I have already written to you, I have accepted boys from the start. You are right, Rovas is a very different place from Jai's homeland. It is not that knowledge is withheld from women here—it is withheld from every-one. Men and women have always done everything side by side in these parts. It would have been very silly of me to exclude boys from the school, I see that now. I suppose that was simply the way I was used to picturing education: schools are for girls; knowledge is for women. But I am learning. I am learning all the time, Sister O.

I have thought a lot about what you wrote about focusing on uniting rather than excluding. Do you mean that I am wrong to protect the villages as I do? But what would have happened without my protection? Your words have fed my concerns, Sister. You said that you cannot advise me or tell me what is right or wrong, for the ways of the Abbey are not the only correct ways. Nor are they necessarily appropriate for a place like Rovas. You are right about this, of course. Yet I believe that I must also recognize my own limitations, must I not? I certainly cannot protect the whole of Rovas from the nádor. That is impossible. I am but one woman and my power is not so great. I wonder if even the Crone's power is great enough. By "uniting," do you mean that I should gather all of Rovas here, within the boundaries of my protection? If only I could speak with you and ask for your advice!

Your letter said to find wisdom within the scriptures, but I do not understand how. I have read everything I brought with me many times over, as well as the books Kárun gave me, but I find no answers.

And yes, I am praying to the Crone, but she is silent. Or perhaps she is speaking from a distant place, beyond a wall, and I cannot hear her words, only a murmur that makes my teeth ache.

My sister is with child again, and I feel nothing but a strong warmth exuding from her. None of the Crone's chill this time. I believe it is the warmth of the Mother aspect I can sense. It glows red on the insides of my eyelids. Meanwhile my own mother's health is deteriorating. The sound of her coughs tears me apart from the inside, and Father has developed a new worry line on his thin face. Sometimes Mother goes to bed in broad daylight to rest. That has never happened before.

Thank you for the paper! It was the best gift you could have sent me. I am always in desperate need of paper.

Thank Heo for her message. Her words were so wise that I barely recognize my little Heo. I suppose she is not little anymore, and novice to the Moon besides. The Moon need not choose, she wrote, and I understand what she means. She means that the Moon carries all three aspects of the Goddess: the Maiden, the Mother and the Crone. But I am not the Moon, nor the First Mother. I am only Maresi, and my path is narrower.

Now it occurs to me that Kárun must have paid that fur-trapper for the letters. Someone like that would never have done a service without asking for something in return. I must be sure to repay his expense.

Your novice,

Maresi

Dearest Jai,

Thank you for your three long, heartfelt letters! It felt as though you were here beside me while I read them. I intend to reread them often, whenever I feel lonely. My longing for the Abbey is different now from when I wrote to you last autumn and winter. It has neither disappeared nor lessened, but I have learned to live with it better. After what I did for the village on the Iron Night, and after finally starting my school, I have found my place here. I even have a new shadow: Marget. Though no one will ever take your place, Jai!

She sounds nice, that Tsela. Strange to think that someone else has come to the Abbey who loves to read as much as you and I! I am sure that you are right: she and I would be fast friends. But you will make certain that she is very careful with the oldest scrolls, won't you? Sister O is extremely protective of them, as you know. It makes me slightly anxious to know that Tsela is particularly fond of reading them. Are you certain that Sister O does not mind her going into the treasure chamber so often?

Do not be so harsh on Náraes. She was right! I do need to ensure that I fulfill my task and mission. Ever since I told you about the promise she asked of me, I have succeeded in keeping it. I gave up my little dalliance with Géros (which, by the way, could have ended very badly for everyone because I was not protecting the villages when I was with him!) and founded my school. With help from Kárun, of course. I am doing what I came here to do, and a little more besides: I educate and I protect. But this does not seem to satisfy you, nor Sister O. You are both scolding me, and I fear that you are angry with me. Don't be angry, please, Jai. I could not bear the thought of disappointing you in any way at all. Especially when I cannot even understand why! You would not want me to marry my first suitor, surely? Like Árvan? You cannot imagine the life of a married woman here. Or, perhaps you can—think of your own mother, with her household and children. Did she have time to spare for anything else? Anything of her own? Could she have run a school, and taken care of sick people, studied and continued learning? No, you know that she could not. And these are all things that I want to do.

Of course there is a part of me that dreams of life with a man as well. After all, I have had a taste of it now, with Géros, so I know what I am denying myself. But it is not so important. And as for children, well, I have my nieces. They are more than enough. My sister is with child again and will soon have a newborn to take care of, so she will need more help than ever. Besides, the children in my school need me.

I am so glad that you light a candle for me every night. Sometimes I am afraid that everyone on the island will forget about me. Others are taking my place, like Tsela. But now I will think of the candle in your window and let that flame warm me in my longing.

Your friend,

Maresi

M y dear Ennike Rose,
    Your impressions of Géros seem funny to me now. The summer I spent with him has become a distant memory. It feels as though it happened to a different Maresi. I am not in the slightest

bit ashamed of what happened, nor the things we did. Everything we shared brought me closer to the Maiden and her secrets, I know that. You describe it so beautifully: "akin to prayer." Those experiences have given me a greater understanding of men and women, the strength and power of the physical body, how these forces can affect people, and their significance for life itself. It is invaluable knowledge to gain, for I believe that I could easily have made a foolish decision.

ᛒ

When I came to the school half a moon ago, to my great surprise Kárun was there. The schoolhouse was cold and dark. I came in to find him lying in his bed, pale and with eyes shut.

"Are you sick?" I cried out with worry. I stamped the frost off my boots (it still had not yet snowed) and came to his bedside. He shook his head.

"My leg," he said shortly. "Broken."

I immediately lifted the blanket, though he tried to stop me.

"Which? This one? Where?"

"The shin," he murmured.

I examined him, just as Sister Nar taught me, and felt a distinct fracture. He made no sound but a sharp intake of breath. His leg was a little warm, but I was thankful that the break felt clean and the bone was not crushed. I did not ask how it had happened. He is a woodcutter: there are a thousand ways he might injure himself in the woods.

"How did you get home?" I asked instead.

"Walked," he squeezed out.

"I'll give you something for the pain, and to prevent fever and infection. And then I had better make a splint." I carefully laid the blanket back over him, and hastily went to light a fire in the hearth. "You can explain to the children. I'll be back soon."

He tried to say something as I left but I closed the door on his protests. I met some of the village children on my way home, and told them

223

what had happened and that I would be late. Once home, I scrambled together the necessary herbs and a few odds and ends before rushing back. I am so proud of my pupils—they had brought in more firewood, and water from the stream, and Péra and Lenna had put water in a kettle on the fire so there would be hot water on my arrival. I took the opportunity to teach them about medicinal herbs, and how best to utilize the plants' various qualities when preparing tinctures and salves. My friend Marget paid close attention to everything I did and was a great help. Kárun was given a brew to drink to keep pain and fever at bay. Then I showed the children how to make a splint for a broken bone, if it is as cleanly broken as Kárun's, and explained how to set the bone straight if it is crooked. Marget helped me to wrap Kárun's leg in soft wool that I had brought from home, and then we splinted it with two thin planks I had gotten from Akios. He took it all very well, said nothing and just breathed through the pain.

With that done, I made a soup for Kárun to drink while he lay in bed. Then I looked at the expectant faces of my pupils.

"It has been a most peculiar day so far. What do you say we forget about our normal lessons and I read aloud from Erva's collection to you and the patient?"

The children whooped with joy, and I took the book out of my bag. Then I read the story that begins: "When the serpent Keal first slithered up from the depths of the ocean, the realm of Lavora did not yet exist, and many small tribes lived in constant battle with each other. Olok, the hero, came from one of the smallest." I am so pleased that I have some books in the children's own language!

The serpent Keal can be a little frightening, and the elder children took the youngest ones in their arms so that they would not be scared—or perhaps so that they would not be scared themselves. Kárun lay perfectly still in bed and listened too. I would have thought he was sleeping, he was so still, but I saw his eyes shining. He did not take them off me.

When I had finished the story I sent the children home, and told them not to come the next day so that Kárun could rest. Marget tidied away my herbs and dressings and cleaned the mess I had made cooking soup.

Then I made sure that Kárun ate a little.

"Your tea helped the pain," he said once he had eaten. "But the story helped even more. You read well."

"I am glad your pain has lessened. You cannot have slept much last night."

"No."

I looked at him closely. His cheeks were so pale that I guessed he was still in great pain. All at once I found I could hardly stop myself from reaching out a hand and stroking his forehead, his hair, his rough cheeks.

"You need sleep more than anything else. I hate to leave you alone."

"Send Akios. He can help me if need be."

I blushed. It had not occurred to me that Kárun would probably need help to relieve himself.

Akios willingly packed a blanket and a few things and set off in the twilight to spend the night at the school and help Kárun. Then I visited this morning and made breakfast for them both. On arrival I seemed to interrupt a serious and intense discussion between them. I have tried asking Akios about it but he skillfully dodges my questions.

Kárun insists that I must continue with the school.

"I didn't build this house for it to become an infirmary," he said in that earnest way of his. "When winter comes into full force the children will have to stay at home. You have half a moon at most before their parents keep them indoors. So let the children come. It doesn't bother me. I might learn a few things."

So the children will come, and the school will continue.

ᚹ

225

For ten days now I have been teaching with Kárun in the schoolhouse. It was difficult at first, but I have gotten used to it now. Used to his eyes permanently locked on me, and the way it makes me feel.

His gaze has an effect on me. I can admit that to you. You predicted as much in your most recent letter. How could you know something that I had no idea about?

Sometimes my knees go weak just from being near him, I have to sit down, and there is a buzzing in my ears that barely allows me to hear what the children are saying. I want to be close to him, for the same reason I wanted to be close to Géros, but for other reasons too. My body desires him, but beyond that I want . . . I am not sure what I want. I like taking care of him, making sure that he eats properly, has clean sheets on his bed and that he is well. But more than that, I simply want to be with him. Talk to him. He has told me all about his childhood. After his mother died little Kárun had to take care of himself. When he was old enough to tend the fire, his father would often go out logging and hunting in the forest and leave him alone for lengthy periods. On these occasions Kárun would wander far and wide. "I got lost so many times throughout the year that I learned never to get lost again," he said once. He always felt at home with Tauer, and it was Tauer and his wife who made sure he was clothed as a boy. I asked him once if he ever felt lonely, and he smiled at me. He is slow to smile and it reminds me of the sunrise over the forest edge, gradually illuminating his serious face, more and more, until the sun transcends the treetops and suddenly bathes everything in a golden light. I feel as though I light up inside as well. I am always hoping to make him smile. "I am never alone," he answered. "I am surrounded by the trees. The birds, the animals, the wind and sun. I always have the best of company." He can recognize every bird by its song, every animal by its paw tracks, teeth, claws and droppings. He has even made friends with some animals, and his voice becomes soft and warm when he talks about the doe that showed him her fawn one spring, or the hedgehog that visited him every evening when he lived alone in his cabin during the first year following his father's death. When his voice warms like that, I wish that he would continue talking forever.

When I read aloud, I am reading to him. Recently I read the love poem "Unna the Seafarer," and every word pulsated between us.

But more than anything, I like the way he looks at me. Whenever possible, his gaze lingers on my face or body for the briefest of moments. The feeling it ignites in me . . . I have no words for it, Ennike. I know that he desires me. I am not so naive. I could surrender to this weakness throbbing in my body, and he would not protest if I joined him in his bed. I dream about it, every night alone in my own bed. His broad chest, his strong arms—I want to feel them around me. I want to feel his skin beneath my fingers and lips. I want to inhale his scent deeply.

I am blushing as I write this. But you are the Rose, so you understand. You know what power is hidden in the body and desires of a woman.

Yet it is not the Rose I serve. I belong to the Crone, though I never officially became her novice. Being with Kárun would be different from how it was with Géros. I would not be satisfied with only his body. I would fall into the trap that Náraes made me promise not to fall in. I must not let anything distract me from my calling.

I am writing about this only to you, and not to Jai, because she would not understand. In her latest letters it seems as if she wants me to choose a different path. I wonder if it is because she is so fond of children? She does love looking after the junior novices. I have never felt that way about children. Of course I adore the little ones at the Abbey as well, not because they are children, but because they are themselves, if that makes sense? Especially Heo. But she is more like a sister to me than a daughter.

My choice is no great sacrifice or sorrow, believe me. But it is with a certain melancholy that I gaze upon Kárun and know that that life is not for me. Maybe it is wrong of me to embrace the pleasure of being close to him, of taking care of him and listening to the tenderness in his voice when he talks of the forest that he loves so profoundly. The pleasure of trying to make him laugh, and that flash of happiness when I succeed. I do not want to hurt him, or lead him to believe that there is a chance of something more developing between us.

Soon he will be healthy again. He will resume his solitary life, and I mine. This is only right and proper. Still I cannot help but feel, my Ennike Rose, that when this happens, my world will be grayer for it.

Yours,

Maresi

WINTER

Venerable Sister O,

Mother is terribly sick. It has become impossible to ignore. Tauer and I have both tried to treat her cough with all the brews and concoctions we know, but they have brought her only brief respite, and even that is getting harder to achieve.

Winter has come and snow has fallen. School is closed because it is difficult for the children to get there, but I would have canceled school in any case. I do not want to leave Mother's side for long. I leave her only to walk around the village with my staff, and Father and Akios stay with her when I do. For several days now she has been too weak to leave her bed, and I fear that soon she will be unable to get up at all. She eats meager portions, and often cannot even keep those down. She had very little extra flesh to begin with, and now she is so thin that I can count her ribs when I wash her with a moist rag and help her into a clean chemise. I try to coax her into eating by preparing the same kinds of food she used to make when I was little. I flavor them exactly how she used to, but it makes little difference. She only takes a few spoonfuls anyway. She has tried—she is so incredibly brave—but it simply is not working.

"It can't be much fun to be mothering your own mother suddenly," she said the other day and patted me on the hand. "I know what it's like to watch a loved one transform into someone you don't recognize."

"You cared for me when I was little," I said, swallowing back the tears. "Now it is my turn to take care of you. And you are just the same as you have always been. You are still my mother. Nothing can change that."

I fear that she will die, Sister O. I believed I no longer feared death. I believed that the Crone was my friend, and I had overcome the terror that affects most people when they stand before her door. I was wrong, Sister O, how terribly wrong I was. I was young and stupid and full of arrogance! It is only my own death I no longer fear. Losing a loved one is a different matter altogether. I have only just got my mother back, after so many long years apart. I refuse to let her go now. I feel that if only I can sit by her side day and night, the Crone cannot come for her.

She still has strength to speak, though she is often silenced by severe coughing fits, and she likes to hear me talk. I read aloud to her and tell her about my time at the Abbey. She listens now in a way she did not before.

"I was devastated when you left," she said one evening as I sat massaging her feet with sheep fat. Her voice was weak and I had to lean in to hear her. "A part of me died. Then when you came back, full of all these things I've never seen or experienced, and calling another woman Mother, I found it very painful. You had experienced so much without me. You were entirely your own person. It felt as if you no longer needed me."

"I do need you, Mother! I always need you—I cannot manage without you!" I could say no more. I weep anytime she starts speaking this way.

"Of course you can," she said. "And it's a great comfort to me to know that. That's what Leiman said to me before he died, and I understand now what he meant. You should know that I don't regret letting Father send you away. Not anymore. Because otherwise you wouldn't be the woman you are today. I'd be worrying about you, and wondering if you could take care of yourself. But now I know that everything will be fine."

Then she started coughing, and I told her to speak no more. She soon fell asleep. It is a relief when she sleeps, for I know that she is not in any pain. I went inside, where Father was sitting before the fire with a knife and some whittling work in his hands. But he was not whittling. He was just sitting and staring into the shadows. I sat next to him and leaned my head on his shoulder.

"She has lived a good life," he said slowly. "She has said so. She said that she's been happy with me. She doesn't blame me for anything."

"She will continue to live a good life," I said. But then Father sat up straight and turned to face me.

"Maresi, you are blind. She is dying. You must realize that. All we can do now is help her to have as good a death as possible."

I could not believe that he would say such a thing. My own father!

"We can't just give up!" I cried.

"You think this is a battle you can fight," said Father, putting his arm around me. "But it's not. There is no one to fight against."

He is wrong, Sister O. Tell me he is wrong! I drove away the frost. I can fight against the Crone. She *shall* bow to my will. I have no intention of letting her in. I walk around the village and beat my protection into the earth, and I know that I can keep her at bay. I sing songs—Rovas songs and Abbey songs—and I feel in my guts and my bones how impenetrable the protective shield is.

This time I am the one who decides.

ᛒ

Several days have passed since I last wrote. Mother has stopped speaking, and it is an effort for her to breathe. I feel powerless. If Sister Nar were here she could surely cure her, but my knowledge and abilities are not enough. All I can do is sit with her. I spoon-feed her water now. Drop by drop.

Akios can hardly bear to come into her room any longer. He goes out, despite the bitter cold. I do not know where he goes, but he takes Silla and Berla with him, for which I am grateful. It is difficult having outsiders in the house right now. Náraes comes to visit every day. Sometimes she brings the children with her but usually she leaves them at home. She wants them to remember their grandmother as she was before, she says. That makes me angry.

"Why do they need to remember her at all? She's right here! She's not dead!"

I expected Náraes to be angry and to argue with me. I wanted an argument. But all she did was take me in her arms and hold me. She said nothing.

Outside a terrible snowstorm is raging. It is beating down on the house so hard that the walls are shaking. It is the worst we have had all winter. Sometimes I think I can almost hear the voice of the Crone on the wind and in the icy drafts that creep in through the cracks in the walls. But I do not see her door, and I cannot hear her calling for Mother. Father and Náraes and Tauer are all wrong.

Father and I take turns to stay by Mother's side. Right now she is sleeping in my bed. Akios sleeps on the ledge above the fireplace and I feed the fire to keep the cold at bay. Sometimes I have to step out of the room awhile, for it is so torturous to hear Mother's gasping, strained breath. Her limbs are ice-cold and no matter how much I rub and massage them I cannot make them warm. I have a pot of water over the fire where I brew various herbal teas, weak ones, that I feed to her. But nothing seems to afford her any relief.

ᛠ

It is one day since Mother stopped speaking. She is so thin that her skull is clearly visible below her sparse hair. Náraes and I have cut it short, to stop it from tangling into knots. Mother lies with open, unseeing eyes, though sometimes her eyes seek mine and it seems that she is trying to ask me something. I know not what.

I barely remember the last time I slept properly.

I have little appetite myself. Father cooks porridge and Náraes brings bread, but I cannot eat. Walking around the village is becoming harder and harder, not only because of the storm that refuses to relent, but because I am so weak. It feels as though something out there, the Crone's murmuring tone, is pressing down on me in the gray winter light.

Father and Akios are busy building something out in the wood-shed. I know what it is. They go out shortly after daybreak. Planing and sanding, sawing and nailing. It infuriates me, but there is nothing I can do. Just keep Mother alive. That is what I am doing. She is alive. Everyone says that she has not long left, yet she lives still.

ʊ

Later.

Náraes came to sit with me this evening, when Father was tending to the animals and Akios was out somewhere, I know not where. I was sitting with my porridge bowl in front of me, and she nudged the spoon closer to my hand.

"Eat now. You mustn't grieve yourself to death. Maresi, Mother has led a good life. Not as long as some, but good all the same. She's had Father and us. Let go, Maresi."

I saw that Náraes was crying. Her tears looked so unfamiliar. Everything inside me hurt. I wished I had tears to cry, but my eyes were dry.

"I miss her," whispered Náraes. "I miss my strong, vital mother. That's how I want to remember her. Not as she is now. All I wished her was a quick, good death, but it doesn't seem that she is getting that."

I pushed the bowl aside and stood up. I could not listen any lon-ger. Mother's room was filled with the sound of her short, wheezing breath. She was lying under several animal hides, yet she was so thin that the bed looked almost empty. When I sat on the edge of her bed she looked straight at me. She uttered a noise. First I thought it was only a whimper, but when I leaned nearer I heard that she was forming a word.

"Out," she moaned weakly. "Out."

"You want to go out, Mother? There is a storm outside. It is too cold."

She looked at me pleadingly. Then I understood what she wanted. By Goddess, the realization cut through me like a knife. It hurt a hundred times worse than when I was stabbed in the belly in the crypt. I was the cause of all of this suffering. The fault was mine, and no one else's.

"Yes, Mother. You can go." I was crying so hard that I could barely get the words out. "Forgive me. You can go."

My tears spilled onto the ring on my finger—the ring you gave me. It glinted like the metal on the door of the Crone. The door that I had not seen, even though Mother was on the brink of death. She had been on the brink for a long time.

I got up and picked up my staff from where it was leaning against the wall. I went out. It was a clear, starry, ice-cold night. The cold struck me like a blow, permeating my nostrils and my chest with every breath. I could feel the protection I had built up during all these moons of walking around the village, like an imprint in the air. It extended down into the earth, among the tree roots deep below. The very air tasted of it: metal and soil. I raised up my silverwood staff to the black sky, high above my head, and I struck. Again and again. With each blow my carved staff met the barrier. The wall. The protection I had made. It was strong, Sister O. It was forged of all my fear of hunger and starvation, my fear of the nádor's men, all my fear of losing everyone I had only just been reunited with. It was forged of my knowledge, of the symbols of power on my staff, of the ancient magic of colors and hair, and the life force of the First Mother. When my staff met the protection and I could feel how robust it was, I understood that it was not constructed by my power alone. No such thing could come from an ordinary human. It was the boundless power of the First Mother and I was merely its channel. It is the same as the power of Anji, the spring that bestowed gifts upon the First Sisters; it is the power that Arra invoked when she sang forth the wind and fire and mountains, it is the energy that Heo's foremother traveled through to restore balance to her people. It is the energy that helped me to open the Crone's door in the crypt and slay all those men. It is a force far greater than any one person: it is the life force behind all things.

But I did break through the wall. With red-chapped hands and my back aching with strain, I breached it, Sister O. I walked around our house and tore down my own work. I was knocked down by the wave of force that hit me when the barrier gave way. The hum, the murmur, the trembling in the ground enveloped me, and suddenly I could hear the sounds it was made up of. *Maresi, my daughter*, whispered the Crone.

I scrambled to my feet and went inside. Around Mother's bed sat Náraes, Father and Akios. Father held one of Mother's hands, Akios the other, and Náraes caressed her head. At the foot of the bed stood the door of the Crone. I walked over to Mother. I bent down to kiss her and whisper my farewell. They are words that I do not intend to share with anyone. They belong to Mother and me. Our final words.

Then I rose and walked to the Crone's door. I had no blood on my hands, not mine, nor the Rose's, nor Mother's. But I had opened this door once before. It knew me. My hand reached for the handle—shaped like a snake swallowing its tail, just like the ring on my hand—and opened the door to the Crone's realm.

This time I spoke first.

"Take what is yours," I said into the darkness. "Free my mother from her suffering."

Maresi, whispered the Crone, and her voice no longer frightened me. It sounded tender, Sister O. It sounded almost like your voice. The handle of the door was cold in my hand, and the air was filled with an odor I recognize so well: the breath of the Crone. But it was different this time, when I had opened the door calmly and purposefully. No blood offering was necessary. There were no screams. I let Mother pass through. She took a short breath and became completely still. My hand was still resting on the handle. There came one final, gasping breath, and then no more. I know that the Crone had received her, and that Mother had been made party to all the Crone's mysteries—and the Crone to hers.

Then I closed the door, slowly and quietly, and with an aching heart. Now my mother is no more.

ᛒ

Náraes and I have prepared Mother for her burial. Washed her, combed her short hair. She no longer looks like my mother. Her facial expression has changed. She is already somewhere else. Once she was ready, we stood and looked at her.

"You got more time with her than I did," I said, unmoving. "Three years before I was born, and eight years while I was away."

"I know," Náraes said, and squeezed my hand. "It isn't fair." She sighed. "We may as well go through her clothes now, so we know what to dress her in."

She opened the lid to the chest by the bed, and we took out Mother's few garments: three blouses, four chemises, one everyday skirt, one special skirt and an embroidered apron for festivals. Right at the bottom of the chest we found an object tightly wrapped in a gray woolen cloth. I reached my hands in to lift it out, and we laid the bundle on the floor and unwrapped it together.

Inside was a sword. It was long and heavy and sharp, and had clearly seen more than one battle. Náraes and I looked at one another. I lifted the sword carefully and examined it. Two words were engraved on the hilt. Not by a smith, but scraped as one does with a nail or other sharp object. Náora, it said. Mother's name. And Leiman. Suddenly I remembered that Mother had mentioned the name Leiman when she was sick.

"She got it from her first husband," Father said from behind us. We turned around. He was standing above us looking down at the sword. "She was carrying it when I found her in the woods. She said his name

236

many times while she was delirious with fever and my mother and I were taking care of her."

"Was Leiman her husband?" I stared at the name on the sword.

"Yes. They married when they were very young. He was already dead when she came here."

"How did he die?"

"I don't know. Náora didn't want to talk about anything that happened before we met, so I didn't ask. We got married, and I was always amazed that she actually wanted to be with me. I suppose she lived a very different life when she was young, but I know her as my wife and mother to my children. And my heart's true love."

I had never heard such words come from Father's mouth. I got up and embraced him. He truly loved her. I barely know who she was, yet I know all I need to: she was my mother.

We are blessed to have each other: Father, Náraes, Akios and I. We are not alone in our grief. We talk about Mother, we remember her, we recreate her as she was before she fell sick. I think about what she said to me, that she no longer regretted letting Father send me away, because it was thanks to the Abbey that I had learned to manage without her.

I know she is right. It is strange, Sister O. I miss her terribly. It is like an enormous black hole in my center. But at the same time she is still very much present. The only difference is that now she lives through me instead of her own body. I carry all that she was inside me: in my body, mind and heart.

ᛠ

Mother has been lying in her bed all day, and the villagers have come to bid farewell with songs and small gifts. Father and Akios have prepared the funeral pyre. At this time in winter we cannot dig a grave in the hard-frozen earth among the roots of the silverwoods, so we must burn the body and scatter the ashes in the burial grove instead.

She is lying in her casket now, which Father and Akios so lovingly made for her. Náraes and I wrapped her up, and the little girls laid down gifts of grain, salt and bread. When dusk falls the men will carry the casket to the pyre outside the village, and in the wintry starlight Father will light the fire.

I do not know if I can witness it. I will try. But the mere thought of the fire that is set to consume what was once my mother is too awful to bear.

When it is all over—these things I cannot think about—the ashes will be taken to the burial grove. It will not be an easy journey, for it is bitterly cold and fresh snow has fallen, making travel difficult. I hear the Crone's whisper again, as I heard her at the Abbey. I could not hear her before through the protection I had built around the village. My barrier shut out even the Crone herself. I did not believe such a thing was possible. But shutting out the Crone could not keep death out of the village.

We could wait before making our way to the burial grove, but both Father and I have a feeling that it must be now. Náraes agrees. "You have appeared in my dreams," she said to me today. "Under the silver-wood trees. But the trees are bleeding."

Father made a simple scabbard for Mother's sword. My siblings and Father all agree that the sword should be passed down to me.

ᛒ

The others are still asleep, but I am dressed and eating porridge and writing to you. I am about to set out to accompany my mother on her final journey. I am thinking of you, Sister O, and I need to share my thoughts with you. It has occurred to me that I am unlikely to be pres-ent when your time comes. I cannot aid you in your passing into the realm of the Crone. I cannot accompany you on your final journey or be there when your bones are laid to rest in the cold dark of the crypt. This hurts. But what is more painful is the fear, gradually transforming into a certainty, that I will never see you again in this life. I hope you can forgive me. I need to write the words I never spoke to you, Sister O. You are very dear to me. You gave me the most precious gift I have: my love of knowledge and the written word. You made me feel safe when I came to the Abbey as a child. I remember how you stroked my hair, and were the first person to touch me with tenderness since my own mother. I can never thank you enough for all that you taught me, or all that you have meant to me. For you allowed me to choose my own path, even when that path led away from the Abbey, and from you.

I have dressed myself in every garment I own, for this midwinter is the coldest that Rovas has ever known. I am taking my staff with me, and the sword. I am reminded of an image I once saw on a silver bowl in the Temple of the Rose, when Ennike, Jai and I were helping the former Rose to polish silver and copper. It depicted the Warrior Maiden, with bared breasts, flowing hair and a ferocious expression on her young face, with sword raised high above her head. It is with this picture in mind that I carry the sword as I accompany Mother and guide her true. The Crone is whispering to me now. I hear her very clearly. *Maresi*, she whispers in every shadow. *Maresi*, she howls in the biting winds.

Something is waiting for me out there. The Black Star is dark, the moon is low, and the longest, darkest night of the year stretches before us. It does not bode well, Sister O. I can feel it in my bones and my blood. I have gathered all my letters in the chest by my bed, and on top lies a note with instructions for Akios, written in large, clear letters so that he might be able to read it without Maressa's help, asking him to ensure they get sent. Just in case I do not return from this journey. For I wonder if this is not what the Crone has been trying to tell me all along. She is warning me of a great danger, but she is also calling to me. Luring me. Now that I can hear her I am no longer afraid—not in the least, Sister O. I know that I walk in the footsteps of the Crone. I know that she will steer my hand, if need be. My actions are my own, and I bear responsibility and blame. Yet I am not alone. I will never be alone, as long as I let the Crone in. I have imagined her before as a hungry, black-mouthed witch with yellow teeth and scraggly hair and scratching, claw-like hands. Even after I opened her door for the first time and learned not to fear her, this image has remained. No longer. Now she has the face of my mother. And what I remember of my father's mother, whom I never saw be wicked or angry. All the wise, strong women who have passed through the Crone's door before me have lent her their faces and wit, their voices and hearts. Why should I fear them? They are with me now, and I am not afraid.

I am ready.

ω

Later.

I am writing this in a shelter we made in the forest. It is very cold. Forgive me if my handwriting is difficult to read; my fingers are frozen stiff. The fire is of little help. Yet I must write now, for soon it may be too late.

I dread recounting what has happened. It is so unbelievable, so awful. I do not know . . . I do not know how we will ever recover from this, Sister O.

When we left the village it was bitterly cold. Everybody in the procession carried something that had belonged to Mother, or that she had made or given them, as is our tradition. Garments, a jar of salve, knitted gloves. I took her sword and my woven belt. I carried the pouch of ashes. Father walked before me, marking the trees along the path to help Mother find her way, and Náraes and Akios walked behind me scattering juniper twigs and singing the songs that prevent her from returning from the realm of the dead. I pondered this as I walked bearing the pouch and beating my staff into the ground in rhythm with the songs. Why are we so afraid that the departed might return? Could we not live alongside them, if need be? Or do we fear that they would bring some nameless terror back with them from death's realm, or else that they would drag us down there with them? Why would they do that? If they loved us in life there is no reason why they would not love us in death.

I am not sure what I believe about death, Sister O. Is it truly a realm behind a silver door, or do I only envision it in that way in order to snatch a glimpse of the unfathomable? Is there really a world under the roots of the silverwoods? Or is death something else entirely? Can we see what happens in our world after we have died, or is contact broken forever?

We came to the offering grove first.

But the offering grove was not there.

As I have already mentioned, the grove lies in a valley. Ancient, enormous, broad-leaved trees grow around a central elder oak where our offerings are made. A stream runs to the northeast.

All that remained when we arrived at the valley's edge in the early afternoon was the stream. The trees were gone. Stumps were in their places, some as large as the foundation of a small house. There were visible tracks on the ground where the trunks had been dragged away, and there were big piles of brushwood and branches all around. We all stopped, quiet, dumb. A ghostly wind whined through the empty valley. There were traces of woodcutters' fires, and I remembered what Kárun had said.

I should have known. I should have seen the signs. Perhaps it was my protection around the villages that prevented me from doing so, or perhaps my mind was too filled with concern for Mother to notice anything else.

Maresi, the Crone whispered on the wind. *Hurry.*

"My father prayed in this grove," Father said slowly. "He honored and made sacrifices to the land. As did his father and mother before him. And I remember my grandmother saying that her mother had done the same, and the elder oak was already great and ancient then."

"Where will we make our offerings now?" Náraes said helplessly. We spoke no more. We continued toward the burial grove, silently agreeing to quicken our pace as much as possible.

Our offering grove is used only by Sáru and Jóla. Other villages make their offerings elsewhere. But the burial grove, that is for the whole of Rovas. Those who live farther afield have various traditions with their deceased. Either they burn the bodies and bring their ashes to the grove, or they bury them close to their villages, dig them up again when only skeletons remain, and bring the bones to the grove for their eternal rest under the canopy of the sacred silverwoods. But all who die in Rovas end their journey in the burial grove sooner or later.

Dusk fell. We continued tirelessly under the narrow sickle of the moon. My hands and feet were like ice, but otherwise the cold did not bother me. I beat my staff into the ground. The earth heeded my call. Rovas responded and bade me hurry.

It was long after sunset when we reached the deep valley where the silverwoods grow. Thanks to the snow, we could still find our way. The path down to the valley cuts between two hillsides. But it was no longer a path; it was a cleared road. Up on the slope of the eastern hill we saw points of light glimmering in the darkness, though we heard nothing. We could only assume that they were the woodcutters' night camps. I held Gray Lady's halter and led her toward the path into the valley, and prayed to the Goddess that she would not feel the urge to bray. The sleigh runners glided silently over the snow. We did not speak; we hardly dared breathe. At the edge of the valley we stopped. A cloud masked the moon, and thick darkness lay before us. I gripped Náraes's hand. We held our breath and waited.

The cloud drifted past and the light of the narrow moon spilled into the valley. Everything glittered and shone as though made of silver. The trees were still standing. I swallowed, and leaned heavily on my staff.

Yet as we descended into the valley, we saw that they had already begun their work. The nearest silverwoods lay felled, with branches still intact. It was too dark to find our family burial tree, so we set up camp among the slaughtered trees and lit a fire. It was a risk. We did not know what the woodcutters might do if they saw it. But without fire we would not survive the night.

ʊ

Early next morning we stamped out the embers and continued deeper into the valley. Father led us to the right tree. Akios sacrificed a chicken, Náraes hung a silverwood spoon in the branches, and I dug away the snow to expose the soil and stuck a copper coin under a tree root. I could not make so much as a scratch in the frozen-solid ground. Father scattered Mother's ashes in a circle around the tree, on the naked soil, while we all sang the song of the earth. As we sang I looked upon the faces of my family, and knew that though we each have our own personal sorrow, none of us needs bear it alone.

Afterward I walked three circuits around the tree, and said a prayer to each aspect of the First Mother, one with each turn. Then I stood for a while and watched the daylight brighten over the snow-covered ground and snow-white trunks and leaves, and silently thanked my mother for all that she taught and showed me.

When Father and my siblings started to pack up, I pulled my red mantle tighter around me and slipped away unnoticed to walk back through the white, snow-silenced forest to the mouth of the valley. The cold bit my cheeks. My staff kept trying to slip out of my gloved hands, and Mother's sword bounced uncomfortably on my back.

The woodcutters had entered the valley by that time. A team of five men was already trimming the felled trees, while smaller teams of two or three were walking around and examining the living trees with axes at the ready. All in all, there were perhaps twenty men. I saw no soldiers.

But I knew that they would come.

"Blessings on your hearth," I said. Some men looked up, and then away without answer, and I knew them to be Rovasians. They knew what they were doing, what taboos they were breaking by even carrying an ax in the burial ground of their own ancestors. The others just stared at me, with fur hats pulled low over their foreheads.

"Seven generations of a Murik family rest below that tree," I said, and pointed at a tree that two of the men had just been inspecting. "And that cluster is the final resting place of every single inhabitant of the small village of Isto in southern Rovas."

"Leave us be," said a beardless man of short stature wearing a knitted neckerchief over half his face. He took a few steps toward me and fingered the ax that hung in his belt, but came no closer. I posed no threat.

"I command you to stop," I said, and planted myself firmly with both hands resting on my staff before me. "This is sacred ground." I raised my voice so that everyone could hear me. "This is the forest where everyone in the whole of Rovas has been buried since time immemorial. Thousands and thousands of bodies rest beneath these trees. The ashes of just as many are scattered on this sacred land. This is death's realm. Turn back and never return, and may you be spared the wrath of the Crone." Then it occurred to me that none of these men were familiar with the Crone. I searched my memory for what I knew of Urundian belief, and the beliefs of my own people. "Great is the wrath of the ancestors," I said sternly. "And the bird Kalma does not guide a traitor true on his last journey below the roots of the silverwood."

The men whom I had guessed to be Rovasians backed away from the trees and exchanged anxious glances. They lowered their axes.

"We're not afraid of some biddy, young or old," said the man who I assumed was the foreman. He spoke calmly and without anger, though bordering on irritation. "We're just doing our job. The young lady should get home. It's cold in the forest today."

"I cannot do that," I said. My voice was also calm. I turned to the Rovasian woodcutters. "This is the sacred ground of Rovas, and you are Rovasians. Shame on you who would raise your axes against the trees of your ancestors. Will you cut down your own mothers' and fathers' trees too? Will you follow orders blindly?" I turned back to the foreman. "This is death's realm, and this realm is mine. The dead are my people, and I am their guardian."

Then I saw the door of the Crone. It stood to the left of the men, high and glistening and silent. All I had to do was walk over and open it. I knew that it would obey my hand. I knew that it would accept the offering. The burial grove is the Crone's dominion, just like the crypt beneath Knowledge House. She would devour the men, just as she did when I opened her door before at the Abbey.

"Oiman, we can't do this," said one of the elder men. The Rovasians had gathered in a group now. They looked at each other and then at the foreman. "It's more than just bad luck to harm a silverwood."

"Now look here," said Oiman patiently. "The nádor said to cut him down some silverwoods. He gets a phenomenal price for them in Urundien. And silverwoods grow only here—we know this. So this is where we fell."

"Then we can no longer work for the nádor," the woodcutter said solemnly.

Oiman shrugged his shoulders. "Fine, but you'll forgo payment for the whole winter's work, mark my words."

The men muttered among themselves, but did not move.

"Suit yourselves." He turned around and pointed at a group of Urundians who were standing by a fallen tree. "You lot can start felling instead."

The man who had answered for the Rovasians shook his head. "We can't let you do that." The Rovasian men spread out into a semicircle in front of the tree, their hands on the shafts of their axes. Oiman's expression grew stern.

"It's like that now, is it?"

He stepped toward the men who remained loyal to him, and they briefly conferred. The Rovasians were all staring at me. I heard another mumble of voices and turned around. Behind me, among the trees, was my family, watching. Náraes stood holding her hands protectively over her belly, and Father and Akios wore stern expressions. They were waiting; they would not leave me alone.

Eventually, without a word, Oiman and his men packed up their tools and ropes and bound everything tight to their timber-horses. Without looking back they set off up the path and disappeared out of sight. Náraes rushed over to me, with Father and Akios close behind.

"You did it!" She grasped my hands. "You drove them away!"

Father went over to the woodcutters and greeted them with a nod.

"They'll be back, won't they?"

"Yes," said a man, a younger one this time, with fair hair and kind blue eyes, but a severe expression. "And more will come."

"With soldiers too," another man added. "Many soldiers." He pointed at my staff. "Are you the frost-banisher?"

I nodded.

"What do you intend to do now?"

I looked over my shoulder at my family. "I think I will send them home, and stay and do what I can."

"Send for supplies from home in that case. Food, blankets, furs. Weapons." He turned to the other men. "We can build a barricade here, with the felled trees. This is the only path down to the valley. Marek, you and Lessas are in charge of moving our equipment down from the hill—if the others haven't taken it. Biláti and Merran, you build shelters for us and the frost-banisher."

But first, the men all stood around the felled trees, and the elder man, whose name was Uvas, led them in an awkward prayer for forgiveness.

Then they set to work.

ш

Three days have passed. The men worked swiftly to build a decent barricade with the trunks of the felled trees. They have put up three shelters. They wanted to build a separate one for me, but I persuaded them to let me sleep in one of theirs.

"You are my brothers," I said, "and I trust you as brothers."

They hummed and scratched their beards, looking humbled and rather pleased. There are five of them. Marek, with the fair hair and kind blue eyes, is the youngest. He and Lessas come from a village in southern Rovas. I believe they are related somehow, cousins perhaps. Biláti is from the west and has three children at home: one son and two daughters. He misses them terribly and talks about them at every opportunity. Then there is Merran, with a beard all the way down to his chest and a large scar across one eye, who comes from a farmstead very close to Murik. Uvas, who led their discussion, has worked as a woodcutter and timber-rafter his whole life and therefore does not consider himself the inhabitant of any one village. I asked if he knew Kárun, which he did. He holds Maresi, friend of Kárun, in higher esteem than he held Maresi, banisher of frost. Kárun has a good reputation as an honest, hardworking man. Uvas said he has worked in the same timber-rafting team as Kárun for many summers.

Father and Náraes were not pleased about being sent home and took a great deal of persuasion. Akios flatly refused, and when it became clear that my brother would stay by my side, Father finally agreed to do as I asked. Then today both Father and Náraes returned with the supplies I had asked for, packed on Gray Lady's sleigh. However, it was not only food and furs they brought with them—the whole village had followed, and Jóla too. Can you believe it, Sister O? They all came! Even the little children were there. Only Kárun with his broken leg and the most immobile old folk had stayed behind. The Jóla horse pulled a sleigh piled high with supplies and little children. Náraes held me in an extended embrace, and I leaned on her, grateful to breathe in her familiar scent. It was almost like an embrace from Mother.

Almost.

Then Marget rushed over and hugged me tightly.

"Náraes told us what you did," she whispered in my ear. "How brave you were. How strong. But you needn't face it all alone, you know. Whenever you need help, you must say so. We do know a thing or two as well."

"I know, Marget," I said. "Though perhaps I never realized it before. For a long time I believed that the Abbey's teachings were the only kind of knowledge that mattered. I was convinced that I had to do everything myself. But you have all shown me that I was wrong. I am so glad for your help."

It is time I put a stop to all this exclusion: shutting out friends and family from my life and the world from our village. Instead I will open myself to those who would help me. And, what is infinitely more frightening, I will open myself to the world. I will not look away. I will at least try to change things. Make things better. It feels terribly presumptuous to write this down—I probably sound ridiculous. In which case please forgive your former student. Write it off as the foolishness of youth, if you wish. But I believe I have finally understood my true calling.

Your novice,

Maresi

Dear Jai and Ennike,

I am writing to you both together now, because paper and time are scarce. We are building a proper camp in the burial grove. How long we will stay here, we cannot say, but letting the children sleep in the open air night after night is simply not an option. The woodcutters have decided to stay. They are helpful, hardworking men, and they have helped us build two log cabins. They are very simple, unsealed constructions of unstripped logs, with fireplaces directly on the ground and smoke hatches above, like in the olden days. Still, it is better than exposure to the elements. The woodcutters sourced the logs from the hills above the valley, of course. No one raises an ax to a silverwood anymore. I have even seen several of them seek out their families' trees and make offerings to their ancestors.

It is not right to take up residence in the burial grove. This is sacred ground, forbidden for anything other than burials and for anyone other than the dead. Here we should speak with hushed voices, make offerings to the deceased and then depart at once. The elder folk, in whom old customs and traditions are deeply entrenched, say that there is a chill here that penetrates their bones to the very marrow. It keeps them awake at night. I feel it too—the Crone's iciness. It is making me sluggish and slow. But we cannot leave the valley unprotected, unguarded, even for a short time. So I have had to help my neighbors get used to living and sleeping among the dead. It has not been easy, for they fear the spirits of the departed. I told them the story of the wolf that ran with its pack, and only when it lay dying did it realize that the others had been ghosts the whole time. It is an old Rovasian ballad that most locals have heard since they were little. I have used it as a tool to illustrate that the dead harbor no evil intent toward the living. Making offerings at the burial trees has also helped. Kild, who is now the eldest in our village, has led everyone in several offerings to our ancestors and to these trees and this soil. This also seems to have brought people comfort.

We have shelter from the cold and wind, and we have food, and we are waiting. We do not know what we wait for, or how long it will take. Uvas, leader of the woodcutters; Grandmother Kild; Kavann, the eldest of Jóla; and I have taken to gathering in the mornings to discuss what we think may happen, and what we must do.

"I can defeat whoever comes," I said during one of our first councils, and nobody questioned me. They believe that I am capable of anything I claim.

"Then more will come," said Uvas, scratching his beard. "The nádor will send more and more."

"And we cannot guard this place forever. Not even you can do that, Maresi," said Kild.

"You are right. So what shall we do? I can create another protective shield to hold them at bay—at least, I believe I can—but it must be maintained continuously."

"We have little understanding of your abilities, Maresi Enres-daughter," said Kavann slowly. "But we must give the nádor enough of a fright that he never attempts to lay claim to this forest again."

"Then it won't be enough only to frighten his soldiers, or even to kill them," said Kild.

She was sitting very straight, with her crutch beside her. She has not been able to walk without it since the soldier's horse crushed her hip. Her wrinkly hands were resting on her embroidered skirt, and she looked like the epitome of an old Rovasian woman at the end of her life, when nothing is expected of her other than spinning by the hearth, surrounded by children and grandchildren. Yet there she was making plans with me and the two men. The Crone is strong in her. I am glad to have her by my side. Our side.

"We must show the nádor himself what we are capable of. What *you* are capable of." She looked at me, determined and somewhat exhilarated.

"Soldiers will undoubtedly come," said Uvas. "And they're bound to send word to the nádor. Can we take advantage of that? We must bring him here."

"I believe I know how," I said.

Then I told them about the comb and the storm and everything that happened on Menos that spring. It felt good to speak about it. I could see that the men grew scared, though they tried not to show it. They stole glances at each other and then looked down at the ground. We were sitting around a little fire under one of the smaller silver-woods, where the woodcutters had rolled over some tree stumps for us to sit on. It was our place for council. The elders' place. And mine.

Kild chuckled in delight when I had finished my story. "That's what we'll do then," she said several times and nodded. "Just like that."

"But these men cannot die," I said. "They must live and tell the nádor of what they have seen."

"So shall it be," said Kavann.

ᚹ

We have been waiting for ten days now.

We have improved our defenses, built a higher barricade and made a plan for how the villagers can escape, if need be.

I have started holding short school sessions every day in one of the two cabins. Many of the adults come in, sit down and follow the lessons for a while. I am pleased that they can see what I am teaching their children. Particularly when I read aloud, whether from one of the school's books or my own, the cabin is chock-full.

ᚹ

The soldiers attacked at dawn. I was forewarned of their coming when the Crone woke me by whispering my name. I got up and stepped over the sleeping bodies on the cabin floor, where several others were also stirring. As soon as I opened the door I heard their approach: the whinny of horses; the clatter of weapons; the crunch of snow beneath horses' hooves. The woodcutters were on guard by the barricade, and I could see the glow of their pipes in the half-light. I went inside and put the sword on my back. I took the staff in my hand, and had everything else I needed in a pouch hanging from Mother's woven belt around my waist. I put one of Sister Nar's leaves in my mouth and chewed on it as I walked slowly outside again. I woke no one, but many sat up when they heard the clangor outside.

I managed to climb to the highest log of the barricade and stationed myself up there before the horses could reach us. The door of the Crone appeared next to me, idle in midair, invisible to all but me. I

251

patted the doorframe to steel myself. I do not want to open the door. I have not told Sister O this yet, and perhaps I never will—I might not live to write another letter. I do not wish to cause more death. There is enough death in the world as it is. Jai, I think you understand this more than anyone. You have also killed. We have never spoken of it, but I know that it torments you. I have heard you talking in your sleep. I have heard you crying. I do not want to open the door to death's realm for any other reason than to help a worthy person have a good death. What I never told Sister O, or anyone, is that I still hear the screams of those men in the crypt. I hear the crushing of their bones; I smell the scent of their blood. They haunt me at night. They had threatened us. One of them had stabbed me. And still I wish that they need not have died.

Yet I must do what I must do. My personal wishes are no longer important.

I positioned myself next to the door of the Crone, took out my comb and chewed on the bitter leaf until my mouth was filled with saliva.

"Stop!" I called, when the first horse came into view. The soldier on its back reined in the horse and held up a hand. The others joined him, and I counted twenty soldiers in total. All heavily armed and on horseback. Many, but not too many. The nádor must not have been expecting much resistance—why should he? As far as he was concerned we were just a few measly woodcutters and peasants.

"This is forbidden ground," I said, and my voice carried far in the quiet winter morning. It resounded between the hills and echoed among the trees. "These trees are sacred. Those of you who come from elsewhere do not understand this, so I am telling you now. Under each of these trees, several generations are buried. This entire forest is a burial ground."

"I recognize her!" called one of the soldiers from the mass. "The whore from the market!"

I could not see his face, but I knew who was speaking. I clenched my teeth, and tried to keep my hands from trembling. I heard the villagers come out of the cabins behind me and take up position behind the barricade. Quiet and watchful. They could do little to help me. But they were there. They did not forsake me. I glanced quickly over my shoulder, and saw that the women were standing a little to the side and were about to let down their braided hair.

I held my staff firmly in one hand and the comb in the other. The sun rose above the treetops. It was going to be a cold, clear, windless day.

The soldiers' captain spoke.

"Surrender and no one will come to harm. The nádor is willing to forgive you, if you return to your homes immediately."

I could hear the soldiers behind him snigger and whisper. Of course he was lying.

None of the soldiers carried bows, from what I could see. To hurt us they would have to climb over or go around the barricade.

"I offer you the same forgiveness," I said. "This is the dominion of the Crone, Kalma, the Great Wolf; whatever name you give her, it is the same thing: death. Surrender, and you may live."

The ground hummed beneath me. The Crone whispered in the shadows. The commander raised his hand to order the others to attack.

I stuck the comb in my hair and pulled several long, hard strokes. Then I turned around and threw the comb to the women who stood gathered in a tight cluster to the right of the barricade. Marget caught it. Her hair was loose and her face wore an indecipherable expression. She stuck the comb in her hair at once. And then came the wind.

The soldiers were approaching. I looked up to the sky, where dark clouds had formed out of nowhere, summoned by our wind. Our call. I whispered to the Crone, to the mistress of darkness and tempest and cold, to lend me her aid and strength. I took hold of the staff with both hands and thrust it hard into the silverwood log beneath my feet. This wood, which had spent its life conversing with many generations of our dead through its roots, answered with a low ringing that reverberated between the hillsides. It penetrated the ground and merged with the hum of the Rovas soil. The masses of snow perched high on the hills replied with a muffled rumble that grew in strength. The soldiers reined in their horses and looked anxiously upward. The snow set in motion in a billow of white.

The women behind me combed their hair, and the wind increased in strength—a dark, unstoppable wind full of ghostly whispers. The snow began rushing down the hillside. The sun was obscured by a dark cloud.

I stood firm and held my staff and thought of Arra the Raven-Haired, who moved an entire mountain with her song, and I knew that I could do the same if I had to. For I was not alone: I had support. The breath of the Crone was seeping through the cracks in the door. I looked straight at the commanding soldier.

"Leave, while you still can! And bring a message to the nádor: this is what the people of Rovas are capable of. We can summon the wind. We can unleash the mighty heavens upon you. See how we conceal the very sun! We will not back down. And we demand that he comes here in person to parley. For no one harms the forest of the dead."

They hesitated for a moment, but the rumble of the snow was unmistakable, and when one of the soldiers at the back turned his horse around and set off at a gallop up the hill, the others soon followed his example. They just barely avoided the avalanche that came tumbling down from two directions at once. I had to leap down from the barricade to avoid it myself. But the mighty timber held. The pass between the hills filled with snow, blocking the way in and out of the valley.

Your friend,

Maresi

Most Venerable Mother,
We are awaiting the arrival of the nádor. Everything hangs on him heeding our summons. But something incredible is happening: many more are coming whom we did not summon.

The whole of Rovas is here.

The first people arrived a few days after the soldiers left. They came from villages in the south, not too far away. They crossed the fallen snow with skis and sleighs to enter the valley. They brought food and tents. Whole families are coming, with children and all. Some have a pig or goat with them.

"Blessings on your hearth," said an old woman among the new arrivals.

"Blessings on your journey," I said.

My own village assembled to greet everyone, somewhat reservedly. Marget and Akios went around offering cups of hot tea. We have no moonshine. Once the old woman had drunk I squatted beside her in the snow and accepted the half-full cup she handed to me.

"How did you know to come?" I asked.

She was the type of woman whose face brings joy to all who look upon it, with round cheeks and the warmest brown eyes among all her wrinkles. She patted me on the hand, in a way that reminded me of my mother.

"The dead called to us," she said. "Night after night. The ones who have made their final journey to the realm below the silverwoods came to us in our dreams. The elders held council and realized that it must be a summons. The dead need us. So here we are."

We told them all that had happened. We decided that the children could sleep in one of the cabins we had built, to keep warm at night.

And day after day, more people come. They have heard the call of the Crone, or the dead, or the earth itself—I could not say. But they are coming. At first it was something like a harvest festival, then an autumn market, and now it is a larger gathering of people than I have ever seen. The atmosphere is strange: somber, weighty. Everyone knows why we are here. We are here to make a stand, once and for all. To show those men who dominate, suppress and exploit where the line is. It runs right here, before the realm of the dead. Before all that Rovasians hold sacred.

Our relatives from Murik have also arrived, reluctantly, drawn by the call. Aunt Míraes is here with her husband, Tan, my cousins Tessi and Bernáti, his wife, Selas, and their children. Bernáti had not wanted to come, his sister Tessi told me when we met. He resisted until the end, saying it was all superstition and it would be foolish to leave the farm empty and unprotected. But the dreams would not leave him in peace, until eventually he refused to sleep at all.

"Every night when he closed his eyes he saw all his neighbors and friends who had died of starvation and disease. Silently they dragged him down with bony hands, wanting to take him below the silverwood roots. He is afraid of them." She shook her head. "My grandmothers called me with the lullabies they used to sing to me when I was little. They sat under their burial trees and sang, so sweet and tender, and the dreams made me very happy. It was like having them here with me again."

Everyone has been contacted in a different way, from what I understand. But everyone has heard the call, some through love and others through fear.

Tessi thanked me for taking care of the orphaned children that her own family had prevented her from helping. I told her that all thanks should go to my mother and father, not me. And then I wept, as I often do when I speak of Mother. I do not weep because I am torn apart by grief, but because tears lighten the burden. I am so glad to have had these last years with her. So glad that we could be together, and that I could see so many different sides to her that I never knew before. I wish that she would visit my dreams and call to me, so that I could be with her again. But it has not happened.

Meanwhile, people are generally in high spirits, especially the young. They have never experienced anything like this before. The threat is abstract and unimaginable to them. They are meeting old friends and new, and all the conversations around all the fires flow back and forth from early morning to late at night. There has never been so much life beneath the crowns of the silverwoods. And not only is friendship blooming, but love too. I am sure that a child or two has been conceived here. So you see, Venerable Mother, all three are gathered here: the Maiden, the Mother and the Crone. They bring me strength and comfort. Whatever may come to pass, all aspects of the First Mother are here with me. I know now that they have always been here, and I never left them behind as I once thought. But now I feel it unmistakably, even physically: the ground is simmering with their power. Though it is midwinter, I feel it—it is life itself, and death, in their eternal dance.

We have passed the longest night of winter and the light is returning. There has been some sunshine and milder weather. It is good. The shelters keep out the worst of the cold. I have even heard birdsong on the sunniest days. The snow crust is hard enough to go out hunting, so teams have been heading into the woods for game, and we are getting by. This is the Crown's forest, of course, but necessity knows no law. Deer and hares and various wild birds are roasted over open fires by teams of cooks. Several porridge pots hang over other fires, and everybody helps themselves as they need, and adds a little flour or cornmeal to the pot in exchange.

But the most magical, wonderful part of all of this, Venerable Mother, is that the parents bring their children to me in the morning.

"If the children of Jóla and Sáru are learning all that reading and writing, then our children certainly won't be worse off," they say.

I have more than a hundred pupils now. It is a miracle! After such initial struggle to convince even people I had known all my life to send their children to my school, I now have more pupils than I can manage! I have divided them into several groups, so that they can all get at least some benefit. One group for the more advanced students, one for the very tiny ones, one for the middle, and one for the elder children. Akios helps me to teach a basic introduction to the world of letters and words. I teach them letters, to write their own names, and to read each other's. I also read aloud to them, and the grown-ups often join us. The whole forest quiets down to listen to my voice.

Venerable Mother, when I speak, everybody listens. Old and young alike. Can you believe it? Do you remember when I first came to the

Abbey, clumsy and ignorant and childish? Could you have envisioned this back then? I certainly could not! The strangest part is that I feel like exactly the same girl now as I did then. I am always a little afraid of making a mistake, of exposing myself, and of people realizing that I am just a child and nobody they should listen to with such attention. It helps to know that the First Mother is with me. But only a little.

So this is the current situation of life in the valley. Nobody's needs are going unmet. But waiting is difficult, and not knowing what will happen when the wait is over is more difficult still.

Respectfully,

Maresi

My dear Ennike Rose,

Kárun arrived yesterday. His leg has healed enough for him to safely put weight on it. A group of people from Murik passed the schoolhouse with a horse and sleigh and he asked if he could ride with them. I did not go to greet them. I stopped doing that a while ago. So many people have been coming that we have had to take shifts to welcome the newcomers, show them where to build their shelters, explain to them what has happened and how everything works in the camp. There are shelters stretching far in among the silverwoods now.

He came looking for me at dusk. I had withdrawn, in need of just a grain of solitude, and climbed up on the barricade, which is hardly necessary now that the snow from the avalanche almost reaches the top. We are building no more defenses. If the nádor comes with an entire army then ordinary defenses will be of no use. We have a different plan altogether.

I enjoy straddling the highest log and watching the sun sink behind the trees on the southern hill (now during winter the sun goes down in the southwest rather than directly west), and then watching the stars compete to be the first to shine. The Black Star is this evening's winner. The Crone's eye among all the darkness. I was sitting up there when someone coughed below me. I sighed inwardly, for I truly need these periods of solitude to cope with all the responsibilities placed upon me during the day. Uvas and Náraes have taken charge of the running of the camp. I am not sure how my sister became the one to take on this role, but she fulfills it very well. She rushes around all day giving out orders and making sure that the different shifts and cooking teams are working and that everything is running smoothly. She seems to be enjoying herself. Father and Jannarl and Jannarl's parents take care of the girls while she is busy.

Anyway, when I looked down I saw a man in a leather waistcoat supporting himself on a crutch. His breath hung in the air around him like white smoke, so I could not see his face straightaway in the shadow of the barricade. Of course it was not difficult to find or recognize me: no one else has my blood-red mantle. Then he said my name.

"Maresi."

I almost fell to the ground. I had to hold on with both hands. His deep voice pierced straight into my stomach. And deeper down.

Now I must be honest: I have been thinking about him constantly since coming here. I have tried to ignore it, tried to suppress the image of his eyes and his hands, and memories of the few times we have touched. To no avail. Something about those memories makes me feel strong. He has shown me such incredible care from the very beginning. No one else has ever cared about me like he has, my dear Ennike Rose.

"Yes?" I said, so softly that I had to clear my throat and repeat my response a little louder.

"Can you come down?"

"One moment," I called. I took a few deep breaths. Then I climbed down.

The wrinkles around his mouth when he smiles are so beautiful. How could I never have noticed that before? He reached out a hand to help me down, then paused mid-movement and realized that this was not a wise idea. I jumped down without help.

"How's your leg?" I asked, and inspected it. He chuckled softly.

"Well, I can walk. But I could never have gotten here if I hadn't been given a ride."

I forced myself to look in his eyes. It is not just that they are kind, Ennike. Oh, I cannot describe them. Neither can I describe the feelings that flow through me when I look into them. I feel happy, and scared, and hot, and heartbroken, all at once.

"My mother and father called to me. In my dreams. I knew that I must come." He looked away. "I just wanted you to know that I'm here. If you need me."

He remained standing there as though he had more to say. My mouth was dry. I wanted him to say it. But when he spoke, they were not the words I wanted to hear.

"I am but a humble woodcutter, Maresi. I know that. I have nothing to offer you. Not like . . ." He trailed off. "But I will try to give you anything you need. Just ask."

He turned around abruptly and limped away on his crutch.

I remained by the barricade for a long time. The place where he had stood smelled of resin and smoke. Or perhaps I only imagined it.

I have not seen him since. The camp is large. Perhaps he is also keeping himself withdrawn. But just knowing that he is here, close by, keeps me awake at night. My whole body feels aglow. My heart starts to race every time I catch a glimpse of someone who even resembles him among the crowds.

Your friend,

Maresi

Beloved, Venerable Sister O,

This letter will be a long one. I am exhausted to my very bones, but you taught me that I must write things down while the memories are fresh. Any detail might be of importance, and human memory is so fallible, especially with things that are painful to remember. This can be a blessing for ordinary women, but a curse on a chronicler. And I have realized that this is the role I continue to fulfill; these letters are the chronicles of Maresi Enresdaughter's return from Menos to Rovas. Moreover, I know that you will add these letters to the Abbey's archives. So it is as chronicler that I now write, and I will endeavor to do so as lucidly and clearly as I am able.

I will begin with the dogs.

ᛒ

Thirty days after the soldiers' departure from the valley, the nádor arrived. I could not say exactly how many people had gathered in the valley camp, but I would guess it was in the thousands. An unfathomable number. Our situation had become very difficult and food was scarce. Yet no one complained, and, as far as I know, nobody gave up and went home. Of course, we were all very conscious of the possibility that we might not have homes to return to. Who knows what the nádor has done with our deserted farmsteads.

We were on our guard; we had been the whole time. Yet the sound of a bugle early one morning took us by surprise. This was three days ago now. Nothing could have prepared me for the events of the past three days. I have had nothing to hold on to, no good advice to follow. I have acted entirely on instinct, and I still cannot be sure whether I have done the right thing, or if I could have done better. We all came out of our shelters and log cabins and looked to the southern mouth of the valley. High above us, against the white of the snowy hills, was the outline of hundreds of figures on horseback. Weapons glinted in the sunshine, and there was a brilliant display of colors: bright red, deep green, midnight blue, gold and silver on banners and shields.

I turned to my people, poised to instruct them to herd the children into the cabins, as we had agreed long ago. But before I could utter a word the bugle sounded again, and its note rang out loud and clear through the valley. And then another sound: dogs.

They came surging down the slopes, fifty dogs or more, with gaping jaws. The snow crust held firm beneath their swift, light paws. I had no time to react, no time to act; my heart was beating so hard that I could barely hear their baying, and my mouth was too dry to speak a single word. The hounds were streaking toward us, I could see their wide-open red mouths, their long, sharp fangs. I heard screams from behind me as mothers tried to usher their children inside or up into the trees. I thought about my nieces. I thought about my pregnant sister. But mainly I was thinking of myself, Sister O, and the feeling of those teeth sinking into my flesh.

Thankfully, not everybody was as helplessly dumbfounded as I. Fathers, brothers and sons rushed forth to the barricade, armed with bludgeons, rocks, clubs or even just silverwood branches. They would not let the dogs near the women and children without a fight. Women were among them too. Grandmothers with nothing to lose, with long gray braids and home-knitted cardigans, stood wide-stanced and determined, awaiting the attack armed with bludgeons and brooms.

The dogs spilled around the barricade, slipping and sliding on the snow. Our barriers were built to keep out men and horses, not dogs.

"Stop," I whispered. Where I found the strength to speak is a mystery. It was an effort to utter that single word. I had no comb, no staff, no sword. Only my own voice.

The dogs halted. They all turned their muzzles to me and regarded me with shiny black eyes. They stared at me for a long time. Then they changed direction, padded over to me and sniffed at my hands. Their tails were calm and still. Then they simply lay down, rested their heads on their paws and whimpered softly.

Standing in a sea of dogs, I looked around. There was a dense silence. Not even the birds were singing. I saw the men waiting up on the ridge, with their bright colors and shining weapons. Nobody knew what to do next.

They had hoped the dogs would chase us away. They had not planned on a mounted attack, for it is too difficult to ride down into the valley on the precarious snow crust. Our defense was not great, but they could not see our preparations from up there. They must have seen that we were a large gathering from the many smoking fires, shelters and people, though most were hidden beneath the white-leaved canopy of the trees. Nevertheless, they surely understood that we were ordinary folk and no warriors.

The soldiers and brightly colored riders retreated. We paused to breathe and regroup: We got the children to safety as far away as possible and armed everyone who was willing to fight in a possible battle with all the weapons we had: clubs, axes, a few bows. The dogs remained lying in the snow, following my every movement with their dark eyes. It was deeply unpleasant. I was in conversation with Uvas about what to do next when the message came. A messenger was skiing his way down into the valley.

As I walked toward the barricade I saw my family among the people preparing to fight. Only Náraes and the children were not there. Father gave me an anxious look, but then smiled encouragingly. Akios raised a hand. His pale eyes flashed with anticipation. I saw Kárun too. He watched me climb up the barricade and station myself at the top next to Uvas. I stood up tall.

The man on skis was a soldier, but bore no weapon. He stopped before the barricade in a flurry of snow. Then he spoke with a loud voice that carried through the valley.

"His Grace Kendmen Thuro, nádor of Rovas, and Queen Voranne of Urundien cordially request the leader or leaders of their insurrectionary subjects for an audience in their camp."

The Queen! Uvas and I looked at one another in bewilderment. What was the Sovereign of Urundien doing here, at the very outskirts of her most insignificant province? The messenger was awaiting a reply.

"Inform His Grace and Her Majesty that we accept the invitation."

The messenger appeared to be expecting more. I glanced at Uvas. He cleared his throat.

"Inform them that Uvas Hammeirsson, woodcutter and fur-trapper, comes."

He looked at me. I took a deep breath.

"Inform them that Maresi Enresdaughter, banisher of frost and tamer of beasts, she of the red mantle, who speaks with goddesses and opens the door to death's realm, comes."

As the messenger skied back up the hill I smiled at Uvas. "Best to make it sound impressive," I said. "So they don't know what to expect."

He grinned at me through his beard. "You, Maresi, are like no other here in Rovas. If I had a son I'd be trying to get you two married."

"I am never getting married," I said, mainly out of habit.

We climbed down. Father, Akios and Náraes came to me. Náraes's cheeks were flushed.

"So you are to meet the Queen herself," she said.

For a moment I thought she was about to braid my hair or straighten my clothes, but instead she passed me my staff. Akios handed me Mother's sword. I had my comb tucked into the belt that Mother had woven. Then my sister, father and brother took turns pressing their foreheads against mine, ever so briefly. They said nothing more. Then came the others; not everybody in the camp, but everybody from our villages and those whom I had gotten to know during our time in the burial grove. They patted me on the shoulder, pressed their foreheads against mine and murmured: "Blessings on your journey." Marget leaned her forehead against mine for a long time. It was almost like having my Abbey sisters with me, Sister O. And then Kárun came. His breath hung around him like a cloud of smoke. He stood before me and looked me straight in the eye, and my heart was pounding nearly as hard as when the dogs attacked.

I took one step forward and leaned in close to whisper to him.

"Kárun, you are unlike any man I have ever met. No one is as thoughtful or kind or strong. I just want to tell you that I love you." He

264

took a deep breath and his eyes grew large and very dark. I smiled a shaky smile. "I expect nothing. I make no demands. I know that I have a difficult path to walk, and I cannot ask anyone to walk it with me. But I just want you to know what is in my heart."

"Maresi," he said in a voice so deep it vibrated inside me. He said nothing more, and seemed unable to move. I turned quickly around and pulled at the straps that held the sword on my back. Maybe he did not share my feelings as I had thought he did.

Uvas and I attached ourselves to borrowed skis. I used my staff as a ski pole. He had his ax. I had my sword. Before we set off I turned to look at the waiting dogs.

"Come," I said, and they rose at once, almost silently, with hanging tongues and eyes fixed on me. And, followed by fifty hunting dogs, we skied out of the valley.

ᛟ

Twenty soldiers with drawn swords met us up at the mouth of the valley. With dark eyes and furrowed brows they looked at the dogs quietly following me, and at my red mantle and my carved staff. They said nothing, but surrounded me and Uvas and drove us along the path into the forest. It was a quiet, windless day with a gray sky. The forest was brooding, dark and secretive around us. I was afraid, but I reminded myself that this was my land. The nádor and Queen had come here to my land. The power of the earth was mine to employ. This thought kept me somewhat calm.

The snow swished softly beneath my and Uvas's skis while the soldiers marched hulkingly through the snow. Uvas peered at me from under his hood and I gave him a nod. I was thankful for his company, though I knew that whatever must be done would fall to me and me alone. This was my task. I had to make the nádor leave the burial grove in peace, once and for all.

Only I did not know how.

After a while we arrived at a glade that had been artificially enlarged by clearing trees. There was a low wall around it, as defense from wild animals, or robbers, or us in the valley—I could not say which. Soldiers in full armor moved between practical shelters made from spruce sprays and animal skins. In the middle of the glade were two large, opulent tents surrounded by striding courtiers in thick, fur-trimmed mantles and fur hats. When we entered the compound—Uvas and I, the soldiers and all the hunting dogs—everyone in the camp fell silent. All eyes were on me. We were led to the largest tent, where two soldiers held the tent flap to one side to allow us to enter.

"Lie down," I said to the dogs, and they lay down together to the right of the tent, watching me all the while. I saw many men and women make the sign against the evil eye. We removed our skis and went in.

It was warm inside the tent. There was a small iron stove by one wall and a pipe to funnel out the smoke. I have never seen anything so efficient. I wonder if there is a smith in Rovas who could build such a thing? But how would they ensure that the metal could stand such heat?

Around the stove were a number of elegantly dressed men and women. I could not guess who was the nádor out of three men with long mantles and high, soft-leather boots. They looked confusingly similar with their close-trimmed beards and hooked Urundian noses. But there was no mistaking who was Queen. She was wearing a long, moss-green dress of the finest wool and a black mantle edged with ermine. Her hair was as black as a winter night, braided and coiled like a crown around her head, and adorned with jewels that glittered in the lamplight shining from a number of tables around the tent. I knew who she was from her posture, and how the others stood in relation to her, always aware of where she was and never taking their eyes off her, even when they did not appear to be looking directly at her.

"Your Grace, Your Royal Highness." The soldier bowed low. "Presenting Uvas Hammeirsson, woodcutter and fur-trapper." He hesitated and glanced at me. "And Maresi Enresdaughter, banisher of frost and tamer of dogs, she of the red mantle, who speaks with goddesses and opens the door to death's realm."

We bowed low.

"So, these are the Rovasian commoners that you failed to subdue, my good Kendmen." The Queen gestured at us to come closer. One of the hook-nosed men puffed himself up.

"Your Majesty did not give me permission to subdue them," he said indignantly. I saw now that his garments were somewhat more extravagant than those of the other two, and that he wore a thick chain of gold around his neck. "There is no reason for Your Majesty to interrupt her hunting trip for this mere . . ."—he searched for the right word and waved his hand in the air—"triviality," he concluded.

"Practically the entire province has gathered in a valley of rare silverwoods," said the Queen, "despite your assurances that it was only a handful of people." She was looking at me the whole time she spoke, not at the nádor. "They are hindering my governor's men from felling the woodland he has ordered them to fell. They have left their farms and homes unattended to protect this woodland. I should not call that a triviality. I should call it a most remarkable occurrence. And I am curious, dear Kendmen. This is far more interesting than deer-hunting."

The Queen inspected me so openly that I ventured to do the same. She was neither young nor old, perhaps ten years or so older than Náraes. I was ignorant of the fact that Urundien had a queen at all, so she could not have been in power very long. As I stood there listening and being watched, I searched my mind for everything I knew about the history of Urundien and its sovereigns, and particularly about its very few female sovereigns.

"So, Maresi Enresdaughter. And Uvas Hammeirsson." The Queen twisted one of the rings on her left hand. "Why are you hindering the royal emissaries in their work?"

"Your Majesty," I said. I hoped that was appropriate—what did I know about addressing a queen? I gripped my staff firmly in my hand.

"We are your loyal subjects. We have never risen up against any nádor that the Crown in Irindibul has appointed to govern us. We keep to the forests where we may hunt and gather wood, and never touch the Crown's land. So has it been for generations. But this valley, it is beyond sacred." I gestured toward the nádor. "He has laid waste to our offering groves, where we make sacrifices to the earth and the air and all that makes up Rovas. These are the places where we have honored the changing seasons, said prayers and given thanks for good harvests for hundreds of years. Though they are situated in our part of the forest, we did not raise our voice when he ravaged them. But this—this is the burial grove of the whole of Rovas. It is death's realm. The nádor orders the woodcutters to raise their axes against the holiest of holies. Under these white trees lie all the dead who have ever been buried in Rovas. And our dead . . ." My voice faltered.

"Our dead are *us*," Uvas said crisply. "We would just as soon die as violate the graves, for what people would allow their mothers and fathers to be violated?"

"Is that why you have summoned all your people there?" asked the Queen. I shook my head.

"I made no summons, Your Majesty. It was the dead themselves."

"Nonsense," snapped the nádor. "Utter nonsense! Do not listen to the babbling of this mad witch, Your Majesty."

"She can read too," came a voice from one of the darker corners of the tent. I did not look. I could not let myself be provoked. I knew in any case that it was the soldier from the market who had spoken. The Queen raised her eyebrows, but the nádor ignored the interjection and continued to speak, more heatedly now.

"Permit me to lead a mounted attack. We have men enough to wipe out every one of these rebellious peasants."

"Is that so?" The Queen directed her gaze briefly at the nádor. She pressed her lips together before continuing to speak, as if to keep hold of herself. "You propose to slaughter all men, women and children in your own province? Who do you foresee working the land, dear Kendmen?"

The nádor glared at me because he dared not glare at his Sovereign. And that was the moment when I first realized that there was hope. There was hope through negotiation, without bloodshed, for the Queen was neither foolish nor bloodthirsty. However, she was proud. I had to find a way to untie this knot without the Queen losing face, because I knew that if she did she could turn against us in a second. I fingered the skull that Akios had helped me to carve on the knob of my staff, and said a silent prayer to the Crone that her wisdom might guide me on the right path.

"What did you do to the dogs?" asked the Queen, turning back to me.

"I do not know, Your Majesty. I told them to stop and they stopped. I told them to come and they followed."

"And the avalanche, did you do that?"

"Yes, with help. From the women of Rovas, from the First Mother, and Rovas itself."

"What else are you capable of?"

I looked at the staff in my hands. What am I capable of? I have no idea. But I knew that I could not say so. Not there in the royal tent.

"I can do whatever must be done," I said, looking the Queen straight in the eye. She looked back at me, weighing my words. The nádor scoffed.

"Empty words. The avalanche was a natural phenomenon, and the dogs have been badly schooled."

"My own dogs, badly schooled? Is that what you are saying, dear Kendmen? And you hurried here personally when the message of this magical avalanche interrupted our hunt, when we were having such a merry time in the forest."

Every time the Queen used his first name he closed his eyes for a split second, as though it caused him great displeasure to hear his name uttered with such familiarity and obvious superiority. I was starting to see that this nádor was indignant about having a woman as monarch and leader. From the frequency of the Queen's use of the epithet "dear," I supposed that she was far from fond of her nádor either.

The nádor turned to the Queen.

"Your Majesty, I beg you, permit me to take care of these insurgents. There is no reason for you to interrupt your hunt. Whatever happens, whatever this witch can or cannot do, I shall take care of it. There is no reason for you to trouble your pretty head with these concerns. I know a forest nearby that is absolutely brimming with deer and wild boar. I believe there is a large pack of snow-white wolves as well. Should that not be quite the trophy to bring back to Irindibul, white wolfskin for all the ladies of the court?"

The Queen looked at him, and her expression of contempt did not go unnoticed by anyone in the tent.

"Why are you so incredibly keen to fell these silverwoods, *dear* Kendmen?"

"Why, for Your Majesty's sake, of course," replied the nádor. He pulled out a silk handkerchief and wiped his brow. "I do not wish to burden these people with high taxes, so in order to meet Your Majesty's stipulated taxation I must find other forms of income from the province. This type of wood has no equal in all of Urundien. It is hard-wearing and white as snow, never darkens or yellows, and is very difficult to burn. It could even be used in the palace. An eternally snow-white pavilion by the palace pond, perhaps?"

Uvas and I exchanged glances when the nádor claimed that his taxes were not a heavy burden. The Queen looked at me, her eyes shining in the lamplight. Then she gave the nádor a brilliant smile.

"I hold your loyalty and hard work for the Crown in high esteem, my good Kendmen. And you are quite right, these sorts of negotiations do bore me. It is better to leave them to the men." She yawned and stretched. "Eara, Talrana, come, let us return to my tent." The men bowed deeply as the Queen swept away.

The two ladies, beautifully dressed in gray and blue respectively, followed. Just as the Queen reached the tent opening, I heard the nádor mutter: "See how fickle she is. I maintain that the realm cannot be ruled by a woman." I did not believe that the Queen had heard him. Then a loud and commanding voice came from the tent door.

"Maresi Enresdaughter, do you hesitate in following the orders of your Queen? We ought to leave the negotiations to the men. Come."

I glanced quickly at Uvas, who gestured to me to go. I turned around and hurried after the Sovereign of Urundien and Rovas, the nádor's gaze burning into my back.

ᚥ

Now my eyelids are too heavy, dear Sister O. I can write no more, not now. I must sleep awhile. My candle is burning down, and I dare not ask for another. I will continue tomorrow, if the Queen allows it.

ᚥ

It is morning, but two days have passed since I last wrote. I am completely overcome by fatigue. They barely let me sleep here. I was in no way prepared for everything expected of me.

I will continue where I left off.

ᚥ

When I emerged from the tent, the Queen was watching the dogs.

"Do they obey only you now?" she asked.

"I do not know, Your Majesty," I said carefully. "I have never done anything like this before. My powers are not my own. They come to me from the Crone, from the land, from the people of Rovas. There is nothing remarkable about me personally."

"You are the first of my Rovasian subjects I have come across who

271

is able to read," said the Queen with a sour smile. "That is remarkable enough in itself. I believe what the soldier said is true."

"Yes, Your Majesty. And I can write and count."

"Hmm. I would appreciate it if you could pass your authority over the dogs to my houndmasters so that they might take them away. They are in the way here."

I crouched down and looked at the dogs. Fifty pairs of dark eyes looked up at me. "Go free," I said quietly.

One by one they got up, shook themselves and padded away in different directions. Men in brown leather jackets ran over, whistled at their dogs and herded them away across the glade. The Queen was not watching the dogs; she was watching me. Then she turned and walked to the second large tent, followed by her ladies-in-waiting.

This tent was a little smaller but more homely, with carpets on the ground, a travel cot by the far wall, a table with folding chairs and a stove similar to the one in the other tent. The ladies-in-waiting quickly lit the lamps. I stood just inside the tent door and looked on. The Queen muttered something to the lady in gray, who fetched a pitcher and poured a red drink into a vessel of real glass. The Queen raised it to me.

"What is it you say here in Rovas? Blessings on your journey?"

She took a sip from the glass and then offered it to me. I, Maresi Enresdaughter, received a greeting cup from the hand of a queen.

"Blessings on your hearth," I whispered. The wine tasted different from the one we drink at Moon Dance at the Abbey. Much sweeter. It tasted good.

The Queen came over to the table and sat down.

"So, Maresi, banisher of frost. Come and sit. We have much to discuss and not much time to do it."

"Was it a pretext then? Was Your Majesty only pretending to be bored?" I heard the question leave my lips before I had time to think it through, and I cursed my impulsiveness. I still have not learned to control it! But to my great relief the Queen only laughed dryly.

"Naturally. I had to find a way to confer with you in peace and quiet without interference from the nádor. The man is an idiot. And I believe that you have much to tell me that he would go to great lengths to prevent me from hearing. Come and sit now. Queens are not used to having to repeat themselves."

I hastened to sit down at the table, on a stool one of the ladies-in-waiting had provided for me.

"I should make one thing clear from the start," the Queen said seriously, waving to the woman in blue to pour a second glass of wine. "I am the Sovereign of Urundien. The nádor and my male advisers do all they can to deny my authority and encourage me to spend my time on more feminine tasks than ruling the realm. They want me to marry, preferably one of them, and let my husband rule. But this I shall never do. So, you can read, Maresi Enresdaughter. Where did you learn this?"

"Have the songs and tales of the Red Abbey reached the palace of Irindibul?"

She looked at me thoughtfully. "Yes, I had a nurse who told me some such stories when I was a little girl."

"They are not only stories," I said. "I have been there. The Abbey is a real place, on an island in the far south. It is a home of knowledge and learning, sisterhood and work. My father and mother sent me there to save me from starvation ten years ago."

"Has there been much hunger in Rovas?"

"Yes, Your Majesty. Three years of true famine within my lifetime."

"That explains the pittance that reaches the royal coffers from Rovasian taxes," said the Queen. She noticed my expression. "Or does it?"

"Your Majesty, I should sooner say that the high taxes are the reason for these famines," I answered, as courteously as I could.

"Really? I have had my suspicions that the nádor is not always entirely . . . forthright in his accounting. I should like to know more about this province, its people, and its ability to pay taxes. You and I shall have long conversations about this anon. But now we have more pressing matters to attend to. What is happening in the valley?"

I explained everything to the Queen as well as I could. I told her briefly about our Rovasian beliefs, and our view of the earth and the realm of the dead. I mentioned my own beliefs, and the Crone, and how I can hear and feel her, and sometimes see the door to her realm as well. I told her the story of how we came to discover that the forest was being ravaged, and about the Rovasian woodcutters joining our fight. I told her about the avalanche, and the departure of the soldiers and the arrival of the Rovasian people. I mentioned the school I had held for the children too, at which the Queen raised her eyebrows. She did not interrupt me once, but I had clearly given her much to think about. Yet she held her tongue and sipped her wine and let me continue. When I had finished she slammed her cup angrily down on the table.

"Kendmen can plead ignorance to all of this, which I am certain he would if I confronted him. But by my father's beard, as nádor it is his duty to know his province, its customs and traditions! As soon as you resisted he must have realized that he was trying to lay waste to your sacred ground, yet he simply does not care. He is out to fill his own pockets. I have long suspected it but lacked sufficient proof. He let me set the dogs on you all in the belief that you were a handful of insubordinates out to disrupt the orders of the Crown."

She rose and I leaped from my stool. Even I understand that one must not remain sitting when a queen is standing. She began pacing up and down the tent.

"Now he has forced me into an impossible situation. If I yield now, after personally ordering the dogs be set loose, I shall appear weak. I lose face, and my reputation is compromised, but what is worse, I lose the respect of those damned old men I have to keep on good terms with all the time. You cannot imagine the ways in which they try to manipulate me, trick me, steal the crown from me. They think it is easy now that the crown sits on a woman's head. I have to be constantly vigilant against people whose job it is to advise and support me in my duties as the newly crowned Sovereign."

She turned to me abruptly. "I wish your people no harm. Your people are my people, and the duty of a sovereign is to take care of their people, not slaughter them. But the nádor wants to set an example. He is clearly terrified of losing his hold on the province, which he would if he surrendered completely. And I cannot lose face, neither before my people nor before my advisers." She collapsed back into her seat. "Of course, I have no trusted advisers to consult. No one is on my side." She angrily tore down one of her braids and began to fiddle with it.

"Your Majesty," I said, and fell to my knees beside her. "Will you not permit me to advise you? I am no shrewd Urundian adviser, I know that." The Queen looked at me from under a furrowed brow. I swallowed. "It is in my interest that this conflict be resolved without you losing face or respect among your own, while also allowing my people to return home unharmed, and preserving our burial grove, now and forever."

The Queen looked at me bitterly. "Have I any choice?" She sighed and shook her head. "Oh, what do I have to lose?"

She ordered more wine for us both, and invited me to sit back down on the stool. I was so nervous that my mouth was dry. I tried to remember everything I had read about the history of Urundien. There was a potential solution. Just one. I wrung my hands, searching for the right words.

The Queen took out a spindle from a basket by her chair and began spinning. The thread was of the finest, softest lamb's wool, and the Queen's hands were nimble and certain. My nerves were immediately somewhat soothed. I pulled the stool a little closer to her.

"I wonder, Your Majesty, if there is anything that stands above the Crown in Urundien. Something that even the Sovereign must bow to?"

She wrinkled her forehead, still holding the spindle. "I had a shrewd father, Maresi of Rovas. He was never destined to be King, for he was the youngest of three. He felt no duty to have sons, and I grew up on his estate in the hills outside Irindibul, far from the intrigues of the palace. My grandfather lived to a very old age and had the great misfortune of seeing both his eldest sons die, one from disease and the other from a most unnecessary hunting accident." She tutted. "And suddenly my father became King in middle age. But he did not live long. And now mine is the head that bears the crown."

While she was speaking her two ladies-in-waiting produced sweet cakes, boiled water on the stove for tea, and served it all beautifully on the table between me and the Sovereign of Urundien. The Queen's hands were moving all the while, and the thread she spun became even and very thin. I noticed that she held the wool a little differently from the way I was taught, more angled. I wonder whether all women spin that way in Urundien, or whether it is a quirk of hers.

"As soon as my father's two brothers were dead and he realized I would have to wear the crown one day, he started to train me for my eventual responsibilities. But he was taken from us too soon, so my training was cut short—something that my opponents take every possible opportunity to point out. But even as a child I learned that there is one thing that stands above the Sovereign of Urundien, and that is the law."

I sighed with relief, so loudly that the Queen gave me a rather amused glance.

"I know a little of Urundien's most ancient laws," I said slowly, searching for the right words and names in my memory. "Unless I am mistaken, there was a king by the name of Bendiro who lived long ago. He married Venna, daughter to a governor of Rovas, to seal the alliance between our little province and your powerful realm." I am afraid that I went on to lose myself in dreamy musings of what I had read and perhaps forgot whom I was speaking to. "Rovas was a very poor province in those times and received a great deal of help from Urundien, especially during the ten years when Bendiro's daughter Evendilana reigned. I have wondered why Rovas even interested Urundien, for we have no great resources to offer her. Might it have been for wood?"

The Queen twisted the spindle against the outside of her thigh. "It may well have been for the sake of wood. Bendiro was an expansionist king, and before his death he tried to conquer Lavora, the coastal realm, to gain access to the great trade routes to the east. He might have planned to build a fleet, and in that case Rovasian wood would have come in useful. But it is more likely that Rovas quite simply functioned as a shield against the Akkade plains in the north. They have not always been as peaceful as they are now, the good Akkade nomads."

"It would be interesting to know more about that time in Rovasian history," I said, and then remembered the true focus of our discussion. "This Venna of Rovas must have been a most remarkable woman, for when the pact between the province and Urundien was made, three laws were written. The first concerned taxes: Rovas shall pay one-tenth of its production in tax, to be collected annually. The second concerned the forest: it was established that most of the southern and eastern forests are royal territory, and preserved for the hunting and timber needs of the Crown, while the remaining woodland is free for the Rovasians to use. But the third law is like no other in the Urundian law book and was written through Venna's initiative. It stipulates that the Rovasians are free to practice their beliefs and traditions without interference from Urundien."

The Queen laid down her spindle. Her eyes were shining.

"I have *heard* about this! It was not Father who taught me, it was . . ." She slapped her hands together. "It was *Kendmen*! He was lecturing me while we were out hunting. He spoke of the forest and hunting rights, and he mentioned that part about 'beliefs and traditions.' Disdainfully, of course. Oh!" She rose. "I came here because I suspected that he was withholding income from the Crown. Never has Rovas brought in so little taxes as now. But this!" She smiled, without warmth or benevolence. "He has dug his own grave. He has acted unlawfully, and knowingly so." I too was on my feet, and the Queen laid a hand on my shoulder. "Maresi Enresdaughter of Rovas, you have shown me how this conflict can be resolved without bloodshed and without losing face. I . . ."

She stopped. There was a commotion outside the tent. In hindsight the noise had been going on for a while, but we were too engrossed in our conversation to notice. It was the clatter of weapons, horses snorting, men calling, but all somewhat muffled. Now it was hooves beating against the hard-frozen ground.

The lady in blue stuck her head out of the tent and then quickly withdrew it, her face ashen.

"They are riding out!" she whispered. "All the soldiers!"

Maresi, whispered the Crone among the hoofbeats. *Hurry, my daughter.*

The Queen swore more filthily than I would have ever thought possible from a lady. She ran to the tent opening but turned back at once.

"They have already gone! Only a handful remain, presumably to guard me." She quickly straightened her mantle. "The maniac. The traitor! He is riding to the valley without consulting his Queen, without my permission! He will probably say that he believed he had free rein to handle the situation as he saw fit. Talrana, my gloves. Eara, fetch my horse. At once!" She rushed out, gloves in hand, with Eara close behind. I followed.

Uvas was waiting outside the tent with my sword. "I didn't dare interrupt you," he said. He was pale and tense. "They drove me out of the tent as soon as you left. I don't know what they intend to do."

"Attack," I said shortly, and attached the sword to my back. "I am going with the Queen. If you can get hold of a horse, ride after us. Otherwise you will have to ski."

Soon the Queen sat astride her horse. She reached down and helped me up behind her, and without speaking we rode unescorted out of the camp. Toward my valley, my people, my dead.

ʊ

Apologies, I fell asleep at my table. I am glad that they have given me a table and chair. I also got firewood for the little fireplace in the northern corner of my room. It must be midnight by now. I can hear the wind whine around the thick stone walls outside. Not the slightest draft can reach me inside, though. I awoke with my head resting on my right arm, so if my handwriting is illegible it is because my hand has been as deeply asleep as I was. I just have to put more wood on the fire, so I can see enough to write. My little candle has nearly burned out. I regret letting it burn down while I slept.

I will continue from where I got to before falling asleep. What follows is of great significance. For it demonstrates the many faces of the Crone, Sister O. She is so much greater than I ever understood.

We galloped through the forest. The Queen was leaning forward and steering the horse while I clung on, my arms wrapped around her waist and my thighs tight against the horse. I had never traveled so fast. I could see nothing but the Queen's black-robed back, so I could not anticipate the horse's lurches or jumps over snow blocks and other obstacles. The Queen's horse must be one of the fastest in Urundien, but the snow and ice were still a hindrance. The soldiers had a significant head start, and they too were going at full speed. The nádor must have ordered them to, for he knew that the Queen would try to stop him.

I gritted my teeth and prayed to the Crone.

When we reached the ravine down in the valley I heard the screams. My people were screaming, and a formless terror took possession of me. The pass was still filled with snow, and the tracks from the soldiers' horses led along the western hillside down into the valley. The snow must be less deep there. They had not even tried to force our barricade. Perhaps they had taken my people by surprise. Dread paralyzed my limbs, and I lost the ability to hold firm in the saddle. I slipped off the horse before we got there. The Queen continued, and perhaps did not even notice me fall. Once I had scrambled to my knees in the deep snow I saw her reach the barricade, where a soldier leaped forward and grabbed her horse's bridle. The Queen shouted furiously, but her shouts could hardly be heard amid the din from the valley beyond the barricade.

Sister O, why do I become so frozen with fear that I can hardly act when it matters most? Why am I so weak? I did not want to go down there; I did not want to face what was happening on the other side of the barricade. I wanted to turn around, sneak into the forest, crawl under a dense spruce and never move again. But I forced myself to edge forward. I crept right up to the barricade. The Queen had dismounted and left her horse and the soldier to their fate. He did not dare raise his hand to the Queen, though he had undoubtedly been given orders to prevent her from getting through. She began climbing the hillside to get around and down on the other side. I climbed up the barricade itself, which no one was bothering to guard anymore. I had been involved in its construction. I knew how to get up. Once on top, I crouched on the highest log and rested for the briefest of moments, with eyes closed and a pounding heart. Then I opened my eyes.

The soldiers were galloping through the crowds of people—my people—and swinging their swords indiscriminately. Their horses reared and kicked. I saw the nádor, riding around in his black mantle, joining in the violence with a cold composure. I saw people huddled on the ground, and people with clubs and axes offering resistance.

I tried to make sense of what I was seeing.

I saw no children.

They had gotten to safety. Or they were hidden inside the cabins.

I saw very few elderly people. Perhaps they were with the children.

Women and men were fighting side by side against the soldiers.

Some of the soldiers were striking with the broad sides of their swords. They were trying to drive the Rovasians out of the valley.

Clusters of people were already fleeing up the hill to avoid the sword blows and horse kicks. But other soldiers were not as scrupulous. They were using their sword's edges. I saw people fall to the ground and not move again. Red-colored snow. The soldiers were pressing the Rovasian folk hard. Step by step they were driving them to the very edge of their own valley. If we left now, we would lose it forever. The nádor would not leave the valley until the last silverwood had fallen. A female figure lay face down in the snow. I could not see who it was, but what did it matter? She was my sister, my friend, my neighbor, my niece, the daughter I would never have.

I sat up. Then I saw it. The door. The door of the Crone stood beside me, shining in the bright winter sun. It exerted the same force on me as it always does. The same lure mixed with terror. It reeked of blood and death. The voice of the Crone muttered through the cracks.

"I do not want to," I whispered. "No more death."

I wiped my tears away with my glove and stood up. The wind took hold of my red mantle and spread it out behind me, like a burning flag. Everybody turned to look. Soldiers and Rovasians. They came to a standstill. Some of the Rovasians fell to their knees. The wind whipped my hair into my eyes. I did not want to open the door, not even in that moment, Sister. There is no shortage of death, pain and sorrow in the world. There is no need for any more.

But it was not my choice to make. I turned to face the door. I reached out my hand. Then I looked at it more closely.

It was not the same door.

This door was made not of silver, but of snow-white silverwood.

Otherwise it looked the same, with the same handle in the shape of a snake with onyx eyes; but this door was carved entirely from rock-hard, ever-white silverwood, grown from Rovasian soil. I have been so blind, Sister O. So foolish. I thought that the Crone's power could only flow in one direction. As if she were so straightforward, so weak! As if death were so simple.

I pulled off my glove and ran my fingers over the handle. The valley held its breath. Then I turned the handle and threw the door wide open.

They came surging out like a raging gale. All the ones we were fighting for. Beautiful and strong and enraged, they flooded out through the door of the dead, appearing as they did in life so that we could recognize them. At the forefront was Mother. My heart swelled. I drew the sword from its scabbard and threw it to her, and she caught it midair. She raised it high and led the dead down into the valley.

The departed souls of Rovas had returned for revenge. The soldiers and Urundians screamed and fled in wild panic. They were struck by abject horror that clawed and ripped at their minds, filling them with darkness and fear. They collapsed in the snow with swords and hands flailing. I saw soldiers claw themselves in the face, or vomit in fear. To them our dead appeared as terrible phantoms with burning eyes and curved claws, with one sole desire: to tear them apart and drag their souls into death. That is how the Queen described it to me later.

Fools. This was the door of the dead, through which no living person could pass. The ghosts continued to flow out through the door I had opened, thousands of them, generation after generation, united in their intention to defend their descendants and their sacred ground.

Horses bolted, some with their riders still on their backs and others with empty saddles. Mother swung her sword, and it was no phantom object—she drew real blood. The Rovasians drew back to the sides, and now it was the soldiers who were driven up the hill and out of the valley. I saw the dead give up pursuit a short distance up the hill. They were probably unable to leave the burial grove. But the soldiers did not stop running and did not look back. The nádor had lost his horse, and Mother showed him no pity as she made her sword dance. He screamed for mercy, but she had no intention of showing him compassion. She knew how to brandish a sword, I saw. She used it well. It was not the first time she had raised it against an enemy.

"Halt!"

A clear, though trembling, voice sounded over the din. The Queen, who had somehow lost her mantle, rushed forth toward the army of the dead. She knelt before Mother and held out her hands. The nádor was lying on his side in the snow with blood running from his cheeks and ears, his mouth wide open in a silent scream.

"We do not deserve your mercy, yet I beg for it." The Queen could not look Mother in the eye, but her posture was proud. "I am their Queen, not yours. Yours cannot be seen by the eyes of the living. But as Queen I beg for your mercy. I swear that no one shall lift an ax against your burial trees without punishment, as long as the realm of Urundien stands, and as long as law-abiding monarchs reign. And no one other than the people of Rovas shall be permitted to set foot on this land."

The army of ghosts had stilled. The last of the soldiers had clambered out of the valley and fled, and only the nádor and Queen remained. A guttural noise came from the nádor, as though torn from his chest against his will. The people of Rovas stood quietly, waiting.

Mother extended her sword to the Queen. Without hesitation the Queen sliced her palm along the edge. Red drops dripped onto the white snow.

"I swear by my royal blood," said the Queen.

"We have heard and we bear witness," I announced, and turned to my people. "Hear the words and promise of the Sovereign of Urundien."

"We hear and bear witness," replied the men and women gathered under the trees.

Mother bowed shortly and turned around. The crowds of ghosts left the Queen and nádor there on the hillside, one on her knees, the other beaten and pitiful on the ground. Then the dead turned to us, and sought out their relatives. They offered no embraces and no words. Yet the living were able to say their final words, the unspoken words that had burdened their hearts and caused so many sleepless nights and such sorrow. I saw my grandmother holding a little bundle in her arms. It was a baby, whom she carried to my sister. Through tears, Náraes whispered tender words into his ear.

Gradually the dead began to return through the door that I held open for them. Several of them greeted me with a nod or a short bow. Suddenly I became aware of someone standing next to me, and I looked down.

It was Anner. My beloved little sister. She looked just as I remembered her, and yet different. She was ... more. Bigger. More beautiful. She was not really my sister anymore. She said nothing, for the dead have no voices in the mortal realm. But a warmth and joy flooded my breast that left me feeling lighter and more blessed than ever before. All the guilt I had once felt for her death dissolved and disappeared.

Mother was the last to walk through the door. She stopped and passed me her sword. It was heavy and solid in my hand.

I had no words to say to Mother, for everything had already been said. Neither did I feel the need to hear anything from her, for she had also said it all. But I felt her love. It was just as strong as when she was alive.

I feel it still.

I leaned my forehead against the doorframe and whispered a few words to the Crone before closing the door, softly and with care.

And so it was done.

Your novice,

Maresi

Dear Jai and Ennike Rose,

It is all over now, but my work continues nevertheless. The first tasks were to bury the fallen and care for the injured. Many were injured, some badly. They had taken sword blows to the head or face, resulting in broken noses, cracked and bleeding skulls, peeling skin and

284

sliced fingers from their attempts to defend themselves. Horse kicks had caused nasty bruises as well. I have never been so grateful for all that Sister Nar taught me about healing, and sewing together wounds, and setting bones straight, and which herbs and plants protect against traumatic fever, and so forth. I was busy from early to late and still did not manage to see to everybody.

We counted thirty-one dead. Our village has lost Máros, my childhood playmate.

There was a certain bashfulness between me and Kárun after my declaration of love. He spoke even less than before, and said nothing about my revelation. But he never left my side. He made sure that I ate at least one meal a day. He forced me to sleep for at least part of the night, when I was determined not to leave the injured even for a moment. He made sure that not everybody came to me with their worries by establishing groups to help those in need, whether it concerned wounds, food, lost family members, settling disputes, or journeys home. He made sure that I was free to care for the severely injured, and nothing else. I did not work alone; there were many knowledgeable men and women to help me. But they all turned to me for the final decisions.

When I was reeling from exhaustion, Kárun's hand was there at once to support me. When I was reduced to tears from hunger and lack of sleep, he made sure that I sat down and ate some food. And when dark memories and thoughts hounded me and prevented me from sleeping, he noticed and took to lying beside me, at a respectful distance but close enough that I could reach out a hand to hold his if I wanted. It was the only way I could get to sleep. It was like having you in bed next to me, Jai—the comfort of knowing that I was not alone. Yet it was also very different. Because as I lay there feeling his big, rough hand in mine, I wondered whether he loves me as I love him. His actions said he did. But he said nothing to confirm it.

ʊ

When everybody started leaving the burial grove to return to their homes, Queen Voranne rode to see me in person, as if I were royalty. She asked to speak to me in one of the log cabins where I was treating the worst wounded.

"Is there anything more I can do for your people?" she asked, and pulled off her gloves. She was dressed just as she was when I had last seen her, and with a white fur hat over her dark hair. Those who were able bent to kneel as she entered, but she hastily gestured to them that there was no need.

"No, Your Majesty. You have already done so much by providing all the food and bandages. Everybody is out of danger now, and they only need to recover enough to get home."

"When do you think that shall be?" she asked, and slapped her gloves against her palm.

I wiped my hands on the apron Náraes had lent me. "Hard to say. That man over there has a crushed kneecap, and his village is—"

"I shall loan out my horses," the Queen interrupted. "Those able to ride can do so, with my soldiers to escort them. Mine, not the nádor's. I shall organize carts for those unable to ride. Maresi Enresdaughter, these people no longer need you, but I do."

"Your Majesty?"

"You must come with me to Kandfall. I require someone to help me examine the nádor's accounts of collected taxes. I must have proof of his deceit. I need no more incriminating evidence against his character, seeing as he led an attack against the very people it is his duty to protect, against my express wishes, and intended to destroy woodland in a valley he knew to be sacred. He has already been escorted to Irindibul and awaits trial. But in order to correct the future taxes I must see what he has done. For this I need you. And then we must draw up new guidelines for how Rovas shall be governed and taxed in the future. I am not overly pleased about your school, for one thing. We have much to discuss. My time in Rovas is running out, for whenever I leave Irindibul I always have a great big mess of loose ends awaiting me on my return."

When she mentioned the school I had no choice but to agree. But I will do anything to defend it, my sisters. Anything.

I packed my few possessions that evening, and the following morning some of the Queen's own soldiers came with horses and carts for the wounded. I would have rather stayed with several of the more serious cases, but even they were getting impatient and wanted to return home. I hope all the injured survived. I gave detailed instructions for how to care for them. But the journey home is long for many of them, and the nights have been cold. Only ten or so people remained in the camp: the injured and their families. My own family had already returned to Sáru with the other villagers. Father did not want to leave me, but I insisted. The farm needs Father and Akios more than I do now. Besides, Akios was among the injured, did I mention that? He had several broken bones in his left hand, and I wanted him to go home and rest properly. Marget received a nasty scratch along her right cheek. It might leave a scar, but I bandaged it well enough that she will not suffer from traumatic fever, at least. Náraes and Jannarl came out unscathed, and they were among the first to leave with their daughters.

The only person left from Jóla or Sáru was Kárun.

On the morning of my departure, a soldier brought me a horse in fine saddlery and bowed low. I turned around and there was Kárun, close by, just as he had been the whole time.

"So you're leaving me now," he said.

His eyes were filled with sorrow, and he met my gaze openly, as he always does, but I could see that it was difficult for him. I gave the horse a pat and asked the soldier to wait, then went over to Kárun. He stood there in his leather waistcoat, with those broad shoulders that I have to stop myself from reaching out and touching. He was wearing the gloves I had given him, as usual.

I had made no plan of what to say. I was unaware that I had come to a decision. But standing there before him, about to ride away with the Queen, I knew exactly what I wanted. I knew what to say. And despite all the help he had given me, I had no idea how he would respond.

I took both his hands and looked him in the eye, and my stomach lurched as it does every time I look at him or touch him.

"Yes, I am leaving you now, Kárun Eiminsson. But if you want, I will never leave your side again."

I held my breath. I needed an answer before I left.

He squeezed my hands in his.

I took a deep breath and felt tears well in my eyes.

"If you will have me, I am yours, Kárun."

"If I will?" He pulled me close and held me tight. "Of course I will, Maresi. I want nothing else. It is what I have wanted since the first time I saw you, beside your brother, with your unbound hair like a shining crown. But I am a humble woodcutter. I have nothing to offer you." His eyes were wild. Hungry.

"I need nothing," I whispered. "Only you."

And then, my dearest Jai and beloved Ennike Rose, he kissed me.

Maresi

Venerable Sister O,

I have just returned from another council with the Queen. I have been here in the nádor's castle for ten days now, and every day the Queen and I have sat bent over scrolls and books filled with columns of numbers. The nádor has been receiving taxes which in some years accounted for almost half of everything produced by the people of Rovas, while sending less than one-tenth to the Crown. He has lived a life of luxury with expensive tapestries, rugs and silk bedsheets, and a table more opulent than the Queen's own. The Queen has already begun to sell the more costly items in order to fill the nádor's coffers with ready money. "To buy seed for the farmers who need it in spring," she says. The Queen is to appoint a new nádor as soon as she has returned to Irindibul, but it will take time to find the right person, and even longer before he arrives in Rovas. The Queen is leaving one of her ladies-in-waiting, Talrana, here to make sure that everything runs smoothly in the meantime.

"I would gladly appoint her as nádor," said the Queen late one evening when we had been staring at columns of numbers for half an eternity. "She is practical and intelligent, and would certainly cause no trouble, at least." She sighed and sipped some wine, which was always available on the table. She drinks a great deal of wine, the Queen. Personally I find it makes the figures harder to understand, so I have asked for malt drink or soured skim milk instead. The Queen says that the latter is an abomination, but always makes sure there is a chilled container of milk for me. "But alas it cannot be. I cannot incur as many enemies as such an appointment would entail."

"Whomever you appoint as nádor, I think it would be wise if he were unmarried, but willing to marry a woman from Rovas," I said.

I have become better at offering uninvited opinions. The Queen specified that I should do so, which I suppose means that they are all invited. It was difficult at first, but she always listens carefully to my suggestions, whatever they may be. Sometimes she gets annoyed, but she takes me seriously.

"You mean like when Bendiro wed Venna? That is a thought." She put down her cup and peered at me from across the table, between the burning candles. "You would make an excellent candidate for marriage. With you by his side the nádor would not dare make one false move." She laughed at my horrified expression and shook her head. When she laughs she looks like a roguish little girl, and those are the moments I like her best. "Calm down, I am only jesting with you. It would never work—men never let themselves be advised and guided by women like you. Or like me." She sighed gently. "Whoever becomes nádor needs a woman who can teach him about Rovas without him realizing that he is being taught."

"Perhaps that is true of the high-ranking men of Irindibul," I said carefully. It is never wise to contradict the Queen *too* much.

"You still have a different opinion of men from me, I see," the Queen said dryly. "So it is agreed. I shall appoint as wise and loyal a nádor as can be found in that rotten palace of mine, and you shall help me appoint him a wife. But for now I need to know how many people you estimate reside in Rovas. I wonder if I could give them all a helping hand now that spring is approaching. You have shown me that manure is crucial for viable agriculture, but to get said manure each farm ought to have a cow."

And so we continued long into the night. We have been referring to those three long-established laws, and writing new instructions for the next nádor. I truly want to help the Queen, and therefore Rovas, as much as I can, but it is difficult when I am constantly made aware of my own ignorance. How many people live in Rovas? I can only guess, based on what I know about the villages and the size of the province. I have recommended that the Queen conduct a census. I have also told her that she should never expect high taxes from this province, for the climate is too harsh and the soil too meager. But if she lets the inhabitants flourish she can count on loyal subjects, and protection from any possible attack from the Akkade people in the north, and many woodcutters and wild hunters, which is probably our wooded province's greatest benefit for the Crown. At least I believe so. Nothing has prepared me for advising a queen in how to rule her queendom. Not even the Crone can help me with this.

We have had long, and sometimes heated, discussions about the school as well. The Queen is not keen on it.

"Subjects with too much knowledge are difficult to govern," she says, pursing her lips every time I stubbornly bring the school back into the conversation. "I have already agreed to aid during hunger, and all manner of relief. You even convinced me to abolish taxation in the worst years of famine. Are you never satisfied, Maresi Enresdaughter?"

"Your Majesty, you are correct in thinking that people who can read and write are not as easy to deceive," I said. "But that also means that no nádor can deceive them like this one did. That makes it harder to deceive the Crown as well."

"I cannot say I am convinced," she muttered. "But how dare I refuse someone who can release the dead among the living?"

She rose, and then laughed. She is not really afraid of me. Not much, at least. And she did yield to the school, eventually. I explained that there is not much time to teach the children because they are always needed for work around the house and farm. Just some letters, some numbers, and the history of Urundien. I do intend to teach them more than that, of course, but there is no need for the Queen to know everything. At least not yet.

In exchange she has demanded fines for hunting in the Crown forest, because the law goes both ways. I agreed, but when I was racking my brain as to how we could ever afford to pay them, she appeared with a signed parchment showing a figure of compensation for the trees felled in the name of the Crown on common land belonging to the Rovasians. The sums canceled each other out.

However, the greatest challenges of my time here in the castle have not been helping Her Majesty with figures and providing sound advice. Apparently a monarch's duties also extend to holding balls and luncheons for important people. On these occasions she has expected me to join her at the table, eating fish and fowl stuffed with dried fruit and rare spices. She has dressed me up in her ladies' garments, which are the most uncomfortable things I have worn in all my life. Talrana washed and combed my hair, but I drew the line at braiding it. "Who knows what storms it could cause," I warned, and she let it be. Then I had to sit next to white-bearded men who spoke of people and events completely unknown to me, or who saw fit to tell me all about Rovasian history (most of which was wrong), or I had to stand in a hot ballroom watching others dance to melodies on pipes and strings, bored and exhausted after all those sleepless nights with the Queen. Her Majesty never seems to be tired. She writes laws and dances with egotistical dukes and eats apple compote all with the same agreeable manner. It is only when we are alone that I can see the wide scope of her character, and the sharp intelligence hidden under those neatly formed braids.

The Queen's master swordsman has told me about Mother's sword. He says it is old, a hundred years or more. It looks very simple to me, but he was impressed by the way it was forged and smithed, and says that it should stay sharp without grinding for another hundred years. It comes from the west, he believes, but he cannot say precisely where. He said it is unlike any sword he has ever seen.

I want to go home to my village, Sister O. I miss our house and my bed, no matter how comfortable the bed is that I am sleeping in now. I miss cooking my own morning porridge, and I want to check Akios's bandage. I want to know if my goat has had kids yet. I want to walk around the villages, not to beat protection into the ground, but to reassure myself that all is well. My school is waiting for me.

The school, and Kárun. Sister O, I will not give him up. I am his and he is mine. I intend to show Náraes that she is wrong—I can have a man, a family, and work all at the same time. If the man is like Kárun. I hope you are not too disappointed in me. There is nothing to say that the servant to the Crone must be celibate. And perhaps I do not want to serve only the Crone. During different periods of one's life, different aspects of the First Mother might become the most important. Sister Eostre was once servant to the Maiden, and now has a closer affinity with the Mother, and neither is better nor worse than the other. Like the servant to the Moon, I can bear everything within me. I am broad enough. Strong enough. I know this, and it is an incredible feeling. I feel that I can do anything. But in order to succeed, to cope, I need someone who loves me, who wants to be with me and help me. Then I can bear everything.

Yours,

Dearest Jai,

What a strange time this has been. For fifteen nights I have slept in a feather bed between silk sheets and had breakfast brought to my room, consisting of soured skim milk, freshly baked bread, porridge with jam and butter, fried pork, and more besides. I have worn dresses worth as much silver as a cow. I have eaten at the Queen's table with a number of important people. And I, Maresi of Rovas and Menos, have helped and advised royalty!

But in fifteen days I have barely been outdoors, and I am losing my mind. I have no notion of how winter is turning to spring. I have tried to steal a little time to myself in the courtyard now and then, but the Queen has been keeping me constantly busy and I have only succeeded a couple of times. There is much beauty to admire here at the castle, but nothing can compare to the beautiful forests surrounding my village. I miss home.

Yesterday morning I was looking through the wordings of the directives that the Queen, with my help, has written for the next nádor. The Queen was busy answering letters from the court in Irindibul. They are clearly impatient for her return. There came a knock on the door and a footman came in.

"There's someone here who would like to meet with the witch." He blushed and began to stammer. "The frost-banisher. The red mantle. She who speaks with the dead . . ." The Queen waved him away, irritated.

"The son of one of my many relatives," she said. "Utterly incompetent, but he needs an education. Having him as a footman here is teaching him something at least. I hope."

In through the door came Kárun. His cheeks were red from the brisk winter air and he was dressed in his usual leather waistcoat and high boots. I wanted to run to him, embrace him, kiss him, but I remained seated, unable to speak. Sometimes I have feared that our kiss was only a dream. Sometimes I feared that he regretted it. Regretted what he had said to me. Yet there he was.

He bowed to the Queen without taking his eyes off me. His eyes were dark, and they revealed a desire that made my cheeks burn. The Queen sighed and put down her quill.

"Kárun Eiminsson. You have come to bring Maresi home, I suppose."

"Yes, Your Majesty. If it please you. She's needed at home in the village."

"Is something wrong?" I felt suddenly anxious.

"No, not at all." He took a step toward me, then looked at the Queen and stopped. "But your pupils are impatient for you to reopen the school. There's time for lessons now, before the spring sowing. Akios's hand is healing well, and Jannarl's mother's knee too, but it would be good if you could come and see to them anyway. Your father is terribly worried about you." He glanced at the Queen and took one step closer. "And I miss you, Maresi."

He spoke these last words very softly. My breath caught in my throat.

"I need her too," said the Queen, spinning the quill between her fingers. "There is no one else who can give such good advice. Or who can be so irritatingly obstinate. Neither have I ever had such an interesting conversation companion." Then she rose with a gentle sigh. "But it is time I returned to Irindibul. From these letters I can deduce that everybody has made a frightful mess of everything. Intrigues and coups have been planned, and my absence is interpreted by many as weakness and neglect. I am going to have to work hard to show them how wrong they are." She smiled at me. "I shall ensure that your belongings are packed up, Maresi, so that you may travel this afternoon. No point in drawing out the inevitable." She turned to Kárun, and the smile disappeared. "Do you intend to marry Maresi?"

"If that's what she wants, Your Majesty," said Kárun. "All I know is that I want to share my life with her."

"Despite the knowledge of all she is capable of? You must be, what? A woodcutter? She can open portals to the realm of the dead. She can call forth storms and calm enraged animals. How will you control such a woman?"

"Your Majesty." Kárun hesitated, and the Queen nodded to him encouragingly.

"You have permission to speak freely."

"I don't want to control her. Maresi can take care of herself." I felt so warm and proud when I heard the admiration in Kárun's voice. "All I can offer her is my two hands. They may be empty, but they are strong. And the work of these hands will be to help her in all that she does. There are some things she still needs help with. Like being brought home, when she is too kind to know what's good for her."

The Queen laughed. "Remarkable men you have here in Rovas," she said to me. "Maybe I should take some of them in tax too." Then she smiled that roguish smile I am so fond of. She came and kissed me on both cheeks.

"Maresi Enresdaughter. My friend. I am going to miss you. You are welcome to visit me in Irindibul whenever you wish. What a scandal it should cause if you swept through the palace corridors with your red mantle and carved staff!" She laughed loudly. "Do not make too much trouble for the new nádor. But do report his activities to me. As long as I reign, Maresi Enresdaughter has the Crown's ear."

"Your Majesty." I curtsied as low as I could. "Thank you for listening to me, and to the people of Rovas."

The Queen left the room and shut the door, and then Kárun and I were alone. I approached him and brought my hands to his face.

"So do you still want this witch?" I asked.

"More than anything," he whispered. "But are you sure you want me? I never said how I felt because you made it so clear that you were devoting your life to the school, not to a husband and children. I respect that, Maresi. I admire you for it. I don't want to stand in your way."

He placed his hands on my waist and, my knees weakened so that I could barely stand.

"You won't," I answered. "You and I can walk this path together."

"Maresi," he said, and from his lips my name sounded unlike it ever had before.

Then no more words were uttered for a very long time.

Your friend,

Maresi

My dear Ennike Rose,

Winter has been fading into spring during my time at Kandfall. There is still snow, and the nights are cold, but the days are mild and much brighter than they were a moon ago.

Queen Voranne gave me an incredible farewell gift. It took Kárun and me seven days to complete the journey home, though it should have been much faster. We had so many animals and objects with us. There may have been other . . . delays to our journey as well.

The Queen gave me an ox. It was standing attached to a cart when Kárun and I emerged into the courtyard on the afternoon he came to fetch me. The cart was stacked with hay for the four cows who were tethered behind—one for each farm in Sáru. And there was much more in the cart besides, things I only discovered when I unpacked everything at home. I will write a letter to Sister O detailing everything that was there, you can ask her. For now I want to tell you about our wonderful journey home.

It was the first time Kárun and I had spent proper time alone together. We spoke of everything and nothing. We sat side by side in the ox-pulled cart, gliding over the frozen earth along barely discernible forest paths, and kissed until my lips were sore. When we could stand it no longer we stopped the cart and made love in the hay under the clear sky of early spring.

The power of the body, dear Rose. It is boundless. I always believed that the Crone was the strongest of the First Mother's three aspects, but this is another thing I have learned here that I never understood at the Abbey—whichever of the Goddess's aspects you are looking at in any given moment, that is the strongest. When I was a child and when I was at the Abbey it was the Crone, because I was surrounded by death, and then by learning. Right now it is the Maiden who wields the most irresistible power. I tremble with desire when I am with Kárun, and when I think of him, when he touches me or I look at him. I want him on me, in me, all the time. I want to feel the weight of his body. I want to hear his breath in my ear.

After the journey home my whole body was aching, and not because the cart was uncomfortable.

Today when we reached Sáru we parted ways—he went to the school and I led the cows to the farmsteads—and it felt as if my heart would burst. I never want to be apart from him. And I see no reason why I ever should.

Yours,

Maresi

Venerable Sister O,

The Queen has provided me with a treasure trove! She had a real chest with iron fittings filled with books from the nádor's personal library! Oh, you cannot imagine the delight I felt on opening it. On top of the books were thick bundles of paper, and several quills and lots of real glass jars of ink. I have shared everything else she has given me with the other farmsteads in Jóla and Sáru. It belongs to them as much as to me. They were there with me in the burial grove from the beginning. But the books and paper are mine, all mine! I keep them on the shelves in the school. I reopened the school as soon as I was back home, and it was a joy to see my pupils' eager faces again. Several of them have carved their own staffs to walk to school with. I suppose they want to be like me.

The most expensive of the gifts were the cows, one for every farm in Sáru. We soon came to the agreement that we would all share the ox for working the land. We have all helped each other with the spring sowing anyway, so the ox may as well belong to everybody. And the Queen gave us even more besides: the finest wool in colors we could never create with our dyeing techniques; linen so thin that you can nearly see through it; several ax heads and knife blades; sewing needles; buttons of silver and bone; and a large pouch of iron nails. She may be the Queen, but she certainly is a practically minded woman.

A new phase is dawning. It is nearly two years since I returned to Rovas, and I can finally relax and feel safe. We will not go hungry this year and, assuming the newly appointed nádor is an honest man, we should never go hungry again. We will always have to work hard, but we are used to that. I no longer need to spend my strength protecting the village, so I can do what I came here to do: educate the children. This summer I will try to travel to another village and educate their children in reading and writing also. Kárun is going to continue working as a woodcutter, but is not going to float timber anymore. I need him here at home. He takes care of all the practicalities of the schoolhouse—firewood, snow-shoveling and the like—so I can direct my full attention to teaching. And when I go out on the road, he is going to accompany me and carry books, paper, abacus and whatever else I need. I believe I will be able to earn enough as a teacher to put food on the table for both of us. Indeed, I am paid in food and provisions. Kárun earns a small income as a woodcutter also, and he can hunt to bolster our diet.

Father and Akios can run the farmstead just fine, even though Father says the house will feel empty without me there. Kárun and I are to move into the schoolhouse in spring. Perhaps Kárun and I can help with the farm work during the busiest of times, and that way we can get a little of our own bread on the table too.

Queen Voranne has promised that once she has appointed a new nádor she will send a messenger all the way to our little village to let me know. And then she warned me that once he has settled into his castle he will undoubtedly send for me, to see with his own eyes the woman who "raised a storm, summoned an avalanche, tamed wild animals and released the dead among the living," in her words. She has a flair for the dramatic.

These years have been difficult, but now I feel safe in the knowledge that there are many good years to come. Good years filled with good work. I will always bear your words in mind, Sister O: I will not exclude, but unite. I will do my best to share the fruits of my work with as many people as possible. And I will pray to the First Mother, and all three of her aspects, and to the Rovasian earth, and know that everything is one and the same.

I have so much to thank you for, Sister O.

Maresi

Dearest Jai,

Spring has come. The ground is dark and bare, waiting for the renewal of growth and life. The deciduous trees have not sprouted their leaves yet, but the first herbs are poking their heads out of the fertile humus.

Kárun is building an extra room at the schoolhouse. A bedroom. Our bedroom. We will live there together as soon as it is ready. We are not going to marry. There is no reason to do so, but I want to live with Kárun for the rest of my life. I could live alone, but I choose not to. Náraes has forgiven me, I think. She is helping us make preparations. She cannot get around easily, what with the baby on its way, so she spends her time sewing bedclothes and other things she thinks I need.

"But hold off on the children," she says decisively. "You can run your school for now, I trust you on that. But having children changes everything, that's all I'll say." And I will follow her advice. I brew Goddess Tongue leaves into a tea because I know that the time for motherhood has not yet come. I am young and there is much I want to do first.

And I do not doubt that I can do it, with Kárun at my side. He is the steel in my backbone. He is the rock on which I stand. He wants to help me in my work, and I am strong enough to let him do so. I am not saying it will be easy, but suddenly it is possible.

I finally feel that I have found my home, Jai. I have always been torn between Rovas and Menos, and never knew which was my real home. But now I know. Kárun is my home. Wherever he is, that is where I belong. He wants me just as I am: Maresi Enresdaughter of Rovas and Menos, who opens the door of the Crone, who walks in the footsteps of the Goddess, who tames wild animals, who causes the earth to tremble, summons wind and storm, and spreads light in the darkness. He is not afraid of me; he is not afraid to see me as I am. Everyone else believes I possess special powers, but I know the truth: he is the truly remarkable one. For he has done something so incredible that I can barely comprehend it—he has taught himself how to give and receive love. No one has shown him how to, as my parents showed me through always loving me, no matter what I did or how far away I traveled. His mother died when he was still little and his father was a callous man. But Kárun did not become callous. He learned to see beauty and love in the world anyway. Every day he strives for the same thing: to make life a little better and easier for me, and I know that he will continue to do so when our children come. He has given me something to strive for too—to emulate him in any small way I can.

There has always been a whispering dream inside me to return to Menos, although that was never my plan. Though I have known deep down that I will never see you again, I have kept wishing that I could. But now I am growing my roots here. I am thinking of having children, Jai. Girls whom I can teach all about the Abbey. Perhaps one day they will travel there. If they do, I hope they can meet all of you. Silla is set to travel to Menos later this spring. She is wild but ready to learn, and the Abbey can provide all the help she needs that I am unable to give. Take good care of her! Of course, I know you will.

I promise to write and tell you how everything is going here, but it will be less often than before. I have to start again, create something new, and not constantly look backward. Besides, my work is going to keep me very busy. We have Berla to take care of as well—Father, Akios and I share responsibility for her. Mik and Eina have become like Náraes's own children. I mentioned that they might be able to move in with Kárun and me in the schoolhouse, but this just angered my sister.

Keep writing to me, beloved Jai, my friend. I want to know how you are. I want to work hard, and know that everyone else is working hard far away at the Abbey. I do not expect you to think of me too often, but perhaps you can send me a thought sometimes, at Moon Dance or when you are all together harvesting bloodsnails on a beautiful spring day.

You will all remain forever in my heart.

Maresi

THE FINAL LETTER

Most Venerable Mother and dear friend,

I have always known that I would never see Sister O again in this lifetime. Your letter reached me yesterday when the first trade convoy of the year traveled through Rovas from the south. You wrote that no one could have guessed her death was imminent, but I suspect she knew. The letter you sent alongside yours, written by her hand not long before she died, mentioned nothing of her health or her death. But there was a sense of . . . longing. She also emphasized that the Crone still had not chosen a novice for her. There is only me. One winter night as I lay awake, I had a strong sensation that the Crone was watching me, and I now believe this was a premonition.

Yes, I will heed your call. I am coming home now. I will take Sister O's place as servant to the Crone until it is my turn to pass through the final door. My sons' wives are running the school successfully with very little involvement from me. There is talk of opening a school in Kandfall as well. Berla, who has been living there for a few years now, says that the time is ripe. I have two grandchildren and a third on the way. Returning to Menos will mean I do not get to see them grow up, which is a painful prospect.

However, my work here is done. Different work awaits me. And I want to work. I do not believe I could live without work. I am not yet old, but neither am I young. If I am going to embark on a long journey, I ought to do it now.

They will miss me here, which is comforting to know. But they can manage, and that is even more comforting to know. My sons have had me for a long while; now it is time I devoted my energies to my sisters at the Abbey.

I am going to miss everybody here in Rovas, that is for certain. Maressa has become so successful that I have barely seen her in recent years. She rarely has time to return home to her little village. I have no words to express how proud I am of her. There is hardly a child in the whole of northern Rovas who cannot read, thanks to her traveling school. She spends every coin she earns on new books that she leaves in the villages so the children have something to read. Maressa has a close affinity to the Goddess. She can feel and hear things few others can. Had she lived at the Abbey, she might have been novice to the Moon. Now she has no such calling, but she is doing the Goddess's work wherever she goes and whatever she does. She has never been very interested in what I have told her of the Abbey's beliefs, nor in the beliefs practiced here in Rovas. She follows her own path, and on that path she accomplishes more than most.

Náraes is busy helping Dúlan and Hélon with their children. They have two and four now, respectively. Mik has not married and still lives with his foster parents. He is of great help to Jannarl on the farm. Hélon, my nephew, has moved into Father's old farmstead with his family. Eina, Mik's little sister, lives in Murik and runs a school there. She has also taken in several orphaned children, who live with her and attend her school. Náraes is incredibly proud of her.

Náraes can grow old surrounded by her children and grandchildren, with Jannarl by her side.

I heard from Akios at the end of autumn. He is in Valleria now, wholly occupied with studying their salt production. Wherever he travels he always finds new things to learn. I think he should come to Menos to teach the Abbey novices about all the things he has seen. I wonder if he could safely step ashore if we performed certain rites and offerings? Maybe I will meet him on my journey southward to Menos. Akios seemed very happy in his letter. He is doing what he always wanted: seeing the world; being a part of the world.

I have already packed the few possessions I intend to take with me. Sister O's ring. The pouch I sewed from the scraps that could be saved from the well-worn cloak you sewed me so long ago. I have given the comb to Maressa. She needs it more than I do. There are still dangers lurking in the places she travels with her school-on-a-cart. But the Maiden holds her hand, and the Crone whispers in her ear. I know that she will be all right. I do not know whether I will reach the Abbey before my letter, but I think that a trade convoy will be able to travel more quickly than I can. I want to take the opportunity to see some of the world during this one last chance I have. I believe this is to be my final journey.

I have said my farewells. I have held my beloved sons and felt my hair become wet with their tears. I have kissed my daughters-in-law's cheeks, I have embraced Dúlan and Hélon and their children. I have caressed and kissed my grandchildren, and those were the hardest goodbyes of all.

This evening I bid farewell to the three I have loved and lost. I will ride through the light spring evening to the burial grove, tether my horse to a tree and walk down into the valley. And there I will sit awhile by Mother and Father's burial tree and thank them for making me the woman I am today, and for sending me to the Red Abbey, to which I will now return and grow old. Father has been dead for many years, but I still find it hard to believe that he is no longer with us. He always felt like such a constant. But the Crone calls for us all, sooner or later. All memories of Father live on in me and all his other children and grandchildren. He is not gone.

And finally I will sit by Kárun's tree. Kárun, my Kárun. My rock, my strength, my home. Writing his name feels like an evocation. I want to evoke him. I want to give him eternal life by letting his name live on. I did not believe I could live without him. The first year following his death was indeed almost unbearable, and the pain that cuts into me every time I think of him will probably never go away. But now two years have passed and, though I miss him, my memories of him bring more joy than sorrow. All that I am today is thanks to him. His love has carried me so far and made me so strong. Náraes once believed that love would mean the end of my work and my mission, but in reality love is what has allowed me to achieve my goals.

I thought it would be difficult to leave his burial tree, and the house that was once our home, and all the places we have been and lived and loved. But I carry it all within me. It follows me wherever I go. The day he died was the worst of my life, but I would not give up the memory of it for anything in the world.

One can live with much heavier burdens than one would ever think possible, my friend. I wish I had not had to learn this.

If Kárun were still alive, I would not travel home now. Instead of growing old surrounded by children and grandchildren, like Náraes, I will grow old together with you and Ennike and Heo.

Now I can finally tell you the truth: I have missed you all so much that sometimes I could barely breathe. I have envied every flock of birds flying south for the winter and wished that I could travel with them. This longing has not diminished with the years.

I am coming home now, Jai. I am coming home.

Maresi

ACKNOWLEDGMENTS

Jenny Sylvin and Fårholmen, Nora Garusi and Dönsby.

Simon Lundin, who helped with wintry ski journeys.

Siv Saarukka, who helped with the history of early schools.

The National Library of Finland, without which this book could not have been written.

Nene Ormes for reading and making comments.

The Secret Badger Society, who brainstormed with me.

Helvetesgruppen, where I was able to let off some steam.

Malin Klingenberg, who kept an eye on me, day in day out, and kept me on an even keel.

Sara Ehnholm Hielm, who also always steered me straight.

Saara Tiuraniemi, who talked through the sticky points of the manuscript with me.

All my fantastic and talented translators.

And then a big thank-you, the biggest of all, to my beloved mother, who passed away while I was working on this book. She is not Maresi's mother; there was never any distance between us. Still, much of her appears in these pages.

MARIA TURTSCHANINOFF was born in 1977 and has been writing fairy tales since she was five. She is the author of many books about magical worlds, for which she has been awarded the Swedish YLE Literature Prize, the Finlandia Junior Award, the Swedish Cultural Foundation in Finland Award, and has twice won the Society of Swedish Literature Prize. She has also been twice nominated for both the Astrid Lindgren Memorial Award and the CILIP Carnegie Medal. The Red Abbey Chronicles began with *Maresi*, which is being translated into seventeen languages and will be made into a film.